The Greenland Vikings

Antonia Staff

Published by Antonia Staff 2015

© Antonia Staff 2015

The moral right of the author has been asserted.

All rights reserved. No part of this book may be reproduced by any person or entity, including internet search engines or retailers, in any form or by any means, electronic or mechanical, including photocopying (except under the statutory exceptions provisions of the Australian Copyright Act 1968), recording, scanning or by any information storage retrieval system without the prior written permission of the author.

National Library of Australia Cataloguing-in-Publication entry
Staff, Antonia
The Greenland Vikings / Antonia Staff
ISBN: 978-0-9943722-0-8 (pbk)

Book layout and publishing assistance by
Publicious P/L
www.publicious.com.au

Cover design by Radiance www.radiancecreative.com

Book is available in print and eBook on most online bookstores
Ebook ISBN: 978-0-9943722-1-5

Dedication

Rose Radiance, friend, helper, family.

Preface

The Vikings were a tough inventive people committed to independence and democracy. They were skilled farmers as well as seafarers and warriors. The islands of the North Atlantic were settled during the Medieval Warm Period which lasted from the Tenth to the Thirteenth Centuries. The Vikings lived in Greenland for 500 years before they disappeared from the historical record. No one knows what happened to them. This story is set in the early years of the settlement when the climate was relatively warm and farming was possible. I have attempted to be as historically accurate as possible in describing the way that they lived and thought. I apologise for any errors.

When Eirik the Red sailed into the deep fiords on the West Coast of Greenland in 986CE he found a land of green pasture and abundant wild life. His son was the first European to visit America. The Norse were such excellent seafarers that it is possible they continued their journeys to the New Country over the next few centuries.

During the Twelfth Century goods from Greenland, such as fur and walrus ivory and hide, were considered vital for the medieval economy and used in the production of luxury items. The kings and clerics of Norway wanted a share of this wealth in taxes and tithes. The cloth wadmal was also prized for its strength and warmth.

The Vikings were skilled farmers and traders as well as seafarers and warriors. Many Irish accompanied the Norse on their journeys into the North Atlantic. They went as slaves, wives, concubines, free settlers and artists.

List of Characters

People who live on the farm called Ebiwaz

Anna Kerldottir Elfspeaker: A young woman pair bonded to Ged. She comes from the Western Settlement.

Asmund Romfortsson: The most senior adult male in the settlement of Hvalsey. He decides what will happen and when. He is married to Skadi, the sister of his first wife. He is called 'lawbinder' by his family and friends. Father of Bjarni and Byggvir Asmudsson.

Athir Berryface: a young bondswoman or serving woman from Ireland. She is called Berryface because of a purple birth mark on her face. She was sold to Sokki for a length of wadmal.

Aud the Ancient: The mother of Asmund and Ged

Bjarni Asmundsson: The son of Asmund and his first wife. He is 14yrs old.

Byggvir Asmudsson: The child of Asmund and Skadi.

Erp: a tomte, a tiny creature linked to the owner of a farm though many generations of ancestors. Mostly the creature is hidden from human sight unless the human is very still and silent.

Ged Romfortsson Dragonfinder: The younger brother of Asmund. Ged is a carver who brings fearful creatures from the invisible world into consciousness and controls them by capturing their likeness in wood or stone; he dreams what cannot be said but is known.

Irish O'Flarty: An old servant of about fifty summers. He tends to the cattle and helps everywhere he can.

Olaf the Unwashed: An Irish monk looking for Iceland.

Short Irish: A bondsman or servant. His ancestors were the Irish who settled Iceland with the Norsemen.

Skadi Olafasson Twistbeaks: The wife of Asmund. Stepmother of Bjarni. She has two large dogs, Geri and Hermond.

Sokki Bluetooth: The uncle of Asmund and the sister of Aud the Ancient. An old Viking who remembers the great raids of his youth.

Thorfinn Markland-Farer: A golden haired stranger who is cast by a whale onto rocks at the mouth of Hvalsey Fiord.

People who live at Thorness, a farm over the hills from Ebiwaz.

Brigitta Sigurdottir: Wife of Scarface. She is a healer and works with rock crystal dust.

Egil Gunharsson: Childhood friend of Bjarni. Son of Gunhar Olvadsson Bloodaxe. Foster son of Scarface.

Eirik Eiriksson Scarface: Chief of Thorness. He is called Scarface because he has a long scar across his face and only one good eye. He is a direct descendent or Eirik the Red and has a similar temper.

Erland Eiriksson Yellowbritches: A bard, nephew of Scarface. He recites the words of Odin and plays music on wonderfully strange instruments he makes himself.

Menglad: daughter of Scarface and his bondswoman, who is now dead.

Old Pa: Uncle of Scarface. Great uncle of Erland Yellowbritches.

People who are at Gardar where the Althing is held.

Elgfrothi Helford: Father of the Irish Princess.

Father Torfi: Priest from Iceland.

Ketil Half-Ear: a tough man.

Sokki Thorisson: The lawspeaker. Elected every three years from an aristocratic or wealthy family, to preside over the Althing. He was responsible for the correct legal procedure in any dispute.

Rhvford Ekvallsson: A landowner who has pledged his loyalty to assist the priest build a church at Gardar.

Sokki Thorisson: Chief of Brattahlid and Lawspeaker of Greenland. The most powerful man in Greenland.

Others

Gunhar Olvadsson Bloodaxe: Landowning chieftain from Hvalsey. Friend to Asmund and Eirik Scarface. Father of Egil.

Sigrid the Tall: Wife of Gunhar.

Table of Contents

Preface v

List of characters vii

CHAPTER 1
The stranger on the rock 1

CHAPTER 2
Anna remembers 8

CHAPTER 3
Thorfinn tells his story. 18

CHAPTER 4
Brigitta comes to visit. 25

CHAPTER 5
Finding the bones. 31

CHAPTER 6
Boiling up the bodies. 37

CHAPTER 7
The treasure is revealed 40

CHAPTER 8
The ghost in the bath house. 45

CHAPTER 9
Spirits in the wood. 52

CHAPTER 10
The grandfather with hair that grew into the ground......... 56

CHAPTER 11
One man can become all men 63

CHAPTER 12
Scarface and Brigitta return to Ebiwaz 68

CHAPTER 13
The birth 73

CHAPTER 14
New life gives hope 76

CHAPTER 15
The blot 82

CHAPTER 16
Anna and O'Flarty go to Thorness..................... 91

CHAPTER 17
The ice cave 103

CHAPTER 18
The battle with the Giants 111

CHAPTER 19
Anna and Thorfinn 121

CHAPTER 20
The men from Brattahlid 128

CHAPTER 21
The local Assembly 133

CHAPTER 22
Preparing for the journey 137

CHAPTER 23
Bjarni's adventure 142

CHAPTER 24
Gardar 149

CHAPTER 25
A new love interest. 156

CHAPTER 26
The Mid-Summer Assembly. 161

CHAPTER 27
An Irish princess. 166

CHAPTER 28
Judgment on the treasure 171

CHAPTER 29
The burial of the bones 177

CHAPTER 30
The waiting 185

CHAPTER 31
The gate to the other world 192

CHAPTER 32
The Nordsetur 199

CHAPTER 33
Ebiwaz. 205

CHAPTER 34
Return to Thorness 214

CHAPTER 35
The hunt 220

CHAPTER 36
The journey through ice. 227

CHAPTER 37
Rhvford Ekvallsson and the bishop 235

CHAPTER 38
Second sight.. 238

CHAPTER 39
Herjolfsness.. 243

CHAPTER 40
Ged sets sail....................................... 249

Glossary... 254

CHAPTER 1
The stranger on the rock

He lay on the rocks, his red hair marking him as a stranger in a land of black and white. The metal around his neck beckoned the two men forward. He was on a beach, just above the level of the sea where the land softened to make an inlet of pebbles and seaweed.

'Norse.'

The men paddled their skin boat closer.

'Stupid Norse,' said the younger. 'He breathes. He is not long on the rocks. Why does the sea not take him?'

'Aglook protects him. Like us when we hunt in the sea,' said the elder. 'He has good clothes. I see little water on his body. Maybe he has come too early to hunt the spring fish. We will take him to the stone house.' He pointed to the land underneath the mountains far away at the end of the fiord. 'There is a family there. They live together in the house with many animals. Headman always wants men to work. Sometimes the roof falls and everyone is wet inside. This Norse is big and strong. We will trade him for milk or knife or clothes their women make from animal hair.'

'Or woman.' The younger man patted his stomach and grinned. 'A soft white woman like the underbelly of a seal.'

They both laughed. All salvage has worth in Greenland.

'He smells like a dead animal,' said the elder. 'They always smell bad. Norse never take their clothes off inside the house.'

They dragged the big man into the umiak where he lay curled around their feet. They fingered the metal on his body and younger man slipped a knife out of the big man's belt and laid it under his own backpack. The old man smiled and began paddling; it was a long journey to the pasture at the end of the fiord. They sang as they paddled, giving praise to the spirits for a safe journey thus far. They were used to hunting seal in the ice flow in the open sea before the water split deep into the land.

This day their boat had flown before a storm down the West Greenland coast and they had come for shelter into the open water of the fiord. It was unusual to find a man alive once he had been in the sea; they accepted that the sea claimed what it needed and returned what it did not. Norse died, Kalal died.

As the time of light closed the men came to a place where the cliffs opened to a bay beneath a sloping green pasture. There was a longhouse sprawled on the land. Grass grew on every surface of the house and attached it further into the landscape like an animal with paws outstretched. There were sheep nosing around the house between racks of brown seaweed that lined the path from the beach. Smoke came from a hole in the roof. A large bird stood and scratched intermittently at the turf where the trickle of smoke warmed the roof.

The old Viking, Sokki Bluetooth, was sitting by the door in the last light of the day when the boat slid into the bay. Years of raiding along the coast of England had taught him caution. He had ears like the watchman of the gods and like Heimdall he too could hear the grass growing and the wool getting longer on the sheep. He was a silver-haired now, still strong but bowed by arthritis. When he heard the lilt of human speech across the water he curled his hands around his sword Stingslove and hobbled down the path to the shore.

The men of the household saw his movement and came to stand beside him. The women watched from the door.

'Pirates,' said Sokki. Told yer lot. English pirates. They come up the coast ter Greenland from Iceland and before that the Far Islands of the Sheep.'

'Thieving southerners who come to steal the stockfish,' said Skadi Twistbeaks to the women with her watching from the doorway. 'Bit early this year. Fish not down yet.'

CHAPTER 1 — *The stranger on the rock*

'Pirates in a ship made of skin and twigs?' said her husband the Lawmaker. 'Pirates ain't brave enough to come though the ice to Greenland.'

The men slid their umiak onto the sand and held up their hands in a gesture of peace. 'No fight,' said the younger man in Norse. 'Find man on rocks. We bring.'

The elder pushed at the man in the bottom of the umiak. 'Still live. Fat. Strong.'

'Pirates? Real ones? Is that what Sokki said?' The boy in the longhouse dragged himself out of bed and stumbled down the path that led to the bay to stand beside his great-uncle and father.

'No pirates here yer young goat. Skraeling.' said his father the Lawbinder. 'Only two men. An old one and a boy. Put down your weapons, kinsmen. We do not fight pirates today.'

The men from the longhouse pulled the boat up onto the beach. They lifted the stranger out of the canoe where he lay on the cold pebbles. His skin was pale. He was young and well fed. Bits of metal strung around his body indicated his wealth.

'He ain't no pirate or slave,' said the lawbinder. 'Too well fed for the likes of a servant. Excepting you lot of Irish servants what eat me supplies all winter and gets fat.'

'Goat's dung,' replied the bondsman Short Irish, who was in truth as tall and as fierce as Asmund. 'We servants, or bondsmen as yer likes to call us Irish, are jest as much owning this land as you Norse.'

The stranger wore seal-skin pants and tunic under his coat. He had light red-gold hair and a red beard. He grunted as they moved him out of the canoe and stared at them with clouded eyes. He groaned and opened his mouth as if to speak but no words came. Skadi marched out of the longhouse and down the path to the bay with two young women and two large dogs following her. Skadi was a tall woman, heavily pregnant under her grey tunic. She had rolled her brown hair into plaits that sat around her head like a crown. The keys of the household rattled on her belt. The dogs barked at the skraelings and sniffed at the stranger.

'Hey, git away you dogs,' snorted Skadi. 'This rotting carcass may look like a load of garbage but he be worth more alive than dead. You women go back in there and prepare a bed,' she yelled into the evening mist. Skadi spoke with an odd accent as part of her upper lip curled without intent towards her nose. She felt the stranger's clothes and winced at the quality of his coat. 'Git him inside by the fire. He ain't no good to anyone like this.'

A whalebone plank was found to carry the red haired stranger inside. The skraelings watched from the path with interest. A tall thin man with pale hair bent over the plank to inspect the stranger.

'He may be from Iceland,' the tall man said. 'He ain't from nowhere round here. I never seen him at any meeting of Norse in Greenland, either in the East or in the Western Settlement when we got me wife last winter.' The tall man looked at Skadi. 'It is not good to see a man thus who has walked in the world of the dead and now returns. He walks between two worlds. I fear he will bring us ill luck.'

'Ged Dragonfinder you is always talking rot,' said Skadi. She prodded the stranger. 'Come from a good family by the looks of him. So we will keep him alive and in this world I say.'

Sokki hobbled up to her. 'Well then you women find them live flies and wrap 'em in butter and put it on his leg now. Git him some ale ter warm the blood. Don't want ter look poor to a stranger do we? Especially if he comes from Iceland.'

'Go away old man. We don't have butter till tomorrow when I does the milking,' Skadi said in her nasal twang. 'And who says we have to show our wealth to the likes of him with me precious ale?'

'Still some of that berry drink I made,' said Short Irish. 'Seeing as you lot are too fine to drink it. Might put a bit of life in him. Does for us lot of Irish servants.'

The stranger was placed on a bed near the fire. 'You women,' bellowed Skadi. 'Look after this man.'

'Beware,' said Ged walking behind her. 'He comes to us from a place known only to the gods. An island that belongs not to the earth nor the sea.'

Asmund the lawbinder pulled at the silver bands in his brown beard.

CHAPTER 1 — *The stranger on the rock*

'Yes. Good fortune for the steading of Ebiwaz to find a man on the rocks alive there.' He slapped the nearest bit of Skadi for emphasis.

Ged took out his carving knife and helped the young women peel off the stranger's clothes. There was a deep cut on the stranger's leg but no bone showed thought the muscle and the bleeding had stopped. The women dried his hair and beard, cleaned the wound on his leg and bound it with moss and honey. They straightened the leg as best they could in case it was broken. On his chest they put a poultice of herbs wrapped in a length of red wadmal. They packed hot rocks covered in wool into the bed and covered him with sheepskin and blankets. He was pale but his breathing was strong if slow. They pressed berries soaked in moss to his lips. The stranger opened his eyes and groaned and Anna watched the way the firelight caught in the red-gold of his brows and lashes. Elfin hair, she thought to herself.

The skraeling stood watching at the door. Anna pointed to the cow byre tunneled into the hill behind the longhouse.

'I've seen the likes of men same as him wif treasure hidden in the bilge of his ship', said Sokki poking a the stranger's clothes. 'Icelanders wot sail to Greenland in their own boats are rich.'

'In Iceland they follow the White Christ,' said Ged. 'Like you, brother Asmund.'

'Husband be he a follower of the Christ god?' Anna asked Ged. 'Like Asmund?' She unwound a strip of wool from her hands and rubbed the cold from the tips of her fingers.

'Take heed Ged,' said Sokki. 'This man don't bring bad luck. Mighty fine silver on him. From them monk houses in England. Fetch a good bargain at the Mid-Summer markets.' He stroked the sheep-skin case that held Stingslove on his belt and grinned through blackened teeth.

Everyone looked at the stranger as he lay semi-conscious in his bed. He had a silver coiled band on his arm and a chain strung with small golden discs around his neck. A piece of silver in the shape of a half-moon was platted into his hair.

'Enough,' Asmund growled and pushed Sokki out of the way. 'I see no sign of the Christ on him. However let us give thanks that his coming to the rocks at the mouth of the fiord will bring luck to the farm of Ebiwaz. We will thank the god who sends him to us.'

Sokki tottered backwards with an agility that belied his age. 'And which god would you be talking about Asmund? That White Christ of yours ain't going ter put his little mincey feet anyways nears where you live. Now if yer talking about the real gods what live in Asgard, I can put in a word for yer.'

Asmund ignored him and made the sign of the cross over the stranger as he had seen a priest do once. He spat on the forehead of the red-haired man just to make sure.

'I trust you to the care of the Christ God,' he muttered.

'Leastways, yer don't have to ask more than one god,' Sokki said. 'Being as it is them gods in Asgard might be at battle and not hear yer.'

'Asgard,' muttered Ged. He held up the carving he was working on, turning the wood this way and that to catch the light. 'What would great-grandfather Viking Hroar have thought of this stranger Asmund?' Ged fixed his brother with ice-blue eyes. 'Great-grandfather carved dragons on ships that sailed the Great Ocean from Greenland to Iceland, to the Far Islands of the Sheep, to the Orkneys and beyond to the Land of the Pitts.' He pushed his pale hair from his face and took up his carving knife. He was a thin man who curled around his work like the endless lines of his carving.

'Husband,' said Anna, moving to stand by Ged, 'here is your meal. Tie back your hair. Do not forget to eat.'

She handed him a bowl of stew and put his spoon case beside him. There were strips of dried seal meat on the side of the bowl and white cheese in the centre.

'And some for the tomte.' An old old woman emerged from the shadows and shuffled to the door of the longhouse. She placed a thimble of sea-urchin stew on the doorstep. A brown hand with four fingers reached out of the evening gloom and snatched the bowl away.

The stranger with the red hair awoke long enough to take a drink of whey mixed with the Irish berry drink. Here was woman, here the smells of household; damp hay and bodies and wood smoke. Animals

CHAPTER 1 — *The stranger on the rock*

and seal oil lamps. A bed with dry skins and blankets. A fire. A cask of dulse by the door. A long room with tapestry on the walls and pallets covered with straw and quilts. A young boy, an old man, men and women around a fire. It was safe and measured in terms of human life. He settled into a dreamless sleep.

The Irish bondsmen came in one by one, took their food and sat to eat at the table at end of the longhouse. Short Irish measured out his fermented drink. It fizzed in the cup as he poured it. From his corner at the table he could see the shadow of the mountain and the sky reflected in the water. Sometimes they brought his dragon wife to him in a ship of soft clouds and she would call to him with her eye hard and bright in the dull wash of the tide.

Anna sat with her spinning by her husband as he poked and scraped at the wood in his hands. All that day she knew something had been waiting to come to Ebiwaz, just waiting. Was Asmund right? Did the gods send this man for a reason?

A wind came through the house and made wild patterns in the shadows from the flickering oil lamps. As Anna dropped her spindle and thinned the wool her mind touched the place far away where her own ancestors were buried, and for a time she was aware of little else but the part of herself that was the sky and the sea that ran deep into the cold fiords of the Western Settlement.

At last Ged looked up. 'The wind comes. Are the skraelings still here? Wife will you take them food?'

Anna put down her spinning. 'They sleep in the cow byre.' She rebound her hands and gathered meat and milk and walked to the byre burrowed into the hill behind the house. When she returned the old bondsman swung the big wooden door shut and pushed the holding beam across so no creatures of the night could enter. The old woman sitting quietly in the shadows arose and drew Jera, the Rune of Beneficial Outcomes, in the ashes of the hearth.

CHAPTER 2
Anna remembers

In the morning the old bondsman O'Flarty opened the door to a light covering of snow on the path to the bay. The skraeling umiak was pulled high out of the water and two sets of paw prints made a circle around it. Anna helped the old woman Aud to the water to relieve herself. The skraelings stood in the distance with only their round brown faces separating them from the whiteness of their clothes and the world around. They pointed to the shed that housed the forge. Anna waved them to the heap of rubbish outside the door of the shed. They descended on the midden with glee.

'Do not go inside,' Anna yelled. 'Do not take from inside that house.'

Metal was precious and only a few people with special powers like Asmund knew the secrets of working with it. Asmund would never let skraeling take even the smallest bit in case they used it to make arrow heads or a knife to be used against the Norse.

The skraeling smiled and nodded. Anna turned to watch the mist lift from the water and move up the rocks on either side of the fiord. There was a pile of driftwood lodged on the beach. Logs like this came from the north where Anna's mother and brothers lived in the Western Settlement. The log had ice in the crevasse of its broken branches. Anna felt her heart fill with longing for her home. She remembered the frost on the ground inside the house and the ice that grew on the walls in winter in the morning if the fire burnt too low, and the way the ground would suddenly shift when the sun came back into the world and the frost beneath the soil melted.

CHAPTER 2 — *Anna remembers*

Her mother used to tell the story of the Icelander, Eirik the Red, the great founder of Norse Greenland. 'Eirik the Red,' her mother would say in the days that knew no light, 'called where we live the Western Settlement although it was north of the Eastern Settlement which is on the western side of Greenland if you come from Iceland.'

Her mother was made a widow by the hunting ground north of the Western Settlement. A place of strange spirits and creatures unknown even to the Vikings who lived in the north.

'Anna,' bellowed Skadi from the house, 'have you seen Asmund's boy Bjarni? He went out after you. He's ought to be bringing me birds. Get yerself up to the smithy and see if he is there, will ye? And bring me that axe Asmund fixed.'

'Locki's balls,' muttered Anna, as she trudged up the hill through the mud towards the smithy. 'Go yerself, yer fat cow.'

'Anna, be quick about you,' yelled Skadi, her voice resonating against the walls of the fiord. 'Woman you is always in a dream. You best get back here and do that carding. Asmund says the knarr needs a new sail. That under wool from the black sheep will make good waterproof wadmal for a sail. As we is known for all over Greenland, eh dogs?' She went off to her tasks, involved in a conversation with the dogs about the skill of them at Ebiwaz who made the best waterproof wadmal from woolen thread that them in Iceland would be jealous of.

The smithy was a building far removed from the house so no fire could ever come from the forge to burn the longhouse. A stream flowed in front of the buildings and past another small structure used for a bath house. Bjarni, Asmund's son from his first wife, sat beside the stream plucking the feathers out of two birds. The skraeling were bum up digging in the midden by the door of the smithy. Anna picked her way across the muddy track.

'Quick now Bjarni. Skadi wants birds for the dogs.'

Bjarni grunted something unintelligible.

Anna returned to the house. She remembered a ship that had come to the Western Settlement. It was a ship of Icelandic men out to follow the way of the sons of Eirik the Red to Markland. There was a holy man with them; a motley-faced creature who told tales of a drink called wine. The bishop said he could find the special berries to make it in Markland. It was necessary, the bishop priest said, for the worship of the Christ god, to find the place where these berries grew that could make this drink.

Bjarni stamped past Anna and heaved the birds into the house. They landed at Skadi's feet. 'Only dogs in Greenland what get birds to eat.'

Skadi snatched the birds before the dogs could tear them to pieces. She carefully removed the best flesh for Asmund and herself. Anna took up her carding and sat by the fire where she could observe both Skadi and the golden stranger. Did they find the special fruit, she wondered. Asmund was a follower of the Christ since he went to Brattahlid last summer. Did he also need this fruit wine to use in sacrifice for his god?

The old woman came to sit with Anna and in silence they pulled the fleece though the carding combs to make a strand that could be spun and then woven into wadmal. As the day warmed and light came into the house the stranger began to rouse. He opened his eyes. His vision blurred. His leg was numb, his foot enormous and aching. 'My leg?' he muttered and coughed.

'Cut,' said Anna. 'Deep. On your thigh. Maybe the bone is cracked. It will heal even if the bone is broken. You will heal. You are strong. Lie still and rest.'

She passed him a bowl of whey and sprinkled moss into the mixture. 'What is your name, stranger?'

'I am called Thorfinn Markland-Farer.' He spoke slowly and touched Anna on the arm as he accepted the bowl. 'My companions?'

To Anna this stranger had a voice that encompassed all things male. 'Did you come to the Western Settlement ever?' she said. 'There was a ship one year came to our farm on the way to the New Country'

'So you was on yer way back from the New Country? Sokki hobbled across the room to perch on the bed of the stranger. 'What was it you had in your boat ? Who was wif you then?'

'Where do you come from Thorfinn Markland-Farer?' Anna asked.

'Iceland,' said Thorfinn. 'We are ten from Iceland on our way back from the New Country.' He began to cough. 'My companions?'

CHAPTER 2 — *Anna remembers*

'Naught but you survived. It was just you on them rocks the skraeling found. And it was luck that brought them to the mouth of the fiord afore you froze to death in them cold seas.'

'May they be safe in Valhalla,' Thorfinn said eventually. 'Brave men. They fought the Great Ocean and lost.'

He lay back, hot and feverish. The house and its inhabitants came to him like a vision from a world he had left long ago. This woman disturbed him with her yellow hair floating in a halo around her face and her soft breasts that pushed against his arm when she held a cup to his lips. He belonged on the sea, with the salt in his mouth and the breath of Thor above him. Grief overcame him. Why had he been spared when all else was taken from him? He was cursed.

He retreated into sleep, rousing only to consciousness with the onslaught of a long forgotten smell, or the sound of splitting wood, cooking utensils banging against each other, and the scratching of small animals around his bed. He dreams were of a woman with long yellow hair and soft breasts. She reached out a hand to him but was pulled back by a walrus behind her who had its jaws clamped on her leg. Often he heard someone singing. Then the dreams came of his son and the women singing to the new born as the life of his wife bled away.

Towards evening the demands of his body to relieve itself drove him to accept the truth of his senses. He struggled to sit up. 'Where is this place,' he said, coughing.

'You is in the house of Asmund Romfortsson in the farm of Ebiwaz,' said Sokki spitting out bits of bark through his the stumps of his teeth. 'Asmund Romfortsson, or Asmund lawbinder as we calls him, is the chief of all the farms around Hvalsey which is, so you know, stranger, the most important place in Greenland. Excepting Brattahlid that is.'

'Ebiwaz?' said Thorfinn. 'Why do you call this farm Ebiwaz?'

'It means we is strong men what live here,' said the boy Bjarni from the doorway. 'What with the ice and the cold and the lack of women and stuff. Or as him the father says, we knows what bad things could happen and we fix them afore they come, being strong and wise as we at Ebiwaz are.'

'Indeed,' said Ged. 'It is the rune of patience and of new beginnings. The gods support us and give us power.'

'Ebiwaz,' repeated Thorfinn dreamily. 'The rune of seeing a problem and fixing it before it occurs. How did I make the ill-judgment to sail when the storm was waiting for us?'

'Thorfinn Markland-Farer, that's who you is, ain't it?' Bjarni said as attempted to drag the bulk of Thorfinn upright. 'You was coming back from the New Country? Where there is no winter and the ale comes in rivers from the caves where the elves live. Black bears as big as a house. Skraelings what has one foot and hops about after a man. Tell us about the Onefoots, Markland-Farer. Egil and me are going soon. We need to know.'

'Listen young Thor,' said Sokki. 'Or Bjarni if that is what you calls yourself today. No one sails in winter. No one goes anywhere when the ice is thick in the sea. Yous know that. This 'ear man and his crew must have spent the winter in the West and got caught in the spring ice drift on the way down the coast. Right stranger?'

'Right,' Thorfinn said and started coughing again.

'Better you walk with a cough like that to move the humors that stagnate in your chest,' Anna said.

She knew this man. On the edge of memory or in a dream. She could see herself turning towards him. Always turning. Then nothing; the image dissolved.

Bjarni wedged himself under Thorfinn's arm. 'Tell me? I want to know about the New Country. I want to go there where the sun shines in winter and the night comes in the summer.'

'You'll need your blacksmith magic then.' Anna smiled. 'I have heard tell that the rocks shine with metal and the streams run brown with the iron plant.'

'Yeah well,' said Bjarni, half-pushing and half-dragging Thorfinn though the house. 'Fuck them dogs by the oath of Odin. I ain't going to be no magic man what deals wif metal like him the father. I got fourteen winters. I am a hunter. It is in me blood. I am grown now. Maybe I don't see far away so well but I knows what I sees when I sees it better then most. He the father can go foster

CHAPTER 2 — *Anna remembers*

some other boy like me from some other farm to come here and learn the magic of iron work. Live wif us like Egil Gunharsson lives wif Eirik Scarface as his foster son at Thorness an' learns him how to make horse harness an stuff.'

'Ay, stepson,' said Skadi as she slammed the birds onto the chopping block. She stood with her large stomach pressed against the table. 'That he does, stepson, and if I had my way you'd be there at the farm of Scarface too. Do yer eyes good to look at them far valleys and mountains behind Thorness. Yer father's too soft on ye.' She cracked an axe through the joints of a bird. 'And this baby better come out soon or I ain't the mother of anyone no more.'

The dogs salivated and snarled at each other around her feet. Asmund and the Irish bondsmen returned for the evening meal.

'I got them birds for Skadi didn't I,' Bjarni said as he saw his father. 'Don't see no one else bringing in any bird for dogs.'

'That ye do, stepson that ye do.' Skadi rubbed her back. Her feet were swollen and there was a dull ache in her legs. 'Only them what will be a great hunter can catch birds like you. Piss in the wool vat, stranger. We needs yer piss ter soften the wool from them sheep what's so old they should be in the pot anyways.'

Asmund grunted and sprawled in front of the fire.

'I am no stranger in the countries of the Norse,' Thorfinn said so Asmund could hear. 'My family comes from Haukadale in Iceland. My father has many cattle and servants. I am a relative of the high chief Njord- Thorir of the Myrkardalr district and my great-grandfather sailed with the Viking Nadd-Odd.'

'Indeed,' said Ged. 'And I am a carver who is brother to Asmund, who is chief in the settlement of Hvalsey, and I live on a farm called Ebiwaz, and I have never been to Iceland but sometimes I go to the place where dragons live. Which is nowhere as grand or important as anywhere in Iceland.'

'Get ale for the man, you women,' said Sokki. 'Him being young and from Iceland will expect it. And mebby we can all have some ter sustain us after such excitement.'

Skadi snorted. Ale was for special occasions and could be made only when a trade ship came with grain and honey. She did not trust the concoction Short Irish made every summer from fermented berries and whey. Once it cracked a cask by blowing itself up. But a small bucket of the real ale she made herself would not deplete her supplies too much before the next ship came. A horn of ale mixed with a little water might ease the pain in her body. The sight of Sokki sucking bark and grubs though blackened teeth made her sick. Ale would calm her stomach. The bondswoman Berryface was sent with a bucket and the keys of the ale cupboard.

'Berryface take him outside with that stinking mess,' Skadi said pointing at Sokki when the bondswoman Berryface returned. 'Why does he do that? We have food. Give him dulse if his jaws won't stop chomping. Get him more willow bark. He can't tell willow bark from berries with those old gums.'

'Listen woman me father and me grandfather sucked grubs for the nourishment all their lives. Till they was older than me. Made their pricks work. Stood up stiff till the end. Stood up straight like them grubs. So don't you young women what know nothing git any funny ideas about what is proper for an old Viking even if yer are pregnant.' Sokki spat the shreds of his meal into the air as the Berryface dragged him towards the door.

Skadi dry retched over the dogs meat. 'Yer disgusting old barbarian. If I catch yer eating grubs again in my house yer can go and live in the hills in a booth and freeze till yer stiff all over.'

Anna took up her spinning. The wool caught on the spindle and made an impassable knot of fibers. She put down her spindle. This knot would be hard to undo without fat to further grease the wool. There were no creatures to be made from the wool ends at Ebiwaz; no laughter and no little dog to cuddle for warmth when her moon pain was bad.

She took a lamp and moved though the corridor to the north store room, her heart heavy with the memory of her family. Although she had been in the settlement as a married woman for one winter this house was always mysterious, the rooms half visible, inhabited by unseen scuttling and whispers. Darkness opened into passageways that

CHAPTER 2 — *Anna remembers*

led to more darkness. 'This house,' Anna whispered to the god Freyja. 'Will I even be welcome here? Am I to live here forever? Is this all there is for me? Will I never see my sisters again?'

The wick had burnt half through the oil in the lamp by the time she returned. Thorfinn lay back in his bed near the fire. He slid his strange golden eyes towards Anna, even as she hid in the shadow of the house pillars.

'Anna' he said softly. 'That's a strange name to find in a settlement of Norse.'

'She is not Norse,' said Ged. 'Her father was a trader from the South Land,' He came to the farm in the West to trade for ivory and the fur of the white bear. He fell in love with Anna's mother and stayed.'

'He called me after his own mother,' said Anna. 'He was a chief in Scotland. He went to the Nordsetur and never came back. He left me this bracelet.'

She held out her arm and showed Thorfinn a black jet-stone bracelet.

Thorfinn took her wrist to examine the bangle. 'Like my grandmother,' he said, smiling though the curtain of his golden-red hair as it fell onto Anna's arm. 'She was sent as a maid to the royal family in Norway. Had to stay at court all her life and never saw her family again.'

'Aye,' said Skadi, struggling with the axe caught in the wood and flesh on her chopping block. 'Good thing too. Anna don't need to go back to that place where she grew up. Half wild she was when she came here, what with that strange blood and growing up with a skraeling family nearbys.'

'You are too harsh on the girl,' Ged said as he turned his wood in the fire. 'She is young Skadi. She has no one here but us. And no child has yet come through me from the world of the spirit.'

Anna made a hump with her stomach and rolled her eyes in the direction of Skadi. 'There was a skraeling family used to visit our farm in the winter, Thorfinn Markland-Farer. They taught me about animals and herbs and the creatures that hide in the earth. That is why I am called Anna Elfspeaker.'

'And wise you are in the ways of the old earth creatures,' said Ged.

'Evil,' Skadi said, and whacked the chopping board with gusto so that bird guts flew about the room and onto the snouts of the dogs. 'Unnatural that's what I say. And them patterns you do in the weaving. Come from a dark place my mother used to call Svartafheim. Has the feel of elves. Not natural for a woman to know about elves. That's what I say about you, Anna, Elfspeaker or no.'

'So yer a follower of the White Christ then like the rest of Iceland?' Ged asked as he brushed a bit of bird guts off his leg. 'Them Icelanders that settled Greenland in the days of our grandparents?'

Thorfinn grunted. 'I don't hold with the White Christ, no matter what the lawspeaker says. Have to ask Thor or Frigg if there is space in the halls of Valhalla for me.'

'An well wif yer, Icelander. Only one of us here follows the religion of the Icelanders in Hvalsey, and that's Asmund and some wimmen folk what don't count. And I hear that Christ ain't one for the sword. No place in Valhalla for them that can't fight or grows old.' Sokki returned to his chair. He laughed so hard he dropped Stingslove on his toes.

'Come, Thorfinn Markland-Farer,' said Bjarni. 'Tell us about the New Country.'

Thorfinn was already asleep, sitting upright in his bed cupboard. The company ate their meal in silence.

'Now we all sleep,' Asmund said when Berryface and Anna had cleared the table. He whacked fondly at the nearest bit of Skadi with his eyes on Anna's breasts. 'O'Flarty, bolt the door. It is time.' He clamped his hands around Skadi's belly and scowled from under black brows at Anna. 'And when, brother,' he said, staring at Ged, 'is Anna going to give us a child to care for the memory of our family when we are gone? She has been here for the passing of one winter already. Brother, do you need me to show you what to do?'

Ged pushed strands of his hair out of his eyes and uncurled to his full height. 'No brother. I am quite capable. Wife, prepare the bed.'

'You think you know him from the West?' Ged said to Anna,

CHAPTER 2 — *Anna remembers*

squinting in the firelight at a curve in the tail of the dragon Jormungard he had been carving.

'I know him.' Anna bent to untie his boots.

'A stranger. Wife his presence bears ill for us. He carries a curse with him.'

'You worry without cause,' Anna said. 'The stranger will finish his journey to Iceland when his leg heals.' She drew Ged into their bed cupboard and he lay still while she removed his belt to play with the soft thing within the curls of his sex. It was always thus; Ged lay extended while Anna moved slowly on top of him. He did not touch her. He did not move. Anna knew that this was her duty, to be a good wife, to please her husband in whatever way she could. Ged held the bed boards above him and sighed as Anna labored to bring relief to the desire that had suddenly consumed her.

CHAPTER 3
Thorfinn tells his story

Thorfinn Markland-Farer remained weak with fever for several days. He slept and was woken by his cough to take a little fish softened in milk with a brew of healing herbs. Anna threw herbs on the fire too, and the house smelt of juniper and willow bark. From her corner in the longhouse the old woman Aud sang the songs of healing when Skadi was not about.

Bjarni took a great interest in the stranger; anyone who had travelled to Markland knew the mystery of great adventure. One evening Thorfinn sat up and smiled. He asked for a drink and leant back into the shadows of the house pillars. His fever had run its course and his breathing was even. Bjarni came to sit by him.

'Well, young one,' said Thorfinn 'Now maybe, if the Allfather Odin permits, I will tell my story.' He gazed at the fire as if it was a window into the past and the glow on his skin and hair drew all eyes to him.

'Yes, we sailed north from the Western Settlement in spring, my crew and I in our beautiful longship. Thor gave us a gentle wind. What a sail we had. The finest wadmal all strung with red threads. But the sea is fierce and her moods cannot be foretold. Oh, my friends, my ship, the treasure.' Tears rolled down his face.

'Treasure. What treasure? In your ship?' Sokki Bluetooth woke up and grabbed Berryface who was resting beside him. 'Them Christ men have a liking for silver and gold. Like this broach I gave to Berryface when she came to be me woman. From one of them monk places wif a Christ priest an all.'

CHAPTER 3 — *Thorfinn tells his story*

Anna pushed the old Viking back into his seat and handed Thorfinn a horn of whey seasoned with the fierce berry juice. Short Irish settled himself in his place by the door so he could keep one eye on the weather and one eye on the proceedings inside the house. The old O'Flarty crept in from the weaving room and inched towards the fire to sit beside Berryface and Sokki. Even the little brown tomte with its long beard ceased setting a trap for Skadi's fingers in the butter churn and came to listen.

At last Thorfinn continued: 'We sailed north from the Western Settlement and the sea was calm and clear, the wind easy in the sail. Many days we were on the sea and happy to be so far out and away from the ice on the coast. But the Great Ocean gives nothing away. Trouble came to us. From under the sea a great turbulence came. A monster as big as an island. It saw us from the bottom of the sea where it lives and waited in the deep hollow where the waves grow till we sailed over. The Kraken it is called. Like a fish with giant tentacles, that monster followed us. But never did it come to the surface so we could fight it. We could see it tracking us when the sea boiled like a storm. Every time we tried to fight it, it sank back down again to the frozen hollow where it lived.'

Ged began to draw a strange monster with enormous tentacles in the ash of the hearth stone. 'I have too seen it. Big as the mountain behind Ebiwaz it is. I have seen the bubbles and the wild currents when the Kraken is rising. When it sinks again to the bottom of the sea, it makes a whirlpool that can pull a whole army of ships with it.'

'Thorfinn Markland- Farer, you is not making sense,' Skadi said. 'Now tell us what was you carrying in your boat when the sea monster threw ye off its back?'

'Aye,' whispered Thorfinn. 'And if you don't get caught by the Kraken there are rivers in the ocean that can pull a ship into the inland sea at the end of the earth and monsters unknown to any on land.'

Sokki thumped his walking stick up and down and glared at Asmund.

'Was it the Margyr?' said Ged. 'All who float in the sea near Greenland fear it. Once I heard it in the sea calling men to their death.' In the soot around the fire Ged drew a picture of a woman with two large breasts and a long beard and hair. 'Did you see this

Thorfinn Markland-Farer? Did the Margyr call you too? Look and see what you escaped.'

The company inspected the drawing Ged made on the hearth. Sokki called for ale to calm everyone in the face of such evil. Asmund nodded. Berryface was again dispatched with a bucket and the keys. At last Thorfinn continued:

'Yes Ged. You too know the secrets of the Great Ocean. We did escape both the Kraken and the Margyr. Oh the sea is bright and the stars brighter above the Great Ocean. It was early summer and the ice was breaking up and moving down the coast. There were many walrus on the ice. What a noise they made. Like a hundred horses on the ice around us as we sailed past. Whale-horse, they are called because of the noise they make.'

He held out his horn for more ale. Skadi filled it with water 'Sometimes Odin came with his Valkyries to hunt at night and closed off the sky in long trails of light. Would draw the soul out of a man's body if you looked at those lights, men said. I say it was a sign that the gods walked on the roof of the world to show us there is an end to things, that the sky and the sea do not go on forever so you cannot ever get lost.'

Everyone inspected the bottom of the ale bucket and looked hopefully at Skadi. Thorfinn squeezed a drop of water from his red whiskers and continued in a mournful voice:

'We sailed till we found a land of rock and ice. Then the eye of Odin told us to go south to the land of trees. Aye, Markland it is called. The most beautiful place on earth. Giant trees like you have never seen. Great strands of moss hanging between them. And so high that when you looked up you could not see the space between the trees and the sky. We found the booths left by the sons of Eirik the Red and moved into them. There was the iron plant growing in the ground. The day and night were of the same length. There was sweet water on the grass in the morning. Fish and wild cattle everywhere. The gods could not have wanted more. There was nothing we needed until the bishop priest who had come with us decided to convert the skraelings.'

'Bishop?' Bjarni bit down on the pendant of Thor's hammer around his neck.

CHAPTER 3 — *Thorfinn tells his story*

'Bishop,' said Thorfinn coughing. 'That rat's penis of a man wanted skraeling so he could find out if they had silver or bear skin and pay him taxes for our protection. Well, we found his skraeling hiding under a boat in a river. Covered in fur, they were, with bows and spears beside them on the bank. The bishop said they had only one leg like the unipeds who live on the edge of the earth. He said they would kill us if they could, being so fierce and not any sort of human. He told my men to spear them to make them tame for it is said that they are not flesh and do not bleed and cannot die. This lot died and bled at the same time. When we were done with the spearing and the bleeding the bishop started to pray over them to save their souls. He said he had to find their settlement to take the story of Christ to them, which would give them human souls.

'Now I thought the skraeling chief would come with boats and kill us in revenge for we were not many. I wanted to sail away then for we had timber and iron and needed nothing else. The bishop priest insisted he go into the forest and find the chief and tell him about the Christ god. Then he said we had to sail south to find the place of the wine berries.'

Thorfinn closed his eyes. 'So the last I saw was him and his men walking into the forest, with the light in front of them through the trees. Men said it was unlucky to leave a holy man there in that forest. We went back to the huts and waited till the winter was near finished and the ice would be loosed a bit on the Greenland coast. That bishop never came back. Not a sign of him or his men. So we left when the sun got warm and the nights short and we come back the way we went.'

'Was it worth it? Sokki said. 'Did ye find any treasure?' He pulled bits of bark through the gaps in his teeth and examined them. 'Pretty Christ things?'

'Wood is the treasure in Markland. This too I know,' said Ged.

'Old man, we towed wood as precious as the carvings of Ged here. And yes, Thor did give us silver, Viking sons that we are. Not far from the coast of Greenland we found a boat. Drifting with no crew. No one on board. No one.'

'The Margyr with her long hands had reached into the boat and dragged them men to its hairy chin and tits.' Ged made as if to cradle the two huge breasts of the Margyr on his chest under his beard so as to act this part of the story out for the benefit of the watchers.

'But by Thor's balls, yes, there was treasure. Much treasure. We found silver under the deck of that ship. Coins and armbands and many precious objects the Christ god needs for sacrifice. A gift to us from Thor and the Great Ocean. So with our boat laden and a good wind behind us we sailed into the Western Settlement and stayed there at the farm of Orm Viflsson.

'Oh tell me,' said Anna. 'Did you see my sisters? Gudrun and Sigrid? Did you see my mother? Maud Juichdottir she is called. Tall with brown hair. And a little dog with a long tail?'

Thorfinn did not hear. 'Aye it was my decision to sail when we did. Down the coast of Greenland back to Iceland. But the gods of the Great Ocean would not be cheated. The ship came into a storm. We could hear the ice groan all around us and the fish rose out of the water with the evil eye upon them. There was a noise like a giant water spout. A monster rose up out of the sea and smashed our boat to pieces. By the strength of Thor I was flung onto a rock. I could hear the cries of my crew but I could not see them.' He ceased speaking and sat rigid, as if stillness could return his crew and ship.

'That's the curse of the bishop,' muttered O'Flarty from his seat by the door. 'Same as my kinsman. Came as crew on a boat from Bristol looking for cod in summer. Had a fight with the priest man and tossed him overboard when he threatened to ex-communicate them for unnatural fornication. He cursed them as he sank into the sea and drowned. Two days later their ship got wrecked on by the ice at the mouth of the fiord where they found you, Earl Thorfinn. Me pa was the only one survived.'

'Go on stranger,' said Sokki. 'By the breath of Locki you is just gitting to the interesting part. Silver was there? Them Christ men have a liking for silver and jewels.' He ran his fingers along the hilt of Stingslove and poked Thorfinn with the tip. Thorfinn remained transfixed on a vision on one else could see. Tears rolled down his face.

CHAPTER 3 — *Thorfinn tells his story*

'Get away all of you,' Anna said. 'The man is not his self yet. But did you see them? My family? The little dog?'

Ged stood and placed his hands on Thorfinn's shoulders. 'Safe you are now stranger. Safe at Ebiwaz. I have caught the demons. They will not harm you here.'

Thorfinn lay back and closed his eyes. 'I saw them. They are well. They live and prosper. Yes, I remember the dog. A small one. Hair over its eyes. And the woman, the mother. Looks like you. Do not fear for them. They are safe. I have no more words, I am sorry.'

Anna pulled the blankets and skins around him 'Rest now. We thank you for your story. You will heal while you sleep. You had the strength to survive such a journey and come safe to Ebiwaz. You are strong and luck is with you. It is a gift from your ancestors in Iceland.'

Short Irish thumped his knee in the manner of Asmund and peered down at the wizened O'Flarty. 'So old man this ancestor of yours, he got stuck in this cursed icebound land with the Norse forever?'

'Ah, yer were accursed afore yer ancestors set foot in this land.' Asmund spoke without emotion. 'Yer bear the sins of yer father, Short Irish. Were not yer ancestors the very men in Iceland who killed their master because he asked them to pull a plough?'

'Aye. And proud of me distant kin I am. Me Irish ancestors have as much claim to land in Iceland or Greenland as any of you Norse. Were not it the black-hearted Norse that slew my proud ancestors in return? Threw them off a cliff, the lot of 'em. Made up the story about the plough to take the land the Irish owned.' Short Irish squinted at Asmund. 'And well yr know me ancestors came on the same ship as those Norse bastards. Got dragged as slaves to Greenland by Eirik the Red. That were a bad day for the Irish.'

'Yer ancestors were nothing but black-hearted Irish thieves,' Asmund replied.

'Lies. Stories made up by the Norse to take all the land. Why me ancestors had to make up Norse names to stop them thieving bastards taking the land what was theirs by right.'

'Indeed? And why were it then that the Irish made up Norse

names? To hide that they were slaves.' Asmund thumped the nearest dog and grinned at the bulk of Short Irish. 'Like yer still are.'

Thorfinn leant back into his sleeping palate. The thought of Iceland made him sick. He felt hot again and his skin damp with sweat. His red hair fell about his face and his skin shone pale and golden. The rest of the company, with the exception of Skadi, who sat glaring at everyone, remained by the crackling fire and thought about luck and retribution and how either came at the whim of the gods.

CHAPTER 4
Brigitta comes to visit

Thorfinn slept the next few days and woke only to relieve himself, eat and request more berry drink. Brigitta came from Thorness with healing rock dust and a secret potion she told Anna to put into the berry juice. Brigitta lived with Eirik Eiriksson Scarface, several children and bondsmen and many horses in a farm under the Grey Mountain.

Thorfinn's coughing became less. His leg remained swollen but the black disease did not set in. The longhouse was always filled with the scent of aromatic herbs and the old healing songs known only to Aud. Sokki even took his turn sitting by the bed of Thorfinn Markland-Farer, for luck, he assured everyone, in case the stranger wanted to relieve himself of the burden of his memories.

Bjarni did not get the opportunity to ask any more questions about the New Country. He was pressed by his father to work in the forge. Bjarni hated the smell of the iron and dirt and the heat of the building where he and Asmund worked. Asmund made him mend or remodel used bits of metal into arrow points and spear heads. He could not see well in the smoke and his eyesight often blurred and deceived him. Sometimes everything looked flat. He could not separate the metal from the mould and burnt himself or dropped things into the dirt. Asmund thought him clumsy and cursed him for his stupidity.

Bjarni comforted himself with stories about an adventure he and his friend Egil Gunharsson would make to the north hunting ground one day. Although Egil lived with Scarface and Brigitta at Thorness, Bjarni often conducted a silent conversation with the invisible Egil about the perils of the Nordsetur. Two years ago four ships went and only two came back. But he and Egil knew the ways of the skraeling. They would be safe.

Asmund decided that although the time of planting was coming, the manuring of the home field could wait. He proclaimed that he, Ged and the bondsmen, would take the knarr and sail to the place where Thorfinn had been found and look for the remains of his companions.

Thorfinn said he had heard his friends calling to him when he lay on the rock. Asmund decided it was their spirit-ghosts calling for a proper burial. The lawspeaker of Iceland had decided the people would adopt the Christ as their god. So even if the stranger was not a Christ man the crew must have been and would need a proper burial. In a cemetery blessed by the bishop and prayed over with the Christ mass.

The spirit-ghosts would not come back to haunt the living then. The people of Ebiwaz would gain much good luck for placing the bones of drowned men in earth where their owners could get to the court of the Christ god that was called Heaven. They could tell the Christ god how they got there and remind him to give good fortune to the steading of Ebiwaz.

It would also be good to see how thick the ice was across the opening of the fiord before the early summer fish hunt began. It would be good to see if the fish had come yet. It was his duty as lawbinder of Hvalsey to do so.

The farmers around Hvalsey had last summer exchanged several narwhal horns, three falcons and a white bear skin for a ship owned by an Icelandic chieftain. The chieftain was related to Sokki and to Scarface from Thorness who claimed to be a direct descent of Eirik the Red. They had spent many a drinking session with the chieftain on this account. The fine boat now lay in a protected inlet and was covered by a shed of driftwood and whalebone. It was a beautiful ship, sleek and strong with the head of a fierce dragon on the bow to announce the coming of the Norse Vikings through the sea. It was called Sleiphir, Odin's horse, by Sokki, who was especially proud that the ship had once belonged to someone he could call family.

CHAPTER 4 — *Brigitta comes to visit*

The day they were to leave Ged painted the rune of Gebo on Sleiphir so any drowned men who floated beneath the surface would know that the salvage was a partnership between Thorfinn Markland-Farer and the men of the farm of Ebiwaz. He informed the fierce dragon carving on the top of the mast that its job was to terrify the ocean monster with one eye that had attacked Thorfinn's boat.

Asmund stuck the Christian crucifix into his belt and Ged hung Mjollnir, Thor's silver hammer, on a chain around his neck. Skadi insisted several cod be hung frozen from a line on the mast so bits could be broken off and eaten to give the sailors strength as in the days of the great Viking voyages. Everyone agreed that a large container of ale must accompany them. With great ceremony the precious iron pot was dragged to the boat and uploaded. The pot was the spoil from an English ship that had frozen in the ice one winter when the sun did not come at all.

Sokki stood on the bank of the inlet and hammered his stick on the ground and bellowed. He wore Stingslove, which hung in a scabbard of wood lined with sheep skin, from his shoulder. He had smoothed his silver hair to fit under a helmet saved from the days of raiding the coast of England, and his silver beard was combed and oiled. Berryface had freshened up the black lines on his face and his blue eyes stared at the world with a mix of avarice and entitlement.

'Shut up you murderous old Viking,' yelled Skadi. 'Git aboard then and jest make sure ye have the strength to stir the bones while the flesh is boiled off them dead sailors. And make sure you find them bodies. Every man what was aboard that boat what the stranger came on. We don't want no spirits around here with half-eaten flesh on their bones to disturb our dreams.'

'Aye and I am the only one who's hearing the ice speak when them fish is about to come,' Sokki told her as he tottered up to the knarr and poked it with Stingslove. 'Remember that, woman.'

The knarr left in the early morning. It was dark. Big drops of moisture slid down the sail. The men rowed till the current linked them into the outgoing tide then the wind took the sail and the mist moved like a shy creature down the fiord in front of them. It was so quiet that every sound echoed off the rock walls above. There were no monsters to be seen, no drowned men trawling in spotted skins beneath the surface of the sea, just the wild falcons calling above and the whisper of the sea spirits as they washed against the keel.

Skadi plucked the hair above her misshapen lips and watched the knarr move slowly out of sight. She rattled the house keys that hung on a string from her waist. No one was going to dig their fingers into the wealth of Ebiwaz while she had the keys. Her husband was the most important man in Hvalsey. Asmund knew the laws of Greenland. He could tell when the fish had come down the coast and were out at the entrance to the fiord. He was a Christ man, which was the new way in Iceland and now in Greenland. He knew the magic ways of metal and he knew the way the Christ god liked things, what words to say. Anyone could ask the White Christ and his family for help, Asmund said, even women.

'A good thing too,' Skadi advised Christ and his women folk. 'Soon I'll need yers ter help me git this baby out being as I don't trust that witch woman Brigitta and the spirits what come at her bidding.'

Luck was not with the women at Ebiwaz when they gave birth. Skadi had been pregnant before and the baby born dead. Her sister had died in childbirth of a seizure one turn of the moon after her second baby was born. The baby died too.

Skadi's sister had married Asmund first. After she died Skadi came to Ebiwaz to look after her sister's first child, Bjarni, who was no older than five summers then. She made fine ale for Asmund with the bucket and stick handed down to him from his ancestors. She tended to the men when they had a wound that needed healing. She supervised the dying of the wool and the weaving and she wore the keys of the farm on her apron. It was a natural progression to the bed of Asmund.

She fingered a magic piece of metal Asmund had given her. It was in the shape of tiny wolf's head, like the wolves that sat with Allfather and guarded him.

CHAPTER 4 — *Brigitta comes to visit*

Bjarni snorted under his quilt. 'Get up stepson and get yerself to the forge.' Skadi thumped him as she passed his bed. 'The fish will be here soon. Make fish hooks from that old knife there. And get them wild skraeling off my farm.'

Bjarni disappeared from the house with his cloak and his hunting knife. He trudged up the path towards the forge. Bjarni decided he and Egil would go to the Nordsetur on foot. They would follow the birds as they flew north in the early summer. They would take two women with them to keep them warm and do the work and these women would never be allowed to speak or order anyone around unless the men gave them permission. And, Bjarni told an invisible Egil, we will build a cairn of stones and carve runes on them so everyone will know we were there.

In the house Berryface quietly maneuvered the big loom into a position out of Skadi's way. She placed it against the wall near the door to catch the wind from the sea. Aud came out of her dark corner to help. Her gray hair fell in plaits to her shoulders and caught often on the cracked beads strung on her tunic. She favored brown clothes, her skin was brown and two small brown clouded eyes watched the world in secret. Aud was the mother of Ged and Asmund.

Berryface moved the yarn though the warp, backwards and forwards, forwards and backwards, never making a mistake as the threads moved to and fro. Aud plied the beaters against the weft and the loom weights knocked together in a comforting rhythm. As always, they moved into a place without thought, where only the texture of the fabric existed in a meditation of repetitive movement. They sang, beating out a rhythm that sustained their unceasing movement. Aud sang the songs of making and of patterning, of loss and of memory. Sometimes Berryface sang the songs of her ancestors too; of green valleys and lords and ladies and young men who pined for love.

Anna sat separately with her spinning, the coarse strand gripped in her mouth so the thread ran through her teeth and did not knot. Now was the time to make strong thread for use when the fish catch came down the coast in summer. She watched the tomte creep around the fire to examine Thorfinn's discarded clothes. A movement caught her eye. Just beyond the door two skraeling stood beaming at her. Both held a dead fox. Bjarni stood grinning at them with an old bent knife in his hands.

'Hunting,' Bjarni said. 'They have been hunting in the mountains and now return. They will show me the secrets of the mountain.' He handed them an old and rusted knife. He bowed and smiled at the two skraeling who bowed and smiled back. They handed Bjarni the two foxes.

Locki's toenails, thought Anna. If Asmund ever found out what Bjarni had done his rage would be terrifying. No one ever gave away metal. Ever. It was always recycled into fish hooks or skewers or useful things like ear tweezers.

'Father Asmund will kill you if he catches you,' Anna mouthed.

'Fox for knife,' Bjarni said and waved the fox bodies in the air. 'Knife good for skraeling but not for fox.'

CHAPTER 5
Finding the bones

At last the men sighted a rocky island near the mouth of the fiord. Brown ice mountains claimed the open sea. They groaned and cracked and fell into the water with a smacking noise. No one could predict where they fell.

'Keep away from that noise,' said Sokki. 'Thems ice is full of spirits from the Nordsetur where they been for the winter. No fish out there yet. I can't hear em or smell em neither.'

Water-soaked timber was piled on a beach of pebbles amongst the rocks on the island. The top of a large box protruded from a submerged ledge. There were two bloated bodies caught in a whale-tale of rocks. One had tendrils of seaweed on its face and strands of something coming out of its ear. The face of the other was as black as the rocks and his eyes were missing.

'Aeh!' squawked Sokki. 'Beware the Nokken who lies on the stones there. He will devour us if we go near. The Nokken makes his self look like drowned man so he can catch live ones. The Nokken has yellow eyes and enormous teeth that clamp onto man's leg and drag him into the sea as silent as a dog's fart.'

'Yer half-blind old bat,' bellowed Asmund. 'It's naught but a dead man whose spirit must be put to rest. Yer never could see beyond yer hands.'

They pulled the knarr into a shallow enclave and used a length of walrus hide rope to tie anchor it to the rocks. Short Irish and Asmund removed the precious iron pot from the knarr and dragged it into a hollow far away from the reach of the tide. Sokki poked at the two dead men with Stingslove. No one wanted to get too close.

'Deal with them bodies in the morning,' Asmund said. 'We need somewhere to spend the night.'

Out here at the mouth of the fiord this time of year the wind was the breath of Thor's goats and Odin and his wolf were as close to a man as the burning ice. Asmund threw his cloak over his shoulder, adjusted his tunic, pulled up his hose and strode off, his hand on the crucifix in his belt. His brown hair flew behind him in the wind and the silver clasps in his beard glinted in the blue light. Before they left Short Irish and Ged dragged the box out of the water and hid it under driftwood in case some hungry ghost might came hunting in the night. It was heavy, inlaid with ivory and silver under a coating of grime.

Asmund led the way upwards along a path to the top of a rocky bluff. Short Irish came next, jostling Ged for second place. Sokki and O'Flarty scrambled after them, muttering curses and prayers. They came upon the shell of house held together with driftwood and salt. The inner walls were intact and the roof held in enough places to give shelter. Inside was a pile of old driftwood next to a fire pit. There was old straw on a sleeping palate and a jumble of wadmal across a hard surface. A large half eaten fish held the door ajar. The runes above the door were crossed through and the shape of a cross scratched on top.

Short Irish lit a lamp. Ged struck a flint for the fire. They sat in silence and bent their teeth on frozen cod and strips of caribou meat as lightning flicked thought the house. They stirred ground fish bone into the skein of berry juice and carefully portioned it out. The ice split and cracked in the bay like thunder and the wind moaned into every crevasse of the old building. Intermittent footfalls, or hail, or hoof beats, could be heard outside the house.

'Thor's hammer,' Ged said. 'This place is like the bridge to Hel with the dragon Nidhogg crawling outside to carry us there in its jaws. Sent by the evil ghosts what live under the sea and Locki who is out to play with us. Listen to them goats drag Thor across the sky and make the thunder and lightning.'

CHAPTER 5 — *Finding the bones*

He curled up in his cloak with only his eyes visible in the tangle of his pale hair and beard.

'It is the Nokken,' muttered Sokki. 'Him who is come for us. The Shape Shifter with his huge mouth and great teeth. Hear him galloping around the house like a horse with his twenty legs. Look in his black eyes and he'll get you.'

The sound of feet stamping a path around the house became more insistent.

'Christ god be with us,' intoned Asmund, who himself did not sound very convinced. 'Protect us for we come to find these men and send them to your Heaven.'

'Be damned with yer White Christ,' said Sokki, his old face skeletal in the flickering light. 'He ain't ever set his soft skin out here with the gods of the Great Ocean. But yer can ask him anyways. The Old Ones are out here where we is known to them. Norse ain't supposed to be out here afore summer and the ice is ready. You knows that Asmund.'

'At least,' said Short Irish, leaning against the lintel of the remaining door, 'the Old Norse did not need a priest to talk to the gods. Why, Asmund, do you think that White Christ god listens to you? He only hears them fancy-dressed clergy. He won't listen to anyone who ain't holy and important.'

'Asmund likes to be a follower of the new religion King Olaf forced on 'em Icelanders like the stranger who came here.' Ged sat turning a half carved fish hook in his hands. 'That great king said he would kill every Icelander in Norway unless their kin gave up the old gods. That stranger says he ain't a follower of the White Christ. But he comes from Iceland don't he?'

'Escaped,' Sokki said, 'like I heard a lot of them did instead of being forced to do something no one wanted to do. That white god don't come ter Midgard and fuck maidens and steal gold stuff and generally have fun like us Vikings.'

'That one god wants less from us than them Norse gods,' Asmund said, getting ready to say a prayer. 'I heard He says everyone is equal when we get to the Court of Heaven. It matters not if you are a woman or a chief or a bound laborer like you Irish. What happens in this life don't count so don't complain yer Irish pagan about your lot in this life.'

Short Irish pulled up his calfskin breeches and stuck his large finger in his large black ear hole. 'Asmund, I hears too that them Christ men eat the body and blood of their god. Always wondered about that, them eating a god who was human.'

The small flame from one oil lamp spread shadows between the men. A penetrating smell of dampness and age arose from the broken walls. Spirit creatures of dubious intent reached long arms towards them from the vast blackness beyond. Slowly the door began to open. Quick as a shoal-fish Ged threw his fish hook at the door where it landed with a thump on the wood. The door creaked wider still.

'Show yourself in the name of Odin,' Ged shouted.

'Nokken be gone,' Sokki croaked.

Short Irish pulled himself upright. He was so tall his shadow reached across the doorway to the other side of the room. A brown thing came slowly through the opening. Short Irish grabbed it. It hung from his large hands wet and dripping. Its feet kicked out into air. It shouted insensible words as the wind came into the house behind it and doused the lamp.

'Hey, yer half-witted Icelandic barbarians, git out of me house,' it yelled. 'Out yer heathens. Out.'

Short Irish deposited the lump in front of the fire. It was a small man dressed in layers of brown wool. He had a few strands of beard and thin white hair in a coil down his back. His feet were bound with seal skin.

'Least it smells like a Nokken,' Sokki said, patting his beard.

'Me name's Olaf,' said the little man in a thick accent. 'I come from Ireland to teach yer pagan Icelanders.'

'If we was in Iceland you'd be in that pot for stew.'

'Makes a noise like a walrus don't it. Ain't got no blubber under its skin. Naught good for the pot being all bone.'

'Face like a walrus as if it were sorry it can't be boiled up for dinner.'

CHAPTER 5 — *Finding the bones*

'Makes a noise like a herd of horse,' said Sokki. 'Whale-horse, are yer? Come in from the sea to find a mate, has yer? Or is yer escaping from the whale-horse queen? Ged can yer make him a pair of tusks like a proper walrus. Couldn't tell the difference then. Be a proper whale-horse then, he would.'

'I am an Irish monk come to teach the word of God and to pray away from the evils of the world,' the brown thing said. 'If this ain't Iceland, where is it?'

'Greenland, yer fool.'

'God help me. I am lost. I ain't never heard of this place.' Words did not come easily. The little man sat cross-legged in front of the fire and stared at them with his lips in a thin line. His eyes were hooded and lines of salt and dirt streaked his face. 'Greenland yer say?'

Asmund fingered his crucifix and scowled. Ged smashed his amulet of Thor's hammer up and down as he kicked at the fire. Short Irish wiped his hands on his breeches and retired to a bed pallet with one eye on the proceedings.

'Papar?' Asmund said eventually. 'So ye are an Irish monk cast off in a leather currach to take the word of the White Christ where ever he sends yer tiny boat? And now ye are in Greenland and yer thinks it's Iceland. Have ye got it with ye then, the Word of God?'

'Greenland yer say?' Olaf shook himself. 'A curse on yer thieving barbarians if it ain't there.' He scrimmaged under a lump of straw, dragged out a seal-skin package and sniffed it with love. Slowly he unwrapped a small book. Gold letters on the cover of the book glinted in the firelight.

'Not for the likes of them pagans,' he muttered to the book and stuffed it back into the sealskin packing. 'Greenland yer say? Are yer sure this ain't Iceland?'

'We'll call it Olaf the Unwashed, seeing as it smells so sweet,' Sokki said.

'Papar do not wash,' said Asmund. 'Shows how holy they are. No vanity, so they says.'

'Bishop must smell a bit then,' said Ged.

Olaf retired to a pallet in the far corner of the room and covered himself and his book with a moldy blanket. During the night Ged woke up scratching at his legs. The air smelt strange, like half cured sheep skin. The others were moving restlessly in their sleep. He went outside to relieve himself. The storm had passed. A green looped ribbon rippled in the sky above the sea and washed the landscape with color. Odin and his Valkyries hunted tonight. Ged stayed transfixed within the glittering landscape until Short Irish disturbed his trance.

'Equinox,' Short Irish muttered as the light turned his long face green. 'Best get inside now for there's work to do in the morning.'

Short Irish settled himself on to a rock to calculate the position of the brightest stars visible and their relation to the mountains. He thought he could see odd-shaped clouds low on the horizon far to the east. He leant back and half-closed his eyes so the lights fizzed about him. One day his dragon lover in the clouds would come and pull him into her softness and he would let her have her fill of him, he would, in any way she wanted.

CHAPTER 6
Boiling up the bodies

No one liked boiling up bodies. They smelt and the guts fell all over the place like dragon spawn and it took ages to get the stuff out of the head. In the morning before light Asmund marched them all down to the shore to drag out the iron pot and begin. He delivered a short sermon, as was the duty of a lawbinder, to the men as they stood around stamping and thumping their bodies for heat.

'Now you men know I follow the way of the White Christ because he is stronger than all the other gods. The king of Norway says this god wants every bit of every person in Iceland and Greenland to be able to get to Heaven. But the Christ ain't going to look for spirits attached to bones what lived in the person unless the Bishop tells Him where to look. He's not going looking here where there's no graveyard what a bishop has not said words over. This Christ god does not want any leftover bits here on earth in a place where he cannot find them. And we Norse do not want any unhappy bits left over to haunt us. So for us to help the men who drowned,' Asmund cast his eyes to the horizon, 'is for us to get their bones to a place where they can go to Heaven and all the bits will be joined up.'

'Yeah and how do a man like you know this?' Sokki asked. 'Who told you? How do you know this ain't a trick by Locki, the Great Trickster? Locki the shape changer. Could change his self into that book, if he wanted, just to trick yers.'

'I was told so by the chief of Brattahlid who is a great man when I went to Gardar last summer. He knew because he had seen it written in gold letters.'

'Words in a language we cannot speak,' Ged said.

'That god can stop the ghosts of the stranger's crew coming back to haunt us with bad luck. Enough brother. Get that fire going under the pot.'

'Valhalla,' Ged said to Sokki. 'Leastways we won't be meeting this half-eaten lot of guts when we gets there.'

'Ah git orf wif yer Asmund,' Sokki shouted, his pale eyes glittering with lust. 'All us Vikings want is a fast trip over the Rainbow Bridge. In Valhalla there's boiled pig and ale to drink every day and wimmen to stuff with yer prick. And yer git to chop off someone's head, day after day. Pity it is I live to me old age.'

He rummaged under his tunic and fondled his balls. 'Trouble is yer have to cark it in battle t'er get to Valhalla and them days are far gone with all this religion and cattle stuff. And you going on about the White Christ what never fought with a sword in all his life. Cursed I am to grow so old t'see this.'

A wave the color of the earth leapt from the sea and hissed on the beach like a sea serpent beside the knarr. The sea was as black as the sky. Lightening cracked on the horizon.

Short Irish stood grinning to himself by the edge of the sea. He felt immersed in bliss. 'One day,' he told himself. It had been prophesied before he was born, his mother told him. His grandmother said the same thing. 'One day a beautiful woman will come for you and ease all your sorrows. She will be soft and white and as delicate as the clouds from heaven.'

Short Irish shivered as the sea swirled around his feet. This being would wind her great soft legs around him and pull him into her secret places. He closed his eyes in anticipation.

'Odin's fond of a fire,' Sokki said and poked Short Irish as he stood transfixed. 'Thor likes his ale, too, and he's got his hands on the winds and the thunder. Sky looks bad. Mebby we could charm them to give us luck on the way home?'

Ged and Sokki decided to make an offering to Odin so his ravens, Thought and Memory, could report back to Allfather that the Norse in this lonely place still remembered their obligations. The two men found a few bits of driftwood and set them to smolder away from the big pot.

CHAPTER 6 — *Boiling up the bodies*

O'Flarty offered a rat he had caught in the night. Sokki threw it on the fire and poured the last trickle of berry spirit from the skein on the rat to please Odin and Thor. The wood smoldered but refused to set ablaze.

A fire was set under the big pot. Sokki stood by the pot and stirred the contents as he had been ordered by Skadi. Ged fed the fire and Short Irish dragged out the bones, one by one. The smell was overpowering. Big birds circled around the updraft of the fire, and called to their kin in harsh tones. Near midday the pot was emptied of all bones, which were then washed and stored in a nestbaggin of goat skin brought specifically for the task.

The chest was far more interesting but Asmund refused to let anyone open it before they got it home. It was a handsome chest, made of whale bone, wood and ivory with a trim of sliver. The water had made the wood swell and dislocated some of the inlay but otherwise it was unharmed. It was carefully loaded onto the ship with the nestbaggin full of bones and the precious iron pot. Olaf the Unwashed, as a representative of a religion with vast cathedrals and colored glass, was invited to return to the settlement especially, Asmund said, as he claimed to carry the words of a god with him. Olaf agreed. He sat in the boat next to Sokki and scratched to console himself regarding the path his god had now set out for him.

The knarr slid with ease through the water between glittering caverns of ice that entranced and enticed. Short Irish informed them that the clouds he had seen on the horizon were thick fat sky beings crossing the Great Ocean to devour the land. 'Storm coming she tells me,' he said and turned so he could keep one eye on the hogsback clouds bumping into the cliff behind them. He pinned his cloak fast and began to wind his hair into ringlets, something he always did when he knew a bad wind was coming.

CHAPTER 7
The treasure is revealed

Light came to the farm of Ebiwaz with the red glow of ghost trails though the angelica and a red sun low on the horizon. Erp, the tomte, sat on the cow bales staring his favorite goat eye-to-eye and waiting for Aud to bring out a saucer of milk.

Thorfinn lay on his bed and the sounds and smells of the morning wrapped him in an unfamiliar sensuality. There was Anna bending over to rekindle the fire, Skadi licking the butter off her fingers and Berryface filling bowls from the water barrel by the door; people and animals all though the settlement absorbed in the sounds of rediscovering their own intimate world.

Thorfinn felt warm with the memory of the good ale this house and its women provided. If there was one thing Thorfinn appreciated it was good ale. The potion Skadi had served was exactly on the horn. There would be more of it, he was sure. If he kept his eyes closed he could be anywhere. In his mind he could see the house where he lived with his wife and parents. His wife was alive and the child still within her belly. He felt the sword Febu at his belt. Unguarded, old emotions enveloped him and opened his heart to a longing he had ignored for years.

There was a scraping and yelling from the bay as the knarr slid out of the mist onto the pebble beach.

'And what have we here?' Skadi marched to the door and rattled the keys on her belt. The men in the knarr stretched and farted. They had rowed hard with the fear of a storm behind them. Now they were stiff and tired. Olaf was pushed off first. He stared at Skadi with grim

CHAPTER 7 — *The treasure is revealed*

determination and began to extract lice from his shirt and crack them between his fingernails. The nestbaggin of bones was thrown onto the shore. It was heavy; an unpleasant thumping sound came from the bag as it hit the ground.

'Well a stinking rat with no teeth and a load of bones with a dead man's spirit attached, I'll bet. Husband, what else have ye got?' Skadi clutched at the sudden pain in her head.

Asmund leapt off the boat, aimed a loving thump at Skadi's arm and nodded in the direction of the chest. Short Irish and Ged carried it into the house. Thorfinn watched. The air was thick with the smell of rain and bird calls. Asmund made the men pull the knarr out of the water and drag it to the boat house. Only when the ship was safe and the boat shed lashed shut did the men come inside and sit around the fire. Olaf was made to drag the heavy goat skin bag after him.

Asmund Lawbinder smacked his wife with affection and lowered his muscled backside into the high seat facing the door. He thumped his wooden spoon against the high-seat pillars: 'From now on, Olaf the monk will live in the shed next to the pig pen and tell the Christ god what we have done. You O'Flarty show him where to go. Now as for the rest of you. We have the bones of the companions of the Icelandic Markland-Farer. I will take them to be buried at Gardar where there is holy ground dedicated to the Christian god. Skadi, them ghosts will not come back and haunt us when I have done this. It will bring luck to the people of Ebiwaz.'

'And my goods?' Thorfinn said.

'Your goods? Who rescued that chest, Icelander? Did not see you out there facing up to the Nokken and its evil breath. We who rescued that chest have claim to what's inside Icelander.' Sokki spat and moved to sit on the chest and pulled Berryface to sit with him.

'Not on Thor's hammer,' said Thorfinn. 'Get off my box you old thief. What's in there is mine and my companions.'

He limped to where Sokki sat on the chest with his arms around Berryface. Sokki pushed Thorfinn who stumbled backwards, his wounded leg giving out under him. He missed the hearth stone and landed on his back in the straw and the muck of the floor. He sat up, stunned. He dragged a large stone out of the fireplace and held it over his head as if to throw at Sokki.

'Enough,' snapped Asmund. 'We have not even looked inside the box yet. Who owns what will be decided by law.' Asmund put on his best lawbinder voice. 'At the Mid-Summer Althing, same as in Iceland, the lawspeaker recites the law and the court of chieftains applies it to what fights are happening. The court makes a decision what is fair before the law. Anything people is fighting over. Land or cattle or women or silver. We don't have no kings to tell us what to do here in Greenland.'

Thorfinn continued to hold the huge rock above his head.

'Thorfinn,' Ged said softly. 'Stranger you are a guest here and bound by tradition to make no violence against us as we are against you.'

'Icelander,' said Asmund, 'take from the chest only your personal belongings and leave the rest.'

'Heathens they were, the lot of 'em I'll wager,' Short Irish said from the doorway where he stood with one eye out for his beloved dragon wife and one eye on the interior of the house. 'Even if the lawspeaker says all Iceland is bound to the Christ men. Most likely turn their mother's hair to sea lice to see 'em bones buried in a Christian churchyard.'

Thorfinn put down the large stone from the fireplace. There was a visible relaxation in the men surrounding him.

'Strong, ain't he?' said Sokki. 'I'm impressed, Icelander. Are not even Asmund what can lift those stones.'

'Open it,' commanded Asmund.

Ged prized the chest open with an axe. Everyone waited. Ged began to remove the articles: a device for telling the direction of the sun, a set of scales, a roll of blue wadmal, a silver box with bone needles and a pair of scissors. To one side he put several cut-up bits of silver, a plaited silver neckband, several silver armbands, rings and a bag of coins. There was also, under the silver, a long sheathed sword wrapped in the skin of a white bear and several bundles of walrus ivory. The sheath of the sword was covered in ancient runes.

CHAPTER 7 — *The treasure is revealed*

'That is Febu, the sword of my ancestors,' Thorfinn said. 'I put it there for safe keeping from the sea. I swear on Mjollnir it is mine. It belonged to my father and his father before him. It has killed for me and will kill again.'

'Have it,' said Ged. 'You will not use it against us, will you brother?'

Everyone except Bjarni moved away from Thorfinn as he unsheathed the blade. It was long and heavy with silver runes inlaid into the uppermost section of the blade. Bjarni remained transfixed as Thorfinn rubbed his hands lovingly along the blade.

Thor signaled his approval as the mountain behind shook with a massive lightning strike.

'She comes, she comes,' yelled Short Irish. 'My darling, I am yours.'

Wind ripped at the roof. Ice and sleet beat at the house and sucked at the smallest crack in the walls.

'The sheep,' bellowed Skadi above the wind.

'Me darling, don't hurt them sheep,' yelled Short Irish. 'Them sheep lay down by the water today. Will freeze to death in this cold if they do not get up.'

He tucked his hair into his cap and disappeared into the storm.

Ged, Asmund and O'Flarty ran after Short Irish. Bjarni sank to his knees and stared up at Thorfinn with admiration. The men returned, dragging several wet sheep though the door of the house where they stood snuffling and snorting. The big wooden door was shut fast behind the animals. Anna and Berryface heaped driftwood on the fire and wrapped themselves and Aud in blankets. Sokki and Thorfinn glared at one another over the fire pit as shards of hail spat though the fire hole. The tomte thought this would be a good time to take a bath in the milk vat and flavor it with a little bit of worm poo which he considered improved the digestion and soothed the complexion.

As the gods of the Great Ocean crashed above the house the tomte removed his clothes and lowered himself peacefully into the milk. Aud in her youth had made him fine trousers from blue wadmal and a little tunic of white bear fur. These he left neatly folded on the side of the vat. His skin was brown from the Arctic sun and covered in soft hair. His eyes glowed in the dark. He paddled his long toes in the milk and considered the recent turn of events at Ebiwaz

Erp disliked dogs and strangers. The dogs pissed on him while he was asleep and strangers brought their odd ways and their odd smell to the farm. One night Anna had tried to spin his favorite bit of bedding, a hank of black wool, onto her spindle. Erp never forgave her. Now another stranger had come to the farm. Ged Dragonfinder was responsible for this, Erp had no doubt. It was he who painted the runes, he who trapped the creatures in his carving. Evil creatures that had better been left in a place unseen by all. Erp decided to teach Ged Dragonfinder a lesson. He paddled his feet in the milk, inspected his toenails from a great distance and thought of revenge.

CHAPTER 8
The ghost in the bath house

Skadi kept a record of the days on a leg bone attached to the top of her dowry box. The box was kept at the back of the food-preparing area and was overhung by great bunches of juniper and berry bush. When the marks reached the number of nine Skadi instructed O'Flarty to prepare the bath house.

The morning numbered nine two days after the men returned with the bones. Skadi told them all they smelt like dead pig and bath day was upon them. Berryface was sent to gather moss and sand. O'Flarty and the dogs went to prepare the stones to heat the bath house. When the fire was lit and the stones heating in the flames, O'Flarty and the dogs sat peaceably together and shared a strip of dried seal meat and a piece of cod. The little stream burbled past the bath house and the tiny flying beasties kept their song out of the smoke.

O'Flarty was on good terms with the ghost who lived in the bath house. Grand Ma Hot-bum they called her, although no one could find in living memory the reason why a grandma would be so dishonored that she had to stay forever in the bath house and not move on to the Halls of Freyja.

It was the job of O'Flarty to shovel the hot stones from the fire into the pit in the centre of the bath house so that the heat of the stones radiated through the tightly sealed structure, making everyone inside sweat. Anna placed a bowl of goat's fat and ash on the stones above the stream and brought into the bath house a bowl of water and a comb made from reindeer antler. Cleansing herbs were sprinkled onto the hot rocks in the fire-pit and the air filled with aromatic steam.

Sokki loved bath days. His old bones reveled in the heat and his teeth seemed to ache less in the proximity of the women of the house in their thin shifts. Asmund went naked into the bath house first. The rest of the men followed likewise and sat to one side of the small low enclosure. The women entered and sat around the other side of the fire-pit which was now filled with steaming rocks. Berryface handed the bowl of water and soap first to Asmund who washed his face and hands and combed his hair and handed the bowl on.

'Grand Ma Hot-bum turned into a rat,' grunted Bjarni from his corner. 'See. Big rat turds under the stone there. Lives under that rock over the stream she does. Comes out when her bum freezes.'

As if in answer, a piece of wood dropped from the ceiling beam and hit Asmund on the nose. 'Mother get outside and tell that ghost Grand Ma to leave us in peace,' he said.

Aud was pushed out of the bathhouse by many willing hands. She stood by the stream, shivering in her bath shift.

'Make an offering,' advised O'Flarty who was sitting outside the bathhouse with the dogs by the fire where more rocks were heating. He went into the storeroom and returned with a bowl of milk, indicating to Aud that she should throw it on a rock near the stream.

'Grandmother to grandmother,' O'Flarty said. 'Only one she'll listen to.'

Aud returned to her space in the bath house. Thorfinn limped to the entrance on his new stick and was helped to enter. His thigh was still bruised and the leg painful to bend. He sat at the end of the men with his leg outstretched. Thick bronze hair covered his chest and his upper arms. Anna imagined running her hands though the hair on his chest. Could she spin it? What would she make? A pair of gloves? She could not look away from him as she tended to Ged with soap and scraper. The planes of Thorfinn's body shone golden in the fire light. She lowered her gaze as she became aware of his eyes on her.

CHAPTER 8 — *The ghost in the bath house*

A squawking from Sokki indicated the ghost was up to her usual tricks of upending the water bowl on Sokki's private bits so they stood up straight and pointed at the space between Anna's legs. The heat increased. The air inside thickened; the walls smelt of long-dead goat and cow. When the cleaning and the grunting and the spitting and the combing was done everyone sprawled together on the floor and tried to forget how difficult it was to inhale the hot air.

'I'll tell you a story from me Viking days,' Sokki said to anyone who was conscious. 'Now some of yous may have heard this story afore but there are some who have not. And there are new bits not told afore.'

'If yer must,' Ged said. 'And take yer eyes of me new young wife or I'll set a demon ter sucky yer prick.' He flicked a line of soot filled sweat at Sokki. He felt heat beginning to rise up his back and set the spirits to thump against his skull.

Sokki scratched his genitals and glared at Ged. 'It's them ghost wimmen in here. Well, when I were young and me long hair curled with the fingers of Odin I went sailing in a great ship. This ship had 100 men. It had carving and runes all over it and a dragon there was to lead us forward. Jest like the ones yr carve Ged, only more fierce.

'We hung our shields on the side of the ship and we were fearsome to see. We feared no one. We left for the south in spring to get slaves and silver. I had Stingslove with me, the sword of me father and his father before him. I were a great sight with me glittering helmet and bear-skin cloak and silver arm bands on each arm.'

A loud snore interrupted his narrative. Thorfinn poked Bjarni who cursed and rolled over.

'We come upon them monk houses when the sea was still and the moon dark. Big were those god houses, with grand hallways and patterned glass in the windows,' Sokki gesticulated. 'And treasure like you have never seen. Silver cups with jewels. Gold and silver on books and rods and plates. Men like Olaf everywhere. They thought their Christ god would bring them luck but Odin was with us and he were stronger. He helped us catch a good load of young men and women and enjoy them we did, the ones that give in with a fight. The rest Stingslove spoke to.'

Sokki kicked at Thorfinn's extended leg and chuckled in an evil way as Thorfinn winced. 'Yes and like you Icelander, we come home and the sea was cold with icebergs all over and monsters just beneath the surface. We had given no sacrifice to Thor and so he tormented our ship. We pushed the slaves into the sea for Thor but he was still angry.

'Jest as we got to the sight of the mountains in Greenland a giant rock rose up out of the sea and smashed the boat and we was all thrown into the deep. Floating we was before death when the Queen of the whale-horse people came up from under the ice. Bigger than the whole of Iceland and Greenland together she is, with a hide that is tough as the teeth of a giant. She has two ivory tusks that reach to the bottom of the world.

'She called out to the other whale-horse in a voice like thunder: Save them Vikings for they are great and strong and beloved of Odin.'

'The other whale-horse swam under us and pushed us up out of the water on to her back. She saved every one of us. Took us to shore half-dead with cold. Put us where the gods put the man from Iceland. On the place of magic wot is not land or sea. Then she gits her son to swim to shore and tell the other Vikings we was on the island. Now I knows that island is a sacred place, it being half of this earth and half of the Otherworld.'

Thorfinn closed his eyes. He felt as if there was a compass pointing to Anna as she sat beside Ged with her shift around her waist, her legs crossed and her long yellow hair falling across her face and between her legs. He could feel her fragile white arms bending around his neck and the press of her nipples against his chest.

'Now listen Ged,' Sokki continued, 'there is a price to pay. The Whale-horse Queen, she says to me while we was shivering on that island: 'If I rescues another Norse from this place, a Norse what has killed my children, you and all your kin will suffer. You will live out your lives as men, but when you die you shall come to me under the ice. Your bodies will fall apart bit by bit and be eaten by the sea creatures you have killed. One mouthful at a time. Year after year. You will not know the company of your ancestors. You will be as the blind and angry ghosts who live under the ice with mouths gasping for air. You will never see Valhalla.'

CHAPTER 8 — The ghost in the bath house

Sokki pulled at his silver beard. 'Listen and ye will hear them, Ged. All those men trapped under the ice, moaning and moaning for us to save 'em.'

Ged stared into the fire-pit through a film of sweat that dripped from his face and scalp. He could see Thorfinn's ship crash against the rocks. He could see the men struggling in the sea and the ice surrounding them, covering them bit by bit, stealing the life from their flesh till they were frozen and floating face up under the ice.

'You hear 'em Ged. I know. The voices under the ice. The moaning,' Sokki inched closer to Anna. 'In the night when you lie half-awake with yer arms around yer new wife. In the morning when you wake, you hear them voices in the wind an' yer poke yer new wife to make them go away. But they do not. Dead men in the sea call to you. You can see their faces in the way you carve. Them empty eye sockets and gaping mouths all twisted up in them lines you carve.' He put his hand on Anna's knee.

Ged saw a huge walrus with yellow skin and huge twisted tusks slide between the dead who floated frozen beneath the surface of the bay.

Sokki continued softly while moving his hand slowly up Anna's leg, 'And you know what she said? The Whale-horse Queen? She said to lift this curse ye must bury the bones of her children beside the men who have slaughtered 'em. In a proper graveyard what has been blessed by a priest man of the White Christ. Ye must show your respect this way and no other if you and yer kin are to have an honorable death and reach the world of the ancestors.'

Anna pushed his hand off her leg. Sokki closed his eyes and sucked at his gums. Everyone was awake now, and listening, since there was naught to do but get up and resume work. The coals in the fire-pit were glowing embers.

Asmund sat up. 'Ignore him brother. He speaks to upset you. Shut up, Sokki, lest you bring the fit on him again. You got your woman. The old goat got a Berryface to fuck.'

'But ye can lift the curse, Ged. Ye must find the bones of the whale-horse children. Take them when yer go to t' Assembly at Gardar. You, Ged, must bury them bones near the church of the White Christ with the bones of Thorfinn's companions. 'Of course,' said Sokki pulling his lips back to reveal a mouthful of black teeth, 'if I was going I would show yers what to do. But I is not going, says Asmund.'

Ged felt confused, afraid. The heat in his skull made vision difficult. He knew there were ghost spirits in the bay. He had heard them, their voices barely audible under the call of the birds. It was true he was gifted with the ability to draw demons out of the darkness and trap their essence in a carving. They called to him from the places he alone could see. All his life he had known that it was his job to protect the men and women of Greenland. Now this stranger had come and brought with him the curse of the whale-horse queen.

'Ged will keep us safe,' said Anna.

'You is known all over Greenland,' Sokki said and pinched Anna's nipple. She swatted his hand away. 'Did not them men from Brattahlid travel to Ebiwaz to ask you to protect them from the evil spirits so no harm would come to them. And them being followers of the White Christ too. Yer know what's to be done Ged. You as the Dragonfinder of Ebiwaz must get the bones of the whale-horse people and bury them at Gardar.'

Ged stared at Sokki. Was this the curse the stranger brought? Thorfinn was rescued from the island. Thorfinn had killed the children of the Whale-horse Queen. And it fell to him, Ged, to protect people of Greenland from the curse of the Whale-horse Queen. He felt clumsy, awkward, as if he suddenly did not fit into the space in Midgard allotted to him. He got up and stumbled out of the bath house. Anna followed.

'Curse yr for an old trickster, Sokki,' Asmund said. 'Yer have brought the fit on him again.'

Sokki clutched at Berryface's breasts and buried his face in her hair. He rocked back and forth with laughter.

'And if he stops carving and cannot sit still and talks to spirits again all day that no one but him can see? Where will we be then when the men from Brattahlid come for their high-seat pillars?' Asmund stood and wrung the water from his hair and beard. His shadow fell across Bjarni.

CHAPTER 8 — *The ghost in the bath house*

'Ged got himself a new wife, ain't he?' Bjarni said. 'That what she's for, yer said. Ter look after Ged when the fit is on him. Why else did ye go so far away as the Western Settlement ter find her, father Asmund?'

'Had to,' Sokki butted in. 'No maid around here would have him, beautiful as he is wif his pale skin and blue eyes. But it was I, Sokki? who should have had the new wife ter help Berryface look after me.'

'Get out. I Asmund, chief of Ebiwaz, will take a second wife before you old man.'

Sokki leered at Asmund. Berryface helped him out of the bath house. One by one people roused and returned to their chores. Thorfinn found his stave and limped off to his rock by the sea. Anna and Berryface set to cooking the evening meal while the men went to inspect the store of seeds from last summer.

Sokki sat by the fire and thumped Stingslove up and down. 'Wasted. Wasted,' he said as the beloved sword thumped. 'It was me as the oldest male who should have got the second woman. Me and Berryface.'

After the meal Skadi went to bed with the child rumbling inside her. The pain was bad. She held the wolf head Asmund had given her. Asmund told her the Christ god would care for her if she asked him. It felt wrong to ask a male god for help with birthing. She wondered if he had a wife who would listen, a goddess wife like Frigg was to Odin.

Ged refused to eat and retired to his bed. He felt on fire, his skin alight with an inner conviction. Anna came to him and lay by his side. She held him and tried to hear what he did, tried to believe that it was so, that it was not so.

'I hear them,' Ged whispered as Anna surrounded him with her body. 'They call to me. They come in my dreams. They beg me with their eyes. I have no choice. I must save them. I must save us all.'

'Brother be at peace,' said Asmund from the next bed. He blessed himself and pushed up against Skadi, who remained unresponsive and heavy.

'Olaf says it is the curse of Eve on yer to suffer thus with the new babe coming,' grunted Asmund and thrust himself into her from behind.

CHAPTER 9
Spirits in the wood

It was rumored that Greenland soon would have a Bishop of its own. Asmund heard it from Scarface who heard it from his nephew Yellowbritches who had spent the winter at a steading in the settlement of Gardar. Some Greenlanders wanted this; many did not. The presence of a religious man meant demands for money and allegiance to some sort of kingly authority regarding trade for, as Eirik Eiriksson Scarface said, them priestly men and kings were like caribou rutting when it came to profit.

'Mid-summer,' Asmund grunted when he was seated on his high seat facing the great door to the bay and the evening fire was smoldering hot. 'Thorfinn the Icelander comes and we takes the matter of the treasure to the courts at Gardar during the Althing.'

'And jest mebbe we all gits to see the color of the bishop's prick too,' Sokki said.

'Sokki, you are stay to guard the farm from pirates and sea monsters what might get lost in the fiord. Bjarni and O'Flarty and the women stay with you. You will be the chief while I am away.'

'Thor's bum to you ancient father,' Bjarni shouted. 'No one is going anywhere near Brattahlid without me.'

He escaped Asmund's fist and jammed himself into his bed.

'It's about time he left off them frozen birds. Be at the cows next if yer don't watch him,' Sokki said. 'Chief there has four young daughters. One of 'em is sure to let him give her a poke. Make a man of him ter have a poke with a real girl. He ain't a bad-looking boy. Got

CHAPTER 9 — Spirits in the wood

a bit of muscle on him now and the beginnings of a beard. Nice long hair. Wimmen like hair.'

Asmund scowled and turned away. 'Son, yer do as I say. Yer can stay and do the hunting. You are the great hunter, is you not, Bjarni Asmudsson?'

Bjarni stuck the tooth around his neck into his mouth and kicked at the walls around his bed until he dislodged a rock from the layers supporting the turf. He threw the rock at a dog.

'Locki curse yer,' Skadi said and drew the enormous dog to her side. This dog had belonged to her sister. Skadi thought a lot about her sister. She wondered if her sister had been sick before the birth when the baby died. Skadi's legs were swollen and she had pain in her head all day. Now the baby moved so fiercely within she called out in fear. Ged held up a small wooden carving of a tiny baby and inspected it with curiosity.

'Oh, Skadi don't cry so'. Anna took the tiny carving from Ged and put it on her altar with the amber beads and the figures of Frejya and Frigg, beside the horn of a narwhale and the feather of a white falcon. 'Look, you have Asmund's god and the Norse gods and spirits of your ancestors and us to care for you. Brigitta will come from Thorness. No one will let you die like your sister.'

Skadi handed Anna a crucifix Asmund had given her. Anna laid it beside the figure of Frejya. She scratched the rune Ansuz on it. Three pieces of elfish driftwood swung from the ceiling above the altar, open mouthed, gaping. 'This is the rune of receiving, of new life. It is also the rune of Locki.' I acknowledge you so that out of Skadi's suffering new life will come,' Anna told the trickster god. 'Keep this child safe on its journey to Ebiwaz.'

Skadi seemed to relax. She smiled her twisted smile at Anna. The old faces in the hanging wood scowled as the updraft caught them and set them spinning, their open mouths gulping with indifference at the suffering of women.

'Skadi I will walk tomorrow into the mountain to find the fruit of the Yggdrasill tree so you will be safe,' Anna said, rubbing Skadi's back. She saw herself walking under the branches of a vast tree that reached from the earth to the sky, the branches so wide they covered the sun and the moon. She imagined strands of golden fur hanging from the branches. Thorfinn's hair. She could show the Norns, who spun the destiny of each person, the golden fur from Thorfinn and . . .'

'Yes, wife, you must do that. Odin hung from the Yggdrasill tree until the secrets of birth and death were given to him in the Otherworld.' Ged looked straight at Skadi with his large eyes staring past any acknowledgement of her pain. 'And like Odin you will hang between life and death. But you will recover and the child will live. For nine days only.'

Anna turned to her altar. Did Ged have the fit on him again? Or was he just lost in that world only he could see? What was she supposed to do? A new set of high-seat pillars had been requested last summer by the chief of Brattahlid, Sokki Thorsson. Asmund had made it very clear in the marriage contract that Anna had a duty to care for Ged so he could complete these carvings. It was the duty of a good Norse wife to support her husband. This way she could contribute to the community; all at Ebiwaz would benefit when Asmund exchanged the high-seat pillars for honey and pitch.

Anna drew the rune of Raido on a stone with charcoal and put it on her altar. 'This is for Ged. Odin, Allfather, I ask you who hung on the ash tree Yggdrasill for nine days and nights to learn the Great Mystery. Help him. Help me to care for him as a good wife should.'

Ged returned to his carving with difficulty. He tried to concentrate but the noise of the dead in the bay distracted him as the wood in the longhouse creaked and moved with the warmth coming back to the land. Every night Anna brought him food and combed his hair. She lay with him and brought his seed within her, although often he did not seem to know her or she him in the time of their coupling.

Ged had made a template of his design with a fine white sheep skin and a piece of charcoal. Thorfinn asked for a skin and charcoal from the toolbox to draw his memory of the coast of Markland. In the smoky evenings of spring the two men sat working together while

CHAPTER 9 — *Spirits in the wood*

Short Irish played his pipe. Sometimes the younger women joined Aud in song as they carded or spun while Skadi sat holding her stomach and staring into the fire, waiting. Olaf remained in his shed with the nestbaggin of clunking bones.

Ged did not show his design to anyone. He had little control of the lines that grew under his fingers. Stranger and stranger shapes arose: twisted serpents, gaping demons and creatures that had no equal in the world of men. Behind every shape there lurked the shadow of a walrus. Nothing in the design seemed to balance, even though he used a marking gauge made out of metal and wood to measure and centre his design. Time after time he stopped to listen, as if listening would make the dead men in the bay quiet.

At last he began to transfer his drawings onto the wood for the high-seat pillars. In the middle of the night, when even Jormungard slept, Erp, the tomte, crept out of the straw and rubbed at the carvings with a nail so the detail of each figure blurred. Ged told no one about this. If he heard the faint sound of scraping, he knew it was the sound of Nidhogg; the dragon made small smacking chewing sounds as if he were feasting on bones.

In the morning, Ged was never sure exactly what he had transferred from his template. The light had been dim, his judgment of space poor. He consulted his drawings to check the accuracy of the detail. His tools began to go missing. The tool box emptied overnight. He spent much time looking for his knives and chisel and smoothing rocks in the rubble under the straw on the floor. He began to doubt his memory. It became as if memory and dreams melted into one and he could not tell the difference. All was real to him but things that required his hands to work with his eyes in the world where he had to speak were becoming more and more difficult.

CHAPTER 10
The grandfather with hair that grew into the ground

Thorfinn helped where he could. If he was not needed in the house, he found himself drawn to the bay and the long stretch of water that led to the end of the fiord. His wound was healing slowly. He could not walk without a stick and his leg hurt if he stood on it for long. Anna watched him in the distance; a tall man in a grey cloak with his red-gold hair in the wind, his form one with the reflection of the cliffs and the water in front of him.

She found she needed to gather fireweed at the same time as Thorfinn left the house. A sense of longing and desperation washed out of the sea and engulfed her as she approached him. 'What are you thinking?' she asked.

Thorfinn picked up a small black stone from the edge of the sea. 'Look, there is a tiny world growing on this rock,' he said. 'Tiny barnacles and the tracks of a worm on the stone. Tiny creatures live in the barnacles. This is how I think of our world. Infinitely small but infinitely big because the stone is part of a world that is unknown to the creatures on the tiny barnacles but still exists with all its wonders.'

He smiled. 'Imagine all the people in the world, each with their own tiny world so far away from each other and never knowing that the other exists.'

'And now you share our tiny world at Hvalsey.' Anna bent towards him and steadied her slight frame against the rock. 'Are you unhappy here, Thorfinn? Have you a wife in Iceland and children who miss you?'

CHAPTER 10 — *The grandfather with hair that grew into the ground*

'I am not going anywhere without my silver and the treasure in that box. Then I will return to Markland.'

'The decision will be made at the Althing at Gardar in Mid-Summer. Asmund has promised.'

'If your thieving relatives don't steal it. I must go back to Markland. It is my destiny. I need silver to get a ship and crew. Otherwise it is the Nordsetur, and Thor protect me in that frozen Hel. I have no wife, since you ask, and my family is far away in Iceland. They care not for my welfare.'

'You would go to the New Country without a woman? Someone to make your ale, spin and weave and give you children?'

'Thor protect me if I have to go alone.'

Anna smoothed her tunic and sat beside him. 'No ships have gone to the Nordsetur in three years and then only two came back,' she said and her eyes were the transparent green of the cold sea when she looked at Thorfinn. 'The rest lie under the ice. It is a bad place where Norse should not go. The animal spirit-gods are too strong. My skraeling friends from the Western Settlement said so. There are sea serpents that live hidden in the ice and white bears that are half human. A dragon with the strength of Thor lives in the mountains of snow. It steals your spirit while you are sleeping.'

'Maybe. I also have heard this.' Thorfinn heaved a rock into the bay. Woman was fragile. Soft and enticing. He saw his hands molded to the white flesh of her body as he spread her thighs apart. 'Oh, woman woman, I am as restless as these ripples to set off into the new world and be part of what is out there. Yes, it is true, I was married once. I owned a farm. Everything went wrong. She died, my wife. Her family took my son. It is a curse on my family. Anyone I love is cursed.'

He felt desire rise within him; this was female, the smell, the shape of her breast, the curve of her hips and buttocks.

'What curse?' Anna said. 'There is magic here in Greenland. The gods protects us. Look how they come to hunt in the sky when the ribbon of color makes a road for them. We are close to Valhalla. No curse will follow you here. Our great ancestor, Eirik the Red, protects all who live in Greenland.'

Anna blushed. Sometimes with this man she felt there was no separation between them. He was as the clear water in the bay to her; it was impossible to gauge his depth and yet the desire to fall within pulled her forward.

'One hundred years ago my family came to Iceland,' Thorfinn said. 'There was a fight between brothers over a woman. One brother set fire to the other brother's house. Many people were locked inside: men, women, slaves, children. All burnt to death. The mother of one of the women inside was a witch – a Hilder witch with an evil manikin from the grave of a dead woman. She cursed all the men in our family from that time on to lose the ones they love. I cannot escape it, this curse. I lost my wife, I lost my son.' He leant heavily on his staff as the pain in his leg descended to his foot. 'I have sworn to Thor never to take another wife, another woman.'

'Things may be different in Greenland. Tell me about them,' Anna said, playing with the braid of hair she wore as a bangle around her wrist. 'What was she like, your wife?'

'You remind me of her. Same age, same yellow hair and delicate hands.' He took her hand in his and looped his fingers though the silver chain wound through the bangle of hair. 'From your mother?' Thorfinn smiled and let her hand fall as he turned back to the homestead. His leg gave way and he fell against Anna. She moved to steady him and he swung her into his arms as they both fell.

'Oh no, no, no,' he said and held her to him with his face in her hair.

She felt the length of him, and he was strong and hard in a way that Ged was not. He smelt like juniper and straw. She pulled away as his fingers found the shape of her breast.

'Anna Kerldottir. Woman. Elfspeaker.'

She could not look at him. She scrambled to her knees and pulled him upright. They stood and took the measure of the space between them. Anna put his arm around her shoulders to support him as they walked together in silence to the house. Thorfinn sat on his bed, took up his charcoal and sheep hide and sat staring at the marks already there. Anna moved her stool closer to Ged who smiled in an absent manner and did not seem aware of anything but the convoluted spiral he was drawing.

CHAPTER 10 — *The grandfather with hair that grew into the ground*

Bjarni ran in from the stables. 'Kazoo! Dead birds bums and cows guts!' He danced in a circle of glee and stopped in front of Ged. 'I saw it. I saw the bird.'

'With wings? And claws the size of a sheep? The dragon of Hvalsey? Tell yr Uncle Sokki, yer mad young Viking. Was it frozen with a little hole in the middle where's you bin poking it?'

'Fair made me skin creep, it did. I swear by the balls of Thor,' said Bjarni. 'A giant black creature what flew towards the mountains.'

Sokki laughed so much bits of shredded willow bark and spit fell down his chin into his silver beard. 'That pa of yours better organize a poke for you soon, young Viking or you'll be seeing them frozen birds ye fuck wherever ye look.'

Skadi felt the sickness rising as she looked at him.

Aud looked up from the sea urchins stew she stirred. 'The black bird comes again,' she sang in a low voice. 'It came the year your grandfather lost his second wife. The year me young sister drowned in the bay. Oh sad day. Dark day. He sat by the stream in grief and never moved till his hair grew into the ground. Oh darkness comes for he who sees the shadow bird.'

'Aye it is a creature that feeds on grief,' said Ged, looking up from his drawing

'Is is naught but an eagle who has flown too far north, brother. Do not listen to old Aud and her mutterings.'

'What are you saying?' Bjarni yelled in Aud's ear. How come you can suddenly hear us? Tells us then what you know.'

Aud continued singing: 'Darkness comes to Ebiwaz. Darkness and the wroth of Odin.' She speared a sea urchin and lifted it out of the pot and threw it into the fire.

'It is a demon that possesses the spirit,' Ged said, suddenly upright. He took up Thorfinn's cane, balanced it across his shoulders and fixed his gaze on Aud as if she herself had appeared in the form of a sea urchin. 'Oh darkness comes to he who sees the shadow bird,' he sang.

'God of the Christ, save us,' moaned Skadi. 'They is all witless here. Olaf,' she yelled. 'Where is that useless thing? Find him, Anna. God help us if it's a demon out there come to haunt us.'

Olaf appeared in the doorway in his cowl and beads. He had managed to shave off most of his beard and little lone tufts of whiskers sprung from his chin. His undershirt was plastered with tiny stains from dead lice and his feet were bound in fresh strips of goat hide. His eyes glittered like red-stained glass as he waved the Word of God at them. 'It is naught but someone is communing with the devil in this household.'

He opened his gold leaf book and looked at the pictures of men made to look like strange letters.

'Yea, gimme.' Bjarni snatched the book from Olaf. 'Hey Olaf they is fucking more than making letters! Look at them legs! They is all twined around one another like they is sexing.'

'Get orf with ye and yer fucking stupid religion,' Sokki yelled. 'Yer the devil around here, Olaf. In the South Land we chopped men like you to pieces for dog meat every time we came to a rats nest of Christians.'

Olaf clipped Bjarni around the knees with his stick and rescued his book. 'You will wake the ghosts of them men not buried in consecrated ground young heathen. And why is it you have not taken the Christ path like your father?'

The tomte, who was at this moment in the roof, pissed on Olaf's head.

Olaf fell on his knees in the straw. 'The angels cry for you.' he said. 'They send their tears to bless us in our ignorance and idolatry.'

Skadi moaned and her legs twitched involuntarily. Any movement was difficult. Anna turned to Ged for guidance as Olaf's mutterings became a litany of accusation, suffering and denouncement.

Ged stood by the loom, perplexed, his eyes focused on a fleeting shadow in the corner. He held a broken tool in his hands. He tried to speak but one thought that could be transferred into a sentence with more than two words eluded him. His fine yellow hair hung in strands around his shoulders and his pale skin seemed as thin as new fire. Asmund indicated that Anna go to him. He put his arms out to Anna as she approached and his muscles clamped around her with the strength of a dwarf. She drew him into their bed and closed the curtains around them.

CHAPTER 10 — *The grandfather with hair that grew into the ground*

Asmund nodded his approval. 'Make a son to pass on our memory, brother.'

Ged sighed with pleasure as Anna straddled him and he moved within her. He did not touch her. He lay still while she slowly brought him to release. Afterwards she pressed against his back to still the trembling of her body. She closed her eyes and imagined diving down into the sea at the end of the path. The water would be cold and clear. There would be soft sand below her. She imagined a line of white light above her like moonlight poured from a silver cup into the water.

'Ah wife, where will I find the children of the Whale-horse Queen?' Ged said hitching up his britches. 'Asmund says only in the Nordsetur.'

'No one goes to the Nordsetur. Sleep now, husband. Your seed is within me and I wish to sleep.'

'Tell me. Tell me, wife.'

'The skraelings say a man becomes a white bear in the Nordsetur, bit by bit, as the frost takes his body.'

Ged saw a creature, half-man, half-bear. Slowly it transformed into the Whale-horse Queen with long yellow tusks. If he found the bones of her children could he save Ebiwaz? Could he save Greenland from the curse this Icelander had released on them all? Anna must be safe. And Skadi with the baby coming. Men brought walrus skulls back to the steading to remove the ivory. He could find them. He listened to the movements of the others in their beds as they scuffled into comfort. It was not the fault of Thorfinn that this had come to be. A man could not be left to die on the cold rocks. The gods had put Thorfinn on their island for a reason.

When the house was quiet and Anna asleep he got out of bed and began to look, overturning clothes and food and old bones in his haste to search for the skulls. The tomte sat in the roof and sang through a small shell flute. His song set the straw whispering: *Ged, Ged. Find the skulls. Lift the curse. Ged, Ged.*

At last Ged stood rigid, his eyes transfixed. The stench of the stale breath of an old sea creature filled the house and mingled with the smell of the straw and the oil in the lamps. He could hear Nidhogg gnawing, gnawing as he ripped apart the foundations of the world and any dead who had descended there. He would not sleep. He would watch and protect the family as was his duty. The gods had sent Thorfinn with a message to tell him what he must do.

CHAPTER 11
One man can become all men

In the morning Skadi did not get up but complained of an intense headache and pains in her womb. Water came between her legs. Anna found Asmund and told him Skadi's time had come. O'Flarty and Berryface left by horse to fetch Brigitta, wife of Eirik Scarface, from the high valley under the Grey Mountain. Brigitta had birthed three children herself. She was known by the women of Greenland for her healing and the rock dust and herb potions she made to help relieve the pain of childbirth, induce love, give courage, speed the mending of a wound or fix a cow that had fallen.

It was possible to travel easy on land again now the ice shards were leaving the rocks with early spring. The earth was awakening and the sun moving towards longer days, with meadows and trees drooping with scented color. From the path Berryface and O'Flarty could see Eirik's farm ahead of them, placed as it was in a wide valley. Water was streaming down the cliff face behind the farm and the sides of the valley were green with new grass.

'A good time to birth with new life coming to the land,' Berryface said as the horses climbed though the birch trees to the high valley.

O'Flarty was, as usual, lost in thought. His horse meandered after Berryface without direction.

Asmund cuffed Bjarni and pointed to the shed that contained the forge. 'Get the good axe, son. We need firewood if Skadi's took in the birthing way.'

He grunted in the direction of Ged. 'Get him out of here Anna.

Fit has come upon him like it was before. He can't do no work like this. Won't be remembered for his carving if he stays like this for long. Better when he can lose his self and his worries in the places where he can't see the end of the sky. His self ain't too good with naught to look at but the world inside his head.'

Anna wrapped herself in her blue cloak and dragged Ged out the door. Thorfinn followed, his leg freshly bound with wadmal and moss. He leant on his stave and limped after them in case Ged's restless thoughts led him back to the hidden spaces of the longhouse.

Skadi was curled in pain and vomiting as they left. Aud stood with her and held her head and sang the songs of childbirth.

'Birth is like a gate that no one else can walk through but you,' Anna said as she dragged Ged into the glowing landscape. 'Look Ged, flowers.' She pointed to a meadow of tiny white flowers. 'Skadi could end up playing with a baby in those flowers.'

'She will be safe,' said Ged . 'The child will come hard. She will rise with difficulty. The Whale-horse Queen tells me.'

Anna turned to Thorfinn who put his hand on her shoulder and moved past to break the ice shards from the ferns on their path. Pain and suffering, Anna thought to herself. That was the life of a woman. You became a giant box where a baby grew. Just an empty box filled with the seed of a man. No one ever said that was where love and desire led.

'We must find the fruit of Yggdrasill,' Anna told Ged and Thorfinn as they moved into the dense forest of small willow and rowan trees. 'And we will ask Odin to guide you in your journey with the whale-horse.'

'I know you suffer with me wife when the vision comes upon me,' Ged remarked to his feet. 'As Odin can see an arrow speeding to its mark, I see your pain. If men hate each other, then I can end it with the wind that calms the sea.'

'Ged,' said Anna, 'can you talk to us in words we understand?'

'Asmund will have another son. The Whale-horse Queen has told me, toad me goad me. Thorfinn wants a wife, wants a pife, wants a knife. Did you know, Anna? Did you know that?'

CHAPTER 11 — *One man can become all men*

Anna sighed. There were no words to answer. Thorfinn walked ahead and with his staff was careful that no branch or ice shard should brush against Anna, no sharp stone wedge under her feet. At times they stood still, each stopping to appraise the words of the other when the need arose.

Ged continued to stumble behind them, his attention fixed on the inland cliffs and peaks.

'So Asmund went to the Western Settlement last summer to get a wife for Ged? What happened before that? When the fit came upon him?'

'Asmund locked him in the cow barn till the visions passed,' Anna whispered.

'Yes,' Ged yelled and pointed to the shadow of a bird against the mountain. 'A white bird. Odin has answered me. We will survive the curse of the Whale-horse Queen. It is foretold. The white feathers of a white bird. I must find the white bones of the whale-horse children. It is the will of Allfather.'

He lowered himself onto the carpet of white flowers by the path and lay there talking to creatures that he alone could see.

'Leave him,' Thorfinn said and took Anna's arm. His strange golden eyes sought her approval. 'He does not know what he says. Come. Let me show you something.'

He led Anna further off the path into the meadows beneath the mountains. 'This is a magic place, eh? A secret world where everything you want can be. Like the path that Freyja walked when she went looking for her necklace and her tears fell as a shower of gold on the path in front of her.'

Anna followed. The secrets of the day opened before them as the mountains spread their shadow across the earth in shapes of the deepest hue. Thorfinn put down his stave and put his arm around Anna's shoulders. She came to his body with ease, and for a time there was nothing in the world but the texture and the contour of the other.

'Oh Anna, Anna. My golden necklace.'

Anna swayed against the pressure of his arms. She felt as if all her life she had known this man: the shape of him, his smell, the texture of his hair and his skin, the lightness that came between them when she closed her eyes.

Thorfinn kissed her again and again. Anna touched his face and her hands played in his red-gold hair. 'What comes between us Thorfinn? Nothing has ever been like this for me before. It is as if I have always known you.'

'Let me come into you. I need woman. I need you.' Thorfinn moved his hands gently under her shift.

'Anna,' yelled Ged. 'Wife. Come. We must find the nest of the white falcon.'

'Leave him. Let his family look after him if he is so helpless. Thor's balls, he can't even find a bird nest by himself.'

'He walks between two worlds. He cannot care for himself when the other world is too strong.'

Thorfinn lifted her shift higher till his hands cupped the roundness of her hips. 'Anna, Anna, I must have you now.'

Anna leant towards him and felt the heat of his body. He was hard in a way that Ged was not. He smelt male. His hands slipped between her thighs.

'Wife,' Ged yelled. 'Come. We must find the bird who gave us this white feather. It is the will of the Allfather.'

Anna twined her arms around Thorfinn as he pressed himself into her body. There was movement in the bushes behind them. Ged appeared out of the forest. His eyes were the color of the sky and his pale skin seemed to stretch in a haze around his long limbs. He not did see Thorfinn and Anna but focused only on the rocks above.

Thorfinn pulled away. 'I need you,' he hissed. 'Anna. Now. I want you woman.'

'Needs a wife, need a pyfe, need a kife?' sang Ged. 'All men must take a second wife, says Sokki. Second pyfe, second kife, second wife?'

Anna stood perplexed. 'Husband, you look like a spirit yourself coming out of the mountain with your hair wild about your face and your eyes shining with the blue light of Odin.'

Thorfinn turned away, beating a path for himself though the scrub

CHAPTER 11 — One man can become all men

with his stave. The mountain ash closed around his form and the birds and insects resumed as if he had never been.

Ged regarded her with mild amazement. 'Do you upset him, wife? He is my friend. He has brought me a message from the gods. Look. Up there on the mountain. Is it a bird with a tail? Or a dragon with wings? Is it black? Or white with the shadow of the mountain upon it?'

Ged scrambled up an incline, dragging Anna after him. He insisted she sit with him and watch the mountain and the creature circling in the shadow of the rocks.

'It is just a bird, Ged. A falcon in the shadow of the mountain. It means nothing.'

'Would you be his wife too, Anna?'

'Freyja. Goddess of cats and gold. How many lovers did she have?' Anna smiled and scratched at the ground. She felt empty, cold without the heat of Thorfinn beside her. 'Oh, Freyja let this man come to me,' she prayed. 'Let this man come into me and fill the emptiness of my body.'

She thought the goddess answered: one man can become all men. She turned to Ged and put her arms around him and touched him between his legs. He lay unresponsive, absorbed in contemplation of the shadows high on the mountain.

'Odin has given me the answer. Wife, we will return to Ebiwaz and I will trap this creature in my carving to protect us all.'

CHAPTER 12
Scarface and Brigitta return to Ebiwaz

'Best get off then,' Eirik Scarface said to Berryface and O'Flarty as they stood and inspected the Grey Mountain behind his farm. 'Hear 'em giants stamping up there and making snow fall from the top of the mountain. I've a few matters to discuss with Asmund so I'll be riding with you. So as yer don't get up to any mischief behind me back, Brigitta Sigurdottir.'

His one eye as blue as melt water flashed into a smile as he appraised his wife. He patted his shining red beard and inclined his head as if in a question. Brigitta detached her youngest child from her breast and partly secured her apron with a brooch in the form of the serpent Jormungard. She had some idea what business Scarface had with Asmund. Whatever Scarface did involved fighting or drinking or having sex with anyone or anything in any place that involved danger, like a rock on the top of a cliff or on the edge of a bottomless blue pool or in the cave of a wild animal with the smell of death and blood all around.

More than once, Brigitta had come home with a cut or a bruise to the flesh on her buttocks and knees. And more than likely after such an excursion Scarface would suffer with itchy balls until bath day.

'Get up then woman,' Scarface said and brushed his hand across the hard nipples projecting from Brigitta's tunic. 'But first come here, wife. I wish to inspect the store house and need you to say what caribou we will take to Asmund for the birthing feast. You bondsman and woman, wait for us.'

CHAPTER 12 — *Scarface and Brigitta return to Ebiwaz*

Berryface and O'Flarty heard him quoting the words of the Wise One as he led Brigitta towards the shed: 'Before a birth, lie with a woman of strength to increase the worth of all women in the eyes of the gods.'

When Ged and Anna returned to the steading the whole world was wet and dripping: the angelica, the small willows, the grass in the home paddock, the roof of the house, the rocks and the seaweed on racks by the path. Moisture fell from all in a steady irregular pattern. Only the beach in front of the house was visible. The sharp walls of the fiord had softened into the mist and the sea lay dense and grey in front of the house.

Ged found his way to the stream where the skins of the animals were cleaned. He foraged in a midden by the cleansing tables. There were bones, small and large, covered with dirt and ice and sheep droppings. Rats scuttled away as he foraged. With a cry of joy he unearthed three large whale-horse skulls, hollow, with the teeth missing. He washed them carefully in the stream and packed them into an old nestbaggin of sheepskin. With his trophy safe he returned to the house with the mist dripping in rivulets from his hair.

Inside the longhouse Olaf leant over Skadi muttering inaudible requests to the Christ god to rid the house of any spirits that might affect the coming birth. Skadi was looking at him with wide eyes, her strange-shaped mouth curled in a silent cry. As Anna entered she rolled over and began crawling around on all fours in the straw on the floor.

'Look to her, Anna,' Asmund said as she came into the house. 'Look to her. I . . .' He stood with his axe on his shoulder and his apron over his arm, his solid form outlined by the fire like a weatherworn house pillar, his mouth slightly ajar with the order of a lawbinder that would not come by his teeth.

'Hey Asmund,' bellowed Eirik Scarface as his bulk filled the doorway, 'your man sent for us. He comes now with a half a caribou for your family. We will trade for goat and seal if you have any. Asmund I've important business with you. As the Wise One says, let the wimmen give birth and let the good men feed their friendship with ale and secrets. Looks harder than it is. Women's work. Not for the likes of us Viking men.'

Scarface clamped his large fist around Asmund's arm and dragged him out the door. 'Now yer listen t' me. Brigitta has birthed three children. She is the best midwife in the West and the East. That woman of yours, she's tough, ain't she?'

Scarface waved a piece of walrus leather in front of Asmund's nose and thundered: 'Now see this, Asmund. A fine a piece of horse harness as you would want. Suit that grey pony of yours. Come on, away from these women and show me that horse.'

Scarface enlisted the help of Short Irish and Sokki to propel Asmund outside towards the cow byre which was tucked into the hill behind the house. There were a few cows munching in the byre and a couple of horses, but room there was enough for men to make a comfortable space in the hay with a small fire in the rocks by the door. A heavy shaft of whale bone could be slid part-way across the doorway to keep out the worst of Thor's anger when the rain and ice blew down from the mountains.

Ged followed the back of Asmund and found his way into a warm place by the largest cow. He lay wrapped in a blanket with his face towards the wall till uneasy dreams claimed him. Short Irish leant up against the other side of the cow and set himself to imagine what it would be like to be a cow rather than an Irish bondsman indentured to the steading of Ebiwaz. The main problem, as far as he could see, would be if he would give birth to small cows or large babies and would they be Irish or Norse.

Scarface settled cross-legged on one of the last remaining straw bales. He rubbed at the long scar that ran from eyebrow to his mouth. 'Now,' he said, 'Asmund, yer know I'm a good man, Chieftain of Thorness and maker of the best horse harness in Greenland. I know the sayings of the Wise One like a pudding of sheep guts by me bed. So I say as the Chief of Thorness that I've a bit of trouble with a tribe of giants that live in the hills.

'Me and Gunhar Olvadsson are getting together a few men to teach them a lesson. This is what happened. You know me oldest daughter Menglad was betrothed to the son of Odd. The field in the

CHAPTER 12 — Scarface and Brigitta return to Ebiwaz

valley behind the Grey Mountain was her dowry. Long ways inland. No settlements near. It's a good field with grass to support the wild caribou that comes in the summer.

'Well, that son of Odd, he went and died just after she married him. His family claims she killed him with magic and so they reckon they should keep the field and the animals in it. But they don't do nothing to stop them giants. I say he died of gut rot and the field is mine and the caribou what come to graze there mine. But while we is arguing, them giants is picking off the caribou on me land and no one is stopping them. None left if we don't stop 'em.'

'Did that daughter of yours sit on the grave of her dead mother one night?' Sokki said. 'Me aunt wot died did. Ghost rose out of the dirt and came into her and gave her the magic way. Not that it did her any good seeing as she died of the fever shortly after.'

'Mad old Viking,' remarked Scarface. 'Thems witches tales, says Brigitta. And no. Me daughter is ugly as a giant's turd and just as stupid, but she ain't a witch. She ain't sat on no grave.'

Asmund stared at the assembled men.

'And we all knows what damage giants can do, being as big and hungry as they is,' Sokki said, coming to sit beside Scarface with an empty bowl that he upended and tapped meaningfully in Asmund's direction.

'Listen well, Asmund. Giants live in the Grey Mountain. You can smell them roasting animals in the valleys where they live. Hidden valleys up beyond the snow. Them is my animals and my land. Odd and his kin refuse to help me. Odd says it is me stealing his caribou and he wants compensation for every animal them giants eat.'

A piercing scream came from the house. Asmund jerked and grunted.

'Women,' said Scarface. 'Take no notice. Always make noise one end or the other. Brigitta now, she yells like a giant taking a shit when she pops a kid. Let 'em alone, Asmund. These giants are men's work.'

'Yer need ale Asmund,' Sokki said. 'We all need ale being as it is a special occasion.'

'I agree,' Scarface said. 'Now who is going in there to get it?'

Sokki got up and moved into the main house as silently as if part of a raiding party. 'Jest getting the crucifix for Asmund,' he said as he fumbled in Skadi's discarded tunic and removed the keys to the ale cupboard.

'I think we could trap 'em in the valley.' Scarface scratched his crotch with big red hands as Sokki returned with a bucket of ale.

Asmund regarded him with a blank look. Short Irish brought himself to consciousness and decided that, tonight of all nights, he must watch what stars first left the shadow of the mountains. 'Particularly important,' he told Asmund, 'to see if The Twins watch Ebiwaz tonight when another Norse comes to Greenland.'

Asmund handed him a horn of ale. Short Irish produced a bucket of his berry fizz.

Thorfinn and Bjarni did not join the party in the cow byre. Thorfinn limped to and fro from the beach to the house with as much driftwood as he could carry till his leg burned with fatigue. Repelled and fascinated, he fed the fire until shadows filled the old house with visions of the birth of his own son and the pain of his wife as she bled to death. He could see the house where they had lived; the walls of Ebiwaz closed around him like a prison of memory. Yet he could not leave now in case the women needed something. He must help if he could this time.

Bjarni sat on Asmund's high seat drinking whey and sharpening the blade of his knife. 'When we go to the New Country,' he told an invisible Egil, 'we need to know what these women know. We had better know what to do if there ain't no other woman around.' He imagined Egil praising him for his wisdom while the strange light of the New Country fell all around them.

CHAPTER 13
The birth

In the longhouse, the women moved around Skadi and for each one it was as if the pain of her birth were theirs again. They helped her into the birthing gown and held her arms as she sat in the birthing way. Brigitta massaged her stomach and her legs with seal oil. Aud caressed her face and sang the old songs of pain and birth.

As Skadi moaned and panted Anna felt the air around them become still, as if there was a presence in the room; a spirit who had come to guide them and was listening with love, with acceptance. Someone prepared to accompany anyone that might travel through the gateway to the realm of the living or the dead. A gate that was so easily opened at this time.

The wind moaned though the house and set the wall tapestries flapping. Skadi bellowed and screamed. She pressed the small metal dog to her stomach and called for the big dogs to comfort her. The women massaged her back and legs. They held moss to her lips and helped her kiss the Christian crucifix as Olaf instructed. They breathed with her and moaned with her. The dogs crept up to her and licked her face as she struggled.

In the byre Scarface told story after story about his famous ancestor, Eirik the Red, and the sound of his voice penetrated even Ged's dreams. 'Women there were to have his children,' said Scarface. 'Even his bondswoman were fertile as me goats. Norse women can give birth anywheres. In a ship on the wild sea if they has to. In a land far away from any known civilization. Squeeze babies out with never a problem.'

Scarface fixed Asmund with his melt water eyes. Asmund thumped his own leg and swilled ale as fast as possible as the sound of Skadi screaming came around them.

Still the women struggled. The mist on the walls of the house was replaced by tiny particles of ice. Thorfinn roused Bjarni and together they sealed all the gaps in the doors and curtains. As Brigitta instructed, they drew runes in charcoal above the doors to forbid entry to all strange beings who might ride the storm and claim the spirit of a child new to the world. Skadi cried and called to the child to come. Brigitta told Thorfinn and Bjarni to open all the chests and cupboards to encourage the opening of the womb. Anna threw pungent herbs into the fire and the scent mingled with the smell of wood smoke and fear.

Towards morning Skadi gave a curdling scream and the baby crowned. She lay still while Brigitta massaged her stomach. The women washed the baby and wrapped it in fine linen and wadmal. They put Skadi on her back and placed the baby on her breast. The placenta came with pain and difficulty. Skadi cried and held onto Aud. One side of her face seemed not to work. One side of her body seemed not to do what she wanted. When it was over she smiled her one-sided smile and cradled the baby to her. The dogs crept up from the fire and nuzzled at her bed.

It seemed to Anna that Skadi and the baby were surrounded by a skein of love; they lay as if bathed in a soft caressing light. There was a feeling of joy and peace around them. The child seemed to be a tiny body with a great spirit around it. Anna sank to the seat beside Thorfinn and rested her head against his shoulder; they had shared this together. Asmund stumbled into the room supported by Scarface and followed by Sokki, Ged and the Irish. The men stood around beaming. Even the stern features of Asmund lit with pleasure at the sight of a small crumpled baby with a thick head of brown hair just like his own.

'There,' Scarface said, grinning in triumph. 'Wimmen knows what to do. The Wise One says, never cross a mountain without the news of a newborn baby. Never tackle a mountain of pasture-stealing giants without the spirit of a new life what has come to your house Asmund.'

CHAPTER 13 — *The birth*

'Makes it up,' said Brigitta and elbowed her husband out of the way to set a stew simmering on the fire.

Asmund sent for Olaf to bless the child. Olaf muttered prayers about the Holy Spirit living within the newborn child who was born good and without evil. 'Honor the One True God, be brave and follow the way of the True Christ,' Olaf waved his arms over Skadi and the baby. Anna could see the outline of a huge shimmering form beside Skadi. The goddess Frigg, she thought, and wondered if this was the presence who had been with Skadi and the baby throughout the birth.

CHAPTER 14
New life gives hope

Brigitta and Scarface stayed through the waxing of the moon. Brigitta made potions of rock dust and herbs for Skadi and supplemented them with ground up walrus teeth.

'Me old mother knew a thing or two,' Brigitta told Anna. 'Women's secrets. Given though the years as each girl became a mother and told her daughters. Those fierce women from the old times knew how to take care of their men when they came home in the winter. They were only with their wives a few turnings of the moon afore they went south again in their longships. Them men had to be fit to make babies. So the wimmen gave them this precious dust and they got all the babies they wanted. Now we in Greenland need babies to grow up and make this place strong so the King of Norway don't take us over and force us to be Christian. Like what happened in Iceland. And who is going to fight Scarface's giants,' she laughed with a wicked twinkle in her eyes, 'if we don't give 'em all the babies we can?'

On the waning moon Scarface told Asmund he must return to Thorness to oversee the seeding of the fodder crop and begin the task of recruiting an army to confront the evil caribou-roasting giants. He left with itchy balls after a short interlude with Brigitta on a cliff on the other side of the bay opposite Ebiwaz.

One night a sweet wind came to Ebiwaz and with it the knowledge that the time of darkness was truly ending. People were happy. Men and women went about their work with a renewed belief in the cycle of things, in the rightness of the world no matter how hard the winter

CHAPTER 14 — *New life gives hope*

had been, no matter how old one was, no matter how much the bones ached, there was always new life to live through again.

The women of the farm took turns to keep the baby warm. Skadi did not walk well and found it difficult to share her body heat with the tiny mewling. Berryface and Anna carried the child in a shawl tied to their back as they worked. Aud put hot rocks on Skadi's feet and held the child to Skadi's breast if Skadi could not manage. The child was strong, a little red faced thing with brown hair and tiny hands and feet he waved around whenever he could. They called him Byggvir Asmudsson.

Bjarni regarded his new brother with a distant fascination. He was pleased he could now escape the sole attention of Asmund and the grime and noise of the smithy. He spent as much time as possible hunting. Ged had seen the black dragon bird again. Bjarni was determined to decorate his bed chamber with its wings.

Thorfinn and Anna kept well away from one another. At night she lay with Ged who remained vague and distracted. Often he would subside within her and leave no seed but sigh and return to his dreams alone. Anna began to look at the genitals of men and long for the feel of Thorfinn against her body. She had no doubt that a child would come to her, rock dust or no rock dust, if she lay with both Thorfinn and Ged.

The women of Ebiwaz had started a new weaving. Anna was responsible for the design that edged the fabric. No matter how difficult the pattern, thoughts of Thorfinn came unbidden into her day: the strength of his arms, the shape of his thighs, the smell and taste of him. The weaving was complicated with a series of knots and forms that grew from the centre of a circle. The patterns came without effort into her hands and told of Thorfinn and Ged in a way that did not need words. 'Could I,' she asked herself, 'not be wife to both?'

Colors and shapes flew before her eyes like the rush of the tide on full moon. She asked the women to set the loom by the door so she could watch the water in the bay below the house. The way the sea moved reminded her of a universe teaming with possibilities; tiny spirits that rushed in upon one another like small fluid creatures involved in the dance one moment, invisible the next. She imagined them all moving toward the shore and together rising out of the foam as tiny white elves and then turning to fly back into the sea.

She longed to be away from Ebiwaz and to be safe in the cold mountain valleys of her childhood, where only the spirits in the rocks and the elves were her companions, and her mother and sisters were waiting at home. Thorfinn was unknown and unpredictable; a fierce man without a family, as strange as his golden eyes that followed her where ever she went.

Skadi's birthing haunted her. Several of her friends had died with the fever after birth. Was this what happened at the end of desire? Did no one understand? The graves of Greenland were full of young women and old men.

At night when she lay beside Ged and used her body to comfort him the pattern came; a thing that grew from the darkness behind her eyes, a swirling black and white thing with no regularity or meaning. It filled the night and stayed before her eyes no matter where she looked.

Ged cried when she told him. 'I will protect you, wife. I will dream your dreams. There is no fear for you in this while I am here. Look, I cry your tears.'

Anna kissed his eyes. 'I will never leave you husband. Protect me. Take this from me.' She wound herself around Ged as he lay stiff and watchful in her arms.

Thorfinn watched the people at the farm and the days of his life in Iceland came back to him. He saw the moment of his wife's death, the blood as it streamed from her body and soaked into the bed. He heard the wailing of his newborn son. He heard the words of his wife's father and mother as they took the child from him because he refused to accept the Christ god. He was so lost in grief he had not the will to oppose them. The lawspeaker had decreed Iceland follow the ways of the Christ god. He was the outcast. He could not in truth give up the old gods of his ancestors. When the judgment about the child went against him he found a crew of strong men who still loved the old gods. He sold his farm and bought a ship. When they left for the New Country he and his men left everything they knew behind.

CHAPTER 14 — *New life gives hope*

He drew endless maps of Markland in the ash of the hearth with his long staff. He listened for the sounds of congress from the bed palate of Ged. He smelt sex on every woman. He could not rid himself of the image of Anna lying beside him. He imagined his hands entangled in her hair as he pulled her to him and found the sweet cleft between her legs.

As the days lengthened Ged returned to his carving. The whispering in the roof became less. The Whale-horse Queen left the house and now watched only from the bay. He could still smell her breath and see the slime of her skin on the path from the door to the water. His tools reappeared in his toolbox. He persuaded Olaf to let him rest his skulls in a nestbaggin near the bag full of human bones in the barn. Brigitta watched him with interest and considered her bottles of rock dust.

Skadi improved. She could only walk with difficulty but still she demanded the keys of the household be returned to her. She fastened them to her apron; one side of her face did not work as it used to and one side of her body was always cold and weak. She spoke with a slur and spat out the words. She dribbled and was unaware of this. She smelt of old blood and fish. The dogs, Geri and Hermod, kept to her side and seemed to want to protect the baby as much as Skadi.

Bjarni continued to supply the farm with ptarmigans from his hunting and trapping in the hills. Berryface had the job each night of thwacking the birds, dead or alive, to provide food for people and the dogs. Skadi supervised the process from her bed. Every night Berryface knelt by the fire with the large hounds pawing and barking around her while she sent the axe through the flesh of the birds. The livid birthmark on her face glistened with sweat.

When he was not hunting, Bjarni spent as much time as he could with Sokki and Thorfinn in the cow byre. As Skadi could not see well out of one eye and must walk dragging one leg after her, Sokki took the opportunity to come and go quietly into the storeroom where Skadi kept the ale. He became adapt at removing the keys to the ale cupboard from her apron when she was feeding the baby. In the dim afternoons of late spring when the earth was still cold and the rocks slippery with rain, Sokki went a raiding again. He illustrated his stories with great slashing and thrusts of his ancestral weapon. He crept from the sea with his shipmates, leapt over walls and captured slaves and silver from the huge stone monasteries of the south lands.

Thorfinn and Bjarni roared with approval as Sokki's sword cleaved the air this way and that and occasionally dislodged a piece of the wall or got buried in cow hide.

Short Irish could hear the noise from the home paddock. 'A curse on them Norse,' he told O'Flarty. 'Thieving pirates, the lot of 'em. Killed me ancestors. Yours too. And took the land what was ours by rights since we came from Ireland same time as them. Same as in Iceland. We Irish won this earth same as the Norse.'

'Irishman, come share the berry drink with us,' yelled Bjarni when he heard Short Irish snorting and stamping around the cattle.

Short Irish came into the byre and glared at all with his black eyes fierce under black brows. Thorfinn handed him a horn. Short Irish dipped it into a bucket by the door and settled himself into a pile of moldy grass where he could look at the clouds and think of revenge. He imagined the way the She Dragon of the Great North Sky would send a ball of lightening down on all Norse in Greenland. Afterwards she would take him into herself, roll him around and suck the seed from him which would fall like stars on the Great Ocean. 'And I will sing the song of victory,' he told Thorfinn and Bjarni.

Asmund decided to ignore whatever was happening in the cow byre behind the longhouse. He was proud of himself to be a man with two sons. He knew it was his duty to produce as many sons as he could for the honor of his memory. Most nights a whimpering sort of burbling could be heard with a rhythmic thumping from the bed cupboard of Asmund Lawbinder and Skadi Twistbeaks.

'I have to go,' Brigitta told the women of Ebiwaz one moon rise. 'That daughter of Eirik's is trouble without me there. Everyone knows it brings bad luck to be living with a woman whose husband died the first night of their marriage, like it happened to Menglad. Son of that

CHAPTER 14 — New life gives hope

Odd never got to plant seed in that skinny cow Eirik calls a daughter. And who knows what that man of mine has been fucking while I's away. Few sheep may have a sore bum.'

Brigitta prepared a bundle of rock dust for Skadi and said farewell. She walked with Anna and O'Flarty to the path at the top of the hills.

'You come and see me as soon as the moon is full again,' Brigitta said to Anna. 'You and I, we will search the hills for secrets. I know what Ged needs to make him strong and give you children.'

She kissed Anna on the lips and walked off at a fast pace.

CHAPTER 15
The blot

A message came from a large farm on the fiord beyond Ebiwaz; the people of Hvalsey Settlement were invited to a blot to celebrate the beginning of new life that had come with the return of the sun into the world. The women of his household, Gunhar Bloodaxe said, had made two huge vats full of ale, one flavored with juniper and one with angelica. A fat pig was to be sacrificed for the feast. All the people in the valleys around would be coming to the celebration, for three babies and two sets of twins had been born and survived in the Eastern Settlement that spring.

The blot was to be held one moonrise after the equinox in honor of Odin and his Valkyries, as in the old days this signified the time of the beginning of the great Viking raids on the south lands. Gunhar Bloodaxe and Scarface would make the sacrifice. Like Sokki Bluetooth and Eirik Scarface, Gunhar could claim ancestry though the settlers of Iceland to a line of men who went raiding years at a time. Gunhar favored the name Bloodaxe, which had belonged to his father's father. His wife was a very tall women with yellow hair in curls that sweetened the eyes of many a young Viking. It was rumored she liked to wear britches and go hunting with her son from a previous marriage.

Gunhar had built a large new hall on his farm to please her. The hall had a fire pit in it where an animal could be boiled in a metal cauldron, which was a marvel to see itself, all shiny and strong like an axe. It had shapes on it drawn by Locki, Gunhar's wife said, so if anyone tried to steal it they would end up roast like a pig themselves as a meal for the Ice Giants.

CHAPTER 15 — *The blot*

Yellowbritches, the poet, was coming too, with a skin drum and a pipe that played so light the feet could not stay still.

The day of the blot was a fine and clear. The path over the meadows and the hills from the inland farms had been cleared of debris; there was new wood on the trees and green shoots promised a good summer. The juniper was in flower and the hills luminescent with the orange berries of mountain ash and the darker hew of the berry bush leaves.

The men and women of Ebiwaz were of importance and their jewels and fine clothes showed them as such. Asmund wore his ancestral sword, Luckspeaker, in its wooden scabbard and a woven cap that made him look twice as tall. The sun glinted on his silver armbands and the ornaments in his hair and beard. Ged chose a tunic of leather with myriad creatures from the dark realm pressed into the hide with blue dye. His hair was bound and secured with silver in the form of a serpent. He had his knife and spoon attached to a belt of walrus leather.

Skadi and Anna each wore a pleated dress embroidered with indigo and gold thread. Each had a set of intricately cast brooches attached to their over tunics with chains hanging between that moved as they moved. Anna wore a headdress of red linen her mother had saved from her own marriage to the trader from Bristol. Aud covered her dark dress with a cloak lined with black fox fur and on her head she placed a woven headdress with a long tail falling down her back. All wore boots of leather and fur trim.

The Irish bondsmen were instructed to stay and care for the cattle and the dogs. Anna ensured they had a fine cut of meat to roast. Ged took Aud on one horse, while Asmund led Skadi and the baby on another. Thorfinn sat with Sokki on another horse while the rest of the party walked.

Sokki glistened in his finest clothes. He had oiled and plaited his beard until his silver hair shone like ice. Berryface walked beside Thorfinn and Skadi. She was not a tall woman, as were the Norse, and she was dark, unlike the women at Ebiwaz, but she walked proudly and swung her hips to the song of the bright day. Sokki watched her with pride.

They arrived when the sun was over the horizon. The wooden door pillars of the new hall snapped and creaked in the heat of the day. The smell of boiling pig mingled with the smell of straw, wood fire and blood. The hall was decorated with long weavings of bright colors; fearful dragons and writhing monsters found their way across the material to frame scenes of the gods, of the fate of men and the great deeds of ancestors. Trophies in honor of battles won in the name of Thor were also strung up on the walls: swords, shields, foreign coats of arms, a bishop's crosier from the south, bits of old silver cut into solid pieces and plates and strings of coins.

There were two large vats of ale at one end of the room. A woman in some disarray dispensed the precious liquid into wooden cups and hollow cow horns. Two fearsome men stood each side of her to supervise the process. All five sipped at their own ale and laughed continually as people thronged around them. Gunhar's wife, Sigrid the Tall, occasionally walked past to inspect the level of the ale.

'Dispatched the pig already,' Scarface said to Asmund. A woman in a green cloak danced past with a sponge and a bucket and sprinkled pig's blood over them both. Skadi and the baby were escorted to the seat of honor with the other mothers and babies. The mothers were red-faced and merry with ale. Berryface held the baby and mopped at Skadi's brow. Next to the mothers on a bench sat old men and women with a variety of teeth filling the spaces in their gums. They laughed raucously and poked at the babies and any other person who passed too close.

Brigitta came to play with the babies. 'There's Yellowbritches and his Aged Pa's about somewhere too,' she told Berryface and pointed to a lithe young man who sang and clapped to the music. 'Now that one should be taking a wife or he'll be off fucking sheep like his uncle Scarface.'

She waved at Yellowbritches and pointed at a girl talking to Scarface.

The ale flowed. Muscles made strong by unrelenting cold and hard work relaxed. Thoughts cultivated in the silence of the land became trade between taciturn individuals. The company linked arms around the cauldron. Gunhar Bloodaxe called the presence of Odin to witness the day. To each person it felt as if the old gods stood with them. Even the Christ men joined with Scarface and Gunhar as they sang the songs of their ancestors to Odin; the melody swelled out across

CHAPTER 15 — The blot

the mountains and the sea and up to the gates of Valhalla. At last each man lit a torch from the central fire and linked arms with a woman to move in a fast stamping dance. The drum beat out an intoxicating rhythm; Gunhar and Scarface bellowed song after song.

The ale flowed. Bjarni got into a fight with Ingibjorg Hrutsson over the color of Gudrun Leifdottoir's hair. The men stood around shouting until Bjarni knocked his opponent out with a kick to his jaw. Attention was drawn to another duel between two old men, enemies since the days of raiding on the Scottish coast. Bets were taken on who could impale the other first with whatever implement. This was much fun to the onlookers as both old men were nearly blind and crippled with arthritis and could barely lift a knife.

Bjarni was dragged by Gudrun into a corner filled with young females who planned to investigate the fertility rites of the Valkyries. Skadi snored in a corner with the baby propped up in her good arm. Berryface sat by her and grinned at all who passed. Asmund decided it was his right as the chief of Ebiwaz to investigate the undergarments of the serving woman who had abandoned her post at the ale vats. Word was out anyways that this woman was the mother of at least one of Gunhar's children.

'The handmaidens of Odin,' she said to Asmund in a softly slurred purr, 'come this day to Midgard to celebrate the creation of life. Do you think I am one?'

Scarface, with a large skein of ale in his hand, came to watch.

'Indeed you are woman, indeed you are,' Asmund said pushing himself up to her. 'Odin's joy.'

'Was the way you dealt the ale that gave it away,' said Scarface.

The girl reached out to stroke Asmund on the chest. Scarface wandered off to a group of men and women settled at a table. 'Now listen,' he said fixing them all with his melt-water eyes. 'We is all kin is we not? Odin's kin. Beloved of Thor. Now I have a problem what needs kin to fix it.

'Giants of the Grey Mountain giving you trouble?' inquired Sigrid. She thumped her drinking horn against the table and bellowed with laughter. 'Come Valkyries,' she said to the women around her. 'I know where this is going.' She stood and the women followed. 'Ale is needed before one finds truth in the words of Scarface. Come my little ones.'

'Well yer know, Bloodaxe,' said Scarface, 'I speak the truth no matter what them women say. Giants is taking the animals off me summer pasture and I need yer help to rid them.'

'Thought that field went with yer daughter Menglad when she married young Odd?'

'Nar,' said Scarface, 'Yer knows young Odd died the night they was married. No dowry has to be given, I say.'

The company grunted and scratched. This had been a topic of conversation over the winter's dark. Asmund left off fumbling with the handmaiden of Odin and reached for the ale skein. The young woman urinated on his feet.

'Well,' continued Scarface with the ale in rivulets through his beard, 'I need me kin to fix this, yer great lot of Vikings. I need that field back before them giants think of taking us over. Always hear 'em rumbling and plotting. I need yers to go ter war with them giants what is a threat to us all in Greenland.'

The men scratched and thought. Yes, the Norse were the match of any giant. They did owe loyalty to Scarface, him being kin of Eirik the Red. And if one giant got away with stealing, then the whole settlement could be overrun. No one was safe.

'If Odd's son died before the marriage was done in bed and there was no magic, then the field that was the dowry Scarface gave with his daughter should go back to Scarface.'

'Aye,' grunted Gunhar Bloodaxe. 'Ain't yer going to take the case to the Mid Summer Assembly?'

'Ter argue with Odd and his lot? Them that never leave the Grey Mountain? Never been to the Althing at Gardar. Can't talk hardly. Wild men. No one knows where they come from. Can't trust anyone what lives behind the Grey Mountain with them giants rutting in the valleys.' Scarface looked severely at Asmund. 'And anyways I want it solved afore mid-summer.'

CHAPTER 15 — *The blot*

'People say Odd married his daughter and she bore a mad child what lives in the caves at the bottom of the Grey Mountain.'

Asmund pushed the woman's dress up to her shoulders. She groaned with pleasure.

'Aye,' said Scarface through a haze of ale and pig skin, 'nothing is there that us Vikings cannot fix.'

'With the blessing of the disir,' said Gunhar, snorting at Asmund who had penetrated the drunken girl. 'Now why Scarface did ye marry off your daughter to someone from a family like them Odds?'

'That girl,' replied Scarface scratching at his balls, 'was never nothing but trouble. If there was something not to fall into to, she be in up to her neck before you could say dwarf's prick. If there was something not to break, it'd be in pieces the moment she walked past. If she was to look after the ducks, they'd by flying halfway to Iceland soon as she fed 'em. If she had to look after the horses, they'd be mats for the giants feet before nightfall. Thor's balls, she had a stink about her. And, as well, she was the daughter of me old bondswoman who was here before Brigitta came to Thorness. So as soon as Odd came over the hill and asked for a women for his son, I knew she was the one. As Odin says, if a wild man comes out of the hills, he will do good to find a woman what has been known by a dwarf.'

Scarface sat with his eyes closed after the exertion of speech. The group of men lost interest and wandered off. Gunhar decided to follow Asmund's example and waved his erect prick at the woman who lay intoxicated on a bench in front of them.

Eirik's nephew, Yellowbritches, set up a rhythm on his skin drum. Four women formed a circle and twirled in a dance around him, their hair swinging loose around their shoulders as they moved. Yellowbritches laughed and sang about the joys of Valhalla as he played. The women held wildflowers they threw to the crowd as they danced. As the dance ended each young woman whirled into the arms of a man and was carried off in triumph.

Thorfinn found the company of other men who had been to Markland. He consumed much ale and sang very loudly to Odin and

Thor. He watched Anna dance from a place that afforded him the best sight of her body.

'What a fierce woman you are,' he shouted as she passed. 'A woman true to your ancestors.'

More good ale was consumed and the pig eaten with duck eggs and angelica. In the early afternoon the music ceased and the stillness of the land returned. People drowsed to the sound of insects and the grunting and giggles coming from shadowed corners of the hall. Yellowbritches was engulfed by a stout young outlander with a flute while Bjarni and Egil disappeared with Gudrun Leifdottoir. Ged was in serious conversation with a carver from the settlement of Hodd, a bronze-skinned man covered with tufts of white hair that stuck up as if attempting an escape from his head and face. They staggered around the hall, Ged in the lead, with a skin full of ale, drawing an endless line around the coupling bodies. 'To define humanity within the limits of Midgard,' Ged told the carver from Hodd. Scarface snored in the straw with Brigitta sleeping peacefully on top of him.

Anna found Thorfinn. There was nothing to be said. They stood bound together with a magnetism that was amplified by the heat and the sensuality of the afternoon. For each there was only the other. Thorfinn put his arms around Anna and she came to the shape of his body. Wordlessly he led her out into the shadowed side of the hall. He kissed her and pushed her against the wall. With one hand he lifted her fine dress and felt her open to him. All that he had ever known he found within her fragility, her touch, the way her hair fell across his face as he kissed her.

Light flowed between them. His hands and mouth gave pleasure as Anna had never known. He lifted and moved her with ease; she followed, delighted at his control. There was no separation, no oneness no self apart from this moment. The Anna who knew Thorfinn folded up into a package to be carried to the halls of Freyja forever.

In the evening, when the moon softened the landscape and a lightness filtered into the hall, people awoke, gathered their kin and prepared to leave. Gunhar and Sigrid gave Asmund two horses so no one had to walk after such a feast. Ged rode with Aud, who looked

CHAPTER 15 — The blot

about in wonder in the world, while Asmund led Skadi and the baby on another horse with perched Sokki behind.

Anna sat in front of Thorfinn, on a stocky grey stallion. To her the land was never more beautiful. The far horizon drew out all concerns, made the self invisible, part of a world without conscious intent. Thorfinn leant against her still drowsy with the quantity of mead he had consumed and the release of a long held tension.

The moon had come more into the sky when they came to Ebiwaz and its outhouses.

'The bird,' shouted Ged. 'It comes. Look. On the roof.'

'Hey,' yelled Bjarni. 'I see it. A cat with wings. No, a bird with legs the size of a bull. A she-wolf with dragon wings.'

'Ah, shut yer gob,' snapped Asmund. 'It is nothing but an eagle. A bird what's shadow has been made long by the moonlit and the shadow of the mountain. Boy, yer never could see straight since ye were born.'

Olaf came out to see what was happening. 'What is it wif all ye heathens? It is the devil of drink pursing ye all in yer unholy lusts.' Olaf squinted at the roof.

Sokki dismounted and made as if to fart in the direction of Olaf. 'Git back to yer bones Olaf. If it's any devils around here its them ghosts of the dead men in that bag what sleeps wif you.'

Ged saw a creature black as night move along the ridges of the house where the shadow of the mountains rested. The creature had wings flattened against its shoulders. It made no noise. It dragged a thick tail through the roof turf as it moved. Ged rubbed his eyes and tried to focus.

'Ged,' said Anna. 'Husband, what is it?'

'I know this creature.'

'It means nothing brother. It is a bird. The shadow of a bird mixed in with the shadow of the mountain.'

'I'll get it,' said Bjarni. 'It will not escape me.' He spat in the direction of Olaf, who gathered his dignity around him with his cowl and returned to his solitude and his nestbaggin full of bones.

Ged spoke softly to himself: 'That creature speaks to me. The demons are known to me. I am strong. I know what others do not. I can see what others do not. I will defeat the evil that comes to threaten Ebiwaz.

CHAPTER 16
Anna and O'Flarty go to Thorness

It was to Anna in the days that followed her union with Thorfinn as if the gods sat in a hall in the sky behind a thin white curtain of cloud and watched her with detached interest. She could not separate her thoughts from Thorfinn Markland-Farer. To be near him brought a strength and a restlessness that took her away from any task. She ached to touch him, to place her hand on his heart, to feel the texture of his skin through the hair that covered his body.

She was still the wife of Ged and, as such, she lay with him at night as was her duty. Afterwards, awake in the dark with only the smell of sex to remind her of her body, the patterns returned; swirling, disembodied, fantastic shapes. 'Does Thorfinn play with me?' she asked herself. 'Does he want Anna or woman, any woman?' Asmund could lawfully lie with her if Ged did not father a child. This was the Viking way. Then she would be bound forever to Ebiwaz. But who would care for Ged if she was not here? Who would lie with him and walk with him in the night when he watched the dragon world for them all? A child would come from the seed of Thorfinn, of that she had no doubt. Ged was weak, his seed barren. But Ged was the brother of Asmund. Ged was her husband. Asmund could kill them all and remain within the law.

Thorfinn too became preoccupied with his inner world. He felt himself encircle Anna's fragility and grow strong. The softness of woman delighted him. He felt invincible. His leg began to heal, the pain on walking less. He still needed a stick but now he had the strength to work again. It worried him that she was the wife of Ged. Still, he told himself, if the gods took who they wanted when they wanted sex and love, so could he.

Asmund watched Thorfinn walk with renewed strength. He decided new whale bone fences must be made so the Giants could not devour the cattle, and the sheep, if unteathered, could not duel with Sieiphir, as they did when the great Allfather rode the white moon on his eight-legged horse to spy on the Norse and their wealth.

'The stones along the path to the work house must be replaced,' Asmund told Thorfinn. 'Then start on the walls in the longhouse. We must repair the holes in the turf on the roof while summer gives us time and before we leave for the Althing.'

Day after day Thorfinn locked the fish-drying racks to the hard ground, carried animal carcasses to the storeroom, dragged vats of urine to the bay and hauled out the sodden wool for the women to wash. When his leg gave way to the pressure of his strength he spent time on the rocks around the edge of the bay. He did not approach Anna although the image of her body rarely left him. It was enough that he had known her, that she would be his again. She would be his, even if she was the wife of another man. It was their destiny to leave Hvalsey and return to Markland together.

Ged became more and more preoccupied with people and objects no one else could see. He padded from room to room and was often seen to speak to the darkness in the corners of the house. He could sit at his carving for short periods only. The creatures he drew were fierce and strange and had the shape of a giant walrus. He constantly checked on the nestbaggin of skulls in Olaf's shed. He ate little and spent much time looking at Anna and the others as if staring out from a dream.

Anna set out spring flowers and polished the amber on her altar. She prayed to Frigg, the wife of Odin, to give her guidance. Did not Frigg have the knowledge of all human destiny? Could she not, she asked Frigg, hold the restless heart of Thorfinn Markland-Farer to her and still care for Ged? The Norns had spun her fate to be the wife of Ged and to desire another man. This was a trick of the gods. Locki was behind this. Thorfinn must stay at Ebiwaz. There was no other way.

CHAPTER 16 — Anna and O'Flarty go to Thorness

At Ebiwaz she and Ged were safe. When the big wooden door was shut nothing could harm them. If evil came in her dreams to torment her, Ged was by her to take it away in his visions. He knew the ways of dragons and strange demons who meant no good to the Norse. Thorfinn always spoke about leaving Hvalsey. Nothing was safe with Thorfinn, nothing predictable.

Sometimes, as she walked in the hills, the creatures of the earth opened to her in shape and form and reflected back to her a path of action without the loss of either man. Only when this happened could she return to the house and know that the creatures who hung in the carvings around her alter would be smiling and benevolent, the spirits floating in the driftwood swelling with increase.

The moon swung through its cycle. The days stretched into a shadow-less twilight. The men went fishing and returned with a load of fat cod. Thorfinn was unable to go with them although he longed for the open sea; his leg would not yet bend into the small place allotted to rowers in the knarr. He spent the time on his rock, waiting for their return, his grey cloak billowing in the wind and the blaze of his golden-red hair flowing behind him. If he was not on his rock he was by the water drawing maps of the coast of Markland in the pebbles with his staff.

One bright day Scarface and his foster son, Egil, Gunharsson, came to visit with two ducks and a new set of horse leather to trade with Asmund. Egil, the son of Gunhar Bloodaxe and Sigrid the Fierce, was born the same winter as Bjarni. Scarface had given Egil a black horse equipped with bells to scare away any ghosts from the mountains who might plot against the family. Bjarni and Egil disappeared on the horse as quickly as they could and the horse bells could be heard as they trotted into the hills behind the farm.

Anna looked at Scarface and his thick red hair and his turquoise melt-water eye and his strong arms, and saw the way he made Skadi giggle like a girl. Well, she thought, if Brigitta can handle this man and make potions to get babies, she must know a thing or two about men and women. Yes, I will go and visit Brigitta. I will go with Brigitta and find the wild elfin sheep in the mountains behind Thorness and make a jumper for Thorfinn so he will stay with me at Ebiwaz forever.

Scarface himself suggested Anna visit Thorness. 'Listen,' he said to Asmund. 'Young Anna there must go and visit Brigitta. Me wife is lonely for the company of women. She is just up there with me nephew, Yellowbritches, who has come to visit with Aged Pa, me father's brother. And of course Menglad, but she don't count, being the trouble that she is.'

'Aged Pa,' said Sokki, suddenly awake. 'He was a wild Viking in them days gone by. Fierce and feared by all what knew him. Travelled the coast of England, he did, like me. Brought home treasure you would hardly believe. Silver bright as the day. And heavy. Had the sword, Algiz, that no one else could touch, so dangerous were it.'

Scarface rubbed at his one eye. 'Old Pa can't hardly see now. Talks to ghosts all the time and has to be stopped from falling into the fire. Yellowbritches looks after him, old fool that he is. What with the trouble Menglad makes and them hoard of kids and the giants roaring in the high mountains, Brigitta needs a woman to keep her company,

'You'll not leave before you pluck them ducks,' snorted Skadi, spitting all over the dogs in her excitement to be able to issue an order in front of Scarface.

'Needs to get out,' said Ged suddenly from behind Skadi. 'Go, wife. But do not approach the dreki that brings the evil spawn to your mind. It lives in the still water beneath the mountain. Take this to protect you.'

He stood tall and concave, his eyes burning in a face curtained by long straggly hair. He rummaged in his tool kit and handed Anna a small serpent made out of metal with runes engraved on the body.

'Yeah, Ged. That's the way for a husband to act,' said Scarface. 'Skadi, you tell 'em young ones.' He put his arm around Skadi and hugged her to his shoulder. 'But let her go today, eh? Brigitta don't shut the door till late when the moon shines full.' He squashed a mosquito affectionately into Skadi's shoulder with his other hand then picked up the insect and ate it.

CHAPTER 16 — Anna and O'Flarty go to Thorness

The full moon was just coming over the mountains when Anna finished her chores. She was consumed by an energy that could not be contained. She persuaded O'Flarty to accompany her though the hills to the high valley where Scarface and Brigitta lived. Thorfinn and Scarface walked with them to the beginning of the track that led up into the mountain.

O'Flarty was made to carry a whale-horse tooth on his cap with the rune of Ansuz carved onto it. This was to ensure that if danger came he would be aware and could take action with his knife or arrows. Scarface put a nestbaggin of seal meat for Brigitta on O'Flarty's back and bid them both to move with caution in case the giants caught their smell. Anna carried a skein of new dyed wool for Brigitta. She wore white feathers in her cloak and the amber necklace under her tunic to claim the protection of the goddess Frigg, wife of Allfather Odin.

As they walked into the hills the light faded into a soft glow that set a myriad of lights rustling across the rocks above them. It was hard to tell where the mountains began and the clouds ended as all shapes above them were rounded and enormous and glowing iridescent. The path seemed to go on and on with the eyes of a million tiny spirits glittering from the rocks as they passed. At last the shape of a house showed itself distinct from the hills.

The steading was small and shadowed by the Grey Mountain, a huge being that sucked light even from the sky and the stars. Anna and O'Flarty walked to the house though an avenue of earth creatures; as the wind moved the trees so did the old ones take shape in the branches, disappearing and reforming in the shifting leaves. A cloud of moths with markings like an owl swarmed from the trees as they arrived at the front door.

Brigitta stood outside in the moonlight with Menglad, the daughter of Scarface and his bondswoman . The door to the house was not yet shut as Scarface foretold. Brigitta looked annoyed. She greeted Anna and glared at O'Flarty as if all men were to blame for her ill-humor. As Brigitta brought Anna and O'Flarty into the house the young woman beside her turned and ran awkwardly away. She was of sallow complexion, her skin loose and wrinkled into folds around her bones. She was dressed in lengths of fur and strips of uncarded wool bunched at the waist and shoulders.

Brigitta shut the door firmly behind her and rearranged the plaits on the top of her head. The sleeves of her under dress were pushed up to her shoulders and secured into bunches with strands of bright wool. She smoothed down her tunic and brushed ash off the hem.

'You've not seen much of Menglad before,' said Brigitta. 'Frigg curse the relatives of me husband, Eirik Eiriksson Scarface.' She spat in the direction of Old Pa who was tied to a bed post in a corner of the longhouse. 'If it ain't his old uncle making me life unbearable, it is that daughter from his serving woman getting up to no good. That girl Menglad. She is like a wild woman from the hills.

'Ain't no kin of mine,' Brigitta continued as she heaved a crying child off a bed and attached it to her bosom. 'Does nothing but piss and drink. Caught her yesterday drinking all the milk. Thin as a moth. Then she goes to the stream and drinks water all morning. Now she can't walk because everything inside is stretched full of water. She gurgles when she moves. Sleeps all day and pisses all night while that disgusting old thing Yellowbritches calls a Viking pisses all day and talks to himself all night.'

Anna offered their gifts and sat beside the fire. The house was adorned with all sorts of instruments and bells and harness for horse care. The smell of horse and walrus leather was everywhere in the warm night. Anna could hear the sound of the horses in their stable at the back of the house. It was comforting to hear the proximity of animals in a house which sat so alone under the Grey Mountain. O'Flarty slipped quietly into the gloom and found himself a warm nest behind Aged Pa.

Brigitta continued: 'Eats everything they can, that pair. Well, by Frigg, if we has to put up with Aged Pa and his ranting and his smell, Menglad can sleep in the shed tonight and not keep us all awake twice over. Scarface built a new shed y'know. Up by the rocks there. Out of stones from the bottom of the Mountain. Show yer tomorrow. His brat

CHAPTER 16 — Anna and O'Flarty go to Thorness

is not nothing to do with me. Child of Scarface and his bondswoman before I came. Thought I had got rid of her when she married the son of Odd. But she killed him the first night with her drinking and pissing. Witch like her ma, if yer ask me.'

'Your weaving is beautiful,' said Anna fingering the cloth of a new weaving. 'Why, you could make this into a dress to wear to the finest court in Norway.'

'Scarface and his ancestors would come to haunt anyone from this house who went to the court of any jarl,' Brigitta said and moved the sleeping child to her own bed. 'We here don't hold with royalty. As you know, Scarface is descended direct from Eirik the Red who was made to leave Norway by the king for something he never done.'

Brigitta knelt and rummaged under one of the beds where a small cupboard was half visible. 'Now it being before the summer grasses are brought in we ain't allowed to have ale, says Scarface. However me loves I have a little something here for an occasion just like this.' She brought out a stone container of sticky brown liquid and a small wooden container. She poured whey into several bowls and stirred some of the brown stuff into it. 'A little something I traded with a man from the hot lands who came here to hunt falcons one summer,' she said smiling.

Yellowbritches sat with them and dug at a hollow piece of wood with his knife. Occasionally he made a note from a piece of animal gut attached to each end of the wood. Aged Pa was tied to a bed palate with a piece of twine around his middle so he could not wander into the fire or find a sword and attack the ghosts that came to plague his dimmed vision. All in Aged Pa's family had died with the sickness last winter. He was set to outlast everyone, according to Brigitta. Most of the time he stood and plucked at the twine around his torso with long veined fingers and mumbled insults at anyone who came near. Both Brigitta and Yellowbritches thought about pushing Aged Pa out into a storm, but that was always for another night.

'Man of yours don't say much,' Yellowbritches remarked as O'Flarty accepted a bowl of the malodorous liquid and pushed himself back under the skins on the bed behind Aged Pa. He turned his face towards the fire in the centre of the long house and found himself drifting into memories of his youth, when the sound of children sleeping nearby was reason enough to live.

'Now Anna my love, what brings you here? Need a potion for that man of yours?'

'Maybe. Well not exactly.'

'Well then?'

Anna could not say the words. 'I want to do a new weaving. I want to make a cloak with the most special magic wool. Can we go up into the mountains, Brigitta, and look for the elfin sheep? I've seen them once, sheep with silver coats that shine in the dark like stars. Their hair is so soft and fine. They have red eyes. They live in the caves of the dwarfs. People say that if you wear a coat of elfin wool you will never leave Greenland.'

'Yes, my love, I know them. Sometimes after a big wind we find bits of their wool on the willow twigs. Look, that weaving over the door has some. I used it for the border. We will go tomorrow with Yellowbritches. Your man and that lazy daughter of Scarface can look after the children. Did you come to ask me that? Is that all?'

'Oh Brigitta, I need some magic to heal my heart. I am frightened. So many women die here when the seed is planted in their womb. Look what happened to Skadi. I am afraid. So afraid.' Tears wet Anna's face.

'Now, now,' said Brigitta hugging Anna. 'It isn't unusual for a young wife to feel afraid of love for the first turning of the seasons. Look at Menglad. She killed her man afore he even poked her. We all have to learn about love. Even Erland Yellowbritches there, he has to learn when his time comes. No one gets it right straight away. Yer need a child. What goes in hard don't come out so hard when it's a wee child. Like these little loves snoring behind me. We women make the men who will be the future of Greenland. We are the ancestors of the luck that will be theirs. Now that man of yours, all I seen him do is wander around the place with a bag full of old bones. Don't cry. We'll go the elfin caves tomorrow, I promise. We might even find some silver

CHAPTER 16 — *Anna and O'Flarty go to Thorness*

wool on the bushes before we get there. You'll see. Won't she, Erland Yellowbritches?'

'Tell me,' said Anna, 'about Eirik the Red, the great ancestor of Eirik Eiriksson Scarface'.

'I will, me love, I will. Eirik the Red was a great man, a wild man who got into trouble in Iceland and had to leave. Came to Greenland with his followers and set his high-seat pillars at Brattahlid. All the kin of Eirik have the anger, except Yellowbritches here. You tell the story, Yellowbritches. It's what you do best.'

Yellowbritches ceased licking the opening of his musical instrument and regarded the two women with curiosity. He picked up a long curved horn and blew into it. A mournful note announced the beginning of his story. Brigitta poured more whey and sprinkled it with a little more brown stuff.

Yellowbritches, who was named by his family Erland Hrafnsson, was the youngest son of Scarface's eldest brother. He wore a bright blue band of wadmal around his yellow hair and a similar band of blue around his fading yellow pants. He had a pattern of blue lines sunk into the skin across his face and the top of the muscles of his arm. He put down the horn and began to pluck out a rhythm on his instrument with the string that stretched from top to bottom of his hollow pipe. He looked into the distance and assumed his bard voice, intoning a rhythm into the words as he spoke.

'This story was told to me by my father and to his father before him. Eirik the Red was the name of our great ancestor. When he was young he lived with his pa in Norway. But the king of Norway told him to fight his own kin. So Eirik set sail for Iceland, land of the mountains of smoke and fire. He met a fine woman and married her. Thjodhlid was her name. He became a great leader in Iceland and was loved well by the gods. But red as his hair was his face and his words when anyone went against him. He got into a fight and cut off the heads of some men who had killed his serfs when they set a landslide down on his neighbor's farm. The men at the Althing in Iceland told him to go and live on an island till his temper burnt out.'

Yellowbritches took a long swig of the mysterious drink. The wind from the Grey Mountain had come to beat at the roof of the house with the call of the night birds seeking food. 'But that Eirik, he was so strong no one could go against him in a fight. He killed another man who tried to steal the great high-seat pillars of his ancestors. Eirik lost his temper at the Althing and told the assembly he would kill them, too, if they did not see the truth as the gods had made it. This time the Assembly made him an outlaw. They said anyone could kill him because he was too wild to live in Iceland with such a bad temper.'

Yellowbritches made a series of dramatic sounds on his instrument.

'See him up there on the wall. That's the great Eirik the Red.' Brigitta pointed to a tapestry hung over the door. It was of a man with wild red hair and a heavy scowl. He had one hand on a very large horse and the other held a very large sword.

'Well, then Eirik had to find another place to live. He took his family to an island off the coast. Then one day as he was sailing out to look for sea monsters to kill, he saw a vision of a great land to the west.

'Now it is told by the kin of Thorgils Thordsson that the coast of Greenland what faces Iceland is haunted by the ghosts of bad men and sea monsters what tear to pieces any Norse who lands there. Thorgils Thordsson knew because he got shipwrecked and escaped with the help of the Seal People. He told his kin that the ghosts of the Norse who had been eaten by the sea monsters sit on the rocks and call out to the men who pass in their ships to rescue them.'

A high mournful call came into the house. A lamp fluttered and died. 'Wolves,' said Brigitta. 'High up on the mountain. They'll not bother us tonight.'

Everyone shivered as if they too could hear the old Norse wail on the rocks.

'So Thor bid Eirik not stop at this place of bad ghosts but to keep sailing till he came to a land more beautiful than Iceland, where the grass was green and there was pasture enough for all. Reindeer lived in the valleys, and the lakes and fiords were full of fish. There were birds and eggs and feathers to stuff as many quilts as you want. Thor told

CHAPTER 16 — Anna and O'Flarty go to Thorness

Eirik that the men who had been there had left; it was for the Norse alone. So Eirik went back to Iceland and told everyone about the new place. He called it Greenland to let everyone know how beautiful it was. Many people decided to go back with him. Iceland was old and tired and the land all used up.

'Twenty-five ships set out with Eirik with women and children and cattle. But the god of Iceland did not want his people to leave. He made the sea wild and come at the ships in three waves that reached from horizon to horizon like the mountain behind us. Eirik called to Thor to save them. Some ships Thor sent to feed the whales. Some ships were eaten by the wild dragon of the North Sea. One ship turned back. But Thor let Eirik and his friends did come at last to our home, to Greenland.'

'And,' said Brigitta, 'it is a safe place for us all, young and old, without the meddling of the king of Norway or the earls of Iceland. Better it is that way.'

No one spoke. The wind continued to wail and scratch at loose turf on the house and bang the shutter across the smoke hole in the roof. The children snuffled in their sleep, the fire crackled and Old Pa scratched. Anna felt warm and safe, happy to be with such friends. Everyone was smiling, their thoughts dancing to the wildness of the wind. Anna gave thanks to Freyja and the ancestors of Eirik Eiriksson Scarface who had come first to live under the Grey Mountain. 'What about the Western Settlement?' she said. 'The place where I grew up? Are we part of Eirik's kin, too?'

'Well they say that Eirik and his wife had a fight over Eirik's second wife and daughter, who was called Freydis. Thjodhlid, his first wife, made Eirik take them others up to the North. She said he could not come into her bed if they was around. Eirik thought it was a good place to leave his second wife, the Western Settlement, being so close to the Nordsetur and all them strange spirits what live there.'

Anna saw the place where she had lived as a girl. All ships stopped at the Western Settlement before they sailed to the Nordsetur. She remembered the way the sheep used to nose up to the door and try to come into the longhouse. She saw her mother and her sister sitting at their work and the puppies; there would be a new litter of fluffy puppies now. She smiled at the memory of them all entangled in a skein of wool, the girls pulling one way, the small dogs growling and pulling in the other direction.

Yellowbritches set up a tapping on his wooden pipe to correspond to the intervals between the scratching of Aged Pa's fingernails. Brigitta began to bang in time on a hollow spoon case. Yellowbritches opened his mouth and sang. Brigitta handed Anna a knife and a stone jar. Soon all who were awake in the room had found something to contribute to the rhythm.

Everyone began to laugh. Brigitta mixed more of her secret herb from the hot lands into another drink. Yellowbritches made up a rhythmic song without words to fill the spaces between notes. Anna found she could not contain her appetite and kept picking at the delicate morsels of food Brigitta placed in front of them. Even Old Pa and his scratching became funny, Anna and Brigitta breaking into laughter at the sight of his wrinkled old-rat face muttering curses at the fire sprites.

The evening became one to remember as a time filled with happiness and song.

CHAPTER 17
The ice cave

Anna awoke with the light of dawn coming through the cracks in the wooden door. She had dreamt of her home, of the ship her father and brothers had built with the men of the Western Settlement. She watched as a walrus with shoe lasts on its tusks, one left and one right, led the ship into deep water, bellowing like a horse as it went. A whale-horse. Her mother stood and waved as the ship drifted under a waterfall.

It was not a waterfall but someone, probably Aged Pa, pissing loudly into a corner while someone, probably Yellowbritches, exhorted Aged Pa to visit the halls of Valhalla immediately and never return. O'Flarty and Eirik's bondsman were already at the door lifting the heavy latch and letting the morning into the smoky house. The children ceased their snuffling and watched as O'Flarty beat at a cloud of mosquitoes surrounding the door.

The day threatened rain; low clouds pressed in a band over the high valley of Thorness and moved down onto the bay below. The sudden violence of the weather was never far from the consciousness of anyone who lived in the highlands, but the grass grew thick in summer on the valley slopes, and little wild ponies and caribou lived there with Eirik's sheep and goats.

No one seemed to be in a good humor after the fun last night. Yellowbritches scowled at everyone and said he would rather face a mountain of dwarfs than one more day with Aged Pa. Brigitta told Yellowbritches she might strangle Menglad if she had to watch her drink and piss all day again. Menglad could be heard sobbing somewhere in the house after her night alone in the store shed.

'Sure to find an elfin sheep or two among them ponies and caribou,' Brigitta announced, while dragging Menglad away from the milk. 'Drank all the milk again she did, the pest. Menglad, I thought I had got rid of yer at last. Git over there and see to them children. Jest like her ma, she is. She what came to no good in them hills after Scarface had finished with her. Sexed a dwarf she did, and only lived one summer after because his sex come out her mouth.'

Brigitta pushed Menglad towards the door and aimed a kick in her direction. 'Maybe you, Menglad, is the daughter of that dwarf with the dangle rooter what come to his knees. Anna, quick. We must go now before the storm comes with a darkness that locks us away in the hills and brings the giants out after us.'

Anna put her nestbaggin onto the shoulders of Yellowbritches and bid him bring his bow and arrow and a sharp knife. She tucked Ged's charm into her tunic and secured a knife in her belt. Dwarfs there might be as in the Western Settlement but no dwarf with a dangle rooter to his knees was going to come near her.

O'Flarty was given the job of caring for Aged Pa, who was tied up to a post in the front of the house because, Yellowbritches said, he smelt like a dead fish and a rotting bird all mangled together. The sun came out as Brigitta, Anna and Yellowbritches climbed up behind the farm onto a rough track. They passed pools of the purest turquoise melt water, enchanting and mysterious. Bluebells and buttercups and spears of long grass glinted in the sunlight around them.

Brigitta marched along, her face held up to the sun. Anna followed. Yellowbritches came behind, humming a ballad to himself about the death of an old Viking who went walking in the hills and fell off a cliff. From no direction and from all directions the wind came softly. It invited the three walkers to walk to a place where time stood beyond knowledge, where there was no Aged Pa, or Menglad, or Ged or Thorfinn. The track curled and dipped. No one knew where it ended, no one cared.

A low rumbling sounded in on the Mountain. Clouds began to curl around the valley and the path was rapidly fading from view.

CHAPTER 17 — *The ice cave*

The wind ceased to caress and scratched with tiny slivers of ice at any exposed skin.

'Just up a bit further,' Brigitta shouted over the noise of the wind. 'Look. See over there behind the rocks. Something's moving. This is the path to where the sheep go in and out of the mountain.'

The path was indeed made of smooth black stones, well used and rounded. Something moved against the rocks of the valley wall.

'Stop, Brigitta,' Yellowbritches yelled. 'If them sheep is looked after by dwarfs I ain't a' fighting in any storm where I can't see where me arrows go. Scarface says dwarfs live under this mountains with them giants. Dwarfs what will be wanting to lie with you women, being as they always are after sex and gold.'

'No further. We must shelter,' Anna shouted as the hail beat at them. 'Look, Brigitta. Where those sheep are there is a ledge.'

Brigitta clambered up the rocks, followed closely by Anna who sought not to be too far from anything human. Yellowbritches followed with his bow in his hand. The clouds hung from the top of the cliff above. The wind stopped, suddenly. Nothing could be heard near the cliff face, not even the sound of insects.

'There,' Brigitta yelled, pointing. A flash of silver showed in a narrow opening in the mountain side.

'Frigg, wife of the Great Odin, protect us,' Anna muttered. There were now two sheep on the ledge in front of them. Both had silver wool falling to the ground. In the shadows of the ledge their eyes indeed glowed red. They were being herded further into the cave by squat creatures no bigger than a wolf. Brigitta disappeared in front of the sheep. Anna and Yellowbritches followed cautiously. The crevasse became narrow, the cliff tops far above them meeting in a thick ceiling of ice. A bluish light came from the ice ceiling and filled the cavern with an unearthly luminescence. Deep inside the crevasse Brigitta stood in front of a pool of water made by the stalagmites dripping from above. She gazed upwards in a trance. The air was dense, heavy. There was the sweet smell of blood around them. A sound like sighing filled the cavern.

'There is a tree up there. A tree. Growing in the ice at the top of the world with roots coming down here,' Anna whispered with one hand holding the back of Yellowbritches.

'Gods in Valhalla, it is the roots of Yggdrasill,' whispered Yellowbritches, 'dripping into the Spring of Mimir. We have indeed come to the land of the giants. Jotunheim I have heard it called. Look over there; that rock is the severed head that Odin sets to guard the well of wisdom.'

As Anna and Yellowbritches moved towards the black pool of water the darkness beyond seemed to become dense, as if something waited there, ancient, unformed, yet aware. Anna felt as if myriad eyes watched them; the old ones of the earth, unknown and undisturbed. She bent down to feel a sheep pressing up beside her. It was hard to remember why she wanted elfin wool, why she was in the cave at all.

Wool. She needed wool. To make a cloak. A magic cloak so Thorfinn would never leave Greenland. She felt reluctant to move and could see the way the others stood that they too felt as if any movement would disturb something ancient, older than the Norse had words for.

With effort she linked her fingers in the matt of wool on the back of the sheep. She turned to Yellowbritches and indicated they should begin to cut the fleece. Yellowbritches shut his mouth and together they set about removing as much of the wool as possible in the bluish light. The sheep continued to nuzzle into Anna's skirts. Brigitta did not move. She remained entranced, staring at the long dripping roots coming though the top of the cave.

'Can you hear that?' whispered Anna as a faint song came from the dark beyond. Yellowbritches nodded and made the sign of danger. Something fell with an echo behind them. Anna expected to see one of the stone creatures poised to send a spear into them for stealing his wool. Yellowbritches was the first to move. He packed the wool as fast as he could into his nestbaggin and held his knife before him. Anna did likewise. She attached herself to Brigitta and pushed her towards the entrance of the crevasse. Soft voices came behind them in a song without words. Brigitta tripped and fell heavily.

CHAPTER 17 — *The ice cave*

Yellowbritches let out his breath. 'By Thor, you've fallen over the stones of a fireplace.' He knelt in the ash and felt around her. 'Look someone's been cooking here.'

Brigitta picked up a long bone from the fireplace, then a skull with the black hair of a skraeling attached in a knot. Both eyes had been gouged out of the sockets but the teeth were intact. At once a long shadow detached itself from the cavern wall and made a rush at the skull. A gristly hand grasped Brigitta's hair and pulled her backwards. Yellowbritches slashed at something with his knife. There was a howl, and whatever it was let go of Brigitta, grabbed the skull and thumped back into the darkness of the cave wall.

Yellowbritches looked at his knife which was covered in a blackish substance. 'A monster from Hel. Out. Now. This place is not a place for the living.'

They stumbled to the entrance shouting threats into the darkness as if noise could encapsulate safety within the boundaries of possession. There were no more attacks from the monster of the cavern. The soft voices stilled behind them. The path outside lay shrouded in mist. There was no wind. Snow clung to the sheaves of grass between the black stones. There were no hills in the distance to entrance. Brigitta clutched the long bone from the fire. It was a human leg bone and had been gnawed up and down the shaft. She turned it over and looked at it with interest.

'What's the matter with you lot?' Brigitta said to Yellowbritches and Anna. 'You ain't cold, is yer? Ain't yers never seen a giant's dinner before? Now yers know what Scarface says is true.'

She rubbed her arms, shook her head and set off along the path waving the leg bone. Anna and Yellowbritches followed with the precious wool. No one spoke. Eventually, Thorness came in sight. There was no movement outside the house; no smoke from the smoke hole; no signs of activity in the stables or barn. Only the bent figure of Old Pa crouched beneath his pole. O'Flarty came to meet them. He pointed to the stream. Menglad lay there with her head in the water and her swollen legs and bum protruding onto the bank.

'Drank herself to death, she did,' O'Flarty said. 'Nothing we could do to stop her. Jest lay down by the stream and drank and drank all day till the spirit took her in a fit of writhing. And she lay there like she is; still and dead. We's afraid to move her, thinking you will want to see what she done to herself.'

Brigitta poked at Menglad's legs. They were cold and soggy. Her face remained in the water. 'Better off this way,' she said. 'No man could've coped with the way she drank and pissed and ate all the time. Frigg take her. Killed one husband. Maybe she were a witch as they says. Gone to be with Odd's son now in the halls of Freyja. Better life for her there than here.'

'Maybe Old Pa needs a drink, too?' Yellowbritches said.

They each took a bit of Menglad and heaved the body out of the stream. The children stood in the doorway with wide eyes. Brigitta decided Menglad could stay in the storeroom until Scarface was notified, being as she was his kin. That evening Brigitta called everyone around the fire. An offering of a horse's head was made to the gods Odin and Frigg, Freyja and Thor. Yellowbritches drew runes of renewal and voyage in the ash around the fire as the horse head roasted. Anna took a candle and drew smoke runes on the walls. Brigitta encouraged everyone to tell a tale about how they remembered Menglad and throw something into the fire to honor the fierce ancestor of Scarface, Eirik the Red, who, Brigitta said, had problems enough with his women folk too.

Anna sat and carded her wool between two sticks. Death must come, she knew, but the voyage was softened by how you were remembered. Menglad was a sad woman. No one had cared for her. Good fortune was never her lot. Anna threw a strand of the elfin wool into the fire and asked her own ancestors that she not be remembered as a evil woman who wanted two husbands.

If the ancestors came that evening to the fireside vigil for Menglad, they came not to protect but to listen to Erland Yellowbritches sing of Hel and sniff the warmth of Brigitta's household.

Early in the morning Brigitta woke the household. Wolves had been heard in the night, and the door of the storeroom had scratch

CHAPTER 17 — *The ice cave*

marks and bites on the wood. One of the children said she had seen Menglad on her horse riding towards the Grey Mountain behind Thorness. The Mountain scowled down upon the longhouse, huge and threatening. Ice filled its shadowed cavities like teeth open with menace. A heaviness came into them all with the thought of Menglad alone on the Mountain. Even if the end of one's days in Greenland were foretold by the Norns, no human knew when the journey through this life might end. Listen as they might for the sound of her horse returning, the valley of Thorness was silent, with only the occasional bird to disturb the mist.

It was bad luck to have a death under the Mountain and leave the dead for the carrion to pick on the bones. There was a graveyard just away from the home field. Being close to the house it was thought the living and the dead could converse without much trouble. One of Brigitta's babies was buried there, along with the bondswoman who had given birth to Menglad. The mother of Eirik Eiriksson Scarface also rested there in the earth and was often heard to give unwanted advice to Brigitta about the running of the farm. She was especially vocal at the winter solstice.

Brigitta decided that Menglad could join her mother in a burial mound and Scarface could talk to them both. She might have something to say to Eirik Eiriksson Scarface, being as she was his daughter. Maybe he could find out why the gods had ordained that she should be widowed the first night of her marriage and then drink herself to death in a stream.

It was not easy to dig a grave in the cold earth. At last they got her in but her feet stuck out.

'A pest to the last,' Brigitta remarked to the bondsman as he struggled with the hard ground. Once the grave was big enough Menglad was folded into the earth and covered with her best dress of blue wadmal. Anna put reindeer strips and a bowl of whey beside her for the journey. With some reluctance Brigitta placed a small metal serpent on Menglad's breast. The children laid ferns and flowers by her head. Yellowbritches made mournful noises on his drum and flute. Brigitta threw Menglad's spindle and an old fleece into the grave with her knife and spoon case.

They filled the grave with earth and placed rocks around it in the shape of a ship for her voyage. Menglad's favorite pony, with rattles on its legs, was let into the graveyard to keep away any demons that might try to claim her spirit.

'Well that's that,' Brigitta said and herded the little girls back to the house. 'You lot had better get back today to Ebiwaz and tell Scarface what's become of his daughter. Jest don't let that meddling Asmund Lawbinder poke his nose into what we've done. He'd want us to dig up her bones and bury her in a churchyard, Thor's balls he knows we ain't holding with the White Christ and them priests of his.'

Anna and O'Flarty left later that morning. The problem of Thorfinn and Ged had not been solved or even discussed. Anna felt encased in her aloneness. The memory of the inhuman universe they had approached in the cavern stayed with her. She wanted Thorfinn, his strength, his smell, his voice; the maleness of him. She wanted Ged to protect her from the demons that lived in the darkness of the mountains.

As she walked, she set her heart to dreaming what life would be like at the court of a great king. On visit with Thorfinn and Ged. Just a visit. She would wear a cloak of red and green and Thorfinn would wear his cloak of elfin wool and it would shine like silver. Ged would be there in a coat of the fur of the black bear from Markland. She would stand between them and curtsey to the king and all his courtiers.

O' Flarty walked behind her in silence. He looked in wonder at the landscape and thanked his god for another day, even if it was in Greenland.

CHAPTER 18
The battle with the Giants

Eirik Eiriksson Scarface was still at Ebiwaz when he got the news of the death of Menglad. He left immediately and returned to have a few words to the ghost of Menglad and her mother who rested in the ground of Thorness.

'It's not that I will miss yer, being such a burden on me good wife Brigetta that yer were,' he addressed the grave mound of Menglad. 'However parts of you were of liking to me. You were good with the horses and did a fine thing getting milk out of them old cows. Now you tell that ma of yours not to let you go consorting with giants. Or dwarfs if it be known. And keep me good name when you get to Asgard so as I'll be remembered with honor when I join you Menglad, being as ye are me kin. Thought I always wondered about that bondsman was here the same time as you arrived in Midgard.'

Brigitta and the children watched from the house till a low rumbling from the mountain sent them inside shivering. 'Giants,' said Scarface. 'Preparing for battle. Menglad's been up to her old tricks and told them of my plans to fight for that pasture.'

Eirik Eiriksson Scarface knew a thing about Giants. They were his enemy, he had no doubt. He had seen their shadows in the mist, which fell on jagged points of rock when sunlight came through the vast halls of the mountain above his farm. He had seen evidence of their passage on the steep mountain passes: a tree felled, a boulder thrown across the track, a lump of dung turned to stone. He had heard their rumblings in the shaking of the earth deep under his farm. He had smelt the rotten smell of giant fart as rock crashed to the valley and left a black scar on the Mountain.

He was a strong thick-set man, the image, everyone said, of his ancestor Eirik the Red. Like Eirik he had bright red hair and beard and eyes the color of turquoise. A scar ran down the left side of his face and he had partial sight in the eye nearest the scar. 'A mark of honor,' he said, referring to an argument he had with an English trader when the last ship came back from the Nordsetur. He was not a rich man but no one crossed Eirik Eiriksson Scarface without good reason.

Eirik loved the old gods, Thor and his hammer Mjollnir in particular. He had changed the name of his farm to Thorness when his grandfather died and his great-uncle had jumped off a cliff after losing a shooting competition to a skraeling. There was a rock on a ledge overlooking Thorness that Eirik loved. It sat beside a down flow of water that moved fast with the spring melt from the secret valleys of the Grey Mountain. Eirik knew Thor came there sometimes to this high ledge and sat on his rock with Locki hanging off his belt to watch the Norse in Greenland. All were forbidden to urinate or spit in the vicinity of this rock, although Eirik's third daughter had begun at this very place. The memory of Brigitta's thighs pointing skywards with the wind in his prick gave Scarface an unaccountably itchy feeling around his balls.

'Now,' he said to the men gathered in his longhouse around the fire, 'as yous all know Odd and his kin think we is stealing his land. Odd says the field is his because it was given to him when his son married my eldest daughter. But Thor told me that son of Odd's was weak and died from fear the night he married Menglad. Turned red and started panting with horror and expired by morning. So that field comes back to me with my daughter because she never got poked. All agreed?'

The sound of the water rushing over the cliff did not break the silence. A rock crashed high up in the valley. A long low moaning note followed.

'Hear 'em. That is them giants after me caribou what live in me field.'

'But how,' said Gunhar Bloodaxe, 'is we going to fight giants?'

'What bloody giants,' Asmund said. 'I never seen a giant in all me life. Maybe heard a dragon bellow in the mountains when a storm

CHAPTER 18 — *The battle with the Giants*

come up but I never seen a giant.' Asmund whacked his own thigh as Skadi's bum was not in sight. Something around Scarface did smell rotten and it was not a giant's fart. Maybe it was the stuff Brigitta was always sprinkling in the whey. Maybe it was the flavor of the dulse they were eating. Asmund munched and considered his friend.

'You knows that something wild lives in the caves in that Mountain,' said Scarface. 'If you had seen the carcass of me animals as many times as I have you know it was not a man eating them. They is all pulled apart and their snouts gone and their eyes gouged out.'

'He's right,' confirmed Brigitta, and Egil nodded. 'Nights when the wind is coming from the deep inside the Mountain. Stamping and grunting. Horrible cries like no human would make.'

'I've seen shadows too, moving on the top of the waterfall,' put in Egil 'Something tall and all twisted. Like a man but not a man. When me and Bjarni was out at Thor's Rock last full moon.'

'Time,' Scarface told Asmund, 'them two young men came out wif us to hunt giants. Those two younglings got good eyes and ears.'

Bjarni felt like the skies of Valhalla were fizzing in his head. It was the first time he had been accorded the privileges of an adult male without censure. He felt so strong he could do anything. He could get rid of that giant. Tear him apart with his hands if he had to. He looked at Egil and saw the same internal storm had set fire to his friend. Yellowbritches sat and chewed at his music pipe and occasionally blew into it.

'It is up to you men to keep us all safe. Protect your women and children and your farms.' Brigitta passed out another round of drinks. 'Where is Ged?'

'Stayed home to protect the wimmen and children with Sokki. Useless in a fight. Cannot see nothing but what is in his head. Stand out like the White Christ wif all that pale hair anyways in the dark.'

Bjarni started dancing around with an unsheathed sword. 'Look Egil. I is the great warrior. Come on Giants.'

'So,' said Scarface without a glance at Asmund, 'the plan is this. We takes a goat and drags it up that track in a night when there is no moon. We slits its throat and leaves trails of blood all over the rocks. We sets up a spit and roasts it on the edge of the cliff above the waterfall. Then when the giants come creeping out of the Grey Mountain where they hide we push them over the edge of the cliff with the spears and the swords of our ancestors.

'Now is you with me or not? Who is there who will not uphold the honor of our ancestors, the fierce Vikings who made this land their own? Who is not as strong as our ancestors who conquered the southlands and ruled all they saw. We are the fierce Norse of Greenland are we not? No one dares go against us. No one tells us what to do.'

Asmund reluctantly agreed with everyone that the honor of the ancestors must be upheld. Everyone knew their Viking forefathers were the fiercest warriors in the world. They protected what was theirs. They looked after themselves, had to, living as they did so far away from the sight of the greedy kings in Norway. They needed no rich chieftain or hungry king to rule them. The Norse gods would give them good fortune and the Christ god, too, if he ever came to Greenland.

The insects hummed and guzzled. A few night birds called to each other over the lonely ice. Brigitta sprinkled their drinks with powder from the horn of a narwhale and the shell of a sea urchin. The night they would attack. The Norse would rid the valleys of Greenland from the thieving giants who stole cattle from the descendant of the Eirik the Red.

Yellowbritches decided that after his altercation with the inhabitants of the Grey Mountain, the women of Thorness would need someone to protect them from magic while the giants were disposed of in the high valley. Asmund and Scarface agreed that someone had to do this and it might as well be Yellowbritches, who was hopeless in a fight anyway, being as he was a bard.

Scarface slaughtered a pig and offered as a sacrifice to the old gods. Bjarni and Egil had their hands painted in blood to give them courage to handle their fear of death like men in battle. Asmund said they must have the blessing of the White Christ before they faced anything evil that lived on the Gray Mountain, giants or no giants.

Olaf, muttering curses about dragons and barbarians, had been dragged over the hills on an ancient horse. He was forthwith dragged inside and

CHAPTER 18 — *The battle with the Giants*

reluctantly sprinkled a little ash and water and said some prayers in Latin, which pleased Asmund. Scarface spat in the dirt as Olaf mumbled.

'Remember,' Asmund told everyone, 'not one of yer fine Viking ancestors but did not take the religion of them monk houses. Ye call the God of the Christians the White Christ but tis a fierce god who helps His followers to win battles.'

'I heard it was the money taken by the priests from the poor farmers to buy arms is what won the wars for them in Ireland,' said Scarface. 'I heard it from that trader what I had the fight with and gave me this scar. Were a brave man too, that man from Dublin.'

The men scratched and considered. Scarface insisted they rise and begin. Brigitta insisted they take a skein of good ale with them as thanks for the war they were about to wage. Scarface agreed. The ale was lovingly poured into a goat's bladder and sealed.

They made their way across the valley, up the hills behind the house to the meadow and then to the cliff face. It was the night of the dark moon. All were dressed in dark colors and armed with axe, knife and spear. Asmund, as lawbinder, carried a flint to light the fire. Gunhar carried the spit. Short Irish had to be prevented from giving a running commentary on the movement of each particular group of stars and how they affected the weather. He withdrew into a brooding silence and decided, instead, to find his beloved in the clouds.

It was a steep path up the cliff with many sharp rocks. Bjarni and Egil were given the job of hauling the recalcitrant goat up the path behind them.

'Me fud, them is got me fud,' muttered the Nidhogg, a tall malformed human who stood concealed in a crevasse behind the rock of Thor. Unwanted bits of bone protruded from parts of his skeleton. His hair flowed in a coat of oily human wool over his skin. He pulled his body with some difficulty along a path behind the rock and blew into a horn. A low desolate tone bounced off the valley walls and set up an echo that traveled far into the Grey Mountain. 'Them is not father,' the Nidhogg grunted. 'Father, where is you?'

It was many days since the ragged man had eaten. He had not been able to catch a horse or a sheep for weeks, his legs being too painful to run and his body crippled by pain. The skraeling he had killed and eaten were too few to rely on for a regular supply of food.

The bony man had been banished by his family. They said he was possessed by a demon that looked out from his crossed eyes. They called him Nidhogg, the dragon from Hel, because of his misshapen body and head. He lived only because his father, the man Odd, came into the valley with his sons and killed caribou for him when the moon was black, like it was tonight. Odd had promised his daughter when she died from the milk fever that he would look after their son, evil and deformed as he was. It was his punishment for committing sex with his daughter even though his wife was dead.

Odd hated Nidhogg. Now, because of his promise, he was in conflict with Scarface and his kin. He wished he had killed the greasy thing when it was born. But his daughter had pleaded with him and in his stupidity he had promised. Now Nidhogg was calling, blowing on the horn Odd had given him. Odd replied with his own horn to let Nidhogg know he was on his way and to wait by the waterfall where starlight from the water gave a small light.

The ice cave was a good place for Nidhogg to hide. Odd knew that no one went there because of the Old Ones lived there in a place as cold as Hel. Scarface rarely noticed the occasional caribou missing, a horse lost, a few sheep less. But Nidhogg had killed skraeling the past few moons. Odd had found their bones. Nidhogg's incessant need for food was becoming a problem.

The problem of Nidhogg's food was solved when the field came to Odd with the dowry of Scarface's daughter. There were wild animals on that field. The man who owned the field owned the animals. Now Scarface wanted his pasture back. That was bad luck for Scarface. His daughter should have stayed and married someone else. Could have married Odd or one of the boys who were all busting to poke something other than each other or the ducks. They could have shared her, being as they were men without a woman among them. A daughter of Scarface's would have been a nice little truffle and he wouldn't mind getting his hands on that fat white wife neither.

CHAPTER 18 — *The battle with the Giants*

A sound like music floated in patches up the valley; human voices. On the Mountain in the dark moon. No one ever came to the Mountain on the dark moon. Not even Scarface and his kin. One of Odd's sons thumped his father and pointed to a tiny patch of light in the distance. Inland folks said that on the Grey Mountain there was a race of One Foots, small and tough with skin the color of the rocks and eyes white with no pupils. They came out only once a year to find men and take their eyes and feed them to their blind children.

Odd and his sons continued with stealth, their thoughts full of tales of unnamed horrors by unnamed men who had heard the tale from those who had survived. Odd had no need to remind his sons that these were the perfect conditions for the appearance of the One Foots with their ice-white eyes. Odd carried his bow and the eyes of his young sons glowed in the reflection of their assorted weapons.

'Cold,' whispered Odd, 'and black as pitch when those with evil in their bellies come out.' The sons of Odd shivered and blew air across their hands. They were tough, dressed in skins and frayed bits of wadmal and only one with a beard as yet. They knew not the softness of woman as their mother had died years ago. Odd always told them, 'Yer right to be hard in this life if yer is t'er survive. Yer has to learn to fight or end up as dog fud for the hounds of Odin.'

Down at the end of the valley Bjarni and Egil had succeeded in dragging the goat to the rock sacred to Thor. This rock balanced on the curve of the cliff, carved out by the gods of Valhalla themselves. The goat seemed to be unaware of its importance regarding the dispatching of the giants and struggled and fought so much Egil had to sit on it while Bjarni sent it's spirit to the halls of Valhalla to provide a ghostly feast for Odin. Scarface collected the blood in skeins and sent Short Irish and his own bondsmen to scatter the blood.

Nidhogg salivated and crept closer. Bjarni and Egil made a fire; the goat was skewered into a palatable morsel for a giant and set to roast. The boys were instructed to hide behind Thor's rock as soon as they felt the ground tremble with the stamp of giant feet. The giants would be pushed over the edge of the cliff by the men lying in wait with spears and knives.

Odd became aware of creatures moving somewhere in the valley. Large creatures, large clumsy creatures, who cast no shadow. He could smell their foul breath and hear them grunt to each other. One Foots! He signaled to his sons to prepare for battle as they walked softly along the path towards the rock near the waterfall where Nidhogg would meet them. Likewise, Scarface and his kin became aware of small stones dislodged, saw in the starlight huge shadows on the valley path, heard the sound of the insects stop as if startled. They too drew their weapons. Bjarni and Egil waited. Nidhogg watched and salivated.

Odd crept towards the edge of the waterfall. The One Foots did the same. A curtain of brilliant light slowly formed over the sea and lit the valley below in shimmering color.

'Be gone, One Foots,' yelled Odd.

'Get away Giants,' yelled Scarface.

'It ain't One Foots Pa. It's that thieving Scarface.'

'Odd . It's you. Creeping up on us in me own land. Git away yer fuck-faced bunch of goat-arsed dwarfs. Git back to them hills and fuck yer own pigs.'

'Our land, yer rancid pack of gum-faced One Foots. Git back ter moo at yer sorcerer of a wife an yer fish-faced daughters. Lest yer want ter give 'em all ter us so we can fuck 'em.'

'Get out of here. I'll not tell yer again, yer goat- arsed old tyrant Odd. Go fuck the skull of that dead daughter of yours.'

Odd spat at Scarface. Scarface threw a spear at Odd. It lodged in his arm. The men fell upon one another with murderous voice and unsheathed weapons and clubbed and stabbed and thumped with grim entitlement. It was difficult to tell who was with what, but bit by bit Odd and his sons were driven to the edge of the cliff. Bjarni and Egil stood beside the burnt goat and jumped up and down, yelling encouragement.

Suddenly Nidhogg could wait no more to calm the storm in his stomach. He ran at the singed goat. As he went to grab the carcass with his mangled hands Bjarni rushed him from behind and stuffed a spear into his back. Nidhogg fell upon the fire and impaled himself upon the metal that secured the goat to the spit. Egil ran at him with a club and

CHAPTER 18 — The battle with the Giants

together they brought the cripple to the ground with the goat attached. The last thing Nidhogg heard of was of a snap in the back of his neck.

'Roll him over the cliff. Quick,' grunted Bjarni. 'With the fuckin' goat if we have to.'

It was not possible to detach the goat from the moaning Nidhogg. It lay impaled in his chest and covered in dribble. As the men fought their way along the top of the cliff, Bjarni and Egil dragged Nidhogg to the edge of the waterfall. He let out one long loud snarling sound as he slid over the gap and was consumed by the rocks below.

Odd and his son remained at the edge of the cliff. There was silence as Nidhogg hit the ground below with a thud.

'Them boys have done it,' yelled Scarface. 'Go on then, send them Odds off the cliff.' He let out a war cry and redoubled his efforts. The fighting and clubbing began again but this time it was quickly over. Scarface and his kin stood back and panted till the earth gave up a snort of acceptance as four bodies hit the rocks and rolled into the pool at the bottom of the cliff.

'There,' grunted Scarface, his face as red as the fire of his hair. 'Hear that. It's them giants again after me sheep.'

Asmund stood and wiped the blood from his knife. 'Ah, shut up, Scarface. What have we done here? Them was just boys. The rest was just that fool Odd and his crippled son. Yer have got us ter fight yer battles for naught. Where's yer Giants then?'

'Up there.' Scarface frothed at the mouth with excitement. 'Come on. We can get them still. Odd was just doing what they wanted. He talks with them giants and helps them steal me cattle orf me land.' Scarface continued to bounce up and down and make stabs with his knife into the dark. He went to drag Gunhar back up the valley.

'Stop fool.' Asmund used his best Lawgiver voice.

'Stop me, will yer, yer black-hearted Norse?' bellowed Scarface and went as if to stab Asmund. Asmund responded with a mighty head butt to the side of Scarface's gut. Scarface bit Gunhar on the arm by mistake. Asmund recovered enough to lay into Scarface with the goat's bladder. Gunhar had Asmund by the leg and was trying to dislocate it at the hip. The rest of the men wobbled on to their feet and eventually sat while the three Norse punched and thumped each other.

'Cease this,' Short Irish bellowed or you will wake them Giants and we'll all be floating over yer Rainbow Bridge soon as a pig's fart.'

He scooped up a pod full of hot coals and threw it over the battling Norse, who stopped fighting and made as if to turn on Short Irish, who sped into the shadows behind the rock of Thor.

'Ale,' croaked Bjarni. 'Give us some of Brigitta's ale. Quick.' Suddenly everyone thought that was the next best thing to do. Scarface sat nursing his gut while Asmund glared at the assembled company to let them know he now was in charge. Bjarni and Egil demonstrated to each other the actions of the doomed Nidhogg. Short Irish reappeared from the dark side of Thor's rock with a scowl and held his hand out for the ale skin.

Gunhar wiped the blood off his hands. 'Law says we must announce their death to someone, falling to their death off the cliff as they did. And cover the bodies.'

'Them is covered by water now in the pool at the bottom of the falls.'

'So who you going to tell then?' said Short Irish, gulping down the ale so fast that bits of liquid dripped from his beard. 'Giants? One Foots?'

'I am the Lawbinder of Hvalsey,' Asmund said, 'and not some Irish slave what has ancestors who never knew a day of righteousness in their lives. I says what the law is and it says a man must tell another man if death happens for a reason. The death here being that of Odd and his sons.'

'Tell each other.' Scarface grabbed the ale skin from Short Irish. 'Be no kin of Odd's left to go to the Althing and demand retribution. As the Wise One says, if evil has been done by bad men, good men must solve it themselves. A bad man's sword cannot talk by itself.'

CHAPTER 19
Anna and Thorfinn

The days of the new moon came to Hvalsey and the community of Norse with the song of the earth sweet in the lengthening days. Each day Anna went gathering herbs in the twilight as the men sat outside playing board games or mending tools. One day Thorfinn walked with her.

'I will come with you and carry your basket to make your burden less,' 'Magic,' he said and his arm swept the length of the horizon. 'Magic for us,' he smiled and they both laughed with the freedom of release. They climbed the rocks by a stream and came to a deep inland melt-water lake. There was always a presence around these turquoise lakes, as if the earth was opening one languid eye to claim the heart of all who passed.

Anna inspected the low willows for clumps of wool as she walked. 'I have a new fleece,' she told Thorfinn. 'I would like to make you something from this wool. I will put a woman's magic in the fabric to protect the man who wears it. The wool shines silver through any color I dye it. I think I will make it blue. A silver blue cloak.' Anna measured the space between them. He did not move away. 'They say, she said smiling, 'that any who wear the fleece of the elfin sheep will never leave Greenland.'

'Your hands.' Thorfinn held them to his lips. Her hands were as usual bound from the wrist to the thumb with strips of wadmal. The skin calloused on the side of her fingers. 'Your hands suffer as you weave and spin?'

'Yes. It is of no matter. I need lichen and the heart of the black flower that grows on the hills behind that lake to make the dye. Ged calls the lake Odin's Eye. This cloak will keep you warm, Thorfinn Markland- Farer. I will make it, for you have no woman to weave for you. And well you should have.'

They walked further towards the mountains.

'Look,' said Anna smiling. She pointed up to a steep ridge where a group of animals bunched together. 'Elfin sheep like the ones that live in the Grey Mountain. The ones that have the magic fleece.'

'You. Anna. You are my magic.' Thorfinn gathered Anna to his body and she folded into him. There came between them the greatest tenderness either had ever known. He spread his cloak on the ground and they lay in each other's arms in a shelter between the rocks. He came within her gently and the sound of the earth beat a pulse with them as they moved together; even the insects seemed to echo a rhythm of ecstasy and lull in a cycle that could be heard with the wash of the water in Odin's Eye. As the ecstasy rose between them there was no separation; they became the sky and the ground, the beings within the rocks and the breath of the gods who dreamed in Valhalla. At last Thorfinn pulled away and lay beside her. As she lay against his chest Anna felt the breath of the spirit rising in tiny thrusts across Thorfinn's skin.

They walked home shoulder to shoulder. There was no need for words. There was no one about, only Bjarni moving like a shadow in the hills as he patrolled the far reaches of the steading. He waved at them with a nestbaggin full of birds slung across his back.

'It is odd how quickly it goes between us.' Thorfinn kissed her again as they paused in the shadow of the house. 'It is not usual for me. I have been alone too long. It is good to know the softness of woman. I will take you with me, beautiful Norse woman, when I get my silver from Asmund. With that silver I will buy us a ship to sail to Markland.'

'Markland is so far away. It is a strange place, wilder than the Orkneys or the Far Islands of the Sheep. I fear to leave Greenland. Could you not stay here and make a life with us?'

CHAPTER 19 — Anna and Thorfinn

Thorfinn gently moved her hair from her neck and stroked the pale skin. 'They say the king of Norway wants all lands in the Great Ocean for his own now he has Iceland. He wants to control the trade between all the places in the Great Ocean. He wants every person to make sacrifice to the Christ god and give money to the Christ Church and pay taxes as well to the king. I do not believe this should happen. There will be fighting and death between those who want this and those who do not. We would be safe in the New Country. It is a place of much beauty. Too far away for any thieving king or priest. Bjarni could come with us. And Berryface if she wanted.'

Anna reached up to Thorfinn and touched his red-gold beard as one would stroke an animal. She remembered this face. For a second she saw a face that was Thorfinn but not Thorfinn.

He rested his face in her hand. 'Woman I cannot be without you. I have spent too many nights alone. I have been thinking. Before the door is shut, I will move my sleeping skins to the cow byre as if to protect the cattle from Sieiphir. I will move the old house blocks from beside the small hatch that leads to the bath house. I have watched. No one uses it. Come to me when everyone is asleep and the wind howls. No one will hear. Ged will not know. I will wait.'

'Freyja keep me safe in my weakness for I cannot resist this life you bring to my heart,' Anna whispered.

Thorfinn held her and kissed her and again the gods of Valhalla sighed the dreams of their pleasure.

That evening Anna sang as she worked and laughed at the pranks of the tomte. She danced around Skadi; she put ribbons of red silk in the long black hair of Berryface and bounced the baby through the house in play.

Thorfinn announced that he would sleep in the cow byre and see that no harm came to the cattle now the days were lengthening and wolves had been heard close by. No one took much notice, it being Thorfinn and him being an Icelander with a stranger's ways. Bjarni half-heartedly offered to accompany him, but he was too young, Sokki said, and would tempt the Nokken with its yellow eyes if it came hunting for flesh now the winter was gone.

Before O'Flarty swung the big wooden door shut and shot across the beam Thorfinn carried his sleeping covers into the animal byre cut into the hillside. 'Cooler,' he said as he left the house. 'Like the sea. I am a sailor. I need to see the stars at night and smell the water.'

Asmund ignored him. 'Ah, ha,' he grunted at the game board as his king smashed down on a knight manned by Short Irish.

Soon the muffled sound of a ribald song could be heard from the cow byre. No one but Anna bothered to listen. It was not usual for an individual to move out of the safety of the longhouse, but Thorfinn had always said he missed the cold white nights of the northern sea.

He liked his new sleeping place although the flies and mosquitoes were a pest. He smeared himself with goose fat and puffed up the straw to make a comfortable bed. He put bits of hide and cloth across the opening of his chosen stall and settled down to wait for Thor to ride his goats across the sky and bring Anna to his bed.

By his own reckoning Thorfinn was a wanderer, wanting only to discover that which no one else had claim to. He was not like his Icelandic ancestors who sat on their high-seat pillars until their bums turned to bone and their hearts became gristle while they did what the lawspeaker said. Cursed they were, like all the males in his family. Cursed by a witch woman. He had seen it more than once. His eldest male cousin had seen his family drown in front of him. Another uncle's son and his family had been killed in a fight with pirates from the Land of the Pitts. Thorfinn remember the death of his wife. Her relatives took the child because he refused to become a Christ man and bring up the child as a follower of the Christ, like the priest said. It would be different in the New Country. There were no kings or priests there. No White Christ to tell him who to fuck, what to eat or who he could trade with.

He rolled over to watch the sky though the folds of the skins. He was at peace. It had not been so for many years. She, who had come so unexpectedly into his life; the stories of their life together in the New Country would be told around the fireplaces of generations to come.

That night, as the fire dwindled, Anna began to spin the silver fleece. She sat with the elfin wool and the fibers flew under her hands

CHAPTER 19 — Anna and Thorfinn

as if her thoughts drew a fine thread from her heart to her fingers. In bed she lay beside Ged and watched O'Flarty swing the door shut and bolt it. All her life she had loved the time when the house filled with the sleeping breath of people around her and the big door of the longhouse was shut against anything evil that roamed outside.

She thought of Thorfinn outside where any hungry thing could find him. Aud looked at her with her clouded eyes and began the song of the Spirit Horse; a creature with black eyes and a mane that flowed behind like starlight. This Spirit Horse came from the bay on the nights of the dark moon when the sea was glass and the stars from its mane trailed in the water. Many cows disappeared when the Spirit Horse came to Ebiwaz. All they found in the morning, sang Aud, were a few white bones. Anna felt tears on her face. Thorfinn was out there. Alone.

She got up and walked to the back of the house with a small oil lamp. The night was still and filled with the song of insects. The blocks had not been moved. Ged stirred and called to her. She returned to lie beside him. She curled around him and watched the swirling shapes and figures fill the darkness until she fell asleep.

The life of Ebiwaz turned with the season and the labor of the people and animals. Anna sat at her loom and started weaving a tunic with a design of sea serpents around the hem. It was a delicate pattern of interlocking circles outlined in blue on the silver wool. She thanked the Norns for her gift; the Norns who sat all day and spun the fate of men in their intricate looms.

At last the dark clouds of a storm came above the fiord. Wind beat against the rocks and pushed the drying racks flat. Thor's chariots crashed above the settlement and set the sea to roar and pound.

Thorfinn wrapped himself in extra blankets and went early to his sleeping place. He took a lamp and a skin of berry juice with him. Anna lay awake beside Ged and listened. Sleep would not come. Her body ached for release even after she had satisfied Ged. She could not take her thoughts from Thorfinn. Was he cold? Did he wait for her? Did the Nokken lie in wait for him? In the cold dark did he hold out his arms for the specter of a woman who did not come?

Anna decided to see if the blocks had been moved at the back of the house. Just to look only. It was the fault of the Norns that she wanted this man so much; her fate was spun with the fate of Thorfinn. She was helpless before the will of the gods. She imagined the voice of her mother foretelling the disaster that came when one went against the wisdom of the gods. What would her mother tell her to do now?

'Freyja save me.' Anna felt an irresistible pull from the direction of the cow barn. Ged was snoring and grunting in his sleep, his hands locked in the bed boards above his head. Anna found her cloak and walked softly to the back wall. One of the turf blocks had been removed. She climbed though the space into a cloud of insects. Just to look. Lightning hit the mountain behind the farm and, for an instant, the hills and the bay below shimmered. She thought she saw a man at the opening to the cow byre. He beckoned to her with great urgency. The light seemed to fizz around him. With the wind wild on the mountain above Anna ran from the house to the byre.

The nights cycled steadily towards the dark moon with a series of storms. Anna worked hard as a good wife to bring the seed of Ged within herself and so send him to a restful sleep. With Ged asleep she crept from the house to the byre, telling herself each time that this would be the last. Once she lay with Thorfinn so late into the morning they heard the bolt of the door being pushed aside as O'Flarty padded softly outside to relieve himself.

'Asmund will kill us both if he finds out,' Anna whispered waited for O'Flarty to return inside. 'I am his brother's wife. He will see anything I do against Ged as an act against him.'

'Asmund wants you for himself.' Thorfinn dragged on his breeches. 'Quick come outside as if you were collecting water. O'Flarty is half blind. He will not know you did not follow him out.'

They moved quickly towards the stream, walking a little apart. Thorfinn sat on a rock while Anna bent to fill a bowl.

'There was a man who came to the steading of Gunhar Bloodaxe. He lay with the servant of Gunhar's wife. Gunhar buried an axe in

CHAPTER 19 — Anna and Thorfinn

them both when he found them. Asmund said there was no crime if the husband did not offer the woman. It is the law.'

'Aye and I will kill Asmund if I do not get my silver back. That is also the law.'

'A man may take two women to bed. Can a woman not bed two men at the same time?'

'Oh, sweet Anna. How would a man know if a son came from his seed then? I will leave Ebiwaz as soon as I return from the Mid-Summer Assembly with my treasure. And you will come with me. The silver is mine, as you are, my beautiful Viking daughter. Thor has given you to me. We will grow fat on honey and wine in the New County and our lives will be told in stories by our children.'

'And if you do not get back what is yours?'

Thorfinn looked at her and considered. 'Yes, it is true. I am but one and one cannot fight Asmund and all his kin at the Assembly. If that happens, I will go to the Nordsetur to buy us a passage.'

Anna held the bowl to her body. An eagle circled far above them. 'There is danger for Norse beyond the Western Settlement. Ghosts there are and strange creatures that live with the skraeling and do their bidding when they hunt. What gods will protect you so far into the cold and the dark of the north? It is not a place for the Norse. Even the White Christ is not known there. Many have gone and many have not returned.'

'Anna, Anna. The luck of Thor is with a man and the woman he desires.'

CHAPTER 20
The men from Brattahlid

When the moon was near dark again Anna held her blood within her to nourish a child. It was expected, she told herself. It could be the child of either Thorfinn or Ged. If it was even a child. She looked at Skadi and her dribbling mouth and dragging leg. She watched Ged muttering to shadows and heard Thorfinn belching and vomiting in the byre. No it was not a child. The being inside her was a thing that had risen out of the secret of her union with Thorfinn, a thing that belonged in the graveyard behind the house and had come into her as she walked on the earth above.

The skraeling had taught her how to prepare a herbal mix to bring on the bleeding of women when a child should not move from the spirit world. Anna spent days in the hills searching for herbs. She beat juniper and hawthorn berries to a paste and added the burnt bark of the willow tree and the droppings of a bird. She looked for elves in the dark places of the rocks to help her. She did not tell either Thorfinn or Ged.

Yet day by day she felt more protective of this tiny creature growing within her belly. She cooked the paste and threw it out. She found new ingredients and made it again. She began to get sick. Food revolted her as did the sight of Ged scratching at his carving and the smell Thorfinn's breath.

One day Thorfinn found her near the rock where he stood watching the sea.

'You don't come to me any more in the storms,' he said with the lisp of alcohol in his teeth. 'I miss you. The nights are cold.'

CHAPTER 20 — The men from Brattahlid

'You're drunk. Thor knows how you are getting ale when Skadi guards it so fiercely.'

'She thinks she guards it,' Thorfinn laughed. 'She thinks it is safe. But Sokki made a key to the ale cupboard. Takes the ale and fills the barrel with water. Says Skadi is too blind to notice now days. It stops the pain in my leg.' He lifted his tunic and rubbed at his thigh. 'It does not heal.'

'Listen to me. Look at me. I'm sick all the time. A child grows in me.'

'A child?' burbled Thorfinn. He beat a little tune on the sand with his staff. 'A child. A gift from Frey. To the gods, from the gods.' He sat down with his leg stretched out and regarded Anna with interest. 'To Markland we must go with haste. I will get that silver. I will not go to the Nordsetur lame like this. I will not hunt in such a place to get what I already have.' He looked at Anna. 'I do not like blood Anna. I do not like to be covered in the blood and guts of creatures who share my path on this earth.' He began to cough. 'Then again it could be my blood and guts covering the animals.'

'You do not hunt. You do not work in the home field. You do not make things like Ged. You do not work with Asmund at the forge. You just sit and draw maps in the dirt with that stick of yours and drink the ale Sokki steals. Or that berry stuff Short Irish makes.'

'Ah, my beloved, I will take you away from all this. We do not belong here, with the cows and the fields and the mud. The world awaits. There is only good luck for me in the New Country. There are no curses, no ancestors, no law to bind me for anything my family did in the past. No lawman to force me to follow the White Christ.' He smiled and looked into the red sun with streaks of red like blood in his hair and his brown animal eyes on fire. 'We will cross the Great Sea from Greenland like Leif Eiriksson before us. I will show you what freedom is really like.'

Anna sat beside him. The wind could be heard in the caves on the far side of the fiord and in the ice. 'The Norns will get us all in the end. Odin and Thor, they just play with us. The day of our death and the manner of our passing are already known. What sort of freedom can we ever have?' She pressed her hands to her stomach.

'You are cold, my love. Come into the house by the fire.'

Thorfinn staggered as he got to his feet. Anna supported him as they walked up the slope towards the house. He limped and leant heavily on his staff. Anna made him sit by the hearth while she and Berryface examined his leg; the bruising was gone but the wound was still red and swollen around the scar. Thorfinn smiled and sang as they pressed a poultice of seaweed and moss on his leg and bound it with strips of wadmal.

That day the men from Brattahlid arrived. They came on horseback across the hills when the sun was low on the mountain. Men from Brattahlid were always important and well received, even if there had been no news of their coming. The two men were thick-set and muscular and had large white teeth in broad faces tanned by the sun and the snow. They were dressed in black fox fur and fine wadmal tunics with an indigo trim. Both wore silver torques and carried sword hilts engraved in gold with ancient runes. Their hair was oiled and decorated with fine silver clasps.

Asmund met them at the edge of the home field and bid them welcome. Skadi and the women hurried to prepare a meal while Bjarni tended to their horses.

'Greenland is to have its own bishop,' one of the men from Brattahlid told Asmund when they were settled with ale and food around the table. 'Sokki Thorisson, the chief of Brattahlid, has sent his son on an expedition to the court of King Sigurd of Norway to request a bishop for Greenland. There was a live polar bear on board to give to the king to show how rich Greenland is.'

'The bishop is on his way,' added the other man, nodding reverently so his silver hair clasps bounced. 'A new church is being built at Gardar. Men and women from all settlements in Greenland must come to help build the church so all in Greenland can worship the Christ God. The priest from Iceland is there now. His Holiness asks for a tithe of ivory and fur to assist in the preparations for the bishop. The priest will send the goods from Greenland to Norway so the Church can sell the wealth of Greenland for money.'

CHAPTER 20 — *The men from Brattahlid*

'The Church must have money,' the second man said, ignoring the look of suspicion on Asmund's face. The man turned to the assembled company and opened his hands in friendship. 'Only barbarians do not use money. We here in Greenland have the fortune to be able to see our goods transformed into money by the agents of the church in Norway. The bishop needs money to live, as does the priest. No one can live on fur and feathers.'

The men from Brattahlid beamed at Asmund, who remained silent with his fingers playing on the edge of the axe in his belt.

'And thus we are not barbarians,' the first man, Snorri, said, flashing his white teeth. 'Asmund you are the lawbinder of the settlement of Hvalsey, the chief, and a representative of the Holy Roman Church I see. You have the Christ crucifix over your door. This settlement is blessed in the name of the Christ. Now it is the time for all payments for the baptisms and blessings you have done in the name of the Christ to come to the church.'

Asmund sat glaring from beneath his eyebrows. His face seemed more aflame than the coals of the fire. 'There is no ivory, no skin or falcons. We have not been to the Nordsetur for many summers. People pay me in food, which we eat. We have nothing to give but these high-seat pillars.'

The men from Brattahlid examined the high-seat pillars. 'Not finished,' they said. 'No matter. Ged Romfortsson is to come to Gardar to work on the church. He can finish these when he returns. The priest has requested it. No finer carver can be found in all Greenland. Ged is to have the honor of placing his work on the new church and his memory will benefit from it. But now, where is your store of fur and ivory and falcons to give to the Bishop?'

'There is nothing,' said Asmund. 'We have nothing.'

Skadi pulled a wolf skin over the battered chest and sat on it with the baby attached to her breast. Asmund stood beside her and aimed a loving slap in her direction.

'I will send word out for the men of Hvalsey to come to an Assembly,' he said

'Greedy, ain't he, this White Christ. If he is so great wot's he want with us in Greenland.' Sokki grunted and scratched at Berryface.

'The men must bring what ivory and skins they have for the bishop,' Snorri said. 'The priest will bless them for their efforts. Greenland is blessed, Asmund, to have this man coming to live with us. We are no longer barbarians.'

CHAPTER 21
The local Assembly

Asmund swore on the mound of the grandfathers that he would help Ged bury the whale-horse skulls if Ged would do as the priest wanted and carve his designs on the church at Gardar. Maybe then the priest would forget about the tithes Asmund and the men of Hvalsey did not have.

The day was set for the landowners from the surrounding farms to arrive at Ebiwaz to discuss the situation. Short Irish informed Asmund of the exact phase of the moon, where the North Star would sit and what clouds would follow the Norse farmers on their journey to Hvalsey. The tomte was annoyed. He hated strangers more than he hated Ged and the red bearded man from Iceland. He set himself to drag thorns into the sand where a big fire had been set within a circle of benches, so if anyone rested weary feet from shoes they would be scratched.

The day of the Assembly came. The male head of each farm, plus his bondsman, came as agreed by custom. No man in Greenland paid a fine if they did not attend, as was the custom of the ancestors in Iceland, but all liked the opportunity to sit and talk. Gunhar brought his wife, Sigrid the Tall, with a brood of her bondswomen. She was dressed as usual in leather breeches and tunic with much silver adorning her person. Sigrid liked the opportunity to inspect the magic Asmund performed in his smithy with the iron plant, and to trade a few household items for whatever metal implements she could get.

The bondsmen sat in a circle behind the landowners while the women stayed apart and watched. Short Irish sat behind Asmund and conversed with his dragon love about the way the devil Norse were really Irish in disguise, and had changed their Irish names and invented Norse ancestry so they could claim the land.

Skadi and Berryface served everyone with white cheese and caribou and passed around a bowl of dulse. Sokki hobbled into the circle to keep an eye on Sigrid, who he insisted, could bewitch any man who looked at her. Short Irish passed a bucket of his berry drink around the circle and then to the women who stood apart. The tide brought waves to sing beneath the mist and the firelight grew on the water near the beach. As of old Asmund threw an axe into the water the declared the Assembly open to the constant rush and weave of the water in the bay.

The men from Brattahlid told of the great church that would be built at Gardar and how each person who helped would be remembered as the one who made this happen. Luck would be theirs forever when the Christ saw how they had given their labor. The bishop from Iceland would make sure their interests were looked to in any trade agreements within the Norse world.

'Indeed?' said Scarface sucking berry spirit though his whiskers. 'Why would us Norse care what the White Christ or his priest does?'

'You is a trader here in Hvalsey as we knows,' Snorri from Brattahlid said. 'You all get rich from what you trade. Cows and horse and leather and caribou hides. Bishop'll stop that trade if you don't do what's good for Greenland and help the people come to the Christian god. Like in Iceland.'

Scarface considered. Tales of the bad things done to traders in Norway and Iceland had come to him over the years.

Asmund narrowed his eyes. 'Don't have to like it Eirik Eiriksson Scarface. But we in Greenland don't want to be left behind and end up the rest of the world thinking we is barbarians and daughter fuckers like them Odd do we?'

Scarface looked around at the assembled men, tough strong men with children and farms and women in their beds. He looked at Sigrid and her women; strong Viking women. He thought about the monster they had pushed over the cliff. No, he said to himself, what

CHAPTER 21 — The local Assembly

did it matter? If building a church for this bishop meant more trade for Greenland, Thor and Odin would allow him to work for the White Christ as long as he told them what he planned.

'Aye,' grunted Gunhar Bloodaxe. 'Long as we don't have ter give up eating horse meat and leaving sick babes out in the cold.'

'And fucking,' said another man.' I heard them followers of the White Christ ain't allowed to fuck who they wants.'

'Fuck anyone you wants,' Snorri from Brattahlid said, 'long as its got two legs and not four.' He demonstrated. Men fell about laughing. The women remained stony faced. Sigrid took out her short wide knife and looked at her reflection in the blade.

Everyone who could always went to the General Assembly at Gardar to make the laws right, to see that what was done was fair and make sure no kings, or bishops for that matter, got to make the rules for how they lived. Although women were not to vote in the Assembly, some women did make the journey with wares to exchange, or just for the adventure. Women were needed to mend and cook and care for any who took ill or got hurt in a fight.

It was a poor Norse family that could not spare one or two people for one turning of the moon in summer, while the servants and the old men and women tended to the cattle and gathered the fodder. No one ever could be sure of how the summer would run in Greenland. If luck came their way the summer grasses would provide a second harvest for the winter when they returned. People had goods and cattle to trade at the Mid-Summer markets, marriages to arrange, disputes to settle and healers to find. There might be news of the outside world and a bit of entertainment as well.

The men banged anything they could and the din of their agreement bounced off the high mountain behind and set more than one spirit loose to calve ice in the bay.

'You,' Asmund said to Bjarni who had been looking after the horses up by the house, 'you and Sokki will stay here at Ebiwaz with the women and do the work on the farm with O'Flarty. Olaf will help where he can. Unless Skadi and the babe wants to come.' He turned to Ged. 'You brother Ged will accompany me to the Assembly with Short Irish and Thorfinn. Anna will stay here and help Skadi. And you all shut up about walrus bones and the treasure till we have been to the law courts and sorted out who must pay for what.' He grabbed the nestbaggin of bones from Ged who as usual had them balanced on his shoulders. 'The whale-horse bones brother,' Asmund said shaking the sack. 'We will bury them the same time as we put Thorfinn's companions in holy ground.'

'Must be consecrated ground what has been blessed by a priest.' Ged grabbed the bag from Asmund. He slung it over his shoulder and sighed deeply. He had about him rapid movements that set his thin frame rippling in waves. Now, because Asmund had touched the bag, he must take the bones out and count them. He moved to a still place amongst the rocks and lifted them out with reverence. He counted them carefully and placed them back in the bag.

'If Ged wants to bury bones in a churchyard then let him,' Asmund told Skadi in bed that night. 'As long as he keeps carving I don't care what he does. Because of him we gets to drink ale all year and sometimes eat barley besides. Maybe that priest will forget his damned tithes. Ged's carving is as good as money to those who want it. What if he can't turn a hand to feed his self? That's what a wife is for. That's why I got Anna from the Western Settlement where they breeds them tough.'

'Ain't good for much else,' Skadi rolled over with effort and dragged up her skirts.

'Aye, Skadi,' said Asmund as he prepared to enter her. 'Will you and the babe come?' he asked as he pushed himself between her soft thighs.

'No,' grunted Skadi. 'We will stay. I don't trust that woman from the West.'

'Ged ain't poked no seed between her legs. If he ain't able to do the job I will.' Asmund grunted as he thrust.

Skadi dribbled with her face turned sideways into the pillow and sent a prayer to the wife of the White Christ, that if it were so she would not have to put up with Asmund grunting and heaving above her night after night.

CHAPTER 22
Preparing for the journey

Preparations began for the trip to Gardar. Skadi sent seven rolls of wadmal to sell at the market, a fine black fleece, four baby goatskins, the down from many ducks and several old household implements and some mended pots from her aunt. Asmund had a box of tools to sell: sharpened knives, axe heads and several spades made from the shoulder blades of a whale. The nestbaggin of sailor's bones was extracted from the shed beside the pig pen.

'Well pleased I will be to be rid of that,' said Skadi. 'It stinks and them bones still carry a ghost voice inside em.'

'Talk to yr, do they?' said Sokki. 'Why jest the other night I swear I heard 'em asking for ale. Keep em quiet it would ter see their friends swilling a bit of ale, woman.'

'Put them bones in a chest with the treasure so no one will hear 'em no matter what they say,' screeched Skadi so loudly the dogs jumped. 'Shut 'em up to be with the silver what belongs to 'em.'

Thorfinn and O'Flarty stuffed the heavy bag on top of the treasure and pushed the box shut. The chest rattled by itself. Thorfinn's face became a landscape of valleys as he listened.

'Come Thorfinn. Your friends are with the gods now. They tell you they are happy. Come with me to the hills to find berries. The bushes have flowered. Come.' Anna stood smiling and held out a pouch for Thorfinn to carry.

'I must go with Asmund,' Thorfinn told Anna as they walked in the hills. 'I cannot see the way with this. If Asmund had not sailed to the island I would have nothing. Yet if I had not found the treasure on the strange ship Asmund would have nothing.'

'He wants your silver to use as a tithe. He has nothing else to give. Let him. He has many friends who will fight for him even if the verdict of the court goes against him.' Anna put her arms around Thorfinn. There was no past and nothing to become; just this moment. 'Thorfinn I am not strong. I do not think I can have this child without you or Ged.'

'O my beloved I will return. We will go to the New Country and discover many strange things. My ancestors would haunt me forever if I do not repay Asmund in some way.' Thorfinn drew her to him.

Anna slid her hands though the golden fur on his body. 'Aye,' she said pulling his hair as if to card it, 'and the trees of the New Country make coffins for the men killed in Markland by many strange things and brought back to Greenland by ship.'

'What stories they will tell about us. Like the great sons of Eirik the Red we will be known by every family in the world of the Norse, from Greenland to the Far Isles of the Sheep. I will not be away long. Weave. Use the wool of the elfin sheep. Make your cloak for me. Spin wool for the child. Make clothes for the days we will spend on the ship. We will sail before the equinox. Wait for me, Anna.'

'So easy for a man. I want to believe you. I cannot do this alone. I am afraid Thorfinn. So afraid of what is to come.'

'Hush now, my love,' he whispered and held her close. 'Come to me.' He drew Anna down to lie with him against the warmth of his body. 'I will not leave you alone with this. I will be back . I will be back for the birth of the child. You must be brave and wait for me.'

They lay within each other on a carpet of white flowers and Anna felt her fears abate. Even the soft footfalls of Bjarni as he padded below did not separate them. Bjarni stopped, looked up towards the high meadow where Anna and Thorfinn lay, then continued past as sun ripped at the grasses underfoot.

The company planned to set off in two days. Bjarni sulked and refused to speak to anyone as soon as he realised Asmund would not change his mind and he must stay and protect the farm and the women

CHAPTER 22 — *Preparing for the journey*

and old men. The muttering of prayers from Olaf's shed became louder each day. Sokki snarled at everyone and continually asked Ged if he was sure the correct number of whale-horse skulls were in his nestbaggin.

A storm came. The wind bent flat the new grass and the cattle were wet and cold. Anna kept to her bed, fear of loss only increasing her nausea. Aud sang the carding songs of love, constantly calling to her lost sons and husband. Sometimes Berryface and Sokki joined in. Thorfinn brought wood for the fire and kept as near to Anna as possible. He carved a drinking horn with protective runes and set it by her bed.

Ged remained unaware of anything but his own need to ensure the walrus skulls were safe. Sokki indicated to Aud that he was ready to take the place of Anna at the warp. He retired to the weaving room with a jar of ale and refused to come out. 'Good for me hands,' he told everyone and rubbed wool fat into the strictures on the palm of his hands.

Asmund spent the days playing board games with the men from Brattahlid. He was still at pains to hide the chest even though Skadi told him the bones from Thorfinn's crew had been put on top of the treasure to disguise it. Eventually the storm abated, the farmers and a few women from the neighboring areas arrived and the day to depart was set. It was decided that some men and women would go on horseback while the men from Brattahlid would go by sea with Asmund and the chest. Ged, Thorfinn and Ged's nestbaggin of walrus skulls would also go in the knarr with the produce from Ebiwaz to be sold at market.

Scarface said he did not like the smell of Ged and his bones and would walk with Gunhar and Sigrid as Brigitta had decided to stay at home with the children. He did put a parcel of old ale making utensils in the knarr to sell for Brigitta, along with two fine horse harness and a loom handed down to Brigitta by her mother but no longer in use at Thorness.

On the day before they left Anna took Thorfinn to help gather sea urchins from the small rock pools on one side of the bay. She was pale, her skin as white as a transparent seashell.

'You must come back, man from Iceland. I need both you and Ged. I cannot do this alone.' She stumbled and fell against a block of ice washed up by the storm. Tears streamed down her face. 'I wish

I was at home with my sisters. It was safe there. Frigg protect me. I miss my mother and my little dog.'

'Think of Markland. You are a Viking, woman. The sea and adventure is in your blood. You are strong. What an adventure it will be. In Markland there is water on the grass each day and the sun shines in winter.' Thorfinn picked her up and carried her back to the longhouse. 'Care for her,' he said to Berryface as he laid her gently on the bed. 'She is not well.'

Ged danced past with the nestbaggin of walrus skulls rattling and his long hair flowing like seaweed behind him.

'Ged,' said Thorfinn, 'Your wife needs care. Look to her. She misses her mother. Look how thin she is.'

'So be it,' said Ged.

Anna felt as if she was stretched above a crevasse. 'How can I survive if you both leave? There is no one to care for me.'

Skadi watched with hooded eyes and considered the possibility that Anna could be pregnant. No matter how many children anybody made, she, Skadi, head wife of Asmund Lawbinder, would always hold the keys of the household.

That night Bjarni did not return. He told Sokki he had seen the strange bird in the valley behind Ebiwaz and was spending the night hunting with Egil Gunharsson. No shadow came to haunt the house, however, but the soft northern light entranced the household into a watchful silence.

The next day the knarr left at high tide with the heavy chest stacked under the seats. The men from Brattahlid had sharp eyes. They had remarked on the manufacture of the box, whale bone and wood with inlaid ivory and silver. Sokki told them it contained the bones of Thorfinn's companions and they should keep well away from it, as the whole thing set up a rattle when anyone looked closely at it.

'Ghost bones,' Sokki had said. 'Want to get back to sea again.'

Asmund did not correct him but agreed it was Thorfinn's companions making their wishes heard. 'Best ignore it,' he told the men from Brattahlid. 'Keep away from it and do not look at it unless

CHAPTER 22 — *Preparing for the journey*

you have to.'

Olaf blessed the people as they set out to walk to Gardar. O'Flarty, Sokki and the women watched from the home field. A violet sky picked out the small figures of the men and women in their dark colors as the line crossed the green pasture of Ebiwaz and moved into a cleft between the hills. The high voice of Aud could be heard throughout the settlement in a song of farewell.

CHAPTER 23
Bjarni's adventure

Bjarni refused to farewell the travelers. It left a black hole in his heart to think he had been ordered by his own father to stay at the farm to protect a few women and an old man. He had killed the Nidhogg. He had been included in the council of adult men. It was an insult of the worst kind to be forced to stay behind. His sight was better every day with the herbs Brigitta gave him. At times he could see the caves in the cliffs on high mountains behind Ebiwaz.

He sat on a hill behind the longhouse with his bow and arrows and pretended to take aim at the men as they set off to Gardar. At last he returned to the house and retired to his bed cupboard. He refused to get up, no matter how much Skadi yelled. He lay on his back and kicked at the treasures lining the walls around his bed: the tail of a white fox, a length of hair from his mother, a mask of scrap metal he had forged, part of the beak of an enormous bird that had washed up on the shore, and a strange new weapon he and Egil had made out of whalebone, seal-skin and cat-gut.

'I'll show yer,' he said to his absent father. 'I'll have the feathers of the dragon bird on my wall when yer return. I'll be remembered as the Great Hunter from Ebiwaz who, before he has a beard grown to his nose, has tracked and caught an animal what has terrified everyone else. They'll make stories about me to tell children at night to be safe. They will forget you, old father Asmund with yer silly crucifix and yer Never-Fail Axe.'

He wanted to get a message to Egil Gunharsson at Thorness to ask him to come hunting but all the good horses had gone to Gardar

CHAPTER 23 — *Bjarni's adventure*

with the men. He wanted to explore the wadmal covering the curves of Gudrun Leifdottoir but he was stuck at Ebiwaz far away from anyone. He imagined the awe on Gudrun's face when he showed her the head of the dragon bird. He wanted that look on Gudrun's face. He wanted a sword like Thorfinn's. His skin was hot with wanting. He lay on his back and imagined Bjarni the Great Hunter hiding outside a longhouse like this one. The Great Hunter would listen with his whole body. Wolves! It were wolves what had moved into the empty farmhouse because everyone had run away in fear.

The wolf with the rattiest coat, Olaf Wolf, was in the byre curled up over a stinking bone. Bjarni could hear him scratching at his fleas. Old Bristol Wolf was in the home field snorting as he tended to the pigs. Slobbery Wolf Puppy had stopped mewling and was asleep, its little paws stuffed in its toothless muzzle. Fat Wolf Bitch was prowling up and down in the corridor as if she had an arrow in her bum. She was dragging her paws through the straw looking for bits of food in the clutter hidden on the floor. Wolf Mother Twistbeaks. Even made Olaf look clean. Always checking to see if someone was trying to steal from her stores.

Sokki got the best of her anyways, seeing as only one side of her face worked properly. As for the others, Bjarni could see the red blotch on the face of the Slave Wolf as she bent over Sokki Wolf and braided his hair into neat lines. Slave Wolf spent all her time licking his wounds and he spent all his time pawing her tits with his clawed hands.

Bjarni watched Anna move towards her spinning and sit herself down with her skirt tucked in so you could see the curve of her hips. Anna and her secrets and her small hands wrapped in wadmal and her sweet voice. Bjarni knew what she and Thorfinn Markland-Farer got up to. Rutting like dogs in season. Ged was too stupid to see what was going on. And him the father was always too busy being important to notice what anyone else was doing. He couldn't even tell the difference between the droppings of an eagle and dragon turds. Bjarni wondered if he looked like Asmund, with his long brown beard and his arms covered with hair as tough as rat's tail.

He examined his own legs and arms. They did look a bit like those of Asmund's: strong and muscular and hairy. He waggled his toes and squashed a rat dropping into the wall. It was time to act. Bjarni the Great Hunter was about to happen.

To avoid suspicion he spent the day moving his hunting gear out to the smithy, piece by piece, so he could leave without explanation. He scrounged what food he could and hid it in his nestbaggin. The creature would be his. In the blue half-light of the summer night when the household drowsed, Bjarni attached his bow and quiver to his back, stuck his hunting knife in his belt and bid farewell to the Mjollnir hanging above the smithy. He covered his feet in shoes stuffed with hay and wound a lock of his mother's hair around the polar bear tooth at his neck for luck. His mother's ancestors protected him. Thor guided him.

Treading lightly so his feet left barely a trace in the soil he moved silently from the settlement. The track led deep into the mountains, climbing steadily though small trees and willow scrub. Bjarni rubbed at his eyes. His eyesight was never good. In the summer light the horizon was a shimmering line at the limit of his vision. He climbed higher and higher into the mountains searching every rock for the droppings of a large bird. It thrilled him to be alone with any challenge the mountain could put before him. The unknown earth stretched around him, white and frozen. He skirted narrow ledges, traversed sharp downward slopes to find the next valley, the next ridge.

It became colder, the light bright air penetrating his very bones. It was time to search for a place to rest. He ate to warm his body and keep his sight from blurring further. Sleep was necessary, too. He chose a small ledge with overhanging rock to give him protection.

Just as he was to climb he caught sight of a shadow moving on the side of the valley. He ran towards it, as swiftly and as quietly as he could, praying to Thor to guide him. The ground was harsh and sharp though his skin boots. Objects around him were beginning to change, to lose their familiar shape in the light that surrounded without shadow. He saw the opening of a high cave. It receded into darkness. The snow looked scuffed around the entrance. He could smell animal.

CHAPTER 23 — *Bjarni's adventure*

He took out his bow and fixed an arrow to it and moved silently to the dark opening.

A round brown face detached itself from the rock below the cave entrance. The face was attached to an arm and a spear poised to strike. Bjarni and the skraeling confronted each other, snarling.

'Norse,' the skraeling said in a high nasal tone. 'You, Norse. Go. I kill'.

'I kill. Norse hunt. Norse hunt dragon-bird.'

Another brown face appeared in the cave entrance. This face was softer, smoother, smiling. She put her hand on the arm of the male and spoke with words Bjarni could not understand. The man lowered his spear and indicated Bjarni should come up into the cave.

'Cold comes,' he said pointing to the pale western sky. The woman smiled and beckoned. She was not young and held a strange tension around her. They both smelt odd, of animal fat and dog urine.

'Ergg,' said the man pointing to himself. 'Woman, Spiri . Friend to Norse.'

'Bjarni. Friend to skraeling.'

Bjarni could just understand. The man moved his lips as if holding a stone within his mouth. He was dressed like most skraeling in a belted tunic of seal-skin with a tail of skin pointing to the ground and a large hood hanging down his back. The woman also wore trousers of leather with the fur against the skin for warmth.

'Friend,' said Bjarni and walked into the cave. Several stones had been moved to make a circle. There was a lamp inside the circle; the moss wick burnt with a flame that picked out lines of crystal in the cave walls. The two skraeling seated themselves on either side of the circle and indicated Bjarni should sit between them. The ground was soft, ancient. The woman took meat out of a pack beside her and offered it to Bjarni.

'Gift from spirit of sea,' Ergg said. 'Spiri say you young. Why you hunt alone so far from family?'

'I hunt animal with wings and long claws. Bjarni illustrated the dimensions of the animal. 'Make me Great Hunter. Always be remembered as Great Hunter.' He pointed at the tooth of the white bear around his neck. 'Make family proud.' He removed his food from the nestbaggin and held it out to share. Ergg and Spiri were as dark forms against the sparkling walls. The light from the lamp inside the circle of stones elongated the features of the skraeling. The woman fingered an amulet of bone and continued to inspect Bjarni from top to toe in a way that seemed to rake through his flesh. He wished Egil was with him.

The woman arranged more stones within the circle. The odd energy she held seemed to come from a power within the stones. The shadows around her kept shifting and changing. She dug into her boots and produced a tiny packet made of seal skin. From this she took a soft black substance. She began to hum a tuneless dirge.

'Call to mountain. Call to animals,' Ergg said. 'Call to Norse.' He patted his genitals.

Bjarni decided his ears were as unreliable as his eyes. He imagined what Egil would do in a similar situation. The woman laughed at his discomfort. She passed him a ball of the black stuff.

'She says now you have eyes and ears of great hunter.' Ergg took a piece of the black stuff and began to chew it.

Bjarni put the strange stuff in his mouth and drifted off into a conversation with the absent Egil. The black stuff was bitter and made him retch. His heart was beginning to pound. He felt as if his face was swelling, his lips enormous. It was becoming difficult to breathe. Ergg pressed him to continue. He sucked and retched. Ergg passed him water. The nausea lifted. The light in the centre of the stones drew him into its brilliance. He was filled with joy. The flames became a series of animals, running faster and faster. They were pursued by a strange creature with wings. He felt the shadows in the cave close behind the watchers at the circle in a protective net. Someone was playing a rattle that sent shivers down his spine. It was a rhythmic beat that did not come from any instrument he knew. He looked at the woman. She was beautiful. Desirable. She smelt enticing.

The woman sat beside him and fingered the bear's tooth at his neck. She spoke soft words and her voice was like the wind in the mountain. She slid her hand inside his cloak and moved her fingers

CHAPTER 23 — *Bjarni's adventure*

between his legs. Bjarni saw a rainbow of colors fly from his sex. She pushed him back against the floor and maneuvered herself on top of him. He thought he could hear the sound of breathing, a great sigh coming from somewhere in the cave. He felt the pleasure of a hand stroking him, felt his tail lift in the air with exquisite pleasure. He had paws and fur. He could smell the sweetness of blood. His mind exploded into flames. Ergg was beside them, smiling.

The rattle began again. Bjarni felt his body dissolve. He was the black bird. He was hunting something, a thing with no claws that carried only a long shining stick. Now he was running. He was strong. He could smell and hear every tiny thing in the snow around him. His eyes were clear and strong. He circled the man and watched. He was hungry. He growled softly but the man did not turn. Just as he leapt for the kill the man spun on his feet. It was him, Bjarni. They rolled over and over biting and scratching at each other until blackness exploded around them.

When the sun was high above the horizon Bjarni awoke. Beside him, on a rock was a necklace of dog's teeth and the dried paw of a black wolf. Ergg and Spiri were sitting in silence at the entrance of the cave. They had moved the stones from the circle into a cairn. Ergg was carving a piece of driftwood into the shape of a man. He held it up and Bjarni could see it was the shape of a Norse wearing clothes just like the ones his father wore. The woman was polishing a harpoon. When Bjarni approached she smiled and handed him the harpoon. It had a walrus tooth imbedded in the shaft.

'Great Hunter now,' said Ergg. 'Ergg and Spiri take home Norse. Not good Norse hunt alone. Storm come with hungry ghost.'

Bjarni was overcome by the brilliance of the world. Objects as he looked at them vibrated in their own skein of being. The landscape had a presence that enveloped him and everything around him. He felt connected to every plant and rock and animal. Nothing existed without the other. He felt as if he had knowledge of the ancient creatures that lived in rock and water, in the flowers in the far meadow, in the animals that roamed the high mountains or lived in deep crevasse.

'Now you know. You understand . Wolf, bird, man. All same.' Ergg handed him an arrow with a polished slate point, and together they climbed towards the pinnacle of a rock. Bjarni thought he could see the shadow of a bird in the distance.

Bjarni handed one of his metal-tipped arrows to Ergg. The woman came to stand beside them. She smiled at Bjarni. Bjarni smiled back, unsure if this was a ghost woman or the woman he had met last night. She gave no indication. Bjarni noticed a pattern of little blue spots tattooed on her face. He had not seen that in the lamp light of the cave. Her hair was long and black and combed into a pattern at the back of her neck. She lifted up her head and made a shrill cry of a falcon.

'No hunt now. Hunt last night. Enough. Spirit inside always help with hunt now. Keep from danger. We take Norse to family. No safe for Norse here alone.'

Ergg indicated the way they would go and that there was no choice. Reluctantly, but with elation in his heart, Bjarni let them lead him down the mountain into the fields of the mist below.

CHAPTER 24
Gardar

The voyage was a thing of delight for Thorfinn so long away from the sea and the rush of water against the hull of a ship. He felt at peace. The smell of Anna was still in his beard with the feel of her body against his. He kept his eyes away from the place the chest was hidden so the ghosts within would get the opportunity to talk amongst themselves, and be too busy to address him. The coastline was blue and green with the sun brilliant on the white mountains behind. He let himself drift into dreams of the New Country. He saw the sunlight on the forest canopy and the great trees, taller than a man could see. The treasure of Markland was wood. Thorfinn saw himself on a ship set for the New Country. He would have the silver to buy a ship. Yes. He would reap the harvest of that wondrous land with Anna beside him and there would be no more family curses on his head.

At midday the knarr slid onto the pebbles of the bay at Gardar. Sheep munched on the remnants of seaweed by the beach. There was the sound of industry, of banging and shouting. Ged leapt overboard first with his nestbaggin full of bones. He stood on the beach and looked around as the rest of the men disembarked. A man in a bright red cape came to the ship. The amount of silver on his body indicated an individual of great importance. His nails were long and manicured; his fingers lit by great jeweled rings. Two dogs appeared beside him and poked their snouts into the sack Ged carried.

'Greetings,' Rhvford Ekvallsson said to the men from Brattahlid. 'You have done well to bring so many. The priest will be pleased. His

Worship the Bishop is still in Iceland. Farther Torfi has come instead to make Greenland ready for the bishop. I am the man invested with authority by the priest to build this church,' he told the others. 'You will take instructions from me in the name of the Holy Father.' He had a tension about him and spoke with a pronounced hiss to his words. He carried a long stick of carved driftwood in his right hand and used this stick to point or prod when necessary. He poked at the dogs who circled Ged and kept just out of the range of Rhvford's stick.

The church building was visible from the sea. It was set out like a stone crucifix on a grass-covered plain. There were long planks of wood lying on the ground around it and a piece of stone was being levered into place over the doorway. To one side of the church there was an oval-shaped yard, outlined with pointed stones to mimic the shape of a ship. A man in a long black robe stood there and seemed to be making signs over a fresh pile of dirt. He stood alone. Further up on the plain men were coming and going from a large rectangular hall. Near to this was a comfortable house surrounded by a field of angelica and summer grasses flowering in the sun. People were setting up market booths in a large flat area near a corridor of granite rocks behind the house.

'Put your stuff in that hall there.' Rhvford Ekvallsson pointed to the rectangular hall. His voice came through broken teeth. Sweat dripped from his skin under his jewels and cape. 'You men will sleep in there.' He pointed again and prodded. 'Food is served at the house when the bell rings. Bring your bowl and spoon and cup. Prayers are said before the meal and mass is every second day. The women can go into the barn over there or stay with their men in the market booths. The priest forbids the continuation of family feuds while on consecrated ground. Go now.'

A little stunned after their journey, the company from Hvalsey moved towards the festal hall. The men from Brattahlid were greeted by the chieftain of the farm who invited them into the longhouse. Asmund followed. Rhvford Ekvallsson barred his way. 'Not for you, lawbinder. The bishop says only for holy men and the family from Brattahlid. Not even for me.' He lashed out at a plank of wood with his stave.

CHAPTER 24 — *Gardar*

Thorfinn came last with Ged. He carried the chest. The dogs followed Ged.

'For Thor's sake, let us get rid of these damn bones.' Thorfinn stopped by the edge of the oval of stones. He opened the chest, took out the nestbaggin of bones and hid it in the shadow of one of the rocks that formed the oval grave yard. He lifted the chest onto his shoulders.

'What are those?' Rhvford Ekvallsson said as he passed, pointing with his long stick at the goat-skin bag in the shadows.

'Bones. Bones of shipwrecked sailors. We bring the bones of shipwrecked sailors to be buried in consecrated ground.'

Ged opened his mouth but was silenced by a thump from Asmund: 'Yes and for the priest to say a mass over.'

'Yes,' said Thorfinn. 'My boat, my companions and my salvage.'

'Yer companions? Yer boat? Well then, you must pay for the salvation of their souls,' Asmund said dragging Ged forward.

'Likes as not they will descend on Gardar as a hoard of hungry ghosts and rip out the heart of any Christian wot interferes with them,' said Scarface walking behind Asmund with Sigrid the Tall.

Rhvford turned his back on them. Sigrid stood like a moth before a flame as Rhvford Ekvallsson waved his bejeweled hands around in the sunlight.

'Payment must be made to the priest for the burial of any bones in consecrated ground.' Rhvford addressed the air in front of him. 'As to who pays for the mass, this will be decided at the Assembly. Once someone pays the priest will bless the bones and you can bury them in holy ground and the mass will be said.'

'Listen,' said Scarface. 'If you get too near where them bones are they start to talk. Someone should listen ter what they want for themselves.'

'And we bring the bones of . . .'

'Shut up, Ged.' Asmund thumped Ged as Rhvford danced in front with his arms in the air. 'I put up with your ranting because you bring fame to the farm with your carving but, by the name of the White Christ, I will not let you bring shame on our family.'

Gunhar approached and stood by Sigrid, his wife. Everyone listened with interest.

'I will never bring shame to Ebiwaz,' Ged fixed his pale-rimmed eyes on Asmund. 'Am I not the greatest carver in Greenland? Brother, do you forget the wealth I bring to our family? Am I not Ged Romfortsson, known though all Greenland? I see into what you do not understand.' Ged drew his thin shoulders down and walked with dignity into the hall.

Thorfinn made a comfortable sleeping place for Ged near the door where it would be easy to get out if necessary. He put the chest on the ground lay a skin over it. Ged settled on a blanket with the dogs panting beside him. There were about twenty men in the hall, new arrivals from distant parts of Greenland and some from Iceland and further south as well. Several men were involved in an argument over what belonged to the bishop when he arrived and what belonged to the chieftain of Gardar who had given this land for the building of the church.

'The chieftain who made this possible must gain benefit as well as the church what is always grabbing goods from honest men,' said Bololf-the-learned.

'Yeah,' yelled Ketil Half-Ear. 'Gardar is the best farm in Greenland. Look at how fat the sheep are. Look at the length of the grass and the lakes up yonder. What's the bishop want with all this land? It belongs to us farmers what have made Greenland our home.'

A young outlander spoke: 'Bishop will bring fame for Greenland. Make us equal with Iceland and Norway. Bring trade from the Orkneys and the Far Islands of the Sheep.'

'Is us who will be telling the Bishop what to do,' Scarface shouted, his skin uncharacteristically flushed and his one eye sparkling with passion underneath his hat.

'Church gets no more land than this what it is built on,' said Gunhar.

'Cease this talk.' The priest stood in the doorway, his black dress stained and torn. 'It is the king and the Church who will decide what you are to give the Bishop.'

'King?' Scarface spat on the ground. 'The men of Greenland at the Assembly, yer means. If I is right midsummer is in a few days when the

CHAPTER 24 — *Gardar*

Great Assembly happens and we all git to say what happens. New to Greenland is yer Priest, not to know this?'

The priest also spat on the ground. He was accompanied by the chieftain and the men from Brattahlid. The men in the middle of the argument ignored the priest and continued their battle. Ketil Half-Ear swung a punch at a younger man with many silver armbands and a fish tattoo on his shoulder. Fish Tattoo retaliated with a kick to Ketil's groin. Men yelled encouragement. Ketil grabbed the younger man's arm and bent it back hard. Someone emptied a pot of brown stuff over Scarface. The pot emptier was landed a punch on the head that knocked him out cold. There was the scrape of metal against a sword hilt.

'Stop,' bellowed the priest. 'I will not have my labor force destroyed before the church is built.' He moved swiftly into the centre of the fighting and it became obvious that it was he who had unsheathed the sword and was using it to stab at the company of battling Norse.

Thorfinn dragged Ged outside while the fighting continued. Gunhar joined the battle. Scarface was trying to invoke a berserk. Asmund appeared with a scowl and knotted brows and head-butted himself into the action. Eventually the priest detached himself from the brawl and dragged a half-conscious man out the door. The man was bleeding from a fish shape on his shoulder and his eyes were shut. The priest dragged Fish Tattoo to the house and disappeared inside. A little later another group of men came out of the hall with something they dumped within the precinct of the oval of stones by the church. The bell rang for the evening meal. No one paid much attention, being, as they were, engaged in a whispered rerun of the fight while glancing in the direction of the house.

Asmund grabbed Ged and dragged him into the house. 'Eat,' he said shoving Ged into the shadows. 'The priest wants you to do work here and all you ever do is babble about them stupid skulls in a sack.'

'I'll do no work until them skulls is in the soil of that church. I told you that, Asmund. The Walrus Queen has been promised.' Ged stared at his brother. 'Speak you like the Midgard serpent? Do not cast Ebiwaz and your family into Hel. I come to Gardar for the benefit of all Greenland.'

Asmund grunted and turned away. He was never sure if Ged spoke nonsense or wisdom.

In the main room of the house two girls and several women ladled stew from a soapstone pot that bubbled with the heat of hot stones within. The room was crowded with men and women. Young women offered yellow cheese and a small serving of fermented whey to all. There was a stream running though the centre of the room where a woman knelt to wash milk pots in the cold water. The room was decorated in tapestry. There were many fine pieces of silver on view. Sigrid stood transfixed in front of a bright sword hung on the wall near the fire.

'Ah,' said the priest, Father Torfi, as he sought out the men from Ebiwaz, 'which one of you is the carver?'

Asmund pointed at Ged, who was on the floor beside one of the dogs. Both were looking with interest into Ged's food bowl.

'Ged the Carver from Hvalsey, I wish to address you. I speak for the Holy Father and Rome.' The priest addressed Ged as he sat with the dog. 'I wish you to carve a design on the mantel of the church. So the congregation can see it every time they enter and know that the pagan devils in this land are conquered by the one true faith.'

Ged stood up and dislodged the dog from its reverie. It nosed at the priest with polite intent.

'Do not let that devil dog near me, young man!' The priest kicked out at the dog. The dog retreated behind Ged with a warning growl. The priest had yellow teeth and more than the beginnings of a beard. He did not carry a weapon now but his sword arm was left free from his tunic and his hands were calloused and very large. He had the habit of shaking them at the ground when he spoke.

'This creature is wise and beloved of the gods,' said Ged. 'Only a man without honor cannot see this.'

'Animals,' said the priest, shaking his fist in the direction of the food bowl, 'animals carry spirits of the damned. Soulless. I cannot abide the bones nor the spirits of the damned near my church.'

'Bones.' Ged spoke almost to himself. 'We come to bury bones in your priest yard.'

CHAPTER 24 — *Gardar*

'Young Erland here need a wife.' Scarface elbowed his way into the group of men dragging Erland Yellowbritches behind him. 'Any of you got any sisters? Wives? Daughters?'

Asmund stepped between Ged and the priest. 'My brother speaks of the bones of the shipwrecked sailors we carry with us, Your Holiness. We come all this way to pay for the burial once the Law has been spoken.'

Ged started walking round and round the dog, humming a tuneless dirge as he walked.

'Well, it ain't your silver yet,' said Thorfinn , 'so it ain't yours to give away.'

'As soon as you have paid the bishop, you can bury anyone in the churchyard and a mass will be said.' The priest had little interest in the dead. He turned away. He needed a live workforce not a host of spirit-ghosts to hinder his workers.

Asmund punched Ged. 'I gave you me word brother. We say no more till the Law has been spoken.'

'Indeed,' said the priest. 'God's law will prevail.'

CHAPTER 25
A new love interest

The next morning Ged and Thorfinn were set to chipping stone blocks out of granite at the back of the plain. The sky was a dome of blue and within it a thin moon fell sideways over the mountains. It was hot on the flat ground. Flies stuck to the skin. Small biting insects picked at arms and legs that were already red and itchy from mosquito bites. The sea could not be heard over the scrape of metal against rock. As the day progressed the men became more and more uncomfortable. Rhvford Ekvallsson allowed little respite, pushing the men to exert themselves more and more.

Thorfinn thought of Anna to distract himself. He hoped his child never had to endure such pointless labor. He would return to the New Country with his son, even if it meant the Nordsetur. 'I must get that silver,' he told Ged. 'Even if it means that I go to that place full of spirits.'

'I will protect you from the Walrus Queen,' said Ged. 'Do not fear Thorfinn. I will save you.'

'Look.' Thorfinn pointed down to the harbor where to a big Icelandic knarr had come to rest in the deep water. It had a blue cross emblazoned on its sail and above that, the hammer of Thor painted in red. 'From my homeland.'

'Good ship that one,' said Boltof-The-Learned, who was standing at the cliff face next to Ged. 'Church in Iceland owns it. Heard it was set for the Nordsetur after the Althing.'

'Thorfinn is going to the Nordsetur,' Ged said. 'The Whale-horse Queen told me. But you are not,' he told someone over his left shoulder and doubled up with laughter at a reply only he could hear.

CHAPTER 25 — *A new love interest*

The law rock was a small cliff where the lawspeaker stood to tell the Law as agreed upon by free men in Greenland and in Iceland before that. All day people had been coming to the area nearby, erecting booths and tables on which to serve food and goods to trade. Sigrid and the women from Hvalsey were working in the heat to set up a booth. The booth was made of hunks of turf with a wooden frame to support the walls. Thick brown wadmal was strung around the frames and across the roof. Colored bits of ribbon and fabric floated in the wind to entice customers. A trestle table inside the booth was laden with skins and wadmal and various implements that had proved their worth in another's hands and were now ready to be owned by a new person. Sigrid had placed a large metal half moon over the entrance to signify the wealth of Hvalsey.

In separate booths carpenters, iron merchants, weavers, leather workers and pot makers worked at their trade. Women selling love charms and healing potions moved through the crowd calling out their wares. Everyone was dressed in their brightest clothes with silver, gold and glass beads decorating their hair. Many had elaborate tattoos on their arms and face. The man selling louse combs made out of reindeer antler was already doing brisk trade.

The women made a circle with green branches of birch near the stream that flowed by the law rock. They sang as they worked: songs to find a lover, or a son lost at sea, or a daughter taken in slavery. The women swayed to the rhythms of the songs and occasionally joined hands around a cairn of stones in the centre of the branches and let out a loud whoop. An old woman drew the rune of Jera on the largest stone to mark the third year of the lawspeaker from Brattahlid. The women then erected two circles of wooden benches for the two courts of the assembly, one on each side of the law rock.

They tied a sail between two poles that stretched between the two circles. The sail was set above a pile of driftwood, which, if lit, would singe the bum of any man who stood on the Rock of the lawspeaker. The old women found this a great joke and spend the afternoon poking each other and chuckling with a secret delight. Far away from the rock and the markets a group of men stood around a clump of birch and willow. A red flag flew above the trees.

More ships came into the bay overnight. There was a general feeling of excitement as people arrived. Yellowbritches stood apart, tuning his odd instruments and reciting to himself the stories he would tell during the festival. Two young women made a point of setting up a food stall close by and giggled loudly whenever he made a noise. People laughed and greeted old friends, or scowled at enemies and hoped for justice before the assembly.

Still the Rhvford insisted the men work at the rock face. At last Thorfinn dragged Ged into the shade of the booths and down to the bay to see if any ships had come from the place in Iceland where his family lived. There was an unusual ship standing in deep water. It was almost the shape of a berry with a hull projecting at both ends. The sail was painted with runes picked out with a black thread. The little ship lay in the water beside the big Icelandic transport ship and rocked to and fro in the tide like a tiny water insect.

Asmund and Rhvford Ekvallsson found them staring at the odd boat. 'Asmund and I have been talking,' Rhvford said in a conspiratorial tone. 'I know you have silver with you. You give me some, the priest a little and bury your companions on the road that leads to heaven.'

'Can we bury them bones afore the priest gets his silver?' Asmund said, swiping at a host of tiny flies around his face. 'We just want to get rid of the burden of them spirits what may be in the bones. We have carried them a long way now. They is hungry to get to heaven.'

'They talk among themselves when no one is watching,' said Ged. 'They are hungry to be in the ground.'

'True,' said Thorfinn. 'This I have heard.'

Rhvford inspected his jeweled fingers. He had come that morning across the bay from his own farm where he lived alone, his wife and daughters dead with the coughing sickness last winter. 'I will ask His Holiness. It may be possible if you show me where the silver is. But perhaps it is not possible since you have not yet given the silver or even told him about it.'

CHAPTER 25 — *A new love interest*

'And you will not, if you want your share,' said Asmund, who was beginning to wonder what came first when you were a priest of the White Christ: money or heaven?

'That man,' said Asmund when Rhvford had minced off in his heavy robes, 'can smell silver like a rat smells water. He scowled at Ged and Thorfinn. 'But never will anyone say that we is burying animal bones in this churchyard. You heard what the priest said about animals what are not holy in the mind of the Christian god.'

'Dwarfs like animals,' Ged said. 'Giants too, but them is almost animals too you could say.'

'You could say, brother, you could.' A herd of hens approached, followed by an irate band of women wielding implements of hen destruction. 'Them bones go into the ground after the Althing, when the matter of the salvage is decided.'

'Maybe they will shut up then,' said Ged. 'those bones Thorfinn hid in the graveyard. Always making a noise when someone looks at them. Soon as I looks they stops.'

Thorfinn watched Rhvford as went out of his way to plant himself in the midst of a group of young women gathered at the door of the main house. Rhvford had made it known he wanted a new wife. He fluttered around one of the chief's pretty young daughters before the priest arrived and instructed the young woman about a particular weaving he wanted for the church.

The evening came with a summer mist. The priest said mass before the meal. Men and woman packed into the longhouse and huddled into corners and behind pillars as the words of the priest became lost in the mutter of the ancestor ghosts outside. After the meal people played board games while the daughter of the chieftain sang. The priest insisted she sit on his lap for inspiration. Everyone joined the song in harmony, the deep male voices blending with the high pure tones of the women. Yellowbritches produced his instrument and sang about Loki and Thor. Gunhar Osvaldsson produced a pipe and set about chasing Yellowbritches though a set of simple rhythms while everyone shouted encouragement.

Rhvford looked with lust on the women present and told the Christ god that he would not spend the rest of his life alone. He pushed himself next to the young woman of his choice and picked up her hand. She smiled.

Some of the men left the house, took off their clothes and started a wrestling competition on the beach around a big fire of driftwood. Yellowbritches found himself tangled up with a sailor from Iceland. He was alarmed at the sensation in his body as he held a handful of his opponents black curls and pushed his face into his shoulder. He smelt delicious. He felt delicious, hard and tough. Better than any female. He pulled away from the youth and they stared at each other with an astonished awareness at the attraction each had for the sameness of the other.

Thorfinn accepted his and Ged's share of the pale ale offered. He watched the wrestling for a while then retired to his blankets in the corner of the festal hall. Ged and a dog slept nearby. One by one the men came into the hall, wrapped themselves in a blanket and slept. Others fell into companionable slumber on the beach.

Thorfinn could not sleep. The smell of the women in the house disturbed him. He remembered with clarity the nights he shared in the cow byre with Anna. The wife of this man who was now his companion. His leg ached from standing so long in the heat and his skin was covered in tiny itchy insect bites. He felt Anna come to him again in spirit and felt again the beat of her heart against his.

CHAPTER 26
The Mid-Summer Assembly

The procession began after the morning meal on the mid-summer solstice. All work now ceased for one half turn of the moon. The lawspeaker, chieftain of Brattahlid, came first with his male kin close around him. All were dressed in fine clothes and silver jewellery, with hair oiled and tied in shining plaits. On each side came a bondsman to carry a shield and flaming torch held high to cast light on the darkness of ignorance and tyranny. Next came the priest in full ceremonial robes with Rhvford Ekvallsson beside him with his torch alight.

Erland Yellowbritches, as the official storyteller, followed, blowing and banging at his instrument. Harald, the dark-haired sailor from the pea boat, walked beside him with his torch. Asmund and the chieftains from Gardar and the many fiords of the West and East Settlements came next, their bondsmen with torches alight, all dressed in as much finery as they possessed. Then followed the men who owned land in Greenland and could therefore vote in the Assembly.

Thorfinn and several men from Iceland and the Far Islands of the Sheep walked last with any man who did not have voting rights but had come to trade. A few odd creatures who did not seem to have a place anywhere limped beside the procession. One man in a tattered grey wadmal tunic scurried forward scratching with fury at different parts of his body. Every few paces he grappled at the man next to him and insisted the man inspect what he held in his hand.

The women watched and sang as the procession circled the Law Rock nine times. A long low note from two horns sounded as the lawspeaker, Sokki Thorsson, walked into the centre of the birch branch circle and set his sword on the earth. Each chieftain placed his sword thus. The lawspeaker gave a signal to his bondsman who picked up an axe and belted it into the rock where the lawspeaker would stand.

The Assembly was open.

The lawspeaker recited one third of the law, as demanded by tradition. The priest stood directly underneath the Law Rock and glared at the company while shaking his fist at the ground to reinforce that the Law supported his presence in Greenland.

The lawspeaker began. 'It is by tradition that the Norse in Greenland, who are descended from the free people of Iceland, claim freedom from the tyranny of kings to determine justice under the law agreed upon by fair and equal process by the people of Greenland. By law we have two courts where men may ask for justice and equality to solve any grievance. The settlement of this grievance may involve retribution for harm occasioned to another man, the theft of property or person or the infringement of grazing rights or any other matter brought before the Assembly. Free men will decide the matter by the voice of the majority and who so wishes to vote will do so by the banging of metal against metal. Grievance will be settled and the Law will be enacted so that all parties maintain honor.'

He paused to take a drink. The mist had lifted and all were beginning to sweat in their heavy robes.

Scarface dug Gunhar Bluetooth in the ribs. 'See any of that Odd's kin here.'

'Only an old witch what said she was his sister. Over there, by the booth serving ale. No trouble from her. She ain't got no men with her. No male kin left. All dead I heard.' Scarface grinned and pulled his hat further over his head. 'She ain't far off the grave herself. Ged, go and ask her where her kin is.'

The lawspeaker continued in a flat sing song voice: 'The lawspeaker will be elected for a period of four years. It is the duty of the lawspeaker to learn the law as decided by our ancestors. The Assembly will also decide matters of trade between Greenland and other nations.'

CHAPTER 26 — The Mid-Summer Assembly

'By Loki, this is tedious.' Gunhar sniffed at the air. The smell of roasting horse meat and warm ale wafted from the stalls surrounding the Assembly. 'So yer reckon Odd had no male kin left after he got attacked by them giants do yer Asmund?'

Asmund decided he had not heard.

The lawspeaker continued, his voice mingling with the wild birds and the drone of insects. Under the hot blue sky, Yellowbritches, nephew of Eirik Eiriksson Scarface, stood beside the Rock and recited the sayings of the Wise One as was the tradition in all Norse lands.

'Praise no day until evening, no wife before her cremation, no word till tested, no maid before marriage, no ice till crossed, no ale till its drunk.

'Only a fool thinks all who smile with him are friends, He will find when he reaches the law-court how few real backers he had.

'Cattle die, kinsfolk die, we ourselves must die. One thing I know will never die – the dead man's reputation.

'Only a fool lies awake and broods over his problems. When morning comes he is worn out, and his troubles are the same as before.

'Better no prayers than excessive offerings: a gift always seeks recompense. Better no offering than excessive sacrifice.

'There is no better load a man can carry than commonsense. No worse load than too much drink. So declared Odin.'

The priest scowled. 'And so declared Christ who taught Odin,' he yelled.

The men greeted this with a roar. Others began to bang their armbands on their shields. Women moved from the stalls to mingle with the men and offer food and drink. The lawspeaker jumped off the rock and began to beat on a large metal bell that had so far been disguised under a covering of wadmal. A man came up to Thorfinn, jabbed him on the back and indicated that he should follow him. The man was continually scratching at little red spots on his face and arms.

The priest hoisted his cassock around his knees and climbed to the position occupied by the lawspeaker who continued to bang the bell. 'This man,' he bellowed, 'the great and honorable Sokki Thorsson, lawspeaker and chieftain of Brattahlid, has sent his son and his friend to the court of Norway to King Sigurd Jerusalem-Farer as a sign of his devotion to the Christian way. The king has agreed to send a bishop to Greenland. The King of Norway has decided this. The holy man is now on his way to Greenland. You men of Greenland are to give him land and tithes. He must have a church to pray in. Tithes are to be given in the form of ivory and skins and falcons.'

'And who'll get them tithes?' Ketil Half-Ear spat in fury. 'Chieftain and his kin there will take care of them tithes by Thor.'

'Church will not see none of them,' Boltof yelled. 'What we give will go to the chieftain and his kin what want the church built here in Gardar on land they claim belongs to them.'

Several men began to speak at once.

'Our kin in Iceland give tithes to the Church and gets protection from the king of Norway in exchange of being Christian.'

'And why did them in Iceland become Christian? Because King Olaf, who we in Greenland do not want, told everyone that the world was going to end.'

'And if them in Iceland did not become Christian the king said he would kill their kin in Norway who would all go to hell instead of heaven and be roasted alive forever.'

A general yelling and clashing of metal against metal met this remark.

'Let the courts begin.' Sokki Thorsson the Lawspeaker banged harder on the bell. 'Who is amongst us that does not want to put his word to the law? Who is it amongst us what do have a case to put to the Courts?'

'What's the word from the rest of the world?' shouted Boltof. 'Hey, priest, what goes with the King of Norway now? How go our brothers in Iceland?'

'Listen,' said the priest, 'and look to your lawspeaker and your courts. In Norway a trader was taken and blinded and his prick cut off by the King because he sold goods to the Danes and did not ask permission from the King first. Last year a giant wave rose out of the

CHAPTER 26 — *The Mid-Summer Assembly*

sea without warning and swallowed two ships from Norway because the fighting was so bad. In Iceland, where the lawspeaker made everyone a Christian, these things do not happen. People have given up the ways of the old gods there. Yes, no one eats horsemeat or leaves babes out to die. A church was built in the Faeroes, the Far Islands of the Sheep, to worship the Holy Father, the chief of the Christians.'

'He's making it up,' muttered Ketil Half-Ear. 'I heard he just got his nose cut orf and got a new silver one instead.'

'Shut up, yer pagan half breed, yer mother fucked pigs afore you was born. He's a priest afore the court of Heaven.'

Ketil Half-Ear was prevented from thumping Sevin Hug-Bear by several burly farmers who dragged both men to the booths for refreshment. As one the Assembly decided it was time to break their fast. While the men wandered to the stalls to drink and eat and reaffirm alliances, Thorfinn allowed himself to be pulled along by the strange scratching man. Yellowbritches and Harald followed to ensure that no bad things were planned for Thorfinn.

CHAPTER 27
An Irish princess

The scratching man pulled Thorfinn towards the back of the plain, where those not involved in the process of the courts were engaged in preparation for the games to celebrate the ending of the Assembly. Thorfinn noted the size of the rocks put out for weight-lifting and decided he could probably win without much effort. The horse-racing track was marked out by a line of flags. Harald grappled with Yellowbritches and told him he could race a horse faster than anyone any day. Both fell about laughing and poking each other as neither believed anyone could ride better or faster than Scarface, horseman and kin to the great Eirik the Red. Sigrid and a few young women passed with bags of silver bits to hide for the treasure hunt. They sang songs about secrets and lovers as they waved at Erland Yellowbritches in his bright clothes.

'What's going on?' Harald asked.

'That man there makes a clue out of runes and then the hunters have to work out where the pieces of silver are hidden,' Yellowbritches said, with his arm around Harald's shoulders. 'The runes are written on a stone. Each man is given a rock with the runes on it when he has spoken a verse. A group of judges decides which man makes the best verse and so should get the next clue first. Sometimes they fight for the rock with the best clue. Then we all get to make bets as to who will win.'

They passed several men in the process of a tethering a fast-running goat to be released for the archers. Short Irish was up on the hill with a large target for the axe throw. The scratching man dragged Thorfinn on

CHAPTER 27 — An Irish princess

and on. He was about thirty and five winters. He was as tall as Thorfinn and Yellowbritches. Brown lank hair fell away from an elongated forehead. His skin was sallow, his body rounded and soft. As they walked the man continued to scratch at his face and body with long black nails. He examined the contents of his fingernails repeatedly.

'Look. Look at this. A live one. See it. There? Alive. All over me body they are. Dog lice. Got them when that black Viking Solof shook his dog blanket over me head last summer. Look, here on me bum. I can feel them moving. Itch the life out of me they do. Crawl around under me skin at night. Nothing stops 'em, not seal oil or whale fat or juniper. I been to every healer this side of Norway, I have.'

He pulled down his pants and stood scratching at his bottom.

'Where're we going then?' asked Yellowbritches.

With some difficulty, the scratching man withdrew his attention from the contents of his fingernails. 'Ah, me lads, have I got a surprise for you lot. Over there, behind those trees. Where that smoke is coming from. See. There is a booth hidden, private like. You can just see the red flag between the trees.'

The scratching man, who was called Elgfrothi Helford, took hold of Thorfinn's tunic and pulled him towards a booth hidden within a crop of birch. A fire burned outside and an old man sat beside it roasting chunks of horse flesh with blueberries. A man came out of the tent grinning. He handed the old man a piece of silver cut from a bracelet.

'I'll take that, Pa,' said Elgfrothi Helford, suddenly distracted from his scratching. 'Well go on in young men. Enjoy yourselves. Pay later. Yer can all go in at once if yer like. Makes no difference to me.'

Inside the tent the light was dim and the space enclosed by a stillness that separated the knowledge of that place from world outside. Smoke rose from a pile of sweet herbs on a brazier and curled about the roof of the tent. A woman sat on a wide bench that was covered with wadmal and quilts of many colors. She wore a transparent shift. Her skin was white; her black air fell to the edge of her shift. A metal chain ran from her ankle to a pole behind the bench.

'Well show them, Celtic princess,' Elgfrothi said, scratching at his genitals. 'Look royal Vikings, here is a princess from the great town of Dublin. Here for your pleasure. She will take you all at once if that'd be your want. But it will cost, mind yers.'

The girl looked with pleading eyes at Elgfrothi who walked into the tent and glared at her with his teeth bared. She raised her shift. Her nipples were bleeding and there were purple bruises on the inside of her thighs. Yellowbritches and Harald glued themselves to the back of the tent with horror.

'Out,' snarled Thorfinn at Elgfrothi. He sat beside the young woman. Yes, here was woman, the softness, the vulnerability, the need to please, but so far away from the image in his mind of Anna and his wife that grief like a knife wound split his heart.

'Please, please,' the woman said in a thick Dublin accent. 'Do it. Now.' She opened her legs and rubbed at herself. 'He will beat me more if you are displeased.' Tears streamed down her face. She placed her transparent fingers under Thorfinn's nose and put her other hand between his legs.

'A drink for the young chiefs,' Elgfrothi pushed a bowl of ale though the flap of the tent.

'Fuck off,' said Thorfinn. He drank half the ale and handed the rest to the woman while gently pushing her hands away. 'No. Not like this. Not ever. Who is he, that disgusting bit of dwarf's piss?'

'Come with us,' said Harald. 'We will save you from your fate, princess.'

'What's going on in there? You lot finished yet? More is waiting here for a turn.'

The young woman refused to drink. 'He is my father. My mother was from Dublin. He beat her to death. Before she died she cursed him and sent the scratching plague on him. Who will be first? Hurry now. He will beat me if I do not please you.'

'More ale, royal sirs?' Elgfrothi asked though the tent flap.

'Come in and I'll split your head with a rock. So will you come with us Irish woman?' Thorfinn was beginning to feel dizzy, his mouth dry and his sight blurred.

CHAPTER 27 — *An Irish princess*

'It's the mother who has done it to us with her curses,' the Irish princess said. 'He can't do nothing without his pa tells him. Can't even remember who I am sometimes.

Thorfinn reached for the ale bowl. The woman put her hand over the opening. 'Careful,' she whispered. 'He puts poison into the ale. He gives nothing for free.'

The woman turned and knelt on all fours and lifted her shift above her head. The bones of her hips were sharp through the skin where there should have been softness; her sex hung raw and open. The chain around her leg pulled against Thorfinn's wound. He recoiled. He felt a rush of anger searing his face and shoulders. He grabbed the axe from Yellowbritches' belt and slammed it into the chain so the metal split. He pushed the woman away, picked up the thick bench and hurtled through the tent flap with the wood held above his head. He swung it hard down on Elgfrothi Helford and screamed with all the force of his frustration and loss. Harald punched the old man by the fire, who fell face first into the ash.

Yellowbritches kicked Elgfrothi hard as he fell to the ground. The men who had been standing by the fire ran off as fast as they could with the sound of Thorfinn's war cry behind them. The woman stood in the sunlight as if stunned.

'Your clothes, where are they?' Yellowbritches said.' Come now. You are free. We will not hurt you.'

Thorfinn felt a blackness approach and recede within his mind. He let out his war cry again and turned round to face Yellowbritches and Harald.

'It is finished now,' Harald said. 'That ale was bad. It is finished. There is no one else but us here. The woman is safe.'

Thorfinn lowered the heavy bench. The woman knelt by the old man and plucked at his burnt skin. Her father was unconscious on the ground in front of the booth. She moved to him and tried to rouse him. Harald held out his hand to her.

'Oh, great sirs, I cannot leave my pa, not when he is so helpless. Who will look after him if I am not here? Who will help the old man who is his father and now lies burnt in the fire? He does not mean to be so bad, my father. It is just that my mother has taken his mind and bought the insect plague upon him. Go now, royal sirs, and leave us to manage the way we always have.' She pulled a blanket across the body of her father. 'I have no one but him. No one wants me, torn and bruised as my body is. I am not one of your pretty maidens. I am only this, what you see, a poor and worthless woman in the sight of the gods.'

She retrieved the bowl from the booth and filled it with ale from a container hidden by the body of the old man. She sat cross-legged by the unconscious body of her tormentor and swilled at the alcohol. Her long black hair fell around her body. She pulled at bits of her hair and stuffed the broken strands into her mouth.

Yellowbritches and Harald looked at her with horror. Thorfinn held on to a tree and tried to keep his thoughts in focus. As if of one mind, Yellowbritchs and Harald took each an arm and led Thorfinn back across the plain away from the devastation in the circle of birch trees.

CHAPTER 28
Judgment on the treasure

The lawspeaker and the priest stood on the Law Rock between the two courts. A circle of men sat in each court on the benches provided. As prescribed by tradition their bondsmen sat in a circle behind. The elders and local chieftains crowded into one court to hear matters of national importance, such as trading rights, the possibility of a church funded expedition to the Nordsetur, and the problem of the tithes wanted by the new Bishop. All other free men who owned land positioned themselves around the second circle of benches. To them fell the task invoking justice in the matter of boundary disputes, marriage problems, inheritance arguments and recompense for murder or loss of stock.

If a matter could not be decided in one court, it went to the other. Asmund, as land owner and chieftain of the farms around Hvalsey, was required by law to assist in decisions regarding national matters. However, as he pointed out to the lawspeaker, there was the matter of the salvage to be decided.

Scarface and Gunhar stood beside Asmund within the circle of the second court. Ged had disappeared. Thorfinn could not be found. It was decided by the majority that any case could not be heard without Thorfinn if there was a dispute over property. Ketil Half-Ear demanded grazing rights from Rognvald Bog-Hunter. The court debated and agreed that Ketil should give his son to labor on the farm of Rognvald as payment during the summer.

Ottar Smooth-Tongue spoke with eloquence about a family feud and demanded recompense for the maiming of his bondsman by an arrow shot by Sevin Asleifarsson. The court decided with a roar of agreement that a cow must be given to him by the guilty party. Romfat Gubnthsson demanded his wife be given eggs all winter because the widow of Haakon Turf-Eater had put a curse on his ducks and the eggs would not come out. There was an argument about the legality of dealing with curses, and if such a curse constituted the practice of magic, and if this should be dealt with in a court of law.

At length Thorfinn returned. Ged appeared with the dogs at his heels. Yellowbritches and Harald positioned Thorfinn next to Ged. Thorfinn kept looking at his hands with a perplexed expression on his face and then back at the dogs as if they had something important to say. Rhvford appeared and took a seat next to Asmund.

Asmund told the story of how he and his kinsmen had found the box in the water next to Thorfinn's dead companions. The priest dragged open one eye at the mention of possible wealth. He had no interest in the internal squabbles of his workforce if they could be solved by the Assembly. This however involved more than magic and cows.

'Silver?' he addressed Rhvford. 'These barbarians from the north have a chest full of silver? Why was I not told?'

'If it weren't for us there would be no chest,' Asmund spoke over the rasp of the priest. 'We is the ones who sailed out and looked for it. We is the ones who dragged it up all the way and put it in our boat and sailed it home. Thorfinn weren't able to get it. Why he was not even in the boat with us.'

'Hid it from us,' said Rhvford fingering a new lump of silver in the folds of his cloak. 'Not worth much I believe.'

'Who says the chest was even belonging to the Icelander? Could be the sea brought it there from a long way aways,' said Ketil Half-Ear.

'Let Thorfinn speak. In truth was all in the chest yours?'

'I will decided what value goods have for the Bishop.' The priest shook his fist at the ground. 'I will decide.'

CHAPTER 28 — *Judgment on the treasure*

The lawspeaker squinted in the heat at the black cloaked priest but said nothing.

Thorfinn rose to his feet with his hand on the shoulder of Ged for support. 'Aye we found the chest in a ship floating without men on the Great Ocean. Taken by the Magyar they were. Not one of them left alive. My companions and me, we carried that chest onto our boat and sailed with it down the coast of Greenland till the monster from the sea rose up and took it from us. If it were not for my companions and me, the chest and the silver in it would be floating in the rivers that flow into the ends of the earth.'

A banging of metal against metal indicated agreement. Thorfinn sat down quickly. He felt dizzy; strange shapes were floating around the edges of his vision. The taste of bad ale lingered in his mouth. He felt unsteady, as if his wounded leg would collapse any time.

'And them bones of your companions?' asked Asmund. 'Who was it got them here to be given a proper burial? Me and me brother that is. And me kin at Ebiwaz what kept you alive all winter. Look at you Thorfinn Markland- Farer. You can't stand without someone helping you. You'd be as dead as your companions if it were not for the luck we brought back from Whale Island. Is that not the way it were Eirik Eiriksson Scarface?'

'Aye, that it were,' Eirik Eiriksson Scarface said from a place of deep thought.

Thorfinn swayed on his feet. Ged rattled his nestbaggin and grinned at the dogs behind him. Thorfinn felt as if a goat's bladder had been shoved up his nose and was leaking blood into his mouth. He could still smell the Irish woman and the burnt flesh of the old man.

Rhvford spoke. 'These men act in truth. The treasure comes from the Great Ocean. It came in a ship owned by the Icelander. Both the Icelander and the men from Hvalsey have claim to it. It is right that the bones of the men have Christian burial. It would be bad luck for this not to happen.'

'Quiet,' said the priest. 'So you north men want bones buried in the churchyard? A place holy to the Christian god? Because they are

Icelanders and therefore Christian? This is what I say to the court afore any judgment is made. The bishop needs payment to finish this church and bring the sacraments of the Christ God to change Greenland into a civilized place from what it is now. Look at you all. Barbarians who eat horse meat and talk to pagan gods. If you have silver I say that goes to the Bishop as tithes. Any left over can be payment for the burial of the lost seafarers what have been brought to me to bless.'

Rhvford hissed. 'Nothing of value in the box Father Torfi. I have seen it.'

'Half of the silver, yer mean priest,' said the lawspeaker. 'Yr holy church don't need all of it, no matter what yer says. I say what treasure came with it be split between the people of Ebiwaz and this man here,' he said, indicating Thorfinn.

'But it were Asmund who got the bones out of the mouth of the sea monster. Be naught to bury if it weren't for him,' put in Gunhar Bloodaxe.' Why should he pay for the burial of the bones of the companions of Thorfinn Markland-Farer?'

'All of us is paying,' Asmund said. 'The question is: do we give the Bishop the money afore we split it, or after? And make Thorfinn pay for the burial of the bones from his share as it were his ship and his crew.'

Scarface spoke. 'Now being a good chief of yer boat, yer would not want the spirits of yer crew not to find peace would yer Thorfinn Markland-Farer? Ged hears the lost men moan under the ice. The ones what never found a proper burial. Never found their ancestors. Yer would not want that for yer friends,

Was it true? Thorfinn could not understand the words. Could this priest bless the bones of his friends and guide them to peace in the spirit world?

'So the Assembly is to consider,' the lawspeaker said. 'I say to you men of the Assembly that the silver should be shared between the priest for the blessing and burial and all the men from Ebiwaz, including Thorfinn.'

'Lot of bones,' said the priest. 'Lot of blessings needed to make 'em safe in holy ground. Lot of masses.' He shook his fist at heaven this

CHAPTER 28 — Judgment on the treasure

time and bunched up his black skirts to look like a warrior for Christ.

Ketil Half-Ear yelled: 'Let Thorfinn give the priest the silver he would have shared with his crew. The rest can be shared wif him and the men of Ebiwaz who saved his life.'

'But I found it,' yelled Thorfinn, swaying on his feet.

'Ay, me lad,' said Scarface, 'but without Asmund there would be no treasure to debate. I agree with Ketil. The silver wot would have gone to your crew goes to the priest here, and the rest is shared between you and Asmund and the people who kept you alive at Ebiwaz. So the priest gets some silver for his precious church and everyone else gets some too.'

A general muttering greeted this remark. The men of Greenland were sore pressed by the tithes the priest and the king of Norway wanted. Thorfinn was the stranger, the Icelander. Thorfinn owed Hvalsey as he had been cared for and brought out of the Great Ocean by them at Ebiwaz. It was to do good that Asmund and his kin had brought the bones of Thorfinn's companions to Gardar to get a Christian burial and a blessing by the priest. Even if they were not followers of the White Christ, this Christ god could look after them on their way to Valhalla or the Hall of Freyja. Or even Heaven if they wanted to go there. It might make the priest less of a pest if he had some silver and treasure to count.

Ketil Half-Ear stood and addressed the lawspeaker. 'This Assembly says half the silver should be given to the priest for a holy burial. Thorfinn, as he was the chief of the boat that was eaten by the sea monster, must accept this. If it were not so the men from his ship would be found by bad spirits and never have no peace. The rest of the treasure must be shared between the people from Ebiwaz, including Thorfinn, excepting the servants and women.'

Thorfinn sat and stared at Asmund. Decisions at the Althing were only binding if you had enough muscle to make them so. If the priest took half the silver and Asmund shared the rest with everyone in Ebiwaz, everyone who was under his control anyway, there would be barely enough for him to get a working passage to Iceland. He could lift up this bench and all the men on it and smash it over the head of the priest.

Seven Hug-bear put his arm around the shoulders of Thorfinn. 'May Thor give you luck, son. Get a good burial for your friends and never will they haunt you for their share of that silver. Why my uncle never did bury the bones of his family when they was drowned by the Kracken and all his life their bones rattled at him whenever he shut his eyes. Like Ged there. Fair drove him out of his wits. Best that not happens to you my friend. In the end he went blind from no sleep and fell into a lake. He died the first moon of spring, he did.'

The priest shook his fist again at heaven in front of Asmund to show he approved of the decision. Rhvford hissed and slid out of the circle.

Asmund glared under heavy brows. The decision had benefited Ebiwaz but had been to the benefit of the priest more. The silver would buy honey and pitch from the Icelandic merchants. All at Ebiwaz would benefit. Thorfinn too if he cared to return to the steading and help with the preparations for winter.

Thorfinn looked at Asmund and Scarface and tried to get his thoughts to focus. They had taken most of his silver. He was bereft again. Alone. His kin had deserted him. He did not have their support to fight this decision. He saw Anna and the possibility of taking her and his child to Markland fading like melting snow. He had nothing. Years of his life empty after so much promise. His crew dead, his woman married to another man. And he now maimed and without the means to fight Asmund or the priest. He was without woman, without children to keep alive his name. Ged could claim his child as his own. He mumbled obscenities, damming the day he set foot in Ebiwaz, cursing the day he ever had trusted his fortune to anyone, the day he had first lain with Anna.

'What?' said Scarface, picking at the remnants of a molar with his knife.

Thorfinn staggered to his feet. Yellowbritches and Harald came to his side. He swatted them away and stumbled out of the assembly to vomit on the ground. He felt as if he was vomiting up the all the hope in his life. His vision blurred. He knelt on the ground and swore at the gods till Yellowbritches and Harald dragged him to his bed to sleep off the effects of the poisoned ale.

CHAPTER 29
The burial of the bones

It was not yet midnight when Asmund woke Thorfinn and Ged. He handed Thorfinn a skein of water. 'Yellowbritches told me what happened,' he said.' It is good what you have done.'

Thorfinn sat up and drained the skein. Asmund handed him a draught of calming herbs and a piece of fine barley bread. 'Come,' he said. 'We have work to do. Now we rid ourselves of the bones of the whale-horse people. I have decided what we must do.'

The sun had barely moved to the edge of the horizon. The settlement resounded to the snoring of a hundred drunken Vikings, everyone being so tired what with the intellectual effort of the courts and the amount of ale and food necessary to sustain the tradition of justice and equality. The lamps burnt low with the shadow of rodent whiskers elongated on the walls above them. A halo of red mist surrounded Asmund as he stood in the doorway. Scarface and Gunhar stood behind. Scarface had his hat pulled down low over his face.

'Listen to me Ged. I have decided,' said Asmund.

'We have decided,' said Scarface. Gunhar chortled

'Which bones?' said Ged clutching his nestbaggin to his chest.

Asmund carried the heavy goat skin sack holding the bones of Thorfinn's companions. 'All the bones Ged. Come now, and softly so we do not wake anyone. And remember I do this for you.'

A few men stirred at the sound of Asmund's voice. Most lay wrapped in their blankets. Asmund kicked Short Irish who grunted and rolled over. Ged got up and threw the nestbaggin of bones over his shoulder. Yellowbritches and Harald were waiting outside in a cart attached to a horse. They grinned at the world as men with a secret. The horse sniffed the air and whinnied. As she pulled the cart past the outskirts of the settlement two big dogs appeared out of the mist to investigate. They too sniffed the air and seemed to like what they smelt. As soon as they saw Ged they bounded up to the cart and followed with tails upright.

Scarface sniffed the air and rubbed at his one good eye. 'Someone's cooking horse flesh. Over there on the edge of the plain. Ain't you this time me lovely,' he said as he patted the horse. 'Fucking bishop will not like that.' He laughed to himself, 'being as it is them Christ men are against eating horse flesh.' A wolf howled in the mountains far above them as they came to the edge of the plain. The long grass caught the sigh of an approaching storm.

'Brother we do not bury the bones here. Where is the Christ grave yard?' Ged sat in the cart rattling as much as the bones in his nestbaggin.

'Thor's goats,' said Scarface, still drunk from the day before, 'by Thor and Odin too I'd like to tell that stuffed bladder of a priest the lawbinder of Hvalsey was out with a bag of animal bones to give them a Christian burial, seeing how he likes animals so much.'

'Shut up yer sodden excuse for a Viking. And keep yer eyes on them bones of Thorfinn's companions so they don't start banging at each other and tell the whole settlement we is here.' Asmund hit the ale sack so hard it split down the front of Scarface's tunic.

Above them the ice on the mountains melted into a luminescent sky. The horse plodded with care, snorting and snuffling. The dogs followed silently. There was no other sound, not the rustle of a leaf, not the hum of an insect nor the crack of ice in the bay; nothing.

Thorfinn thought it was as if some ancient earth spirit had come to settle nearby. One of the old creatures of the earth, older than the gods themselves. He watched the hair on his arms bristle and felt for his knife. The horse stopped at a circle of trees. Ged pointed up onto the mountain behind with a look of speechless horror.

'It comes to watch. It waits. Up there.'

CHAPTER 29 — The burial of the bones

'Off,' grunted Asmund and pushed Ged off the cart. 'Not with the ranting now brother. Over there. Soil is deep. Dig. Throw as much as you can onto the cart.'

'It follows me.' Ged began to shake and make wild grimaces with his face.

Thorfinn stood beside him and placed a hand on Ged's shoulder. He felt as if this witless fool was the only friend he had in the world.

Everyone else, with the exception of Scarface, who continued to roll around in merriment, got off the cart, grabbed a shovel and began to heave dirt into the back of the dray. The strange stillness continued. It was cold in the silence, dense, secret.

A mist rose up from the centre of the trees and hovered over the cart. The granite of the rocks behind added to the illusion that this was a huge creature with an enormous black eye focused on the occupant of the cart. A shadow passed overhead.

'Odin's raven, what's that?' Ged stood transfixed, his pale skin glowing like silver, his pale eyes glittering with passion. 'The beast Nidhogg. It follows us. Listen brother. It breathes. It grinds its teeth. It comes from another world than the one on which we stand.' The carving of Thor's hammer bounced up and down on his chest.

Harald threw a rock into the bolus of mist. It bounced off the rocks and flew back, hitting Scarface on the arm.

Scarface stood up and waved his arms 'Thems is what you can't hear coming,' he shouted. 'Thems is what yer can't see coming. Not one of yer made a sacrifice ter the gods ter get protection for this night did ye ? Fuck all this priest stuff. Feel that? The eyes of them what can't be seen. The ancient ones. Not even Ged has magic against them.'

He stopped as the beating of wings came though the mist. The dogs bristled, each looking the opposite way. The mist was so thick now the cart was barely visible and each man a white form moving in a land with no contours. There was a sense around them of a presence alien to the knowledge of any European.

'We dig in the grave of the mother of a giant. Her spirit bids us not ter disturb the land.'

'It is the shadow of the black beast who has followed us. Look at the dogs. They see what we don't.'

'An ancient god of the inland guards this mountain. Odin protect us. Allfather warns us not to ignore him. We will give sacrifice to yer, Great One.'

'Dig. Now. We don't come all this way for nothing. Dig yer black-hearted Norse. Tomorrow we give sacrifice.' Asmund took up his shovel and continued to heave dirt into the cart. 'To one god or another,' he muttered.

Everyone except Scarface pushed dirt as fast as possible onto the cart. Scarface continued to stare with his one eye at the rock face and mutter about Odin. There was the most uncomfortable sensation that someone or something was watching. The dogs continued to growl at things invisible to human eyes.

At last the cart was full. Everyone climbed in and sat on the soil. Scarface beat at the horse. As they rattled and banged back along the track the mist lifted and the rain came upon them with vengeance. Sleet flew before the storm. The cart crashed through the settlement to the wall beside the graveyard. Asmund handed Thorfinn the nestbaggin full of his companions.

'The Whale–Horse queen has told me what to do,' said Ged. He got off the cart and dragged his precious burden over the graveyard wall. He emptied it out and began arranging the walrus skulls in a linear formation down one side of the enclosure.

'What are you doing Ged?' muttered Asmund. 'Here we are and you are making patterns?'

'Witless,' said Scarface. 'Like you all from Ebiwaz. Mother walked over a grave when she was pregnant.'

'Leave him,' said Gunhar as Asmund went to push Ged out of the way. 'Bones is happy to be in any holy place. Just stuff Thorfinn's bones into the old graves. Dirt is dirt. Priest will not know the difference.'

'Stuff 'em into as many graves as possible' said Asmund as Ged became increasingly preoccupied with his task.

CHAPTER 29 — *The burial of the bones*

'Bones will be in a Christian graveyard. Bones is bones,' said Yellowbritches.

'Do it then before that priest wakes up and sees me out here with you lot.'

Thorfinn, Harald and Yellowbritches took the human bones and one by one shoved them into the dirt of old graves. Asmund came behind and covered the place so it looked as if some animal had been rooting there. When Ged was finished Scarface and Gunhar threw the dirt from the cart over Ged's bones so it could be seen that a new grave mound had been added to the graveyard.

Asmund disposed of the horse and cart. Everyone was covered in dirt and wet to the skin. Ged stood grinning from ear to ear. As they trudged out of the graveyard the priest came to the door and peered outside at the sodden men.

'So we have done it Earl Priest,' Asmund told the face of the priest separating the heavy door curtains. 'Just like you said we could. Buried the bones of Thorfinn's companions in holy ground.'

'We brought fresh dirt to cover the bones of the shipwrecked companions of Thorfinn Markland-Farer,'

'All that is needed is for you to do the blessing now,' said Ged rattling his teeth in the cold. 'Thorfinn has the silver. We have done the burial as the decision was made by the courts. Come with us to the place where the silver is.'

The face disappeared and reappeared attached to the body of the priest in a thick felted cloak. The priest followed Thorfinn and Ged through the rain to the hall. Thorfinn rummaged in the chest and dragged out a bag of silver bits and coins. He spread it on a skin. The priest counted it and stuffed it into his cowl.

'Silver yes,' he said. 'Tithes. And an offering for blessing and five masses. Indeed let us bless those who will rest in heaven for all eternity.' The priest walked to the churchyard. Asmund appeared with Short Irish. Ged and Thorfinn stood in the rain while the wind beat at everything. The priest came into the graveyard and stood beside the fresh mound of dirt. He waved his arms around, said words in Latin and sprinkled holy water on the ground. Ged smiled in beatific glee as he stood beside the fresh grave.

Everyone escaped to shelter as fast as they could. Thorfinn and Ged sat together.

'I am at peace now,' said Ged wrapping himself in his blanket. 'I shall carve the story of the Whale-horse Queen on the lintel of the church to show my love for Asmund and the way he has helped me.'

The storm continued. It was too wet for the games to begin; the sky was grey and hung close to the ground. Scarface and Asmund made a fire in the hall and sat glaring at each other. Thorfinn drowsed in his corner, pleased at least that he did not have to listen to the clunking bones of his companions. His leg ached with the damp. Here there was no Anna or Berryface to apply a hot poultice. No soft bed with the smell of woman in it. He hated Gardar. He had lost his ship and his crew were now lying in the grave of a god they had no interest in. He cursed Greenland and all who lived there. Yet he had found woman. His woman, Anna. The wife of this witless soul snoring beside him. She would give birth without him. He had no choice but to go to the Nordsetur if they were to have any life together at all. If he was to get the ivory and skins that he could trade for a ship to take them all to Markland.

A screeching brought everyone to stark awareness. The rain had stopped but the bellowing increased. People stumbled out from their places of rest. On the steps of the church a goat had been killed, its throat cut as in a sacrifice to the ancient gods of the Norse. Beside the goat, on the granite in blood, was a drawing of Thor's hammer, Mjollnir. The priest shook his crucifix above him and called out to his god to avenge this heresy. The chieftain stood beside him, sword unsheathed.

'Someone will burn for this,' said the priest pale with fury. 'Let him who is consorting with the devil come forth'.

There were grunts and snorts from the crowd. Most turned away, more interested in the possibility of games now the rain had cleared. Scarface stood at the back of the crowd and grinned. Thorfinn glared at Scarface.

The young woman who had sat on the priest's lap ran up to the priest: 'Father

CHAPTER 29 — *The burial of the bones*

Father, it is but a childish prank by an uneducated fool. Is not the God of the Christ strong enough to cope with this?' She took a rag and drew a line across the rune to make the hammer into a cross.

The priest turned bright red. 'There will be no more building, no more food or drink until this devil is gone from our midst.'

The women from the farm flooded out of the long house behind the lawspeaker. They stood in a circle around the priest and sighed and wrung their hands on his behalf.

The lawspeaker nodded his head and indicated this would be better handled indoors where there was less to anger the priest and fewer to watch. 'Come,' he said. 'This is not unexpected. Do not let it dissuade you from your purpose. We will continue building the church as usual after the games to end the Assembly. The gods can sort it out amongst themselves. Let us prepare now for the competitions. Let us find out who is the strongest of all these men so we can make him work harder than all the rest.'

The priest allowed himself to be led inside.

Scarface poked Thorfinn. 'That Icelandic ship over there me lad, the big one next to Harald and his dad's boat. See that. Captain's wanting men to go on the hunt to the north. Cleared it with the lawspeaker and the Assembly. Said they could leave when the storm finished. Been waiting they have. All legal in the eyes of the priest. Might be a place for two men who know the way of the Walrus Queen.' Scarface chuckled. 'Or in the words of the Wise One, if a shoe fits badly or a shaft snaps, make another one. Go in a different direction.'

The ship rode in the sea long and fat with a sleek keel visible through the water. The captain watched from the deck. He wore a black tunic and britches with a silver crucifix stuck on a belt around his belly.

'Up here men,' he called. 'Need to make a bit of loot this summer? Or be you fond of working at that stone wall up yonder? I need strong men to row me ship and strong men to come with me to the Nordsetur. Men who can handle a weapon and who know the way of the Great Ocean. Belongs to the bishop of Norway, this ship does,' he told

Thorfinn and Scarface. 'Be back just after summer's end with a load of ivory and skin for each of you. Space for two more. You can manage a spear and an ore and by the look you two ain't no stranger to either. Leaving as soon as I get me crew together. Only need two more men.'

Thorfinn came again to know the heavy thing in his heart that had troubled him at Ebiwaz. 'Anna,' he raged to himself. 'Woman I have no option now. I have lost everything but you. You and my son will come to Markland when I return.'

'I will come,' he yelled. 'To the Nordsetur. You say I keep a share of the ivory and skin we catch?'

'As much as you catch. We share all,' yelled the captain. 'You will return a rich man.'

Thorfinn felt Anna by his side. He felt her presence, her softness and warmth. Anna with breasts the color of new milk and hair as like the line of light on the horizon. 'Damn you woman,' he muttered. 'I go for you, I go for us all.'

He wrapped what was left of his share of the treasure in seal skin and wadmal and tied it to his belongings. He could not speak to Asmund. He grunted farewell to Ged and Yellowbritches and followed Scarface onto the ship.

Yellowbritches watched Thorfinn and Scarface climb onto the big Icelandic knarr. He had little protection now from the priest and his ranting, being as he was a man from the pagan north and a bard of Odin. He had never seen Iceland. Harald and his father needed another man to sail with them across the Great Ocean.

In the first light of the half moon after midsummer, the big Icelandic knarr and the tiny pea shaped boat sailed the still reach together from Gardar to meet their fate in the wilderness of the Great Ocean.

CHAPTER 30
The waiting

Anna spent the days waiting. She waited for Skadi to feed the baby so she could wrap the little thing in fur and attach it to herself. She waited for O'Flarty to make a pile of driftwood next to the hearth. She waited for the cod to freeze, for the milk to sour, the wool to dry, the spindle to turn. She waited for the warp to move backwards and forwards in the loom and she waited for the summer to end when Thorfinn and Ged would return.

Some days she could feel the child moving within. Berryface was pregnant too but Anna told no one she carried a child. Was it the day of the dark moon when Aud began her chant of birthing? Berryface sang with the old woman but Anna remained silent. No one yet knew she carried a child as the folds of her tunic disguised the hard swelling of her stomach.

As often as she could she returned to the memories of her time with Thorfinn; the way he held her, the shape of his arms, his hands, the feel of him as his seed burst within her. She made up stories as she sat weaving with Aud and Berryface at the loom and listened to the rush and pull of the sea on the pebbles in the bay. She saw herself with Thorfinn in a ship on a brilliant blue sea. She was heavy with child. As they sailed down a wooded coast as they searched for a place to build a home, a settlement. There were others with them. Men from Iceland. Bjarni too, perhaps.

Then there were the days when she set the milk to ferment and skinned the fish and she felt Ged around her like wood sap, as if his memory was sticking to her like a cloak of syrup. Constant and prolonged nausea plagued her. When it was bad she went to the place she had lain with Thorfinn. The byre smelt of him, a musty male smell amongst the juniper branches. Once a long red hair appeared from the straw. She wound it into the bracelet of hair her mother had given her when she left the Western Settlement so those she loved most would always be with her.

She found a hank of black bear fur in the back store room. The fur was matted and full of rat droppings. Slowly and carefully she pulled it into bunches so that the fibers could be spun into a yarn. 'To protect you my love,' she told the Thorfinn in her imagination, 'with women's magic that knows the patterns of strength and the runes of protection.'

There were trees in the New Country and sweet water on the ground, men said. She imagined Thorfinn and herself and a child living in the house built by the sons of Eirik the Red. There would be no snow. Her hands would not be cold. There would be no ice on the water in the house. Light in the day all year. No winter. How strange that would be. No other women; no Berryface or Skadi or Brigitta. No Ged to keep them safe from the wild creature of other worlds. Her own family lost forever. Everyone lost forever. She and Thorfinn and a baby in a place where there was nothing and no one to help if things went wrong, not even the gods of the Norse.

It was safe at Ebiwaz. As she spun the silver thread with the black fur of the bear from Markland, the birds sang and the women of the house plied their voices together in companionship. There was comfort in the sounds of belonging. She had come to love the patches of moss on the walls and the stones at Ebiwaz, the grasses that grew in summer, the wild things that owned the sea and the song of the insects at night. The spirit creatures in the bay were known to her. She was safe. Ged would return from Gardar when he had carved his creatures in stone for the priest. Thorfinn would return with the silver he so wanted. It would all be as it was, as it was meant to be.

Ged would always care for her, protect her from the demons that roamed the wild mountains and came to Ebiwaz to tear at the dreams

CHAPTER 30 — *The waiting*

of the living and the dead. Dear brave Ged. She saw him with his pale hair knotted and his bright eyes focused on a place no one else could see. It was her duty to care for him when the burden of holding the dark side of everyone's dreams became too heavy. Ged was precious to the people of Greenland. How many chieftains had come to seek his magic for their high-seat pillars, the symbol of their leadership? True, sometimes the demons were so strong and so many that they could not be held the art of Ged but flowed into the day to torment him with lies and tricks. She was his wife. That's how she would be remembered. The child must be his. It was a trick by the gods to think she carried the child of a stranger.

She would think no more of the man with the golden eyes and red-gold hair. She would wash into the bay the feel of his body against hers. Let him return to the sea from where he belonged. She would give Asmund and Ged a child to ensure the memory of their lives would continue. She would rid herself of the memory of Thorfinn.

Then there were the days when the nausea lifted and she was able to walk into the hills. The bright summer light came to her as she wandered amongst the flowers and her heart was filled with hope. Then the land cried with the eyes of Thorfinn and the trees spread his hair in the wind and the stream called yes, yes I am coming with you, I am with you always; on the Great Ocean, in the forests of Markland. Yes, yes, I am with you always.

A deep love for the tiny being in her body enveloped her at these times and she knew the child to be from Thorfinn.

Then vomiting returned and would not go away. The child inside her became a changeling, an elfish devil come to answer Olaf's ranting. This was not the child of Thorfinn but a strange creature given life from the dank bed she shared with Ged. She could sit at her loom for the length of one candle flame only. She was alone with a devil inside her. She could not drink, although thirst drove her to try again and again. The skin on her face and hands shrunk into witches wrinkles. She felt like the brittle shell of an egg within which the unborn grows. She cursed herself for allowing this pregnancy to happen. She could not imagine the child, any child. There was only an emptiness that came to her mind when she tried to call the image of a baby to her inner sight.

It became increasingly difficult for her to stand. Ged was not there to protect her from the evil when it came at night to fill the darkness with a myriad of forms. Thorfinn was not there to hold her when the dizziness came. There were no visions in the fire. The spirits in the wood above her altar leered at her frailty with bared fangs. They were bloated and savage and glared with disgust at the woman below. The wild flowers wilted and the dogs chewed the feather from the white falcon.

When she did get out of bed to look at the sea and the mountain, Skadi limped after her and berated her for her lack of diligence. Skadi had discovered the stores of her precious ale had diminished while she had lain in with baby Byggvir. She was furious. Ale was a luxury and not to be shared unless sanctioned by the lawbinder himself.

Skadi invited Olaf, a righteous man who never dipped his whiskers in stolen ale, to the hearth in the evening to tell stories from his gold-leafed book. Skadi was curious about the god called the White Christ. Asmund had told her she must find out about this god; a god who listened to women and cared about children, Him being once a child and able to cure the sick and not interested in thieving nor fucking neither, she told the dogs.

Sokki kept well away from Skadi's wrath. He taught Berryface board games and sat outside in the sunlit evenings to play with her. Mostly O'Flarty was out in the fields with the cows and the sheep. That left Aud, who was deaf, with Skadi and Anna as the audience Olaf had been promised. Bjarni disappeared and only came home when the moon was dark. He spent as much time as possible with his friend Egil at Thorness plotting a hunting trip to the Nordsetur.

Olaf told his audience of a faraway place called Jerusalem, where the Christian god had been buried, had risen from the dead and would return again one day soon. If one went to this place, Jerusalem, one could be absolved from all sins against god and man, said Olaf. Sin was something that men like Olaf knew about. The worst sin of all was not believing in the Christ god.

CHAPTER 30 — *The waiting*

The chief of the Christians, Olaf said, was a man called Pope Urban. He had called for all Christians to go to this city called Jerusalem and fight the people who had killed the White Christ when he was a god who walked on earth as a man. Olaf knew this because the men from Brattahlid had a letter from the Bishop and showed it only to him because he could read Latin.

Night after night, Anna, Skadi and Aud sat in front of Olaf as the world without shadow turned towards the equinox. Anna thought the Christ god might help her. Olaf said that god looked after lowly people, even women, as well as kings and princes. He was strong and an army of saints and angels protected those that loved Him. The Norse gods only played with humans. Odin was the god of war. He thrived on conflict and stirred up mischief between men. Thor was handsome and strong but what interest had he in a pregnant woman? In love that did not involve him mating?

'Dear friend,' Anna said as Berryface held her arm and they walked to the bay together. 'What would we do without you? And yet you have been forced by your birth to live here among us as a servant.'

'What would Sokki do without me you mean,' laughed Berryface and the red mark on her face creased into lines. She took a stick and reached for the seaweed stuck on the ice nearest the shore. 'And now a child comes for him.' She patted her stomach. 'He is as pleased as an old sea lion. But you, Anna, you are so thin and pale. I never see you eat. Be you missing the love of a husband?

'Ged? Who chooses who we love?' Anna and turned aside to retch onto the stones. 'What is love anyway? The gods play with us. They always have. Love is sickness and despair and loneliness. That is what we are left with. The amount of good time with love is the same time as the pain that it brings. Like the wave that speeds the boat throws the boat upside down.' She saw in her mind's eye Thorfinn being flung into the sea and something within her felt satisfaction. 'They are both gone now. And I am left with this in my body.' She sat on the ground and put her head in her hands. 'Berryface I am also with child.'

Berryface looked at Anna anew. She smiled and embraced her. 'Dear one, you are sad because you are ill with this child. It will pass. When I am sad I think of all the women in my family and they give me strength. Think of the women in your family, the mothers, the grandmothers. They suffered through pregnancy and heartbreak and the loss of many loved ones in the Great Ocean and in battle. Slaves and free women alike. They stand behind us now and give us their strength. See them in a line reaching back to the very first woman who came to Greenland.'

The two women washed the seaweed in silence and bundled it up. Anna found she could imagine a line of her female ancestors standing behind her, each with one hand on the shoulder of the woman in front and one hand on her belly. She could feel the love and strength Berryface spoke of flowing from woman to woman into her.

'Does Ged know?'

'No.' Anna smiled. 'He thinks only of his old bones.'

Aud had a pot of urchin stew boiling on the fire. The smell mingled with the rancid dulse and set Anna vomiting again. 'Now what?' Skadi lurched towards the store room jangling her keys in one hand and waving a knife in the other.

'I am with child,' Anna stared into the smoke that curled like a spirit though the hole in the ceiling. Skadi wiped her knife on her tunic and motioned to Olaf to join them.

'About time.'

'It will please Asmund to have another child at Ebiwaz,' said Berryface.

Skadi grunted. She was the wife of Asmund the lawbinder of Hvalsey and her child would be in control of Ebiwaz once she found a way to get rid of Bjarni. Maybe he could go off to the Jerusalem place. 'Being pregnant ain't any excuse for lying around here and doing nothing. When I was pregnant I kept a good house, I did.'

Berryface put her arm around Anna while Aud continued her song. Anna thought a face stared from the fire. A strong masculine face with a patch of darkness over one eye, stern and unforgiving. 'Allfather,' she whispered. 'If Ged and Thorfinn are precious to you, help them return to me.'

CHAPTER 30 — *The waiting*

But no message came from Gardar in the days that led to winter. O'Flarty and Bjarni brought in the fodder. Berryface tended to the cows and the goats roamed at will through the dying grasses. Short Irish disappeared on a trek to discover if the setting stars led to a nest of Onefoots behind the Grey Mountain. Secretly he thought he might find the place of pirate ship in the sky, the place where the She Dragon of the Clouds waited. Skadi limped after Sokki and snapped at everyone. The tomte gave up his attempt to make Skadi stumble into the dung pit and spent as much time as possible with Aud for he sensed her time was near.

CHAPTER 31
The gate to the other world

Anna lay in bed and was conscious only of a world gradually turning to shades of grey and white. She longed for the heat of a man, to rest in the arms of someone strong and know that she was safe. Black and white patterns swarmed through her mind when she closed her eyes. Her back ached. Her legs felt like ice. Pale figures moved across her vision. Berryface sat with her in bed when she could.

'Berryface, I loved them both,' she whispered. 'What good was it? No one is here to help me now. It is I who must suffer. I did not make this child alone.'

Berryface held her hand and placed it on her belly. 'This is life. Your child will live. You will live.'

'I do not fear death dear friend,' Anna said softly. 'The day of my passing was set with my birth, as it is for all of us. My fate is set. But I am not ready. It is not time. It is not time. Oh, I am betrayed by the gods. Why did this happen to me?'

Anna agreed to allow Olaf to baptize her if that would bring her luck from the White Christ. Olaf smiled in triumph. 'You do right. The White Christ holds his arms out to all, even women though they bear the evil of sin within their sex.'

He indicated all should kneel at the end of the bed and remain silent with bowed heads and eyes downcast. After a waving of hands and a shaking of cold water, he regarded all around him with stern countenance.

'I am cold, cold,' said Anna. 'So much pain. I cannot see.'

CHAPTER 31 — *The gate to the other world*

Berryface held her hand. Anna's body was convulsed with violent tremors. She called out aloud for Thorfinn again and again. Then silence. Not even the sound of her breath. Only the wind from the mountain told the tale that the frailty of women must carry. Aud sent out a long keening note and began the song of death to call the ancestors to come and collect their own. Skadi snuffled into the baby's clothes. Even Sokki moved to comfort Berryface in the presence of such mystery.

Anna felt herself lift above the bed into darkness. There was no pain, no cold, no fear; just the awareness of light and a great freedom from the weight of her body. She floated into darkness above the house. Something delicious caressed her. She felt herself drawn to the smoke coming from the smoke hole in the roof; it caressed and nourished with the most delicious smell, as if everything that had given birth to it remained within it in essence, the wood, the trees, the tiny animals that once lived in the tree, the water that had fed it and all that had ever lived within it. She knew them all.

The tomte crouched on the turf, shaking. He held up a tiny shoe and batted at Anna. 'Be gone witch,' he spat. 'Evil wife of the man who loves demons.'

'Go,' whispered Anna as softly as the wind. 'You, tomte, are the nasty evil thing. You harmed Ged. You sour the milk and knotted the wool. You try to harm us all.'

The tomte ran. Anna followed, her thoughts twisting with grief and anger. She did not want to die. She wanted to be with Thorfinn and Ged. It was not her time. She was young, in the first winter of her marriage. She did not want this child who had taken her away from the place she loved. She moved faster than the north wind, round and round the house until the space inside became a cave in the centre of a world where nothing could live.

Berryface got up and fought her way to the door. She held onto the door frame and shouted into the tumult outside :'Be gone whatever you are. Leave us in peace. I call on the ancestors to protect us. Go, Anna, if it is you.'

The sight of Berryface in such distress brought compassion to Anna. There was no anger. Just a terrible terrible grief. It was not her time to lose these people. She watched the spirit of the being who was to be her child move above the house into light. The being that was to be the child swelled to an enormous seize, then dissipated into the air around them to become a shimmering transparency.

Anna felt herself encased in light. Now she knew everything was as it was meant to be. She let her life at Ebiwaz go with ease. She felt the presence of others around her in a vast unending space. Of the Christ God and his army there was no sight. Where were the ancestors? Where were the gods of the Norse?

The ancestors, when they came, came softly. There was her father and her mother's brothers with the sons of Aud; there was her grandmother and the sister of Skadi and many others she did not know. By her feet was her little dog from the West, its sweet nature embracing her. There was the Grandmother-ghost from the bath house and her baby. Grandmother had flowing red hair and held a pale child to her breast. She had the blue crescent moon of a wise woman painted on her forehead.

'Many gods, many paths,' Grandmother of the Crescent Moon told her. 'For the spirit is in each of us to teach us lessons. It is only in the body where we find the ability to learn. Be at peace, Anna, as I never was. You are exactly where you are meant to be in this life. The Norns have spun your fate not to come to us yet. Spend the days you have in love with the man you love.'

Now Ebiwaz was as an opening to a cave far below her in the darkness. She felt a great tenderness for Thorfinn and saw their union stretching back into another place, where there were hills and trees taller than the house. Ged stood beside them. He held out a carving and strange forms writhed and contorted within the bounds of his drawing. She called to him, to both of them. She felt herself falling into blackness. Immediately she found herself anchored to her body. The pain was intense, coming in waves now. Berryface and Aud hung over her. Brigitta appeared as if from nowhere and dropped something

CHAPTER 31 — The gate to the other world

into her mouth and pushed at her heart. Berryface gasped as Anna opened her eyes and yelled.

'Now,' Berryface whispered. 'The baby comes. Push, Anna.' Brigitta held her from the back while Berryface stood to catch the child. At last it came in a rush of bright blood. The baby was tiny and malformed with a blue tinge to its skin under the blood and mucus. It did not breathe. Berryface held it up and gently smacked its tiny feet without result. Anna felt herself drift again to the place without pain. The women pushed rags soaked in astringent herbs into the birth canal and laid the small malformed baby on the bed.

'It does not breath,' said Berryface. Aud took it and wrapped it in a seal skin harvested from a female seal. She began the song of mourning while scratching the blank rune of Odin on the shroud.

'Thorfinn', Anna moaned as the darkness came and receded, 'Thorfinn, we came together. Where are you now? You said you would not leave me.'

She saw Thorfinn. He limped and his skin was cold and sallow. He leant on his stick for support as he moved across the ice with the skraeling. He was angry. He yelled to Scarface and pointed to a huge white bear. Icebergs groaned around them. The ice was thronged with shimmering animal spirits that towered over Norse and skraeling alike. A skraeling woman walked among them with a rattle made of whale bone and bear skin.

'Thorfinn?' Skadi sat up, suddenly alert. 'Anna is the wife of Ged. Why does she call for Thorfinn?'

'By all the legs of Sieiphir, since when was a good Viking woman not supposed to sex all them men who was the friend of her husband?' spat out Brigitta while slapping Anna's face.

'I knew she were up to no good with him. Right in front of Ged and Asmund. Now you is the wife of no one, Anna Kerldottir and an evil spirit has taken the child of No Father to Hel to punish you.' Skadi sucked at her lips.

'You fool Twistbeaks,' Brigitta turned on Skadi. 'Bad words bring bad spirits. Us Norse fucks who we wants. When I want a man I takes him, Twistbeaks, with the approval of me husband. And dare you not say a word against Scarface, Twistbeaks. More women he has is easier for me. So shut yer moo arsed face or I'll stick you with me knife. As if all men ain't the same.' She turned back to press a charm into Anna's abdomen and to clap her hands in the air around the bed.

'Now, Anna,' Brigitta continued while rubbing ground-up crystal into the skin over Anna's heart, 'leave them spirits alone. Come back here and stay. Spirits never done anyone any good while we walk the paths the ancestors made for us in Midgard.'

Aud and Berryface took the bundle of mother seal skin outside and placed it on the earth. Aud held a piece of charcoal and drew the rune Dagaz next to the bank rune of Odin on the stones near the dead child. 'A great change for you,' she sang to the child body. 'Return to the world of the spirit. Your passage to this life is not safe.'

'Anna Anna. Come back,' shouted Brigitta, pressing her hands over Anna's eyes. 'You do not need to go. It is not your time. Stay with us. Ged needs you. Thorfinn needs you. Those Norns ain't spun you out of this life yet.'

'Thorfinn, Thorfinn ,' the wind whispered in the Nordsetur, 'it is I, Anna.' Thorfinn looked around as if he had heard. The skraeling yelled and sent a harpoon over the ice. Thorfinn returned his attention to the hunt.

'Let me go. Thorfinn calls,' Anna moaned as the tears streamed down her face.

'Who?' said Brigitta. 'Thorfinn? He ain't dead yet by my reckoning. Do a spirit call from the grave out yonder? Who says them ancestors know anything better than we Norse women who is living now? Jest because we can't see 'em, we think they see more than we do, and they do not. Them spirits know nothing. Come back and a pox on them what call you away. Send 'em to Ged to put in his wood. We have enough of them pests around here what with Olaf's ranting.'

Anna spent the days drifting in and out of awareness. Brigitta stayed with her and put strange smelling drops and tiny bits of crystalline rock into her mouth. She massaged her body while Aud fed her warm sea-

CHAPTER 31 — The gate to the other world

urchin stew. Berryface told her long stories about the place of her birth and the wild women of Ireland. She wound Anna's feet in hot wadmal and sat with her hands on her body to give warmth and healing.

The men walked cautiously to the bed as Brigitta bid them and addressed Anna with kind words. Some stayed to listen to the stories of Ireland as Berryface remembered from her mother. Some stayed to tell their own stories of sea voyages and discoveries and treasures won.

As Anna drifted, her spirit continued to fly with her thoughts. She thought of Ged and suddenly she was at Gardar. The land was covered in snow. Ged was in a half-built church on a broad flat plain. Curled beside him was a large dog. Both were peaceful, both as if in a dream watching the snowflakes fall on the stones surrounding the graveyard wherein lay his precious bones. Anna saw many strange forms flow around Ged, but neither he nor the dog were bothered by this. The dog looked up to acknowledge Anna, then moved closer to Ged to protect him. Ged had his tools beside him. He had been carving on a large stone. He wrapped his arms around the dog and thought briefly of the wife he had left at Ebiwaz.

When Anna thought of the farm on the inland fiord, deep in the Western Settlement, her mother looked up from her spinning and smiled. A man unknown to Anna sat in the high seat of her father. A child lay in a basket beside the spinning wheel. Her mother seemed to be aware of Anna but try as she could Anna could not communicate with her. It was the same with everyone. All acknowledged her presence when she came to them and accepted this awareness as a memory, or a thought that flew from one to another over the vast lands that separated them. No one spoke, no one called her by name. Only the beloved small dog of her childhood offered companionship. The dog barked with delight each time Anna's thoughts caressed it.

'Old Pa could use these pants,' Anna heard the rasping voice of Sokki as she struggled to stay with her body. 'And who is looking after the fierce old Viking, Brigitta, while you is here? Yellowbritches and Scarface ain't come back have they? Why did you not bring Old Pa with you?'

Anna saw Old Pa staggering though shards of ice in a high valley. He rattled an ancient rusty sword and muttered incessantly. Menglad rode behind him on her favorite horse. She spat and bared her teeth when she became aware of Anna.

'Old Pa escaped,' said Brigitta loudly and drew Anna back to Ebiwaz. 'Went off to fight them giants in the Grey Mountain. Got up one day, took his sword and said he was going to rid Greenland of 'em forever. Not been seen since. Disappeared he did. Tried to catch him, but the old Viking was too strong for us.'

Sokki glared at her and rattled Stingslove. 'Time were that Old Pa could fight any man alive and then more. But now he don't see well, Brigitta, and his hands is all cramped up like mine. He and I, cursed we were not to die in battle but to grow old and frail.'

'He be a disgusting old fart Sokki Bluetooth and do not say otherwise. Pissed his self all the time in the house. Dug shit out of his bum and ate it even if his hands don't work proper. Yellowbritches may have sailed off but I am not looking after his kin while the Norns weave me life away. Scarface said afore he went that Old Pa were now my responsibility and I would know what to do when I had to.'

This set the Menglad and the ghost horse laughing.

Anna saw Old Pa enter the Hall of Freyja on a high plateau behind the Grey Mountain near a lake that shone with an iridescent glow. The Hall of Freyja was enormous, made of fine white stone and hung with tapestry and silver ornaments. There was singing and feasting from golden plates and spoons and the scent of roast meat and herbed ale. Yellowbritches was there, too, seated next to a young man with black hair who played music on a horn. Old Pa stood behind them holding his sword with both hands and made little passes at the fruit and flowers on the table. He wore a dead cat on his head and the tail came between his eyes like the nose plate from a battle helmet.

Anna drew back. Yellowbritches smiled and beckoned her to join him. Not yet, not yet. I must wait, she said to him. Brigitta calls me. The little dog attached itself to the leg of Old Pa and tried to draw him away from Yellowbritches and Harald.

CHAPTER 32
The Nordsetur

Thorfinn was angry. He felt betrayed by everyone at Hvalsey. Except perhaps by Ged who wished harm to no one. Now he was in as cold and desolate a place as Hel. He did not remember ever being so cold. His leg refused to bend and carry his weight. His hip hurt. His teeth ached and his eyes ran. The skin under his beard felt like it was crawling with insects and, to make it worse, his whiskers were becoming silver white in the centre of his chin, just like his father. His cloak was damp, the soles of his boots rotten. He thought bitterly of the elfin cloak to be made from the magic sheep from the Grey Mountain. Why had Anna not finished it and given it to him? Why was it not on his back now? Why was he not in the New Country with his woman and child? He could not call the face of Anna to his mind, let alone imagine what his son would look like.

There was nothing to drink in the Nordsetur except a hideous skraeling concoction that left a layer of fat on his whiskers. The skraelings infuriated him with their fast speech and unfathomable eyes. He cursed everyone at Ebiwaz for keeping him away from Markland, which was now so close yet so unattainable. He railed at his ancestors for the curse they had brought upon him. The captain and his crucifix annoyed Thorfinn. The animals on the ice annoyed Thorfinn. They bled too much and made too much noise. After a day of hunting the ice was slippery with blood and the seabed full of predators that watched a man with hungry eyes.

He wanted ale to sleep and to deaden the pain of his life. At times a great weariness overcame him but still he could not sleep. His hands shook. He spent the nights in a lather of sweat while Scarface fucked a dour-faced skraeling with concentrated exertion and exhorted Thorfinn to do likewise.

They had pulled the ship high onto the land and built a booth around it to use as a shelter from the northern summer storms. It was comfortable and dry but did little to protect them from the swarms of biting insects that decided Norse blood was a rare feast. When sleep did come to Thorfinn the dim light of his dreams was full of the Bishop of Markland and his boat of bleeding Onefoots.

Thorfinn thought about Ged whenever he had to bundle up a walrus skull with the tusks intact. The old white walrus that floated upright in the water around the ice shelf reminded Thorfinn of the Whale-horse Queen. The bones of her children were buried in holy ground as Ged said she wanted. What had happened to them all at Hvalsey without Ged to hold the spirits who haunted their dreams? Could a creature like the Whale-horse Queen be held in the vision of one man?

The captain of the ship exhorted the Norse to kill and kill for the good of the church. Animals, he said, and that included the skraeling, were made by the Christ God for the benefit of those who worshipped the correct way. They did not have the capacity to know the divine. Their only value was to help human souls on their way to Heaven.

Hunting white bear was the most dangerous; as much as white bear was hunted by Norse, white bear hunted Norse. The bears were cunning and savage and had no fear of humans. The great bears moved across the ice with a host of spirits behind them; bad spirits who forced anyone who had wronged the earth onto thin ice where the sea claimed back what it owned. One day the man who had sat next to Thorfinn in the longboat was pushed by a spirit bear into the sea. He died immediately; one breath he was walking beside Scarface and the next he disappeared into a hole in the ice. The skraeling woman from the Norse camp came to stand at the hole and muttered over it and made strange movements with her hands.

'You go now,' she said. 'You have taken enough. Aguta has taken him. Aglooik bids you go now. Aglooik cannot save you all.'

CHAPTER 32 — The Nordsetur

'Fool,' shouted the captain. 'The devil take him and his carelessness.'

The frozen eyes of the drowned man stared though the ice. His brother began to beat at the water with a spear as the body slid into the depths. The men refused to hunt anymore. They let go the white bear they were tracking. Both bear and Norse moved cautiously away from each other, sniffing the air as they went.

The men retired to the ship and spent the next few days cleaning and winding long strips of walrus hide, organizing the walrus skulls with tusks attached carefully into piles, and scraping fat from bear hide. They spoke little and sat close to the fire and each other while the sun drew from the rocks long shadows that no light could dispel. Scarface told everyone that the man who died would tell the spirits of the old dead Norse that a new ship had come to the Nordsetur. The ghosts would come from under the ice and float beside the ship to find their way home. Bloated they would be, and spotted like narwhale; the ghosts would follow them home to bring bad luck to the families of the men who had left them in the cold desolation of the Nordsetur.

Suddenly the air was colder, the days shorter. When the light did come across the horizon it cast small lines of color and distorted the planes of rock and ice into inhuman shapes. Home and the gods that protected them were far away. The mountains behind the bay seemed to encase a town full of mystical creatures, some with evil faces and horns that could impale man in his bed, some with tentacles so fine they could float in the air like the hair of a child and suck the life out of a man without him even knowing. In the twilight the water was a mirror that could upend a man's senses and tip him into Hel if he could not determine which was land and which was reflection.

Two men became sick with the vomiting and diarrhea after a day when it was too wet to light a fire and cook the meat. Walrus sickness, the skraeling called it, and said it came from eating raw flesh. One man died and was put to rest under a cairn of stones. The men were sullen and irritable. The equinox passed and already the snow threatened to engulf the summer settlement of the skraeling. The Norse had ivory enough and skins of the white bear and narwhale horns and not a few falcons beside. The horns were wrapped carefully in blessed cloth for the captain said these could work magic if not contained by the magic of the Christ. Scarface had a walrus penis hidden in his belongings, promised as it was for Brigitta. Bags there were too of walrus hide and gut collected when the creatures were skinned on the ice.

The captain decided it was time to leave. The bishop would be pleased with his tithes, and if the king of Norway ever got any he also would be pleased with the wealth Greenland provided. Thorfinn traded a knife for bear skin pants and a vest with a pointed hood for the sea journey south. Scarface told the captain his skraeling woman wanted to come. She could, Scarface pointed out, take the place of the man who was under the ice. Everyone laughed as the woman showed with gestures that she liked Scarface because of his large bum. Scarface gave an axe to her father.

'Might cheer them ghosts up to hear the sweet tones of a woman's voice over the moaning of them bergs,' Scarface announced to the crew.

No one said a word. Anyone with any knowledge of any way to placate the gods of the Great Ocean was of use, be it Christian, Norse or skraeling. A flock of birds led them from the bay to the open sea. By caverns of blue ice the ship slid, and the only noise was the moaning of the wind across the walls of ice and the occasional drop of a calving berg. All watched the water save the tiller man, who watched the winds.

The land passed like a giant claw with black fingers of rock stretching into the water. It was never safe on a ship that carried such a cargo. Beasts of the Great Ocean, pirates and gods of the sky desired rich gifts from a place known only to a few; treasure from the lair of a cold dragon with a tail that wrapped around any who sailed within its reach.

The wind was behind them but the ice crept around the boat so no one could see where danger waited. They pulled into the lee of a frozen ice floe when the darkness became intense. No one but the woman slept. The ship rested in a shallow bay where the melt water had come to the sea in spring and frozen into a wide arc with a small inlet beside. They anchored their boat to a rock and tried to find some peace within

CHAPTER 32 — The Nordsetur

the hands of the wind and the tiny particles of rock dust that filled the air. They left with the day that had become half evening.

As the boat slipped from the coast, all gazed in horror at the creature watching from the rocks at the bottom of the sea. It had crawled from a place under the arc of surface ice. It was white and as long as the boat, with two curling crab like arms in the front of its body and round red eyes on the end of a stalk on each side of its head. No one spoke. When the dark seabed opened under them the helmsman took up his horn and it sang of victory; a long low note, once and once again.

The skraeling woman became more and more agitated as the day wore on. The cold increased, a frost seeping into their hair and growing in the strands of their long beards. Thorfinn was glad to take his turn at the oars for at least here his body could heat with exertion. The woman rocked beside him in the space made by the dead man. She made little comforting noises to herself and every now and then pointed at Scarface's bum and laughed. Towards the second night she began to jump up and down and point at the shore. The ship passed under an almost transparent ice palace. Through the opening of an arch in the mass of ice the men saw a flickering light high up on a cliff. The light bounced off the ice like a beacon.

'Norse go, Norse go.' The skraeling woman pointed to the top of the cliff.

'Knows something we don't,' advised Scarface. 'Better for us we do what she says.'

The captain with a sour expression indicated that the tiller man should maneuver the ship across the current and into shore under the massive cliffs. As soon as they landed the skraeling woman punched Scarface on the bum, levered herself from the boat and ran up a steep track to the light. The men followed. With much cursing and sweating they eventually came to an encampment nestled in amongst some large caves. Skraeling men stood around a fire with bows and arrows in hand. The skraeling woman ran to one of the men and embraced him. She made a gesture of thanks to the Norse. The skraeling lowered their weapons.

'Well I eat Locki's turds,' said Scarface. 'Thought she liked me bum but it was just a way to get to here.'

The captain rubbed his silver crucifix against his nose. The skraeling offered meat and space in a rock shelter not far from the fire. The captain knew his crew wanted to get home but they also needed time away from the moaning ice and the dead men floating under their ship.

In the morning they left, each with a belly full of seal meat and the smell of fire in their hair. The journey was a easier now with the knowledge they were soon to be at the shores of the Eastern Settlement.

CHAPTER 33
Ebiwaz

On the second moon after the equinox the ship came to the entrance of Hvalsey Fiord. The sea was clear around them, although the fiord itself was filled with ice that groaned like loose teeth in Sokki's mouth. Scarface and Thorfinn disembarked with skis and long sticks to guide their way. They crossed the ice to find the ancient track to Hvalsey. For months now they had been attuned to every shape and sound in a landscape of ice and snow; it took but caution and the shared knowledge of the skraeling and the animals they had hunted to walk the frozen path to Hvalsey.

Scarface led the way with a thick rod of driftwood to break the shards of ice that fell like knives along the path from the dead branches of the summer plants. Like Thorfinn, he wore his white bear-skin inside out on his shoulders and seal-skin trousers over boots of walrus leather.

It was immensely pleasing to Thorfinn to be moving along the winding track with the mountains in front of them. Both Thorfinn and Scarface carried a nestbaggin hanging from their shoulders with narwhale horns and walrus ivory wrapped in sacred cloth. As the bag thumped against him Thorfinn thought of the animals who had given them such riches. He remembered their eyes, in particular, at the moment of death. In truth, Thorfinn said to himself, it could not be that man alone lived in Valhalla in the realm beyond death. The animals he had killed had looked into his eyes with awareness as he waded in their blood and dragged the skin from their bodies.

The track wound between the rocks. Thorfinn felt Anna with him and his thighs sang with anticipation. He remembered her in the nights when the wind rent the world outside in storm and lightning as they lay together. He could feel the shape of her sex in his hands, the feel of her as he kissed her. He imagined slipping within her. Would she be different after the birth? His son would be born. Would she have called him after his father? He ached for the sound of someone calling him father. As he walked he imagined a tall youth beside him. How they would talk! They would share wondrous adventures in Markland. He would be clever too, with bow and arrow and harpoon.

When they reached Hvalsey Scarface did not come into the farm but decided to continue on to his own steading. A few sheep grazed in the home field around Ebiwaz, a few rows of cod stiffened in the freezing air. The farm and the mountains behind were softened by a faint glow from the water in the bay. The rattle of the drying racks by the house reverberated against the walls of the fiord. A few birds called overhead. There was a fresh mound amongst the ancestor graves.

Thorfinn called out before pushing the door open. The hall was quiet. The wall hangings were still there, as colorful and intricate as ever, the silver and the precious Viking swords. Only they seemed to hang in a way that spoke of emptiness, of stillness. It was as if it some strange still creature had taken up residence in the house and swallowed all noise. Skadi sat by the fire with the child at her breast, her eyelids drooping. Olaf sat beside her and mouthed words silently from his book of gold leaf. Sokki rocked in a corner and did not hear Thorfinn enter. Berryface lay beside him with a new born on her lap.

Olaf looked up as Thorfinn entered. He still wore a tattered brown cowl and a crucifix hung under a few strands of beard hair. 'Thorfinn Markland-Farer,' he said. 'A sinner back from the place of the heathen. Have ye tithes for the bishop in that sack?'

'I greet you. And I ask you for shelter at Ebiwaz during the winter. I have walked a long and hard path in the Nordsetur this past summer.'

'You have suffered as did the Christ. Be thankful for your pain.'

CHAPTER 33 — *Ebiwaz*

Skadi snorted suddenly as if waking from a dream. 'Thorfinn Markland-Farer. We have been waiting. Asmund has been waiting. He goes to the mountain to find falcons for the tithes. The priest sends messages on the full moon to ask for the ivory and fur we do not have.'

'Welcome back stranger,' said Short Irish appearing suddenly in the doorway. 'Never get enough, those greedy priests.' He produced a bucket of berry ale and handed a bowl to Thorfinn.

'Ged?' said Thorfinn. 'From memory Ged could find falcons faster than anyone.'

Skadi indicated an inner doorway with a toss of her head. 'Stays in Gardar to work for the priest.'

As she spoke a woman came to the door of the weaving room. Her figure was softened by hair that fell loose and fair to her shoulders. She was pale, almost translucent.

'Ged has not returned,' said Anna. 'I welcome you Thorfinn.' She was thin, the light around her shimmering as if the edges of her body were already fading into the spirit world. 'Thorfinn,' she repeated. 'You have come. I am pleased to see you. Our house is your house, our wealth is your wealth.'

'Your house.' Skadi sneezed and snorted. 'Your wealth? Listen to me, Anna of No Husband, Ged is not here. You ain't got no say here until you gives us a child like a real wife of Ebiwaz. Even the servant has given birth. Look at Berryface with her baby. Otherwise you is worthless.' She held up her baby up and waved it in the air.

Anna lowered herself onto a bench and addressed Skadi without malice. 'Twistbeaks, I spin and weave till my hands are thick with grease and my arms ache. Aye it is a sweet babe that Berryface has.' She picked up the baby from Berryface and held it to her. Tears came to her eyes as she looked at Thorfinn. 'Your leg troubles you still? Come sit and be warm. You are thin. Your hair is well grown and your beard. I would not know you. Berryface, fetch drink and meat while I hold the tiny one.'

Thorfinn felt the watching presence in the house again. This was not the Anna he knew, this creature with luminous eyes and wild hair. Where was his son? What was going on here? Anna held a child but called Berryface the mother. Where was his child? Anna was not pregnant. She called no babe her own. She held no babe to her own breast. Thorfinn steadied himself against a house pillar. Berryface came to embrace him. Thorfinn found comfort in the warmth of her body, in the milky female smell of her.

'Best you eat and drink,' she said. 'We have meat. Bjarni is with Gunhar Olvadsson but he still hunts for us. As you see Short Irish has made a fine batch of berry spirit this winter.'

At the sound of her voice Sokki sat up and groped around him.

'Thorfinn has come back from the Nordsetur,' Berryface said and moved to guide him. 'Come sit Thorfinn with your drink. You see Sokki has a new son.'

Not again, Thorfinn's thoughts raged . The curse of his family. He could not look at Anna and not betray his feelings.

Berryface served bowls of stew and dried curd. 'We have ale too now from the trade Asmund made at the Assembly.'

'You have changed. I would not know you,' Anna said softly, staring at Thorfinn.

'Sokki is not himself these days.' Berryface spoke while smoothing Sokki's hair. 'He was so excited by the birth of his son he tried to climb onto the roof. He fell and has been within himself since. Does not seem to see what we see. Talks to spirits no one else can see. Will come good with time. Just have to let him rest. Teeth hurting him bad these past few weeks too.'

Olaf made the sign of the cross as if to ward off evil. Skadi did not move but continued to glare at Anna.

'Well, Thorfinn, what have ye got to tell us about the treasures of the North,' Olaf poured ale for himself.

Thorfinn had his mouth full. 'Who lies out yonder?' He pointed in the direction of the graveyard.

'Aud. Died end of summer. Buried with the child Anna lost. Both together to look after each other in the next world.'

'You lost a child?'

CHAPTER 33 — *Ebiwaz*

'Near we was to losing Anna, too, if it were not for Brigitta.'

'Do not mention that witch woman in this house,' Olaf squinted at Thorfinn. 'If a child is not ready to live in this earth, it is because it seeks to sacrifice itself for the sins of the parent, St Patrick says, as did the Christ for the sins of humanity.'

Thorfinn felt a grief without end open before him. Anna laughed quietly to herself in the manner of Ged.

Skadi pushed at one of the dogs sprawled in front of the fire. 'Mind you keep a Christian tongue in your head, Anna of No Husband. You took the faith of the Christ remember, afore you told us of your evil.'

'You lie, Twistbeaks.' Anna turned calmly to Thorfinn. 'I remember nothing. I do not trust this god Olaf talks about.'

'Thorfinn, you sleep over there.' Skadi pointed to an empty bed palate. 'Take the quilt from the bed of Bjarni. Asmund will see to you when he comes in from the mountain.'

Before he slept Thorfinn thought he caught the faint sound of sad voices outside somewhere. Were these the men Ged heard calling from the ice in the bay? He was not sure if it was the sound of the wind in the ice or the lament of the Grandmother-ghost in the bath-house. Or even the cry of his dead wife.

When Asmund returned from the mountain the household was asleep. He noted with satisfaction the evidence of Thorfinn in the house. After some time of sleep the household awoke into a darkness as dense as the one which had soothed their weariness. Thorfinn remained asleep.

'It is well done for him to return,' Asmund said looking at the sleeping form of Thorfinn. 'I have work enough for another man here during winter.' He collected his tools and left with Short Irish to work in the smithy.

Thorfinn awoke with the clatter of the household.

'Your hair Thorfinn,' Anna said as he struggled with the long tangled strands catching in his clothes. 'Do you need help? I have a new knife. Let me.'

As she lifted the matted hair from his neck she felt the power begin again between them. 'Come. We will sit outside.'

'You have not been well?' Thorfinn said as they seated themselves at the gaming table. Anna saw the shape of his head; the soft curls around his neck as if she had seen it thus every night as he turned his head from her face to sleep after they had lain together.

Thorfinn had longed for the touch of this woman. Now he had no words.

'I finished the cloak from the elfin wool. Asmund says I may give it to you in exchange for some walrus skulls with the ivory intact.'

The air between them was heavy with unspoken thought.

'Over there Thorfinn.' Anna pointed to a heavy woolen cloak on a peg by the door.

Thorfinn took the cloak and tried it on. It fitted well. It was thick and light with a border of black and silver. He could see tiny fragment of black bear hair woven into the material. He wanted to take this frail woman in his arms, to tell her how it was for him all the time he had been in the Nordsetur, how the one thing that he had believed in was the thought of his son. His arms became tangled in the cloak. 'Anna,' he said. 'You lost a child?'

'The baby could not grow. Its spirit did not want to come to me. It made me sick. I could take no food or water. I could not walk, I could not see.' She spoke with no grief. 'The spirit of the child died inside me. There was no one to help. There was no love to give me strength.'

'Oh Anna.'

'Asmund comes.' Anna pointed. Asmund and Short Irish could be seen moving towards the house.

'Thorfinn,' said Asmund when he arrived. He embraced Thorfinn. He was as Thorfinn remembered; his body heavy with contained strength, his hair tied in a sliver clasp and his eyes noting every small variation in the world around him.

'As lawbinder of Hvalsey I welcome you back from the Nordsetur. It is good to see you, friend. Have you news of Scarface?'

CHAPTER 33 — Ebiwaz

He gripped Thorfinn firmly by the arm and steered him away from Anna. 'Now this is talk for men. These women know only the business of the house and its children. You hunted well?'

'Aye,' said Thorfinn. 'It is not the business of women. I bring ivory and skins. I need a place to stay this winter. I offer ivory in return for your hospitality.'

'No matter. It is well done,' Asmund smiled. 'You may stay here and help since Ged stays at Gardar . The chief of Brattahlid sent word to say he stays with the priest and carves the lintel during winter even if the weather is bad. Friend, your contribution to the bishop's tithe will be well received, for we at Hvalsey cannot make the quota no matter how we try.'

'Dragon of the mountain tells me of Ged,' Short Irish said. 'Since he did not come back the ice moans for him. Like those ghosts under the ice were still there, waiting.'

'Maybe he were not as witless as we thought.'

'I too have heard them,' Thorfinn said.

The men settled themselves by the fire with Sokki. It was wet and dark outside. The cows had been boarded up till the spring ice melt. There was a good supply of grass laid in. O'Flarty had made a drainage system to collect the runoff and prevent an evil smelling mould from growing under the cow tails. Now the hunting was done for the day no one had the inclination to do more than drift into the color of memory. The women worked slowly at their carding and spinning, the babies snuffled and Sokki responded to the conversation of the shadow people.

Anna sat at her weaving but nothing came under her hands as she planned it to be. She could not take her thoughts from Ged and Thorfinn. She wanted to care for them both, to tend to Ged, to keep him safe from the strange creatures that stalked his dreams. She ached to touch Thorfinn, to lie within the strength of his arms. Could she not be wife to both of them? Asmund spoke of taking more than one wife. It was the way of the Norse gods to love many. She watched the way the men moved around Berryface, now so warm and female in her motherhood. Today she wore a dress Anna had given her. It pinched in her waist and her milky breasts flowed out of the neck line.

Olaf joined them for the evening meal.

'Tell us about the hall where the Christ lives,' Skadi asked. 'What is it that the White Christ would have us do for him to look after us women?'

Olaf pulled at his beard. His eyes glittered. 'Give wealth to the True Church to care for the priests. Them is the only ones know words the True God understands. The priests say who can live in Heaven because they know if you have done what the Christ wanted here on earth. If you have given up unlawful fortification and the flesh of the animals with a cloven hoof. And ye must get your men to go to fight the infidel in the name of the Lord.'

Olaf stopped, wiped the spit off his whiskers and took up his drink. No one spoke. The tomte crept to the hearth to pluck at Olaf's boots.

Thorfinn scratched his beard and looked thoughtful. 'I left Iceland because I fought with my kin who took the religion of the White Christ. Will this Christ listen to them when they tell Him about me? How will the Christ understand the words of the priests from Iceland if He speaks the language of the Holy Land?

'Aye Thorfinn,' continued Olaf. 'He will understand. There is only one language in Heaven. Like it will be when the heathen has left the Holy Land and the one True God can return to Jerusalem. When this happens Heaven on earth will return and everyone will be united with those they love. And all curses will be no more.'

Asmund carved the hair off his forearm with his knife. 'Your leg Thorfinn? How was it on the ice?' He spat into the straw. 'Lame you may be friend but I ask you to help me. We can only meet the tithes the priest wants for this bothersome bishop if we can find a falcon's nest in the mountain. And there is word of a blackbird with a tail like a lizard that lives yonder in the mountains. A wild thing, enormous with wings as wide as a house. Diamonds grow on its feet I have been told. Such a bird would please the bishop. It is said that those who have been to the Nordsetur and looked into the face of the spirits on the ice are the only ones who can hunt such a creature.'

CHAPTER 33 — *Ebiwaz*

'You have been to the Nordsetur. Are you not able to see the animal with the diamond claws to give to your bishop?'

'My sight is not good in the dark. This creature can be seen only on special times when the moon is absent. I have hunted many times on the mountain and found nothing. I fear to mistake the diamonds on its feet for the frost on the skin of a giant. Or a Onefoot. Or a dragon. Which well it might be. And I have no wish to start a war with such creatures. No I must have a strong companion with good eyesight on such a hunt. Someone who can see well. Will you come with me as the guest of my house and make my burden less?'

Thorfinn was fascinated. He felt compelled to go with Asmund to hunt this fabulous creature. 'My leg gives me pain when I climb but that does not stop me. I will go with you. It is my honor as a guest to assist you.'

The two men sat in silence until Thorfinn limped to the bed where he had his belongings. The stiffness in his leg had indeed never left but the pain was lessened by the warmth of the house and the care of the women here. A shadow from the fire fell across his bed and formed the shape of Ansuz, the messenger rune, the rune of Locki, a warning to be aware that change was coming. This was a message from the gods. He would receive help but it might come as an unwelcome gift. He curled into his furs and slept.

CHAPTER 34
Return to Thorness

Bjarni arrived the next day on skis with a message from Thorness. He carried a load of peregrines on his back with a nestbaggin full of fox fur. Bjarni had grown tall and muscular over the summer. He wore a cloak of wolf skin. His beard was a pattern of wiry tufts on his face. He carried himself with dignity. He had as always the tooth of a whale-horse within a harpoon around his neck. His knife was sharp and hung in a sheath of leather from his belt.

'Asmund Lawbinder, Father.' Bjarni spoke in a voice that, like Asmund, indicated great physical strength. 'Eirik Eiriksson Scarface bids me tell you that Brigitta wishes for Thorfinn to come to Thorness with Berryface and the child of Sokki. She wishes to see if the child thrives.'

'That witch will not come here again,' said Skadi. 'Olaf says she has magic from a devil god.'

'Not married yet young Viking,' said Thorfinn. 'Is there not some young woman who you desire?'

Bjarni grinned and felt the color rising to his face. 'Not yet. Maybe I will go south in the summer. It is said the richest landowner in Herjolfsness wants a husband for his daughter. She is said to be beautiful like one from the court of the English king. They say she wears clothes of the silk and to sing like a goddess. Her hands are white and her skin has no sores.'

Anna looked at her own hands, bound for warmth in brown wadmal. Her fingers were red and calloused, the skin split with cold.

CHAPTER 34 — *Return to Thorness*

'Herjolfsness? I was there,' Thorfinn said. 'Two long arms of rock take a ship into a fine beach of sand. Many ships come there from England looking for cod. They have iron and jet to trade.'

'It is a good place for Norse,' said Asmund. 'It has been so since the Eirik the Red came first to Brattahlid.'

'And from there you can get to Iceland and Norway and join the Olaf's fight against the enemies of his god,' put in Short Irish. 'Or sell your unwanted house guests to the pirates who roam around that coast.' He frowned at Asmund and punched the nearest bit of himself.

The day Bjarni, Berryface and Thorfinn set out to Thorness the clouds hung low across the bay and the water kept its form under a grey mantle. Anna sat at her loom and watched them climb the path into the hills. Thorfinn waved as Berryface drew him forward into the music of her hips.

Brigitta came to meet them. She was pregnant again. Her face shone with health and her shift stretched over a body as tight and fluid as ever. She descended on the baby with glee and drew Thorfinn and Berryface into the longhouse. The place was in turmoil, leather, hides and wadmal covering most surfaces. It smelt of ale and sex and animals.

As Thorfinn entered the room one of the piles of material came alive to reveal a small child mending stockings. More children materialized from the mass of articles piled in front of the fire; they sat quietly sewing or polishing. The smallest one began a song about a cat and the others joined in making cat noises.

Brigitta handed Thorfinn a stone cup of whey and sat back to observe him. 'Any news of Yellowbritches? Word has it from a wandering hunter that he set out for Iceland in a ship with two men after Mid-Summer.'

'Yes,' Thorfinn said. 'He left Gardar in a small ship to sail to Iceland.'

'The gods love Yellowbritches. Maybe he sits in the halls of the gods already? Maybe the gods were jealous of his music.'

Both remained silent. Brigitta picked up a piece of blue ribbon and turned it over in her hands. Thorfinn settled himself into the sweetness of the household bustling around him. It gave him much peace to be surrounded with the things of domestic life; the herbs hanging from the roof, the stone bowls and cooking pots, the clothes thrown everywhere, the bits and pieces of ancestral treasure hidden in the general tumult of belongings.

Bjarni went to talk to the horses. He did not return till the oil in the lamps had burnt and been replaced twice. Scarface and Egil came in from the hills with a small caribou carcass. Brigitta served her excellent ale as it was a special occasion to have both Scarface and Thorfinn back from the Nordsetur. Berryface left the baby with the eldest child and was compelled to demonstrate her skills as a cook. Scarface bellowed with laughter and sat Brigitta on his lap whenever he could.

When everyone was sated and melting into the general chaos of the house Thorfinn and Berryface took their leave. Thorfinn carried the child. As he walked beside Berryface he inhaled the sweet smell of baby. He was overcome by a great sense of loss. Scarface had so much joy and happiness around him in his home, so much love and ease of being with his kin and his children and his horses. As the stars moved across the Mountain, Thorfinn considered his life. Would it always be like this? Would he always be the outsider, the traveler looking for comfort with another man's wife? Never to have his own woman, his own longhouse? Never to hear the sweet songs of his own children?

Ribbons of green light shimmered in the darkness above the mountains and reflected off the melt water lakes. Thorfinn felt old and alone. It is not enough, he told himself, to be in the world thus, a man separated from kin without wife and children. Misery enveloped him as never before. There was no one. He had taken the wife of another man to what end? He thought he could escape the family curse in Greenland. He was mistaken. His son had died. The woman he wanted would not talk to him. His life was cursed.

As the path dipped to the pasture surrounding Ebiwaz, Thorfinn saw someone beckoning to him from the bath house. He bid Berryface go

CHAPTER 34 — *Return to Thorness*

on alone with the child. As he got close to the opening of the bathhouse, Anna came out of the shadows. He took her into his arms. She laid her head against his heart and they remained silent for several minutes.

'Anna Anna. I thought you had no need of me. I have missed you.' Thorfinn pushed her through the flap into the interior. 'It has been too long. What happened to the child? Oh, woman, I have missed you.'

'It was not meant to be.'

'I have let my curse come to you. It is the curse of my ancestors to cause me pain and lose ones I love. Anna I have done this to you.'

'The spirit of the child left in peace.'

'I cannot live like this anymore.' Thorfinn held her face in his hands. He kissed her and pulled her down to lie with him on the ground. His hands found the smoothness of her body. It was as if they had never parted, each dissolving into the ecstasy of the other. Thorfinn felt an outpouring of light that reached deep into her body. They clung together until Thorfinn moved and bliss broke over them both.

Afterwards he leant against the rocks and cradled her in his arms.

'Ged stays at Gardar? There is nothing to stop us leaving together for Markland now.'

'You have no ship. I cannot travel in winter over the ice.'

'We will stay then till the spring thaw. Asmund has asked me to help him hunt the falcons in the mountains. I will not leave you again.' Thorfinn cupped her breast in his hand and brushed her nipple with his thumb. 'So beautiful. My Anna.' He bent to take her breast in his mouth.

'There is danger. Do not trust Asmund. See how he sharpens his axe. You do not see the way he looks at you. Skadi told him I called for you when the child came. He will never forget anything that damages the memory of his family. He wants me to have his child.'

'No Anna it could not be so. I have said I will give him ivory in exchange for staying the winter at Ebiwaz. I worked at the church in the name of Hvalsey. I took care of Ged. I bought luck for Ebiwaz with my payment of silver to the priest at Gardar to bury my companions. And the bones of the great Walrus Queen.' Thorfinn smiled. 'Besides I am his guest. He is bound by tradition not to harm me.'

'The treasure of the Nordsetur is great. Few make the journey and few return with the riches you have. If he kills you he need only announce his deed to Gunhar Olvadsson and he is within the law. Asmund can claim everything that is yours. He cannot pay the tithe the bishop demands unless he has your ivory and skins.'

'The rune of Locki came to me in the smoke last night. It is a warning. Come, let us not waste this time together. I have been away many turnings of the moon without you.' He lifted her so she sat astride him. He moved her in a slow sweet rhythm against his body. Anna felt again the delight of his strength; so unlike Ged who insisted without knowledge that his pleasure was hers.

Afterwards as they walked to the bay together, their thoughts became the secrets of the wind. Anna collected seaweed from the rocks while Thorfinn picked up driftwood frozen at the edge of the ice. Asmund watched them from the doorway of the house. Thorfinn paused on his old rock to stare out into the sea. The wind blew his red-gold hair back from his head and he pulled the grey cloak around him. To Anna for a moment, it was as if he had never left.

'You must go.' Anna pulled at the opening of his cloak. 'You must go to the land that Olaf talks of, the place where all is forgiven by the Christ God and rid yourself of this curse.'

'If it is true,' Thorfinn said to the wind. 'Olaf says the White Christ can change the pattern of the ripples here, the path allotted to me by the Norns. If I got to Herjolfsness before midwinter I could stay with a farmer until the ships from Iceland and England come in the spring. But only a fool travels in winter and I have had enough of ice and snow. I cannot go again without you. You must come with me.'

'You left me. Ged left me. The child died. I will not be alone again.'

'Thorfinn,' Asmund yelled from the house. 'Where are you? Come. Bring wood. I need fire to mend the axe before the hunt.'

Before he walked to the smithy Thorfinn whispered: 'On the breath of Thor I will never leave you again. We will go to Gardar and get Ged if that is what you want.'

'It is winter. No one leaves Ebiwaz in winter.'

CHAPTER 34 — *Return to Thorness*

He watched her walk into the house then limped across the stones to the smithy. Asmund was not mending an axe; he was sharpening a new blade to fit into an axe head. It was the finest and strongest blade Thorfinn had ever seen. The floor of the smithy was littered with broken tongs, part of a scythe, an old frying pan, bits of discarded metal and lumps of a spongy substance Thorfinn could not identify. He narrowly missed catching his arm on a jagged hook that stuck out from a shelf. There were pieces of wood piled near one wall.

Asmund kicked at the mess. A piece of wood flew into Thorfinn's leg. 'Widow Maker this place is called. But then you ain't got a wife so if you die you ain't going to make a widow is yer Iceland man?'

Thorfinn did not answer but bound up his leg with a rag while Asmund continued to rummage through the contents of the shed. The furnace was a small stone frame covered with clay and set over a shallow pit in the ground. It was not yet alight. On the other side of the hut another pit held wood Asmund was burning to charcoal for the furnace. He directed Thorfinn to place his driftwood into this pit and use the bellows to increase the heat. It was cramped in the smithy and Thorfinn found it difficult to keep his balance. It took all his concentration not to trip and fall across the fire pit.

'Not too steady on that leg are you?' Asmund held a hammer and banged at a piece of iron until it resembled an arrowhead. 'Easy to fall in here. Need to be careful when we go into the mountain.'

CHAPTER 35
The hunt

Every night Asmund sat with his new axe and reminded Thorfinn that come the night when the moon was darkest he must be Asmund's eyes and guide him through the mountains.

'Ye must give Ebiwaz a child by next spring,' he told Anna, as he looked along the blade at Thorfinn. 'If the seed sown last winter was bad, ye must get a good one. Children we must have from every woman to continue the memory of our family. If no children are here to recall our name when we are dead, then we are damned.' He placed the axe beside him. 'Well, woman, get these boots off me and prepare my bed. Ged knows the line of our family must be continued by the man who is fit to do it.' He took hold of Anna's breast as she bent over his leg. 'Small but it will grow fat for a baby of Ebiwaz to suck. 'Why do you stare, man from Iceland?'

Thorfinn turned away. There would be time, he said to himself. When the winter had gone, there would be time. He did not approach Anna again. He found the idea of stalking the mysterious black beast drew him to it. He allowed himself to dwell on how he would catch his creature, especially when his thoughts berated him about the futility of loving another man's wife. Where did the strange beast sleep? Did it only fly in the dark? Was it a creature such as Ged spoke about? Could he and Asmund trap such a being? Would it be possible to enter the realms of Hel as Ged had been able to do to keep them all safe?.

The house began to draw in with the depths of winter. The land was silent, claiming the knowledge of all life. The birds were silent

CHAPTER 35 — The hunt

in the time of wakening. Strange bones came to be washed up on the shore and strange shadows were seen around the dark ice floating in the bay. Some days the snow came so high up around the house that people did not get out of bed except to fuel the fire and remind themselves that there was a time when the land smiled, and the wind was so warm the doors could be left open.

Sokki remained perplexed by figures only he could see. Berryface tended their child and looked to his needs as well as she could. Sokki told her he spoke to the children he had with a bondswoman who had died a long time ago. The children had left Greenland as adults and now came only as specters to watch their father before he too moved into the shadows.

Asmund continued to insist Anna prepare the bed for him and Skadi. He followed her to the storerooms and pushed his sex against her when she passed him with a load of goods. In the corridor when he was not there it was as if a lascivious ghost waited, and made the hair bristle and the skin creep of any woman who walked that way.

Anna thought of lying with Asmund. He smelt of dung and fish oil and shit. She had heard the way Skadi grunted at night till Asmund was finished with her. Skadi never had a choice except when she bled. Anna found Ged's white feather and invoked the protection of Freyja. She found small shells and lit a lamp again to the old Norse gods. The spirits came back to the driftwood hung over her altar. With their odd wooden noses they pointed to the door and the bay beyond.

The men of Hvalsey came to Ebiwaz to discuss the tithes. What they had was precious to them and few trusted the protection of the White Christ if they had to pay for it so dear. Gunhar Bloodaxe said the priest was in league with the King of Norway and wanted the tithes from Greenland to make them poor so he could send his soldiers to govern them and take what he wanted any time.

Scarface raged at the bishop and royalty in general and advocated war with Norway on behalf of his ancestor, Eirik the Red. Iceland had been forced to become Christian. Gunhar said the king of Norway had threatened to kill every Icelander in Norway unless all men and women in Iceland became Christian.

Asmund cleaned his nails with the axe blade and considered; just how much did the Bishop and his priest expect? Farming land, falcons, ivory? Trade rights over Greenland itself? Night after night Olaf berated them with the need to support the clergy as the only men who knew the way to address the Christ God, until even Asmund told him to cease. Was not the presence of Ged at Gardar enough but they had to listen to Olaf and his endless dirge about the material needs of the priests and his bishop?

Thorfinn watched and listened.

Anna packed a nestbaggin with dried seal meat and berries and cheese and put it in the furthest storeroom. She asked Thorfinn if he could mend a pair of skates made from the leg bones of an old horse and put them with the nestbaggin of supplies.

'Asmund is desperate. The men are desperate. They cannot give to the White Christ what they have not,' she told Thorfinn. 'Give him what you have now or he will find a way to take it.'

When Thorfinn was not using the bellows for Asmund he spent the days removing ivory from the skulls of the whale-horse he had brought from the Nordsetur. The memory haunted him of the old white walrus floating upright by the edge of the ice. He saw again the lifeless eyes of his dead companions and heard the words of the skraeling witch. Had he not faced the wrath of the Great Ocean to get this ivory? Had he not battled with the white bear and the spirits of the ice? While Asmund stayed in the warmth of his bed, his needs tended by the women around him.

He could not rid his mind of the last night he had spent at Thorness. He remembered the children singing as they spun and sewed and the way Scarface beamed at his pregnant wife. Could he ever have this with Anna, he asked himself.

Sometimes the smell of horse took him back to his home in Iceland. He tried to imagine what his son looked like now, how old he would be, if he would be tall and strong, if he was a good hunter, if he had his own bow and spear yet, if he ever asked about his real father.

Anna worked at her weaving with difficulty. 'Grandmother Ghost,' she said as the wool knotted and split and her fingers cracked in the

CHAPTER 35 — *The hunt*

cold, 'you have tricked me. I cannot leave Ebiwaz. He cannot stay. How can we ever be together?' Tears blurred her vision as she thought of Thorfinn on the mountain with Asmund. Would Asmund wait till Thorfinn stood near a precipice? Would he send an arrow into the dark so it found the heart of Thorfinn and claim that he thought he shot an animal? Would he walk behind and slip the knife into Thorfinn when his leg gave way?

Asmund announced that the time approached when the hunt for the bird with the diamonds on its claws would take place. He would carry the weapons to lessen the load on Thorfinn's damaged leg. He instructed Berryface to ensure all clothes and boots were rubbed with fat so to be as waterproof as possible, for it was cold and treacherous in the high mountains and a man could slip easily and fall to his death at any time.

Berryface and Sokki found a dead albatross in the home paddock while they were out secretly looking under rocks for a nest of frozen grubs. Sokki told everyone it was a sign from the gods of the Great Ocean. Short Irish made dire predictions about the weather, insisting that all of Greenland would soon be frozen solid because of a new constellation that had risen above the Grey Mountain.

Thorfinn was feeling more and more uncomfortable in the house as the darkness and the cold intensified. 'I will be safe on the mountain,' he told Anna. 'I am strong through my leg is painful. I must go. I want to catch this creature as much as Bjarni does. It will be a good hunt.'

Thorfinn did not see the tears on her face.

That night Asmund told O'Flarty not to push the beam across the big wooden door but to leave it unbarred. He instructed Short Irish to prepare the bow and arrows. The wind pushed black smoke though the louvers of the smoke hole where the tomte sat warming his toes. A piece of driftwood in the fire burnt in the shape of a raven. The form hovered in the fire and faded with the flames as the wood burnt.

Something set up a banging on the big door, forcing it open.

'Who's there?' Asmund stood in front of his high seat with his axe in his hand.

'We come to speak to the Lawgiver of Hvalsey,' a voice came above the barking of the dogs and the wind. 'I am Rhvford Ekvallsson.'

Two large human shaped bundles threw themselves through the doorway and into the warmth of the longhouse.

'I am here with a message from the priest at Gardar. We demand the protection of your hearth.'

'And don't forget me. Ketil Half-Ear from Gardar. Come with Nose-Saw, the sword of me ancestors.'

The two men shook themselves and stood gaping at the color inside the longhouse. Their skin was spotted red with cold. Ice fell off their clothes.

'Who? Who?' said Sokki. 'Who comes here in the dead of winter?'

'The priest's man from Gardar and a wild Viking who accompanies him,' replied Ketil Half-Ear.

With much cursing and stamping the visitors were relieved of their outer clothes and fur hats and settled with food at the fire. Ketil Half-Ear had lost one eye as well as most of the hair from one side of his face. 'Fell in a fire drunk,' he said when he noticed Thorfinn staring at him.

'Yes,' said Asmund. 'Well I remember you. You met us at the bay of Gardar and bid us work in the name of the priest Father Torfi. How goes my brother?'

'Asmund Lawbinder,' Rhvford Ekvallsson lisped through his broken teeth, 'Ged Romfortsson has stopped carving. He mutters to himself all day about bones and dances with devil dogs. He brings fear to the other workers. All work on the church has stopped. The Bishop of Greenland will arrive from Iceland in the spring when the ice clears. The church must be finished.'

Ketil Half-Ear walked up to Asmund and thumped the table. 'This brother of yours knows the spirits behind the world. The ones what want to harm us Norse. He tells us he can hold them away, trap 'em in his carving. But he don't carve. He don't do nothing but talk about bones and something about a whale-horse.'

'The Holy Father is unable to cast out the demons that possess my brother?'

CHAPTER 35 — *The hunt*

'The Holy Father has failed. Ged Romfortsson does not eat. He does not wash. He does not sleep. He calls for his wife and this man here, Thorfinn.'

'The Holy Father bids you send the wife of Ged Romfortsson to Gardar with the man Thorfinn Markland-Farer to act as their protector and …'

'And yer t'bring wif you the tithes from the Nordsetur,' put in Ketil Half-Ear with a grin at Thorfinn. 'When yer left us at Gardar yer sailed under the banner of the Christ did yer not? We all need ter break the back of the tithes, Viking son. The demands of the bishop are too much for us farmers of Greenland. Jest in case you was thinking of doing something else with what you got in the Nordsetur, that is Thorfinn Markland-Farer.'

Thorfinn regarded Ketil with suspicion. 'Indeed?' he said. 'Why is this so?'

Asmund scowled. Thorfinn alive might still be of use, especially if he took his treasure from the Nordsetur to Gardar to appease the priest. 'If the Holy Father says it, then it must be so. Thorfinn you will go and offer your services and your ivory in the name of Ebiwaz. You will care and protect the wife of Ged while she cares for my brother.'

'What will be left for me Ketil Half-Ear?' Thorfinn said. 'You ain't stealing my treasure from the Nordsetur, try as you may.'

'Yer git what the rest of us get from this fucking church. Nothing. And may the Bishop of Greenland find his bed at the bottom of the Great Ocean before he steals any more from us.'

Rhvford Ekvallsson was too busy inspecting the firelight on his rings to join the conversation. Things had not gone well for him at Gardar. The priest had refused to let him bed the chief's daughter until the church was finished. The priest hounded him daily to get the men left at Gardar to work on the building. Supplies were short. Ale was rationed. Few people hunted and most of the cows and pigs had died. The men were slow now, slow moving and slow thinking, more concerned with surviving the cold then anything to do with the coming of bishop they neither knew nor cared about.

Anna sat on her bed. These men had decided her fate. Why did she not get up and say, no, this is my place. I will stay here. With Berryface and Brigitta and Skadi and the babies. With one thump Asmund could send her sprawling into the fire, subdued, obedient. He could demand she lie with him as his brother's wife. The black and white pattern floated in front of her eyes. She could not move. She lay back and let the pattern eat at her consciousness.

'Yer say the Priest wants this man Thorfinn too? As well as me brother's wife? And how am I to hold this farm with all me labor gone?' Asmund kicked the nearest dog who snapped at his foot.

'Yer brother wants this man Thorfinn. Calls for him to help him with someone called the Whale-horse Queen. Says he knows what has to be done.'

'Send him Asmund,' put in Sokki. 'We can look after his stuff while he is gone.'

'O'course if you don't want to send them both yer can give ivory and silver so the priest can pay for another carver to come to Greenland. Few in Iceland I hear.'

'Does not eat yer say? Stands and calls to devils all day? Aye they had both better go then to me brother and care for him so he starts carving again.'

Sokki took the opportunity to stuff a grub into his mouth while Berryface fed him softened bark from the willow tree.

CHAPTER 36
The journey through ice

It took but a day of fine weather for preparations for the journey to be completed. Asmund decided that Thorfinn may be of use to him alive after all. He could look after Ged long enough for Ged to finish the carving on the church. He had ivory and skins to take with him. The priest knew this. Likely the Icelandic man would get himself fastened onto another man's wife and come to grief. That was the way of strangers.

The sun now only came into the day for half the length of an oil wick if that. Thorfinn told everyone he was disappointed the hunt for the creature with the diamond claws had to be cancelled. He told Asmund he would return the following winter to help him catch this beast. Short Irish observed that the new group of stars on the horizon had moved to the north of the Gray Mountain and thus travel was favorable.

The sledge was packed with provisions. Asmund had arranged for them to take the fleece from a good sheep, a needle case and sheers, the pieces of a loom, an old spindle whorl and a new tunic and boots for Ged. Skadi saw there was food and drink for all and a small skein of ale and whey to keep them warm when they stopped. The horses were harnessed and shod with iron nails to tread the ice, their long hair carefully arranged by O'Flarty. Short Irish gave them horse coats to use when needed.

Anna sat in the sledge with the treasure from the Nordsetur carefully packed beside her in an old nestbaggin. The household clustered around to bid farewell.

'Will I ever see you again?' she said sadly. 'I lost my family in the West and now I must leave you all. I fear I will not see Byggvir grow. And Bjarni come to his first love.'

'You go to Ged,' said Berryface. 'A child may come to you yet for the spring. We will wait for you.' She passed the carving of a pregnant woman to Anna. 'From Brigitta. You have them both now.' She smiled a secret woman smile and her black eyes sparkled.

'Take this,' said Skadi and reluctantly handed Anna the metal wolf's head. 'You believe in them old gods more than me. Better you have it so they can protect you.'

'I will miss Ebiwaz. Miss you all. The moss on the path. The wind in the roof at night and the insects in summer. I have come to know the spirits in the bay. They talk to me Asmund, they do.'

'It is your duty girl,' said Asmund. 'The spirit ancestors of Ebiwaz are your ancestors now. They go with you to protect you.'

'Grandmother Ghost? Do you think she travels with me?'

'Jest like the old witch ter send yer off into the winter,' said Sokki.

'You will come back,' said Berryface. 'People do. They come back. You will be safe. That grandmother will guide you. And Thorfin's ancestors will run before the horses and show the way over the ice.'

O'Flarty came to the sledge. 'That god of Olaf's will also take care of you.' He pressed a stone cross into her hand.

'I will come back,' said Anna. 'Byggvir will be walking then Skadi.'

'Aye he will. And you might have a baby with you. A baby for Ebiwaz,' Skadi thought it best to add.

Then they were gone. Rhvford Ekvallsson and Ketil Half-Ear walking beside the horses. Thorfinn walking silently beside the sledge; Thorfinn, with the grey elfin cloak on his shoulders, never looking sideways or behind after he had bid them all a curt farewell. Strands of his long hair curled out from under his hat; his face and beard were wrapped in wadmal. He leant heavily on his staff feeling for rocks under the snow.

He found it difficult to say farewell to these people when in his heart he wished never to see them again. It did not matter. The gods brought people together at whim and they found a path together for

CHAPTER 36 — *The journey through ice*

a while, or they separated. It was the way of the Norse and always had been. He let a feeling of release and lightness sweep though his body. Now he and Anna travelled together. He watched the bowed form of Anna as the sledge moved beside him.

Anna saw the lands of Ebiwaz disappear into a frozen whiteness. Thus it had been when she left the Western Settlement. Now she was losing everything and everyone she loved again, travelling to a place unknown, to a husband who was also unknown and unpredictable. An image came to her of Ged, stretching with release on the quilt under her, his skin as ice, his white hair in strands around his face, the sickly smell of him on her body, like something not human.

A fine dry wind flew over the ground around and behind them, pulling the surface of the ice into writhing tongues that flicked around their bodies and stung their flesh. They moved slowly, the air forming tiny crystals of ice on their clothes and skin. Birds clumped frozen in the snow or huddled together in a crevasse of rock. The sun did not come; the moon came instead and hung close to the horizon to send liquid fire onto the ice in front of them.

Thorfinn almost fell when they crossed the surface of a lake. His hand slammed against the back of the sledge in an effort to regain his balance. He made little of it but Anna insisted he ride in the sledge to rest his leg. She tied the skates to her boots and kept her hands swathed in wadmal and fur and blindly followed Ketil and Rhvford.

They stopped in a deserted house to light a fire and take a meal. It was colder than Anna ever remembered. She felt her thoughts become slow, unclear. Rhvford pushed them to continue after a short rest. Anna felt his anger when he spoke of the priest, which he did only to curse the man and his connection with the royalty of Norway. Ketil trudged on with his legendary strength; he leered with his scars white and threatening whenever Anna caught his eye.

Anna imagined the family at Ebiwaz safe around the fire, with the big door shut fast and the demons of the mountain hungry outside. The same demons that pursued them now in the dark lonely world. Yet she travelled with Thorfinn to be with Ged. They would all be together again. This was her prayer. Now Freyja had granted her wish. She felt her thoughts dull with the cold that penetrated even her mind.

Exhausted and stiff they came at last to the plain of Gardar. Anna thought she could hear the faint sounds of a flute though the roaring of the Arctic wind. As they slowly crossed the plain towards the farm and its buildings it was impossible to know if it was the time of sleep or waking. The festal hall was silent, covered in ice where water had frozen in jagged planes. The windows were bound in pig skin and the smell of fire was all around the farm. Rhvford dragged his charges to the house and banged on the door. The Chieftain of Gardar sat with his bondsman polishing a fine metal sword. The priest dozed upright in his bed cupboard. The women were not in sight.

With a loud hiss Rhvford announced his entrance. Thorfinn staggered into the longhouse with Anna and Ketil. Everyone was suddenly awake. The priest, Father Torfi, leered though swollen lips until his gaze came to rest on Thorfinn and Anna.

'At last the heathen comes from the larder of the Nordsetur. And this is the woman who will heal the carver from the fit that will not let him work?'

'Yes,' Rhvford Ekvallsson pushed a shivering Anna in front of the priest and moved to the fire pit.

'Then take her to him and let us be rid of the devils that inhabit his body.'

'He calls for the Icelander as well.'

'Well take them to him. Now! This church will be finished afore the summer, Rhvford Ekvallsson. And you, wife of Ged Romfortsson, get that carver working. Lie with him. Let the devils that torment him come into your body if you must. If you and your family are to have any luck for the rest of your life you will get him back to work. Thorfinn Markland -Farer, Rhvford tells me you have come from the Nordsetur. Good. We will talk.'

'The carver refuses to come into the house. He stays in the hall with the other men who rest here for winter,' said Rhvford. 'You will have to go to him.' He dragged a thick fur off one of the vacant beds

CHAPTER 36 — *The journey through ice*

and threw it at Thorfinn. 'You will need that in the hall. It is as cold as Hel in there. I stay at my house across the way. You can find me there if you want me.'

'Come.' Ketil beckoned Thorfinn and Anna to follow him. 'We need food.' He picked up a bucket of cheese, a large malodorous quilt and a bowl of dried seal meat and led them out the door.

Anna followed with her hand on Thorfinn's arm to steady them both. Ketil took them to the hall a little way from the longhouse. The workers who had decided to stay at Gardar during the winter had erected a domed tent of wadmal and turf in the middle of the hall. Smoke came out of an opening in the top of the tent, blackening the stones of the ceiling above. It was grimy inside but warmer than the empty space outside. There were a few long haired horses in one corner of the hall and a sheep beside them. Most workers had returned to their farms for the winter, but some men had stayed and built sleeping booths inside the tent to be as close to the fire as possible. There was thick straw on the floor. The hall smelt male, and of animal.

Ged stood outside the tent, jigging up and down to keep warm. There was a walrus skull on a stick beside him poked into the ground. He had a half rusted sword attached to his belt. He smiled his angelic smile and placed his fingers around Anna's neck. She reached to kiss him. Although his face was partly covered by long flowing hair, his skin and eyes held a peculiar luminescence. He looked at Thorfinn with interest.

'Husband. Come to the fire. Your flesh is frozen.'

'Ah ha. Frozen. The children of the Whale-horse Queen. Wife, have you come to help me bury the bones of the whale-horse children? Too late. Too late. Thorfinn comes too. Do you have a message for me? You are the man sent to the sacred island by the gods. The bones have been dug up. Look at this.' He indicated the walrus skull on the stick. 'Dug from the precious grave we made. There are evil ghosts at work here. I have a plan. You come with a message. I know.'

'Oh my husband. How thin and cold you are. Look, Thorfinn. Look how dreams escape and come to torment him. Oh Ged.'

'Dog dug up that thing on the stick,' Ketil said. 'After the rains came and washed it back to the surface. Now he won't leave it alone day or night. Jest stands there muttering to his self. Possessed by the spirit of them wild men what died at sea and whose bones be buried in the churchyard there. Look at his skin. Spotted like he was a dead man already. Its them spirits wot he can't control talking to him.' Ketil emptied the cheese bucket and left the hall quietly.

'Ghosts? Demons? I take your fears. I dream your dreams Ketil Half-Ear. They come to me now even when I am awake. Bad dreams. Bad creatures. I take them from you and live your fears. Anna. Wife. Do not cry. I will save you and all of Greenland from the demons who come from the spaces between the stars.'

Anna stood helpless in front of Ged. 'What do you want Ged? How can I care for you?'

Ged turned away and walked up to Thorfinn.

Anna followed. 'What am I to do Thorfinn? I cannot lock him up like Asmund used to when the fit was upon him.'

'Listen son of Iceland who travels too long.' Ged began to circle around Thorfinn. 'You Icelandic man who came to us from the island of the gods. You seek wife and steading. Soon you will have all. The Whale-horse Queen walks amongst us again. I hear the dead moaning in the bay under the ice.'

'Yes husband. We hear you. But first come to the fire.'

'They tell me I must take arms and fight her. On the open sea I must kill her so when she dies her blood will not foul the shores of Greenland and poison the sons of Eirik the Red. Do not fear. It is me she calls for. Listen to me man from Iceland.'

'You must be strong to go on such a journey. Come do as your wife says.'

Ged allowed Thorfinn to lead him into the booth. Anna fed him bits of cheese and warm reindeer stew. Ged opened his mouth for her like a baby. He was very thin and smelt odd, like old meat. His clothes were ragged and two of his fingers bruised by the cold. The sword at his side scraped his clothes as he moved.

CHAPTER 36 — *The journey through ice*

The few men left at Gardar from the working party stared at Anna with lust, then looked away as Thorfinn met their gaze. His red-gold hair hung in thick coils and the strength in his arms and shoulders was accentuated by his wet cloak.

Ketil returned with the bucket full of ale. He waved it under Thorfinn's nose. All were suddenly alert. They crowded around Ketil.

'Nothing but what them servants won't do for a bit of silver,' said Ketil. 'Wot we all puts in for,' he said as he sloshed the bucket at Thorfinn. 'Silver or ivory. Thems inside is not particular.'

'And we all gits to fuck the maid too does we?' asked Boltof.

'Help yerselves,' Ketil said laughing. 'Me silver's still good and apparently me prick is too.'

Anna filled a horn for Ged and held it to his lips.

'I gets it out the back door for a bit of silver from them servants what looks after the ale for that priest man and the lawspeaker,' said Ketil. 'Now Ged here ain't slept the past moon but a candle or two. Keeps muttering about music wot comes in the night. Says it is played by Yellowbritches in the hall of Freyja. And some shadow bird wot follows him.'

'Git him to lie down for a start, wife of Ged,' said Boltof. 'Needs a woman here to look after him. All them women left when the winter come. Except of course the women inside the house, but they don't count for workers like us.'

Ketil threw the covering onto a bed pallet near the fire. 'Place for you lot over here. Jest because the dead want to freeze don't mean the living have to. You'll all have ter fit in there, in that bed cupboard where Ged is supposed to sleep. The priest don't want us workers in the house wif his precious women.'

'Not even Rhvford can get his hands on 'em women inside the house.'

'Ged have you news of Yellowbritches?' Anna said.

'I hear the dead,' Ged said and waved his hands in the air. 'He plays in the hall of Freyja.'

'I thought I heard his music on the wind as we came here. Why do you say he is dead?'

Ged began jigging up and down and laughing. 'I hear it now. I hear it now.'

'I saw him in a dream the hall of Freyja once. He was happy.' Anna smiled at the memory of Yellowbritches and Old Pa in the hall of Freyja. 'He was with Old Pa. They were both happy. Old Pa wore a cat hat like a helmet. Yellowbritches was playing music with a black haired man. Is that how you see him husband?'

'You know nothing,' said Ged. 'You see nothing.'

With much coaxing and direction Anna and Thorfinn led him to the sleeping booth by the fire and made sure he could still see the stick with the skull on top through the wadmal curtain. Thorfinn put the fur on the bed boards and lay the quilt on top. They pushed Ged into bed and squeezed in beside him.

Anna lay between the two men and gently stroked Ged's forehead. Thorfinn pulled the elfin cloak over them all to trap the heat from as many bodies as possible. He lay with one arm across Anna and Ged to still Ged's restless movement. At last Ged slept, his face free of pain and shadows. Thorfinn drew Anna into the circle of his arms and they lay together while the light of the Arctic stars glittered over the plain of Gardar.

Thorfinn did not sleep. He wanted this woman. He stroked her breast and let himself drift into memory. There was a fire; it was warm. There was grain on the table, and mead and yellow cheese. He saw his wife at her loom in the house of his father. She was pregnant.

He bent his head as Anna shifted against him in her sleep, and kissed her hair. Ged stirred. Thorfinn looked at the pale malodorous body lying so soft and unresponsive beside Anna. Ged and Anna, man and wife? Was this a union in the eyes of Thor? A marriage blessed by the White Christ and his followers? Thorfinn thought again of Scarface and Brigitta. How did Ged know what he wanted? Witless as he was he said the truth at times.

CHAPTER 37
Rhvford Ekvallsson and the bishop

Rhvford Ekvallsson thought he knew the men from Ebiwaz. He had worked with them during the summer assembly. He had been to the house of Asmund. A good house, a wealthy house. He had watched Thorfinn and Asmund during the judgment. He had noted the sacrifice on the steps of the church and the immediate departure of Thorfinn and Scarface. They were strong men who did not scrape mud off the ground before the priest walked. He would have liked to offer Thorfinn the comfort of his house across the bay; someone to talk to other than his sons, who only grunted at him. The problem was Ged. And the woman. Thorfinn would bring them both.

Rhvford's wife had died of the coughing sickness last winter. His eldest son had travelled with Einar, son of the chieftain of Gardar, to the court of King Sigurd Jerusalem-Farer in Norway. They took a polar bear, fine ivory and many skins to show the king Greenland was a rich country and could support a bishop. It was important the King of Norway knew who the people of Greenland wanted for a bishop. Rhvford's son carried this message.

Rhvford and his kin, however, had no say in who that bishop was. Instead the bishop had sent a priest, Father Torfi, to issue orders and ensure that all was done in a manner that benefited himself. Rhvford had helped the priest, but the priest's conduct was becoming irksome. He demanded the local farmers provide tithes for the church and taxes for the Norwegian King. He demanded the best land for his cattle and as much food as he wanted.

'Is there no end to the things this priest wanted?' Rhvford asked himself. Was there any need for this meddling priest to still be in Greenland? All building had ceased in the darkest time of winter. Everyone waited for the return of the sun. And Rhvford waited for a wife. 'When the church is finished,' the priest told Rhvford, 'there will be no taking of wives before then.' He commanded the women at Gardar stay by his side and receive communion every day.

Rhvford polished his rings against his robes and hissed though the gaps in his teeth. He stood in the opening of the hall and surveyed his workforce. The priest was, as usual, tucked up by the fire in the long house with the women. The sun was below the horizon and a curtain of frozen water closed every opening. Ketil pushed past him to piss in the snow. Ketil's piss vaporized in the cold air.

'Where is that man from Hvalsey?' Rhvford asked. Ketil pointed. Rhvford strode into the hall and banged against a large metal shield. The silence in the hall deepened. He banged again, holding the shield against the bed Ketil indicated. A muttering came from within. Ged stumbled out of the bed. He ignored Rhvford and walked to the walrus head on its stick. He began to pat it and look into its mouth. He put something into his own mouth and sucked on it. The man from Iceland came next, followed by the wife of the carver.

'You, Thorfinn Markland-Farer.' Rhvford frowned and waved a piece of paper in front of Thorfinn, who was busy struggling with something under his tunic. 'Father Torfi bids me show you this. I have a letter here from the King of Norway. It says you are to give ivory and skin to the bishop as tithes from the settlement of Hvalsey. There have been no tithes from the Eastern Settlement so far. The bishop will have nothing to sell in Norway.'

'Norway, yer piece of dragon's piss? Iceland, yer mean,' said Ketil.

'Quiet dwarf's spawn or I will have your guts wrapped around the bishop's boots.'

A few men peered out of their sleeping cupboards. Ketil bristled with the excitement of a fight. Thorfinn put his hand on Ketil's forearm. 'Let it go friend. The earth will claim us all in the end. Let it go.'

CHAPTER 37 — Rhvford Ekvallsson and the bishop

'You have goods from the Nordsetur, Thorfinn Markland-Farer? You wish to exchange these goods for silver? You must take them to Norway or give them to the priest who will sell them for you. The King of Norway has made a law that all trade from Greenland must go to Norway. No goods will go to Iceland. All trading ships from Greenland will go to Norway where the King of Norway will offer a safe harbor. If this does not happen the King will take the ships from Greenland to be his own as the Greenlanders will be against the law of the King and the Church of the Christ in all the lands of the Norse.'

'Ah go piss yourself,' said Ketil. 'Church and King can go fuck each other. If Thorfinn goes to Norway with his treasure that greedy king will gobble it all in taxes and what is left will be grabbed by that bishop o'yours.'

Ketil took hold of Rhvford and heaved him out the door into the wind. Rhvford stumbled into the frozen landscape. The wind had blown the snow into little peaks as if the plain of Gardar was a choppy sea of solid waves. Rhvford fought his way back to the longhouse. There was no sign of the priest or the chieftain. He decided to wait until the wind dropped and he could return to his own house across the frozen bay.

There was an Irish bondswoman scrubbing at a pot near him; long black hair fell to her waist over a loose shift that covered the fragility of her body. It was said the wife of the chieftain of Gardar had found her wandering alone though the hills after mid-summer, calling out to her father. Now she worked in the house in return for somewhere to live.

Rhvford could hear the priest and the chieftain snoring loudly. No one else was around. He pulled the woman into the darkness of a corridor. She put up no resistance to his need. With one hand tangled in her hair he lifted her tunic, pushed her against the wall, and found some comfort for his bad temper.

CHAPTER 38
Second sight

Thorfinn watched Ged avoid the bits of food Anna was trying to get into his mouth. Ged moved like kelp under water; a slow fluid dance to music only he could hear. For one flame of the candle Ged laughed with Anna as they both stood and regarded the walrus skull on the stick. As Anna went to uproot the stick to bring it closer to the fire, Ged hit her hard on the breast.

'Leave it, woman. It is mine, mine. Only I can hear what she says.'

Ged menaced Thorfinn with his sword as Thorfinn approached. He made as if to stab him, then let the sword drop. He sat on the straw and looked up at them with tears in his eyes.

'Thorfinn. Forgive me. This woman annoys me beyond measure. I know you care for her but I am sore pressed to find a way to do my work with her around me. Night and day. Day and night. I must build a boat. In the ice cavern where the spirit of the dead moan for release, I will find her. I will fight her and win. We will all meet in Valhalla.'

'Leave 'em,' said Ketil. 'Ain't no one going t'er get him to do the priest's work today. Least he is out of the snow and safe in here wif us. Git back t' yer bed or warm yerselves by the fire here.'

'Cold one today,' said Boltof the Wise who lay in the bed next to Ketil. 'Priest will stay in house with women ter took after him and feed him ale. Leave the food for Ged there by the skull. He'll calm when the dog comes and sits with him. Thinks the dog's his ancestor come back to help. Thinks it tells him things.'

CHAPTER 38 — *Second sight*

Thorfinn guided Anna away from Ged and his skull. They sat in front of the fire and tried not to listen to Ged sucking and scratching at the skull. Anna took up some mending to disguise her tears. At last Ged came to the hearth and began drawing in the ash. 'Valhalla,' he muttered kneeling over his drawing. 'This ship must take me to the Hall of Odin if I die in battle with the Whale-horse Queen. I must protect the people of Greenland. Thorfinn and Ketil and Anna and Asmund and Skadi and Sokki. It is my sacred duty Thorfinn Markland-Farer. The demons have escaped. It is my duty to capture them. But I cannot carve anymore. I am not strong enough.'

He looked up at Anna who was staring at him with her hands helpless in front of her. 'Take her, Thorfinn. I do not want any. And well rid I am of the ways of women and of the world. Listen. They call. They call me. I am coming. I am coming.'

'At least wear this.' Anna put the cloak she had been mending around his shoulders. Thorfinn put a bowl of hot stew by the side of his drawing. Ged threw off the cloak and knocked over the stew. The wind howled, the fire spat and smoked as a storm encircled the steading. Anna thought she could again hear the faint sound of a flute when the hail was loudest.

There was nothing to do but wait till the storm had been swallowed by the red rocks of Gardar. Ged remained scribbling on a piece of hide as the men returned to the warmth of their beds. Thorfinn drew Anna into the comfort of his arms. They lay together in the dark under the elfin tunic; this time the wind did not freeze the tears that fell on Thorfinn's shoulder. He kissed her tenderly, enraptured by the smell and feel of woman, this woman, his woman.

'He pushes me away Thorfinn. What am I to do? I am less to him then one of the demons he chases in his dreams.'

'Leave him. Come away with me. We could get a ship. From Herjolfsness. Ships come and go from there all the time. Travel to that place Olaf talks about, where curses are lifted. He does not want you.'

'We would be outlaws. Cursed by the priest and the Law. It would be wrong to leave him when he is like this. I gave Asmund my promise with Frejya as my witness.'

'Olaf says that the Christ God forgives everything when you fight for Him. And all bad things the ancestors did go away too. There is a curse on my family. I told you once.' Thorfinn brushed the hair from her face and rolled her on top of him.

Ged stood alone by the walrus skull, oblivious to all around him. He chewed and spat and made odd gestures to frighten away the dangers he alone could see. 'Listen,' he said suddenly. 'Yellowbritches plays.'

The priest came into the hall. 'I come to speak to you men. To all you traders and hunters. Is Rhvford here?'

'Gone to his steading. Lonely wifout a wife.' Ketil rolled over and pushed his head under a bunch of furs. 'But yr would not know about that wif all them wimmen in there, would yer priest?'

The men stared blearily at the figure of the holy man. Ged looked up, his skin and hair the color of snow, and smiled. He held up a piece of hide with the drawing of a neat row of walrus skulls down the centre. Thorfinn and Anna sat up. Anna began to search in the bed for wadmal to bind around her hands. No one looked at the priest or said anything. The priest read from a document written, he said, by the Harbor Master of Bergin.

Thorfinn felt the old anger rising: 'What pig shit is this Priest? Who are you to say who we can trade with and who we cannot?'

'It is sanctioned by the King of Norway,' the priest said, shaking the document at the recumbent figures. 'And sanctioned by the Bishop of Greenland. You men will do as they do in Iceland and trade only with Norway. As the Bishop says and the King says. Or you will starve and your wives will bring forth no issue.'

'You might as well return to the graveyard and talk to them bones priest. An' what do Scarface say?' Ketil emerged from his pile of furs. 'Odin says never listen to a priest in a black mood without a horn of ale to soften the blows?'

'Or poison to salt the meat,' came a voice from somewhere.

'Listen.' The priest shook his fist at the ground and raised his voice. 'I will have that church ready by summer. The witless carver

CHAPTER 38 — Second sight

from Hvalsey will finish the carving. It is his design. It shows the pagan devils overcome by the light of prayer. Why the fuck does he not work ? His wife is here. His friend is here. But he does nothing. He stands all day by the graveyard and mutters and bangs.'

'Building a dog house for his friends.'

'Got a ghost inside him. Men are scared of 'em. Think he swallowed a ghost what was put in the dogs dinner. No one wants it ter get inter them too.'

The priest shook his fist again. 'Let the wife go to him,' he shouted. 'Let the devils within be cast out by the sacrament of marriage. You woman. Be as wife to him. Release the devils within his body into your cunt. Cursed be woman for this reason!'

Ged stopped his flowing dance and walked outside. Anna got out of bed and followed. The black and white pattern was forming at the edge of her vision, making movement difficult. There was little escape from the freezing wind. Her face burnt; she could barely feel her hand and feet. It was never as cold as this in the Western Settlement. Thorfinn could take her away from this cold Hel forever; protect her, make her laugh, give her the keys of his house, make children with her. They could go to Iceland together. But there was always Ged. And her contract with Asmund. Would it be like this till the end of her life?

'Go woman,' said Ged as if he could hear her thoughts. 'Leave me to my task.'

Thorfinn came behind Anna with a cloak he placed gently over her shoulders. The priest spat at the dog following Ged and returned to the house. Ged stopped by the graveyard wall. He had accumulated a large amount of wood and whalebone. He began to rearrange this in a determined manner.

Anna and Thorfinn stood and watched him.

'Leave me. Both of you.'

'No, not this time.'

'Go. Useless beings.' Ged waved a knife. 'Go. I have no need of any of you any longer.'

'Husband, 'Anna said . 'Ged Romfortsson from the steading of Ebiwaz in Hvalsey. I Anna Kerldottir. I am your wife. Thorfinn is your friend.'

'I have work to do. I do not know either of you.' Ged bent his long body around his work and the wind pulled his clothes into dark wings behind him. Anna and Thorfinn stood watching. A shadow moved above them, like the passing of a low cloud.

Rage boiled in Thorfinn. Why should this man have a wife? Why should he not trade with who ever he wanted. Had he spent time in the Nordsetur to come back to this? He turned from Anna and Ged and walked into the hills unaware of the pain in his leg. He climbed until the sky and the rocks and the settlement merged into a blue glow on the surface of the earth below him. It seemed to him that his life had not changed since the day he was found on the rocks at Hvalsey. He had no home, no family. He had lost his son. Markland seemed like a dream, or a memory from another life.

No one, king or bishop, could control the trade in the Great North Ocean. Ships came and went without the knowledge of anyone. Regardless of kings and priests and wine soaked bishops. Thorfinn had seen for himself the ships made by the Greenlanders. The Viking fathers knew the secrets of the Great Ocean better than anyone. Timber was there for the taking in Markland. And iron to make nails.

He sat glaring at the world until the bell rang for the next meal, then slowly walked back to the longhouse.

CHAPTER 39
Herjolfsness

That night Thorfinn sat in bed with his arms around Anna. Ged lay unconscious in the bed place nearest the wall, drugged with ale and a mysterious black syrup provided by a healer woman from Rhvford's farm over the bay. The men grunted in their cups with the pleasure of Ketil's ale and the company of the Irish serving woman who had come to sit with them and the ale bucket in the hall.

'Irish princess, yr say?' Ketil said. 'We in Greenland don't hold with royalty. 'Beautiful you are but I never seen a princess with black under her toenails and marks on her hands like yerself.'

'You ain't never seen a princess,' said Boltof.

The princess smiled and twisted her fingers through Ketil's beard. Ketil took her upon his knee.

'I was once in Herjolfsness,' Ketil said. 'There is a harbor where trading ships come before the summer ice. It is a good place with a wide beach and a narrow opening to the harbor where ships can be safe. Yr know Thorfinn a man and woman could get a passage from Herjolfsness for the price of a bit of ivory.' Ketil grinned and rubbed his face against the Irish princess.

Thorfinn held Anna and stroked her softly and with passion as Ketil became increasingly preoccupied with the Irish woman. It was easy in the dim light with the smell of sex and the earth around them. Gently, silently, he implored her and she came to his longing with Ged snoring beside them. Silently they moved together and a sweet peace came to them both.

'Oh, Anna, I have missed you. I had such dreams of you and my son in the Nordsetur. I want to take you to Iceland and claim what is mine by birth. I want to find my son. He is a lad of many seasons now.'

'Come with you to Iceland? How could I leave Greenland? It is everything I know. You must go and find your son because he is your son.'

'You Anna will give me a son to be his brother. The child you lost awaits a home with me. You are already the mother of my children.'

'It was not shown to me who was the father of that child.' Anna reached for the small cross O'Flarty had given her. She felt herself lift from her body as she had done when the child died. 'It could have been Ged. It could have been you.'

Thorfinn felt as if bolt of wadmal had jammed itself in his guts.

'You mean it could have been the child of Ged?'

Anna pressed O'Flarty's cross into her heart. 'I cannot tell you anything but the truth. Freyja demands only the right of the mother to bear. It is unknown who fathered the child.'

Thorfinn pushed himself away from Anna and into the circle of men by the fire. Ged remained snoring in the bed.

'Witless?' Thorfinn asked himself. Perhaps not so witless if he could push seed into her womb. His seed? This was not the knowledge of life given to man. It was beyond his awareness. This was business between women and the gods. He preferred to get as much ale as possible into him to further understand the situation. He reached for the ale bucket abandoned by Ketil for once.

Ged flung his arm across Anna, emitted a loud howl and scratched his way out of the bed. He ran out of the hall. Anna lay as if in a dream, all thought dissolving into the pattern sprawling though her mind. When the snow had covered the stones in the graveyard, all men were in bed and the last oil lamp finished, Thorfinn pushed himself into the bed beside Anna. He lay with his face turned away, the gray cloak wrapped tightly around him.

Ged stumbled back in the door towards the fire: 'The gates of Valhalla await. Heimdall awaits.' He brandished his ancient sword. 'I challenge the evil Walrus Queen. Whale-horse woman, I will silence

CHAPTER 39 — Herjolfsness

your threats. I have done all you asked on land and yet it is not enough. Brothers be at peace. I will save you.' He smiled at no one and let his cloak drop to the floor. His skin seemed to glow white as ivory and his eyes burned.

Ketil awoke long enough to shake the Irish woman beside him. She who was well used to words of anguish awoke, roused herself to push Ged into the bed cupboard where he lay shivering and chewing under the furs next to Anna and Thorfinn.

The time of waking witnessed a loud argument between the priest, Father Torfi, and Rhvford. The priest wanted part of Rhvford's land to use as his own on behalf of the Church. He said it was necessary, as the clergy who would come with the bishop and were not able to grow food for themselves, but would spend all their time at prayer for the redemption of the heathen Greenlanders. Rhvford wanted a body of strong men to remove the priest from Greenland forever. Someone started banging outside the hall which intensified the voices of the priest and Rhvford.

Ged had dragged his construction to the outside wall of the hall where he was sheltered from the worst of the weather, and was hammering nails into wood. 'I progress,' he told the dog watching. 'Soon the battle will begin. Listen. Yellowbritches plays music for the coming of the battle. It is beginning.' He held his head as if listening to something.

Anna cautiously approached with food. 'I hear nothing. You must eat husband.' Ged took the food and shoved it into his mouth. 'Go woman. I have had with women. Leave me to the music. Go to your new husband.'

'He is not my husband. You are. At least he is kind. Can you not see how hard it is for me?'

Ketil and Boltof walked up to inspect what Ged was doing.

'Least he be quiet. And out of the way of the priest. Look he has even started carving on that piece of wood.'

Ged looked up and smiled. He had bundled a precious store of nails at Ebiwaz and carried it in secret with him all summer. Now these lay on the ground beside the rough carving of a huge grotesque bird.

'The fit is passing husband. You carve again.'

Ged smiled his angelic smile and bent to his task.

That night Ged came to bed and lay peacefully beside Thorfinn and Anna. When the wind ceased he returned to his project. For days he labored. He would not let anyone see what he made but kept his work covered by an old sail. At the time of sleep he came to the bed cupboard with the walrus skull and the dog and lay beside Anna and Thorfinn with glazed eyes. He ate what he was given and quietly drank his ale with the dark syrup concealed within.

Rhvford took his meals now with the men in the hall. He wanted their allegiance in a fight to send the bishop's representative back from where he came. He had no intention of giving the best of his land to the bishop. The workers mumbled and farted. Why could not Rhvford just ignore the priest like the rest of them? Why make all this fuss? Rhvford was the one, after all, who had sent his son to the King of Norway to request a bishop for Greenland.

'Rhvford,' Ketil said, 'is angry because his son was not made the bishop. But some outsider from Norway comes instead to be the Bishop of Greenland. Only the women folk of Gardar will talk to him. So the White Christ is for the women what are the only ones are interested.'

Mid-winter came. In the long house they sang songs to the Christ god and the women made twisted bread from barley seed. The priest told stories about the wondrous deeds of men beloved by the Christ. Saints, he called them. The stories were about some woman or child dying in a way that made the Christ God love them more. Mostly it involved torture and mutilation. Rhvford stood as far away as possible from the priest and made sweet talk with the woman he wanted for a wife. He hoped the priest might like to get closer to the Christ god by following the example of the saint persons.

When the stories were finished and the priest drowsy with ale and bread, the men returned to the hall and built a wild fire there. They set food out for the creatures of the dark who came to the living this night. They cut themselves so the blood of their ancestors ran as a

CHAPTER 39 — *Herjolfsness*

sacrifice into the fire on this, the darkest night, when the space between the living and the dead dissolved. No matter what the priest said, this was the time when the ancestors spoke to the living. The Irish woman stayed with Ketil. She cut herself twice for her father and his father, she said. Not for her mother who had sent the scratching plague.

Boltof asked her if the rattling in the pigs bladder covering the window was her father or her mother come to chat.

Gardar now became two camps: that of the bishop and his minions and that of the worshippers of the old gods. Work on the interior of church ceased without Rhvford to prod the men. Everyone avoided the priest and his ranting. The men and women in the hall took their food from the longhouse but nothing else.

Ged remained calm with the dark liquid from Rhvford's farm. His skin fattened and stretched. He continued to chew ceaselessly; as if he were eating himself, Anna thought. He spent the time working at his secret project near the graveyard. He refused to talk to anyone, and could not be drawn even on the subject of saving Greenland from demons and whale-horse. He just looked out with his ice bright eyes and bit his lip. His pale hair hung in long ringlets to his shoulders. He wore a fur hat with a long rat bitten tail that hung over one ear. He did converse with the dog and always wore the rusted sword on his belt. Sometimes a dark shadow passed above the graveyard. Most who saw thought it was but trick of the light, or the brush of a low cloud against the roof of the church.

People became slow and thoughtful as the winter silence absorbed past and future. Thorfinn thought of Ebiwaz and his life there. Had anything been real? Was Anna really pregnant? Did the bird with the diamonds on its claws exist at all? Was it his child or the child of Ged who moved into the spirit world? Did it matter? Did it matter what the king of Norway said? Did anything matter beside a warm bed and a soft woman to hold?

He had not lain with Anna since she told him the father of the child was unknown to her. He could not speak to her, nor lie within her arms again. He found a sheltered cave by the bay and spent much time there in his gray cloak waiting for the lights of Odin to change the landscape into the strange colors of the land that led to Valhalla.

Anna sat by the fire and played with her spinning, her movements numbed by the cold and the dark of the world outside the booth of wadmal. Spirits from her time at Ebiwaz stalked outside the small protection of the fire. She felt the pain of the birth again, the wrath of Asmund, the longing for a man that was neither Ged nor Thorfinn to protect her.

The wind came thought the half built hall, water and ice dripped from the walls and ceiling and small evil creatures leered at her from the patterns in the cold stones. Once a woman from the house came to ask her help with a tapestry; apart from that no one spoke to her. She was as alone as she had ever been at Ebiwaz, but now there was nothing to comfort her: not the solidity of belonging, nor the burbling of Skadi's baby, or even the smell of Skadi and Sokki.

Sometimes she felt as if her father stood by her side or was it grandmother ghost? If she sent her thoughts to Thorfinn the shadow of Ged fell across her mind. The only thing that brought her peace was the memory of her dog from the Western Settlement. She took a piece of the fleece Asmund had packed in the sledge and made a tiny dog doll of wool. When she felt most alone she stroked it and thought she could feel the softness of the little dog's love surround her again.

CHAPTER 40
Ged sets sail

The priest decided conflict with his work force was not going to build a church. Norway and the king were a long way over the sea. The priest knew his own success would be measured by the greatness of this church at Gardar. Trade between Greenland and the King of Norway could be sorted out by the cunning of the Norse sea captains. No fools were they when it came to custom and deceit. It was not his business as long as the men worked and he managed to extract a small tithe from the farmers and hunters for the clergy who would follow.

He decided to prepare a feast for the Norse who were always ready to eat and drink. He told the women in the longhouse to prepared caribou and seal and white cheese and bring out their spiced ale. A musician was found, a grand fire prepared and invitations sent. The priest told the women to dress in their best clothes. He sent Rhvford a message to say he would consider his need for a wife if it helped him get the men back to work.

Men came from the dank chill of the hall into the longhouse. The big room was sprinkled with sweet herbs and filled with the scent of warm ale and wood smoke and females. The music enticed, the ale and the food provided a soft place to rest from the strange beings who walked the winter nights. Even Ketil and Boltof joined the singing around the fire with the women. Rhvford smiled at the one he desired; she smiled back and patted his rings. Anna sat by the fire and warmed her hands. The Irish princess was too busy cleaning up the remains of the feast to join her. Farther Torfi beamed at everyone.

Ged refused to enter the house. He stayed in the grey light and worked at his secret. 'I finish today,' he told Thorfinn.

The priest requested the company begin to recite a verse or two now that silence claimed most of the land outside the longhouse, and all were done with singing and feasting. 'As in the tradition of your ancestors,' he said. 'I salute them, brave men, strong men. And women too. Never forget the women.'

One by one the men took a turn to recite a verse. Thorfinn sat by the young woman Rhvford wanted as a wife. She had hair like Anna. And blue blue eyes whereas Anna's were green. Thorfinn could not but imagine those blue eyes waking in the morning soft with sleep and sex.

But where was Anna? He got up and looked around. She was not at the fire, nor helping keep the horns supplied with ale. There was the sound of scraping outside, as if something heavy was being dragged on rock. Thorfinn saw Ged dragging a heavy object along the path to the bay. The dun landscape framed his figure. Huge blocks of ice marched behind him to the grey horizon and the sea. The ice mirrored no light. Ged moved with purpose and strength. Anna ran behind him. She grabbed at his clothes, his arms; anything. He writhed out of her touch. A black shadow flew on the ice before him, leading him; it had the shape of a bird the seize of a dragon, like the shadow of the mountain as the sun left the earth in summer.

It was a boat. Ged was dragging a boat; a small thing with no keel and the carved dragon-bird stuck on a pole and inserted in the middle of the hull. The sword on his hip swung unsheathed. The dog followed, tied to the boat by a long rope. Ged dragged and pushed a path to the frozen sea. The dog whined and tried to escape. Anna tried to grab the dog but it snarled and pulled away. Ged took his hands off the boat and pushed her. She fell onto the mud and ice.

Ged skimmed the boat over ice so thin it cracked behind him. He carried a nestbaggin on his back. He pushed the boat into a narrow path of free water in the middle of the frozen bay. With one look at Anna he lifted the dog and shoved it shivering into the boat. The ice cracked and sent streaks of black water to the shore while the boat and its passengers were encased in shadow.

CHAPTER 40 — *Ged sets sail*

'Farewell,' said Ged in a tremulous voice. 'I fight the Whale-horse Queen and her evil dreams. I will save you all. I will save Greenland.' He swung the sword in a wide arc around him. 'Only the enemies of Greenland will try to prevent me. Tell Sokki I have done it. I will see him in Valhalla. Let my fight be the memory of my life. I go to battle with the monsters of the Great Ocean.'

'No. Come back. Ged. Husband.' Anna dragged herself to the edge of the bay. The ice cracked and floated. 'Oh what shall I do? What shall I do? The ice will not hold me.'

'Ged,' yelled Thorfinn. 'Come back. Ebiwaz needs you. Asmund needs you.'

'Tell Sokki I go to fight. Tell Sokki.' His voice was overcome by the screeching of the shadow bird flying in front of the boat as it moved slowly into deep water.

'Thorfinn get him. Do not let him go. Ged come back. Thorfinn, Ketil. Do something.'

Thorfinn lifted Anna off the ground. She was covered in ice and mud. Ged and the boat floated in the channel of water opening through the ice. The ice had cracked so much in the bay that it was impossible for anyone to follow without falling into the freezing water. The howling of the dog mixed with the screech of the black thing above the boat. People came out of the house and stood amongst the ice and the stones on the edge of the bay. The women held their skirts out of the mud. Some men carried their ale horn with them.

No one spoke. The enormity of Ged's actions overwhelmed them as Ged and his boat slid into the sea mist.

'We cannot follow,' Boltof said at last. 'Them boats is up on land covered in pitch.'

'The carver. The carver has gone. Gone in a boat on the sea.'

'Get a boat and follow him,' Anna cried. 'There must be a boat.'

'Boats on shore for the winter repair,' Boltof said again.

The faint voice of Ged came over the ice. 'We meet in Valhalla.'

'But he ain't died fighting. How do he get into Valhalla wifout being dead in battle?'

'He goes to fight the Whale-horse Queen.'

'He goes to fight the creatures of our dreams, yer mean.'

'Well I never saw a whale-horse in any dream of mine,' said Ketil.

'Because he kept them away from us. Out of our dreams. Locked them up in his mind.' Boltof the Wise considered. 'Maybe he spoke true. Always said he kept the demons out of our days by dreaming them for us and carving them in his art.'

Anna shook and bit at her fingers. Thorfinn took her hands in his own. 'Let him go. It is what he wanted. Ged goes to his fate as we all will when the Norns have finished weaving our lives.'

'I tried to be a good wife. I tried. Why does he desert me? What will happen to us now when he is not there to hold the demons for us?'

'Odin and Thor will protect us.'

'Says he is going to Valhalla.' Ketil farted with excitement. 'Better he be wif Odin to give advice on what is happening here in Greenland wif all this orders from Norway.'

'Which we as Vikings is going to ignore.'

'Get him back.' The priest was as red and pulsing as the innards of a seal. 'Does no one here but me care for the fate of the carver? Woman he is your husband.'

'An how is we to get 'em back?' yelled Ketil. 'You go yerself on that thin ice and end up frozen dead in the sea. Boats all up on land. He weren't no good to you anyhows. Better be off helping us all from the world of the gods what has called him. Fighting he will be when the end comes.'

'Farewell,' said Boltof the Wise 'Brother I honor you and your voyage. Farewell Ged Romfortsson, brother of Asmund Lawbinder of Hvalsey, wife of Anna Kerldottir. We will remember you with honor.'

'Let him go priest,' Rhvford hissed softly. 'Greenland can do without the carving on the church. We don't want no land grabbing followers of the White Christ here anyways.'

Someone blew a horn and the mournful sound blended with the cry of the birds and the wash of the sea against the rocks. The enormous bird had disappeared into the sea mist with Ged and his boat.

CHAPTER 40 — Ged sets sail

'I speak for this woman now,' said Thorfinn. 'As father and protector. I will care for her.'

'It is done then.' The priest shook his fist at the ice. 'You Thorfinn Markland-Farer must repay any debts the carver and his wife accumulated here.'

Slowly the watchers dispersed. Thorfinn held Anna. She was wet and shivering.

'The sea has taken him. Truly I am woman of no husband now.'

Thorfinn put his arms around her and pressed her face into his shoulder. Still she shivered. 'Odin has called him to battle. Ged has gone to face his fate on the Great Ocean. A brave man. And he will win. He will find Valhalla.'

'He will never come back. He is gone into the Great Ocean. Like my father. I tried. I tried. Oh Ged, Ged, Who will protect us now? Who will hold the shadows for us now?'

'Ged wished you to be safe Anna, safe with me. He knew. You will come with me. It was his will. You will always be with me now.' Thorfinn carried Anna into the hall. She lay in her wet clothes on the bed palate staring into emptiness.

'Oh, my beautiful Viking daughter. What would you have become of him? To stand forever tormented by visions and dreams of hideous demons? Now he has gone with pride to honor the name of his ancestors.'

'Aye. Let us honor his action and find good memory in his passing,' Ketil said, reaching for the ale bucket and the Irish princess.

Thorfinn held Anna to his heart. He pressed her face into his hair and his beard and she felt again the safety of a small thing surrounded and engulfed. It was thus to be safe. It was thus to be woman. Thorfinn would care for her. Thorfinn would protect her.

That night the men and women in the hall heard the faint sound of a flute in the wind. Troubled dreams came to all in the house; the priest awoke with the feel of the foul breath of a sea creature on his face and the chieftain dreamt of tusks coming forth from the womb of his wife.

Glossary

<u>Althing:</u> An annual assembly that could be attended by all free men.

<u>Asgard:</u> The realm of the gods where the gods have their great halls. Valhalla was situated here.

<u>Blot:</u> a ceremonial meal, sacrifice and dance to honour the Norse gods at the seasons of expedition and return.

<u>Brattahlid:</u> (Steep Slope) The name of the first farm in Greenland. Built by Eirik the Red on the shore of Eiriksfjord, or Tunulliarfik, as it is now called, a little after 986 CE. A place of importance to the Norse as the Lawspeaker for Greenland lived there in the early years of the twelfth century.

<u>Bifrost:</u> A flaming rainbow bridge that connects Asgard and Midgard.

<u>Booth:</u> A temporary construction , tent like, made of wood and wadmal.

<u>Burial:</u> Pagan societies buried their dead with the objects important to the person who had died. Christ men were buried with the things that accompanied them into this life; nothing.

<u>Currach:</u> Small boat constructed of hides and sewn together and stretched over a wooden frame. Irish monks seeking solitude set off in these small boats with only their faith to guide them. Many ended up in Iceland before the Vikings.

Glossary

Eastern Settlement: Group of farms clustered around the original farm Eirik the Red built. The farms were situated at the end of fiords, where in summer green grass grew with willow trees, birch and rowan trees, bluebells and buttercups.

Ebiwaz: A rune that indicates growth and movement can happen through perseverance and wisdom even though there may be adversary. The name of the farm where Ged and Asmund live.

Eirik the Red: The founding father of the Norse Greenland settlements. A strong man and a good leader. Originally from Norway, his temper fuelled deeds sent him to Iceland where he again got into trouble and was made an outlaw. He sailed to Greenland with his wife and his followers.

Freyja: Fertility goddess. Goddess of love, she sold herself to the dwarfs for a golden necklace, the Necklace of the Brisings. She collects the dead and takes them to her field of the afterlife, Folkvangr, and her own hall, Sessrumnir. Her chariot is drawn by two cats. She is sister to Freyr.

Freyr, a god who symbolizes male fertility. Represented by a statue at Uppsala of a small man holding a giant penius. He provides prosperity.

Frigg: Wife of Odin. A maternal goddess who helps women in childbirth.

Ghosts: Considered in Medieval Greenland as being able to converse with the living.

Christians: Christ men sailed with the first ships to sail from Iceland to Greenland. Christianity took hold slowly in the countries of the Norse. Ari the Learned in a book called *Islendingabok* describes the possibility of a conflict between Christ men and pagans in 1000CE in Iceland. The Lawspeaker of the Althing, recognising civil war would end self-government, decided Iceland would become Christian but with some old customs remaining, such as the exposure of children and the consumption of horse meat.

Heimdall: The watchman of the gods. He has super sensitive hearing and sight. He lives in a hall where Bifrost, the rainbow bridge, meets the land of the gods.

High-seat pillars: A pair of wooden poles placed on each side of the seat of the head of the household. According to the sagas, the pillars were taken on voyages of exploration and thrown overboard when good land was sighted. Where the pillars came to shore was the place the travellers built a permanent farm. The high-seat faced the main door of the longhouse.

Icelandic Sagas: These were written in the Twelfth or Thirteenth Century and express the interest of the period in which they were written. Some were written about contemporary events and some about the history of the Norse in Iceland and Greenland.

Jormungandd: An enormous serpent that lived in the oceans surrounding Midgard, the world inhabited by humans.

Knarr: Viking cargo ship. Could be up to 27m long and could carry about 50 tons. Clinker built and single masted with a square sail. They could be sailed or rowed and were fast and sturdy.

Kracken: A sea monster said to live off the coast of Greenland. It usually dwelt on the bottom of the sea. When it rose it caused a great turbulence in the water; when it returned to the bottom of the sea it created a whirlpool that could suck ships into it.

Lawspeaker: Presided over the general assembly and considered the leader of the Settlement. An elective office but the individual was chosen from the most powerful families in the Eastern Settlement.

Glossary

Lief Eiriksson: the son of Eirik the Red, was the first European to set foot on America as described in the Saga of the Greenlanders.

Locki: A god with a sense of humour who worries little about consequences. He brings change to the world of gods and humans alike. He is unpredictable and cunning.

Norns: The three goddesses of destiny, Urd,(Fate), Skuld,(Being), and Verdandi, (Necessity). They live by the Well of Fate and Wisdom under Yggdrasill and water this great tree every day. Every day too they spin the destiny of each person and weave their fate in a way that cannot be undone.

Markland: Forest Land. One of three places in North America mentioned in the sagas; Helluland or Slab Land, Markland and Vineland.

Mjollnir: The hammer of Thor. Made by dwarfs. Has magical properties.

Nestbaggin: back pack.

Nordsetur: The northern hunting grounds of Greenland, Disco Bay. It was always a source of fear and challenge to the Norse, being so far away from any god that could protect them. However it was a rich source of polar bear pelts, walrus ivy and skin rope.

Odin: Allfather. Foremost of the gods. Ruler of all. God of war and god of poetry. Two ravens, Huggnn and Muggnn, Thought and Memory, sit on his shoulders. Two wolves, Geri and Freki, sit by his side. His horse is the eight legged Sleipnir who sometimes comes to Midgard to duel with sheep. In his hall, Valhalla, fallen warriors could feast and drink and fight as much as they desired. He has one eye and wears a wide brimmed hat. For nine days and nights he hung upside down on the world ash, Yggdrasill, to learn wisdom.

Papar: Irish monks who travelled in their curach through the North Atlantic, seeking solitude and trusting the Lord to guide them to a place where they could spend time in prayer and contemplation.

Skraeling: A term used by the Norse to describe the Amerindians and Eskimo peoples. The word was first used in the 1120's by Ari the Learned in regards to the Dorset Eskimo remains found by Eirik the Red when he settled Greenland. It was also used to describe the Thule Eskimos who moved into North Greenland about the same time as the Norse.

Thor: Son of Odin and Earth. Seen to bring justice and order to the world with his hammer Mjollnir. Loved by the common people. His chariot riding across the sky created thunder. His chariot was pulled by goats.

Tithes: Goods paid to a religious organisation for the upkeep of that organisation.

Valhalla: is a hall located in Asgard, where Odin rules. Many warriors who die in battle are led by the valkyries to Valhalla, while some go to the goddess Freyja's hall, Fólkvangr. In Valhalla dead warriors fight each day and feast each night. Before the hall stands the golden tree Glasir, and the hall's ceiling is thatched with golden shields.

Valkyries: Women who carry warriors from the battlefield to Valhalla, the hall of Odin. The handmaidens of Odin.

Wadmal: A tough woollen cloth. It was made from fleece and used for sailcloth and clothes. It was woven on an upright loom with weights attached to the warp. Mostly women did the weaving indoors on looms that were about one meter wide. The cloth was coated in animal fat when used for a sail.

Western Settlement: The second Norse settlement in Greenland, settled about the same time as Brattahlid. North of the Eastern Settlement, in the Nuuk district.

Whale-Horse: walrus. Called this due to the noise they make when on the ice. Prized for ivory and their pelt, which was made into rope.

White Christ: A term first used by Icelanders during the conversion to Christianity in the early 10th Century. White denotes complexion and refers to the white robes of baptism. Could be seen as a term of derision as white was associated with weakness. Thor was called Red Thor.

World view: To the Norse the world had three structures placed one above the other; Asgard was on the top. The Aesir, warriors gods, lived here in fabulous halls, as did the Vanir who were fertility gods. The second world was Midgard where humans lived as well as the giants in a place called Jotunheim. An ocean, where the great serpant Jormungard swum, surrounded Midguard. The land of the elves, Svartalfheim, was also near Midgard. Asgard and Midgard were connected by Bifrost, the rainbow bridge. Nine days ride downwards from Midgard one came upon Niflheim, a cold place of death. The dark city Hel was here. Yggdrasill, the world tree, connected all worlds. One of its roots grew though Midgard into the Well of Fate where the Norns sat weaving the fate of humanity. Another root grew into Jotunheim and dripped into the Spring of Mimir. From here came wisdom. Another root grew into Niflheim. The dragon Nidhogg lives here and munches on the roots of the great tree of life.

www.ingramcontent.com/pod-product-compliance
Ingram Content Group UK Ltd.
Pitfield, Milton Keynes, MK11 3LW, UK
UKHW041414180426
11947UKWH00007B/137